THE GIRLS OF HEATHERLY HALL

Also by Julie Houston

Goodness, Grace and Me
The One Saving Grace
An Off-Piste Christmas
Looking for Lucy
Coming Home to Holly Close Farm
A Village Affair
Sing Me a Secret
A Village Vacancy
A Family Affair
A Village Secret
The Village Vicar

THE GIRLS OF HEATHERLY HALL

Julie Houston

HEAD of ZEUS

An Aria Book

First published in the UK in 2023 by Head of Zeus,
part of Bloomsbury Publishing Plc

9 7 5 3 1 2 4 6 8

A catalogue record for this book is available from the British Library.

ISBN (PB): 9781803280059
ISBN (E): 9781803280035

Cover illustration: Robyn Neild

Typeset by Siliconchips Services Ltd UK

FSC www.fsc.org
MIX
Paper | Supporting responsible forestry
FSC® C013604

Printed and bound in Great Britain by
CPI Group (UK) Ltd, Croydon CR0 4YY

Head of Zeus
First Floor East
5–8 Hardwick Street
London EC1R 4RG
WWW.HEADOFZEUS.COM

For Debbie, Jo, Tracy and Helen –
The best ever writerly wordy mates who eat my lasagne
and supply the wine and wisdom while doing so!

1

The garden, its half-acre of lawn set squarely in front of the eighteenth-century vicarage in the pretty village of Westenbury, West Yorkshire, was alive and buzzing with the first signs of spring. Actually *thrumming* with the new season, Rosa Quinn realised before smiling at her indulgently romantic choice of words. A wooden bench towards the far end of the lawn was in need of something: paint or creosote, or whatever gardeners and handymen did to benches abandoned for too long by the previous incumbents of All Hallows Church. Doubtless she'd be the one to roll back her sleeves and rescue it.

The vicarage, adjacent to the church itself, sat steadfast, regal almost, behind a dense yew hedge which, Rosa also knew, if she didn't do something to thwart its obvious intention to take over the garden, would continue to run rampant. Resolving to tackle the burgeoning greenery once that morning's wedding was over, Rosa lifted the hem of her best white surplice and, relishing the feel of the damp, daisy-strewn grass beneath her bare feet, made her way across the lawn towards her church.

Her church. Rosa loved those two words. *Her church*. Alright, it was, she argued, *God's* church, God's house, but she still got a thrill of pleasure, seven months on from taking over at the helm in what had been, many years before, her grandfather Cecil's church. Miserable old devil that *he* was, Rosa remembered with a grin as she bent to pick a still-blooming specimen from the last of the daffodils before threading it through the top button of her surplice.

'What are *you* smiling to yourself about, Vicar? And you need a carnation in your buttonhole, not a manky daff from the garden.' Hilary Makepiece, churchwarden and mainstay of the parish council, wafted an expensive-looking cream and gold-bordered order of service in Rosa's direction before frowning at the shoeless state of the vicar's feet. 'This is a pretty important wedding, you know, Vicar. Do you not think you should put some shoes on?'

'I'm enjoying the feel of God's good grass beneath my feet, Hilary.' Rosa grinned. 'Communing with nature you might say.'

'Well, commune all you like, love, but you might want to smarten yourself up a bit: the groom's the nearest we've got to *royalty* in this village. The bell-ringers have been at it all morning. I had to go up there with bacon sandwiches and coffee to keep 'em at it when they appeared to be going off the boil a bit. So, yes, the most important man in the village.' Hilary ran a hand over her own neatly tied-back blonde hair and down her professionally laundered best choir surplice before nudging Rosa to make sure she was taking in what she was saying. 'He'd probably always had equal ranking with the Marquess of Stratton but, you know, Rosa, since your dad passed over before Christmas...' Hilary paused and Rosa wouldn't have been surprised to see her piously cross herself '...God bless his soul, your groom today is solely in the number-one position. And, as such, I reckon you should put your shoes on before you go in there to join the pair in holy matrimony.'

Hilary had been one of the naughtiest girls in school – bar Rosa's own sister Eva – when she'd been Hilary Caldwell, and they were all fifteen-year-olds at Westenbury Comprehensive, not averse to smoking in the toilets or legging it down to the town centre instead of sitting through an RE lesson. She always made Rosa want to laugh with her veneer of respectability now she was one of the churchwardens and married to Duncan Makepiece, the village's family butcher, and mother to a troop of little Makepieces.

Hilary's face softened and she patted Rosa's arm sympathetically, looking long and hard at her face for any tell-tale signs of sorrow. 'Do you miss your dad, love?'

'As you know, Hilary, the marquess was mine, Hannah and Eva's biological father and we miss him very much. But *Richard* is our dad, our real dad, and *he's* very much alive and kicking. In fact, he's wanting to come on a trip to Paris with the three of us.'

'Paris?' Catching the potential smell of village gossip, Hilary raised her head, her ears on high alert like a sniffer dog's, and Rosa wanted to kick herself. 'Paris?' Hilary repeated. 'Why Paris? Is it *Disneyland Paris* you're off to? Getting some ideas for Heatherly Hall now that you three are in charge up there? Hey, that'd be a bit of alright, wouldn't it? Disney Westenbury? I can see that.'

Rosa knew she had to stop Hilary in her tracks before the whole of the village had it on Hilary's good authority that that's what the Quinn triplets had in mind, now that Bill Astley, twelfth Marquess of Stratton, had bequeathed his fifty-one per cent share of the estate management to his three biological daughters: Eva, Hannah and herself. A theme park was the last thing she, Rosa, had in mind for Heatherly Hall, although she wouldn't put it past Hannah, who was already mooting the idea of *Westenbury*, a Yorkshire rock festival to compete with – and even trounce and surpass – its southern rival, *Glastonbury*. 'No, no, honestly, Hilary, I can't see the Estate Management Committee agreeing to a theme park up at the hall. It would have been the last thing Bill would have wanted, and just think how expensive all those rides and equipment would be to install.'

Hilary nodded sagely. 'And the insurance? Blimey, my car insurance is bad enough. Insuring against someone flying off the Rollercoaster Galactica or the Beastie Nemesis into the hall's shrubbery would soon eat into all that money Bill left you and your sisters.' Hilary raised a hopeful eyebrow in anticipation of finally finding out just how much the Quinn triplets had inherited. 'Bet all that money will come in handy, now that you're no longer earning the thousands you were on when you were in London and heading Rosa Quinn Investments?' When Rosa deigned not to answer, Hilary went on, 'I've always wondered why you washed your hands of your high-flying career to become a lowly vicar earning a pittance back in your grandad's old church. Something happen down there? A broken heart, was it?'

Ignoring her churchwarden, Rosa bent to pick another daffodil, adding it to the first in her buttonhole and set off walking, Hilary in her wake.

'So,' Hilary opined, hurrying to keep up with Rosa and, as the latter appeared unwilling, as always, to confide anything re her years away from the village, changed tack. 'You might find it all a bit difficult? A bit of a conflict of interest you could say?'

'A conflict of interest?' Rosa turned. 'In what way?'

'Well,' Hilary went on, her tone confidential, 'I reckon you'll be trying to keep God happy by persuading folks to get married in the church? You know, like they always used to? Or...'

'Or?'

'Or, now that you, Eva and Hannah have inherited the place, pushing Heatherly Hall as the wedding venue of choice? Hmm? Difficult decision, Rosa,' Hilary added sagely. 'As I say, conflict of interest and all that? I mean, you don't want to be seen to be putting financial gain ahead of what the Lord dictates. I've overheard more than a few conversations in the pub and in church.'

'Which lord exactly are we talking about here, Hilary? David Henderson?'

'No! You know exactly what I'm getting at, Rosa, so don't play the innocent with me.'

'So, David Henderson? Village royalty, you reckon?' Rosa smiled, neatly sidestepping the conversation about any conflict of interest she may have re her position on the management committee of Heatherly Hall. As the village vicar, wanting people to marry in her church, should she, at the same time, be endorsing and celebrating the wedding venue up at the hall?

'Oh absolutely. You can't get much posher than David Henderson.'

And now, lovely, charismatic Grace Stevens, teacher across at Little Acorns, the village school, was about to walk down the aisle and she, Rosa, would join her and David Henderson together in matrimony. There were times when Rosa just loved her job.

The heady smell from masses of creamy longiflorum lilies was soon fighting for survival amongst the plethora of expensive perfumes wafting down the aisle, as beautifully dressed women, some holding children's hands, others partners' arms, made their way to the front of the church, taking up seats on either side dependent on whether they were 'bride' or 'groom'. Rosa, now sporting a pair of black court shoes – as well as her brightest lipstick, in honour of the occasion – stood watching and smiling, welcoming everyone in as her church filled up with guests. Daphne Merton, All Hallows' stalwart organist, was giving it all she'd got thumping out Elgar's *Salut d'amour* – determined, it seemed, to rival the church bell-ringers who, obviously on a caffeine high, appeared to have upped the ante even further.

While both David Henderson and Grace Stevens had told her they'd wanted a really quiet wedding – it was, after all, they'd argued, a second marriage for both of them – it seemed the village had other plans and, on this beautiful April morning, the week after Easter, Rosa didn't think she'd ever seen the church so full. Of course, she realised, it was still the school holidays. And as Cassie Beresford, head teacher of Little Acorns school, a shocking-pink hat set jauntily on her fair hair, walked through the huge open oak doors at the back, Rosa caught sight of what must have amounted to half the pupils of the village school excitedly waiting with mums and grannies, eager to see Grace arrive at the church. There were older kids as well, wanting to see their favourite primary school teacher arrive at church, now gathered somewhat uncertainly and self-consciously, smiling their newly straightened and whitened teeth and showing off their designer gear while still finding safety in numbers.

Delighted to see them, Rosa walked quickly up towards the vestibule, ready to usher them in just as David Henderson, accompanied by his best man, made his way down the aisle towards her.

'Good morning!' Rosa welcomed the pair of them with a huge grin before walking out into the spring sunshine. Oh, but it was glorious out here. Looking forward to an afternoon in the vicarage garden bullying the yew into submission whilst hoping to catch a few rays to chase away her winter pallor, she uttered a quiet: 'Thanks, God,' before opening the heavy doors as wide as they'd go and beckoning those outside in. 'Do join us inside. I know Grace will be delighted to see you all.' The kids stared, shuffled, giggled a bit at being addressed by the vicar and then, following the lead of the more confident, walked en masse into the church.

'She's here, Mummy,' a little tot shouted as a gaily beribboned Audi swept in front of the gathered onlookers and Rosa gave the thumbs up to Daphne on the organ before hurrying down to take up her own position in the sanctuary at the front. As Handel's *Arrival of the Queen of Sheba* hit the fifteenth-century church rafters, heads turned as Grace Stevens, on the arm of her father, walked forwards. Attended by her six-year-old daughter, Pietronella, as well as Grace's best mate since school days, Harriet Westmoreland, Grace appeared overcome with emotion, her shoulders below the cream silk of her dress heaving, the hand not holding her simple bouquet of spring flowers wiping surreptitiously at her eyes. And Harriet wasn't faring much better.

It was only when they were standing in front of her that Rosa realised the pair of them were actually having a total fit of the giggles and Rosa laughed herself, delighting in their joy and humour. David turned to Grace, his eyes raised in surprise as she gave a final squeak of nervous laughter, before smiling down at her with such love and adoration that Rosa could only feel a bolt of pure envy. She, Rosa, had once been looked at in such a way by a man who'd loved her; a man whom she'd loved back unconditionally until it all went wrong.

Shocked and disappointed at herself for allowing such an unpleasant and pernicious emotion as envy to enter her mind on such a glorious morning, and on such an occasion as this, Rosa offered a repentant *Sorry God* sent up in a silent prayer of contrition to her boss, before turning to the congregation with a smile and saying: 'Dearly beloved we are gathered here today, on this wonderful spring morning, to join this lovely man to this fabulously lovely woman…'

'So, what was it making you laugh so much as you came down the aisle?' Rosa asked as the main wedding party moved into a side room to sign the register.

'Sorry about that, Rosa.' Grace started laughing once more. 'Harriet and I have always got each other into trouble, giggling at inappropriate moments. You know, we've been mates…'

'Joined at the hip,' David Henderson interjected fondly.

'…mates since our first day at Midhope Grammar,' Grace went on. 'When we were eleven? We've had our fallings-out but Harriet's always been there for me. Anyway, just as I was about to come down the aisle, on my best behaviour, she goes all gooey and sentimental and whispers: "You do know how much you mean to me, Grace, don't you?" and I turn, a tear in my eye and she goes on: "Love you always, Grace. You know, I'd take a bullet for you?" At which point I'm about to dissolve in snot-ridden tears and ruin my mascara when she adds: "I mean, you know, not in my *head*, or my *heart*, Grace, but, you know, in my *leg*…" and that made me laugh so much I couldn't stop… Sorry.' Grace obviously wasn't a bit sorry and as David, laughing himself now, scooped both Grace and Pietronella up into one big hug, Rosa knew that here was a marriage made in heaven. A morning's job well done.

'Come on, Grace, there's something lovely waiting outside for you.' Harriet's eyes were shining.

'Oh jeez – sorry, Rosa – you haven't commandeered a big white horse to take me up to the restaurant, have you, Harriet? Because you know, much as I pretend not to be, I'm terrified of the great beasts. And I'm probably allergic as well…'

'Come on, or they'll be getting tired of waiting.'

'Who'll be getting tired of waiting? For what?'

'For you and David. Come on.'

Rosa followed the pair back down the aisle, the guests filing off behind them to the strains of Mendelssohn's *On Wings of Song*.

'Oh, how lovely.' Grace laughed in delight as she saw the guard of honour waiting for her and David at the church door. Cassie Beresford had obviously organised the children from Little Acorns into age order, the tall Y6 pair commencing the guard – not with an arch of sabres of steel, but with flower-festooned yellow plastic metre rulers – and finishing with the little ones from Reception.

'We've been practising this for days,' Cassie confided to Rosa, as David and Grace bent themselves almost double to go through the guard, at its conclusion five-year-olds who'd been standing stalwartly, attached to their rulers with pride and impatience, until the big moment. 'The nursery staff were a bit put out I wasn't prepared to include the three- and four-year-olds but, thank goodness I didn't. David would have ended up on his hands and knees…'

Cassie's words ended up floating somewhere round Rosa's head, their meaning lost as the blood in her ears started to pound. Joe Rosavina. He was there. She'd not seen him since before Christmas, when she'd agreed to have dinner with him in a fancy restaurant to hear him out. She'd managed both to hear him out and to finally convince herself she'd put her relationship with the boy she'd fallen in love with when she was sixteen behind her. Joe, the boy who'd followed her to Durham University; the man who had stood shoulder to shoulder with her in London as she worked every hour God sent – and some he obviously hadn't – establishing Rosa Quinn Investments. Cheering her on and so proud of her when she won Businesswoman of the Year.

Joe Rosavina: the man who'd broken her heart when he'd slept with her PA and best friend, Carys and who now accompanied the result of that one-night stand, his beautiful daughter, six-year-old Chiara, as she determinedly held on to her metre ruler until David and Grace finally emerged, slightly pink-faced, at its conclusion.

As the metre ruler guard of honour was led to one side by Cassie and its respective parents, Chiara ran over to Joe who swung her up into his arms, kissing the top of her blonde head. Rosa saw that Joe's eyes were searching, searching the faces of the guests as they filed out, laughing and chattering, into the warm sunshine. And when his gaze finally met her own, unable as she was to reverse back into the cool safety of her church because of the people still making their way out, she was unable to decipher the emotion held in his beautiful blue eyes.

Rosa saw him raise a hand and realised he was about to come over to speak and her pulse raced – when a different hand was placed on her arm and a head bent to kiss her cheek.

'Hello, Rosa darling. How's my favourite vicar?' Sam Burrows, Rosa's partner for the last six months, stroked her back through her surplice. 'Just popped over from the surgery to catch the last of the nuptials. Did it all go OK? Quite a responsibility, I bet, marrying the Lord of the Manor?'

'Marrying him?' Rosa turned, feeling slightly anxious. Or was it irritation? 'As far as I'm aware, I'm still single – the spinster of this parish.'

Sam laughed, kissing her once more as the crowd of wedding well-wishers exiting the church behind her finally thinned to a trickle. 'You know what I mean, Rosa. Look, the press is out in force. I bet that's *Hello!* Magazine over there.' Sam pointed towards the church gate where photographs were being taken. 'Quite the jet set here in Westenbury. I never thought, once I came to work at your sister's dental surgery, I'd be hobnobbing with the rich and famous.'

'I think you'll find its Darren from the parish magazine,' Rosa said drily, trying to concentrate on what Sam was saying whilst attempting to work out where Joe Rosavina'd gone.

'Isn't that your ex over there?' Sam asked, his head resting firmly on her own, his arms snaking possessively around her waist.

Rosa glanced towards the old timbered lychgate at the entrance to the churchyard where Joe, holding his daughter Chiara's hand, was now heading without a backward glance. Joe had kissed her for the very first time under that gate's covered awning, as they'd sheltered there from a sudden autumn downpour when they were both just sixteen. 'I don't know,' Rosa smiled, taking Sam's hand. 'Was it?'

2

Seeing Joe Rosavina outside her church had unsettled Rosa and, rather than spending the afternoon visiting her elderly parishioners before battling the yew tree as she'd originally planned, she wanted nothing more than to pull on her walking boots and tramp over the surrounding fields by herself in an attempt to erase the image of him standing there, gazing across at her. She knew she also needed to work out what she was actually feeling for Sam. She'd been convinced Joe was about to come over and talk to her but Sam, appearing at her side, his arms wrapped somewhat possessively around her, had put paid to that. Well, it would, wouldn't it? No one's ex-lover is going to come across and tell you he still loves you when you're in a tight clinch with your new man. *Still loves you, Rosa? Dream on, you daft vicar.*

Meeting Sam six months ago had made her think she could move on from her past – could start again with a new love. But, deep down, if she was being totally honest, shouldn't she acknowledge that she must share some of the blame for her break-up with Joe seven years previously? She'd obstinately – almost feverishly – refused to listen when, determined to be head of the best investment company in London – in the UK – Joe had implored her to slow down, to take time out for their relationship. She'd known he wanted to have a family with her, wanted to perhaps move out of London, quit the hectic life they'd made for themselves, but she'd steadfastly turned a deaf ear to his ideas, to his appeals for their starting-to-crumble relationship.

Instead, she'd continued in the same vein, driving herself on, ignoring his pleas, keeping herself awake with the uppers she regularly downed with her black coffee. And which Joe, once he'd found them, just as regularly – and furiously – threw down the lavatory…

Rosa reached up into her kitchen cupboard for a new pack of coffee, sniffing at its contents in an attempt to exchange the addictive, albeit often bitter, sensory pleasure of remembering past times with Joe, for that of her addiction to caffeine.

'Penny for them?'

'Sorry? Oh?' Rosa jumped as Sam appeared at her side. 'What are *you* doing back? I thought you'd appointments all afternoon?'

'You were miles away.' He gave a little laugh, patting her arm. 'Obviously deep in thought about something? *Someone?*' Sam looked at her meaningfully.

'Your appointments?' Ignoring Sam's raised eyebrow, Rosa held up the cafetière in his direction and he nodded. 'I thought you were rushed off your feet over at the surgery?'

'School holidays. Two families I was supposed to be seeing have apparently taken advantage of some last-minute deal to Majorca and cancelled. I've a couple of hours free…'

'Both of them? Bit of a coincidence that, isn't it?'

'…so, I thought I'd come back over and give you a hand with that yew.'

Rosa glanced across at Sam, taking in his fair hair, his classically handsome face that had, according to Eva, made him such a hit at *Malik and Malik*, her sister and brother-in-law's dental surgery in the village. 'Actually…' she smiled, indicating her walking boots '…change of plan. I'm going to walk across the fields and then call in to see Mrs Whittaker and Mr Dobson. They're both just out of hospital and could do with a visit.'

'I'll come with you.'

'To see Mrs Whittaker and Mr Dobson?' Rosa frowned. 'Why?'

'We need to show your parishioners we're a couple and that we're serious about each other.' Sam smiled. 'You know, with your being a single woman vicar...' Sam trailed off. 'Well, I'll come for a walk anyway. I want to be with you, Rosa.'

'In those shoes?' Rosa glanced across at Sam's polished brogues.

'In any shoes,' Sam said seriously.

'Right.' Rosa inwardly sighed and then berated herself for not wanting Sam with her. She was in a relationship with him, for heaven's sake. Wasn't she seriously thinking of settling down with him? Her last chance to have the children of her own she so badly craved? With two years to go to her fortieth birthday, and with ten of her eggs frozen in a laboratory in London, prior to her undergoing the chemotherapy that had saved her life, she just had to work out what she wanted. Where she and Sam were heading. And whether she even still wanted to be on this journey with him.

And, she *had* to get Joe Rosavina out of her mind. She suddenly felt cross that her ex had dared to intrude into the life she was trying to make for herself back here in Westenbury. The sooner bloody Joe Rosavina left the village and moved back to London, the better for both of them; she could get on with her new life with Sam. 'OK, listen, Dad left his wellies here last time he was helping me in the garden; they'll probably fit you.'

The April afternoon was surprisingly warm and filled with perpetual, insistent birdsong from frantically occupied nest-builders. Newly emerging carpets of bluebells unrolled below their feet as they left the village and made their way through the adjoining woodland and, once they were back onto the country lanes, daffodils in differing hues of orange and yellow, banks of tulips and gloriously creamy magnolia, azalea and cherry blossom vied with each other in the cottage gardens basking in the unusually warm spring sunshine.

Rosa began to relax and enjoy the walk, loving being outside on such a glorious afternoon. She took Sam's hand in her own, feeling a happy contentment with her life as the village vicar, and being this lovely man's partner. She took a surreptitious glance in his direction as they walked. He really was amazingly good-looking – conventionally tall and handsome as the hero of any good romantic story must be. And didn't Sam fit the bill of the romantic hero in this, her own particular story? He'd come into her life just as she'd returned to the village and the vicarage, whisking her off her feet so that, six months later, it was assumed by her family and the church parishioners who saw them together that they were a couple. And she really wanted them to be just that. To be with Sam and try for the family they both so very much wanted.

Encouraged by the offer of her hand in his, Sam appeared also to loosen up. He smiled down at her, but she could tell her dad's wellingtons were too small for his feet and, although he was making an effort to hide it, he was in some discomfort.

'Look, you go back,' Rosa advised after a good thirty minutes' walking. 'Those wellies are pinching, aren't they? You can double back here and go down past the post office and across the cricket field and the village green. You'll be back in fifteen minutes.'

'What about you?' Sam was obviously loath to leave her. 'Why don't we both go back? Have a cup of tea and a bun before I go back to the surgery? I don't seem to have managed to get you all to myself for ages.'

Rosa was equally loath to leave this quite glorious afternoon and return to the piled-up admin waiting for her in her office. 'I'm just going to carry on for an hour or so, and then I can do my round of visiting on the way back.'

'I'm not leaving you by yourself.' Sam frowned. 'You don't know who's hanging round these woods.'

'Don't be daft, Sam. I've walked these woods and meadows since I was a kid…' She broke off as Sam came to a standstill, holding a hand up to his eyes against the afternoon sunshine, and almost leaning forward as he focused his vision on three figures up ahead of them, walking across fields separated only by drystone walls.

'Isn't that your ex over there?' Sam repeated the question he'd asked outside the church a couple of hours earlier.

'I think you're manifesting him when he's not actually there.' Rosa managed a laugh as she squeezed his hand.

'Oh, I think it's him alright.' Sam gave her a look. 'Is that why you didn't want me to carry on walking with you?'

'Well, your eyesight is a lot better than mine if you can make out an ex-boyfriend of mine at fifty paces,' Rosa tutted. 'And, to answer your question, Sam, I didn't want you to carry on walking with me because my dad's wellies are obviously a size too small for you. No ulterior motive. And I didn't really want to inflict old Mr Dobson – who is as deaf as a doorpost and bloody hard work – on you, knowing you've got to get back to work at some point.'

'Well, come back with me now, Rosa. Come on.'

'Sam, I *love* these fields. I want to carry on across them and head back home that way.'

'There's cows up there,' he started. 'I'm not overly keen on them.'

'Good job you're a dentist then and not a vet,' she said cheerfully.

'They can be dangerous. I was only reading the other day…'

'Oh, you big townie.' Rosa smiled but inwardly sighed. 'You live in the countryside now. Cow shit on your shoes and badgers under your back wheels, if you're not careful. You go back. I'm fine.'

'No, I'm not leaving you. I'll carry on with you. Make sure you're alright.'

'Why wouldn't I be? OK, OK up to you.' Rosa was beginning to feel irritated. 'Come on, if you're coming.'

'Why don't we go the other way?' Sam was insistent.

'Because I've been looking forward to going *this* way.'

'Because you've seen your ex across there? Hoping to bump into him? Unfinished business from outside the church this morning?'

'Sam, please don't do this.' Rosa shook her head and set off towards the fields. 'Come with me; I *want* you with me, but not if you're going to be so ridiculous. I haven't seen Joe – apart from outside church this morning – since before Christmas; since I had dinner with him and it just wasn't working. And now, I'm seeing *you*...'

'But wishing you were seeing Joe Rosavina?'

Rosa shook her head once more. 'I'm off. Are you coming or not?'

Without another word, Sam moved back to her side and in silence they climbed the first of three wooden stiles that took them across acres of farmland. Most of the fields were empty apart from a couple of large red tractors drilling oilseed rape in the adjacent one, and dressing and spraying cereal crops to their right. On their left, lambs that had been born at the beginning of March were already leaping around like teens at their first rave, headbanging with their mates, and Rosa gloried in the sight, laughing and pointing out their antics to Sam who remained sullenly unresponsive as they walked.

They'd just climbed over the fourth stile and were heading towards the lane leading back to the village, when two figures came towards them, one moving awkwardly and shouting, the smaller one running, but also screaming.

'Have you got a *phone*?' the taller one shouted down the field towards them. 'We need a *phone*. We need an *ambulance*... Oh, Rosa? Rosa, it's Joe...' Rhys Johnson, Joe Rosavina's almost-sixteen-year-old stepson, was limping towards her, completely covered in mud, while holding on to Joe's six-year-old daughter, Chiara, who continued to scream hysterically.

'What is it, Rhys? What's the matter? What's happened?' Rosa set off at speed towards him, pulling out her mobile from her jacket pocket as she did so.

'Daddy! Daddy! My daddy's dead. And Ron's poorly...'

'It's the cows...' Rhys managed to get the words out before suddenly swaying and sinking to the ground, holding his ankle. 'Think it's broken... my phone's broken too... left it in the mud...'

'The cows?' Rosa's heart was pounding as she took the hand of the little girl who was incoherent with crying.

'They've killed my daddy!' Chiara turned, pulling herself from Rosa's grasp, and started back up the field, running in hysterical circles, before racing back and pulling at Rhys's hoodie. 'Rhys, come and get *Daddy* and Ron...'

'Ambulance please... Cows... Yes, one man... actually, there's someone called Ron as well... I don't know... hurt as far as his children can tell...' Rosa couldn't believe this calm woman was herself speaking, when all she wanted to do was run and run and get to Joe in the next field. 'Erm, I don't know... Where are we...? Sam, where *are* we?' She turned, frantically appealing to Sam who, looking dazed, shook his head, unable to name the area and then to Rhys who had gone deathly white and appeared to be about to throw up. 'Head between your knees, Rhys,' Rosa automatically instructed, while pulling frantically at her hair, trying to get her bearings.

There was a swirling thick fog where her brain had once been, but she managed to tell the calmly questioning woman on the other end of the 999 call that they were in a field... 'Which field?' Rosa demanded of poor Rhys, who was obviously in some sort of shock. 'Come on, Rhys, which *one*?'

Rosa took some deep breaths, turning her back on Chiara who was continuing to shout, 'Daddy! Daddy!' and then 'Mummy! I want my mummy!' hopping pitifully from one to the other of her shiny red patent wellingtons while pulling at Rhys's clothes. Rosa scanned the landscape. Oh, thank goodness, there was Bracken Folly to her left and White Dean Farm next to it.

'OK,' she breathed, 'the field off the lane that leads to Bracken Folly and White Dean Farm, about half an hour's walk out of Westenbury village. He's in the second field above the farmhouse… no, there's no one with him… well, yes, someone called Ron… no, I'm going there now… I'll keep my phone on… you've got this number…'

Rosa turned to Sam who was attempting to calm and reassure the children, his arm held protectively around Chiara. 'Come on, we need to get up there.'

'Is that a good idea…? I mean… the children…?'

'A *good idea*?' Rosa breathed, trying to remain calm. 'You stay and look after these two, Sam. I need to get down to the lane to direct the ambulance…' She turned to Chiara. 'It's alright, sweetheart, it'll all be alright. The ambulance will come and help Daddy… He'll be fine…' She set off up the field at a run, knowing that if Joe *wasn't* fine, if he'd gone, *she'd* never be fine again. Instead of staying with the shocked children, Sam ran with her, trying to catch at her hand, to slow her down, but Rosa was having none of it.

'Sorry, Rosa, blisters… shit… hang on…' Sam was obviously in pain and Rosa stopped, but only to tell him to walk and catch her up, and she was off once more.

She frantically climbed the high wooden stile, missing her step and grazing her hand as she fell and then, pausing to scan the landscape from her vantage point at the top, saw something that looked like a bundle of rags under a huge oak tree at the very edge of the field ahead. The herd of around twenty brown cows – not the black and white Friesians Rosa'd been expecting – had moved towards the far corner of the field and were nonchalantly grazing once more. A slight movement from what she now realised was Joe, his blonde hair and white face lying awkwardly and standing out against the dark-coloured trunk of the tree, filled her with hope.

'Thank you, God,' she muttered. 'Thank you, thank you, God,' only to be plunged into despair when she saw the movement was from a small blonde dog. Since when did Joe have a dog? This, then, must be Ron.

'Rosa!' Sam called from behind her, as he hobbled painfully over the stile. 'Don't even think about it. For God's sake wait until the ambulance comes. Those cows are looking over here again. Come back,' he ordered. 'Shit,' he added, his right foot missing the last bit of the stile in the ill-fitting wellington, before following in her wake.

The tiny blonde dog – just a puppy – flung itself at Rosa, crying pitifully as it did so, its back leg hanging at a strange angle.

'Joe?' Rosa knelt at his side, took his hand, scanning his face for any movement. *Please, God, let him not be dead. Please, God, let him not be dead.* Rosa sent up prayer after prayer in her head as she scanned his deathly white face, the huge ugly blue-black mark on his temple – testament to the injury he'd received. Blood was congealing in his fair hair and his left hand was bruised, cut and bleeding.

Sam hunkered down beside them, ignoring Ron who was whining and attempting to climb into his lap. 'Just move out the way, Rosa,' Sam said brusquely, taking over. 'Stand up, go on, stand up so the paramedics will see you from the lane. He knelt at Joe's side, tilting the other man's head back, his own face centimetres from Joe's as he looked and felt for any signs of breathing. 'He's OK, Rosa, he's breathing.'

Oh, the relief. Rosa sent up her silent thanks to God.

Sam moved Joe on to his side and into the recovery position.

'Should you be doing that?' she asked. 'I mean, what if his neck or back is broken?'

'Rosa, I'm a dentist. Do you not think I've had training in every single bit of a head and neck's anatomy.'

'Oh yes, sorry. Of course.'

'He'll be OK, I think. Possibly got several broken ribs. Look, you can see hoof marks on his middle…' He broke off as Joe stirred, his eyelids fluttering before he opened them.

'Rosa?' Joe frowned, attempting to sit up. 'How come…?

What are you doing here? Shit... the kids?' His voice was panicked. Are they alright? Is Chiara OK? I told them to run...'

'It's OK, mate.' Sam's voice was calm, reassuring and, more than anything, kind, and Rosa glanced across at him, remembering just why she'd been so attracted to him when he'd come into her life the previous year. 'Lie still – you've had a nasty kick to the head and possibly broken ribs.'

'I told Chiara to let go of Ron, but she wouldn't,' Joe muttered. 'They just appeared from nowhere. From behind that hedge... and sort of circled us. One of them kicked out at Rhys and he went down... I wouldn't have taken them across a field of cows at this time of year... calves...'

'You're better not talking, mate,' Sam soothed.

'...and I had to get between the herd and Rhys and... fuck it... totally surreal.' Joe put a hand up to his head, obviously frightened by the amount of blood that continued to seep from a cut there.

An incoming ringtone – the Backstreet Boys' 'Don't Go Breaking My Heart' – made them all start, and Rosa scrambled to her feet from the long, wet grass, pulling her mobile from her jacket as she did so.

'Over here,' she shouted into the phone, waving her arms above her head towards the lane where a police car, and an ambulance, blue lights flashing, were just pulling up behind a rapid response vehicle. 'Over here!' She continued waving and gesticulating, before heading off towards them.

'Rosa, the cows,' Sam warned. 'For God's sake, are they still there...?'

'It's OK, they've moved right back into the far field and...' Rosa strained to see '...I think there's a Land Rover and a couple of farmer types with them now.'

'Arrest that cow,' Joe muttered with a slight smile before wincing in pain. 'Rosa, can you see to the kids?'

'I'll stay here with Joe,' Sam offered, and Rosa shot him a look of gratitude. 'You go and reassure that little girl her daddy's

OK.' Rosa realised Sam was probably remembering the horror of being told his own twelve-year-old son, Ollie, had died in a freak avalanche in Italy, several years earlier.

'Anyone else hurt?' A young paramedic, accompanied by an even younger-looking policeman took her to one side as two more, older paramedics, knelt down to attend to Joe.

'A possible broken ankle,' Rosa said, 'and shock, I would think. Two kids... they're in the next field. We need to get over to them.'

'Hang on, we can't just walk across this field with that lot...' The young officer indicated the herd of cows now calmly grazing up ahead, before surveying the patchwork of fields below. 'We're near enough here to the lane. We should be able to drive across the field from the bottom entrance.'

'I'll go and see to Rhys and Chiara, Joe,' Rosa said. 'We'll take them back to the vicarage and I'll ring your mum and dad from there.'

'I'll go to the hospital with Joe,' Sam said. 'I just need to ring the surgery to cancel my evening appointments.'

'That's so kind of you, Sam,' Rosa breathed. 'Thank you.'

Five minutes later, the police car was making its way through the gate at the bottom of the lower field, bumping painfully across tussocky grass and molehills, tyres churning up puddles and mud and splattering windows.

'There, over there,' Rosa shouted as the two figures came into view halfway up the meadow. Rhys was sat against a drystone wall, his arm around a white-faced Chiara who was now eerily quiet.

'It's OK, OK, Chiara. Daddy's fine,' Rosa shouted, carrying Ron over to the pair of them. 'Look, Ron's possibly got a broken leg, so we need to get him to the vet. Daddy's gone off in the ambulance, but he'll be fine.'

'Right, young man, let's have a look at this ankle of yours.' The young paramedic was all breezy bonhomie as she examined Rhys's legs and feet. 'Yep, looks to be broken; we need a pot on that.' She grinned. 'You'll have all the girls writing their names on it by this time tomorrow.'

'Not sure how I'm going to work down at Rosavina's if I can't stand,' he said gloomily. 'I'm trying to save up to get to Australia to see Mum.'

'I'm going too.' Chiara wiped a filthy hand across her tear-streaked cheeks. 'I want to see Mummy too.'

'Right, OK, Vicar,' the police officer said, taking in Rosa's dog collar before looking at his watch. 'What do you want to do with these two?'

'So, if Rhys can go with you up to A and E…' Rosa smiled at the young paramedic '…I can take Chiara back with me to the vicarage and ring her grandparents from there and tell them what's happened. That OK with you two?'

Rhys nodded. 'Thanks, Rosa.' He turned to Chiara. 'Your dad's OK, Chiara. Go with Rosa and she'll look after you. She's a vicar; that's what she does.'

3

A week after her sister Rosa had found herself rescuing ex-boyfriends from angry cows, Eva Malik snapped an angry *Fuck it* at the traffic diversion signs ahead of her. The first of the Quinn triplets to be lifted unceremoniously from their birth mother, world-famous artist Alice Parkes, and handed immediately over to Alice's older sister and her husband, Susan and Richard, for adoption, Eva had come to a standstill at roadworks parallel to *Malik and Malik* Dental Surgery in the heart of Westenbury village. Impatiently tapping her fingers on the steering wheel as she sat in the burgeoning queue of cars pulling up at the temporary traffic lights, Eva realised the huge hole in the road was probably the surgery's fault – well, her husband Rayan's fault, determined as he was to expand his village surgery into something resembling those one might expect to find in neighbouring Midhope, Leeds and Manchester.

The new gas and water pipes needed at the extended surgery were in the process of being updated at the mains, plus a veritable spaghetti-load of updated electricity cables to operate the latest dental paraphernalia, hydraulic beds and chairs Rayan had insisted upon, were being threaded onwards and upwards to where they were needed. These, as well as a healthier and redirected broadband, had resulted in a five-day closure of the roads and pavements on this side of the village.

On her way to a meeting of the Estate Management Committee up at Heatherly Hall, several miles out of the village – and now late because of the roadworks – Eva reflected not only on the changes to the village, but on the recent changes to her life as well. Newly separated from Rayan, her husband of fourteen years, she contemplated the huge adjustments already brought about by the split of just a few months' duration, as well as those that were obviously still ahead for her, Rayan and their family.

The village was very different now and Eva wasn't totally convinced it was all for the better. Just as she wasn't completely able to reassure herself that the separation from Rayan, now that it had actually materialised after months – possibly years – of her secretly debating the idea, was what she really wanted. Sitting impatiently at the wheel of her Evoque, she took a good look round at the village of her birth; the village she'd never really expected to return to after training as a dentist.

The road across from the village school – where her own seven-year-old daughter, Laila, was now in Y2 – appeared busier than ever, controlled by a series of pelican crossings, more traffic lights but, as well, on school days, a traditional lollipop lady.

Laila seemed happy enough at Little Acorns and, whenever Rayan had suggested that they might think of moving their daughters into the private sector, in line with how he most certainly *hadn't* been educated in the Little Horton area of Bradford, Eva had demurred, quoting league tables and statistics to bolster her argument that Laila was just fine where she was.

Eva reached into the glove compartment for the half-eaten Crunchie she knew was still in there. She might be a practising dental surgeon and not allow her girls sweets except on Saturdays, but she wasn't averse to a sneaky chocolate treat herself when no one was looking. Eva sucked almost lasciviously at the chocolate, poking the tip of her tongue into the sweet honeycomb while gazing across at *Malik and Malik* and remembering how the now extended building had once housed one of the last remaining branches of Freeman, Hardy and Willis.

Eva could hear her four-year-old self begging to be taken to where the branch had, apparently, stood since the turn of the last century. It wasn't so much the shoes themselves that fascinated her (although one glance at the number of shoeboxes that graced Eva's fabulous walk-in wardrobe might, she conceded, have suggested otherwise) but that the black-skirted, white-bloused assistants had the enviable job of climbing little ladders to reach the high-up shoeboxes. Eva knew that, one day, this was what *she* was going to do and she remembered Bill Astley, their natural father, on one of their very rare earlier visits up to Heatherly Hall, laughing with glee when she'd told him, quite determinedly, that when she was a big girl, she was going to be one of the ladies up the ladder in Freeman, Hardy and Willis. For months, even years after, Bill had continued to collectively label the triplets Freeman, Hardy and Willis, which had annoyed her five-year-old self intensely, her sisters getting in on the act, on *her* ambition to be the one up the ladder, touching the ceiling.

God, she missed Bill. She'd never imagined his death would leave such a hole but, almost six months after his death, she missed his eccentricity, his refusal to bend and adhere to the social norms befitting those born into British aristocracy, as well as his devilish sense of humour. And, of course, she missed the obvious love he'd had for his natural daughters, over his two remaining legitimate children, Jonny and Henrietta Astley who, despite Bill's desperate efforts to keep in touch with them once they'd left with their mother and her lover to America, hadn't appeared, over the years, to want to have anything to do with their father. Until the will was read of course.

Eva frowned, remembering the bombshell of the reading of Bill's will, immediately after his funeral. The shock of the revelation that, although Bill legally *had* to pass on the inherited title of Marquess of Stratton to his legitimate son, Jonny, he'd also tied up his own fifty-one per cent share of Heatherly Hall and its surrounding estate, handing it over to Eva, Hannah and Rosa while leaving nothing, apart from the title, to Jonny and very little to Henrietta. Eva smiled at her reflection in the car mirror, remembering with love the man who had played such a major part in her life. She even missed that damned greying ponytail of Bill's that she and her sisters had threatened to cut off for years. Too late now, Eva thought sadly. And too late, as well, for her to be up the ladder in Freeman, Hardy and Willis.

Instead of becoming a shoe-shop girl (as well as not following her heart and Bill's encouragement that she go to art college in order to realise her dream of being an artist as famous as the girls' birth mother, Alice Parkes) Eva had gone to Sheffield University, trained as a dentist, met and married Rayan, and given birth to their two daughters. She still wasn't sure why she'd decided, at eighteen, to go down the scientific route and become a dentist rather than the artistic road to being a professional artist. She'd not liked to admit, even to herself, that she'd wanted the security of earning a good wage, having a posh car, a lovely house which, with four girls to bring up on one average wage, her adoptive parents had never aspired to. Artists, so often, ended up on the breadline, starving in the proverbial garret. And, what she'd now achieved, materially, as well as being blessed with a steady husband and two beautiful daughters, that should have been enough. Surely? *More* than enough.

And yet it hadn't been. Guilt – actual shame – that her loving husband, her daughters, her career as a dentist and her large modern five-bedroomed house up in Heath Green on the edge of the village *hadn't* been enough, sometimes threatened to overwhelm her. Flatten her, almost with shame, that she hadn't worked harder at her marriage. And yet, when both Rosa and Susan – their mother – had suggested she sit down with Rayan and work out just what it was she wanted and why and where the marriage was floundering (it's lack of sex, Mum!) part of her, just a tiny part of her, didn't want to do that because she wanted to see what was out there for her in the big wide world; was excited – albeit terrified – at what she might discover about herself.

Once the lights turned green, Eva took the diversion around the village before re-joining the main road out to Heatherly Hall and put her foot down, disregarding the speed limit. Hell, she might as well be hung for a sheep as a lamb now that everyone appeared to hate her. She was persona non grata with Rayan's extended family in Bradford who couldn't countenance the fact that she and Rayan had separated, as well as with Rosa who, despite her support and seeming non-judgemental approach to the breakdown of Eva's marriage, was, Eva knew, distressed by the whole situation. Susan, their mother, was also terribly upset with her while Virginia, their eldest sister, had been straight round on more than one occasion with a sympathetically handed-over casserole or lemon drizzle cake, hoping to find out exactly what was going on in Eva's life.

And when Eva refused (as she always had) to open up to this big sister of theirs, Virginia, it appeared, wasn't averse to reminding anyone listening that, of course, the triplets' *real* mother was that Bohemian Alice Parkes and, really, was it any wonder Eva was now following her artist mother in going off the rails? The whole affair appeared to be becoming everyone's main topic of conversation.

Affair? Ha? There wasn't and never *had been* any *affair*. Maybe if she'd had a bit of a fling, put into motion an actual real-life marital affair rather than the erotic fantasies she'd built up over the years as a result of Rayan's lack of interest – sexually – in her, she'd have got it out of her system and been able to get on with the rest of her life. The rest of her marriage.

Eva slowed down, taking the next turn on the right before leaning out of the car window and swiping with her lanyard to gain entry into the grounds of Heatherly Hall and driving through to her allocated parking spot. She still felt the same thrill of ownership, of pride she'd had ever since the three of them had learnt of Bill Astley, twelfth Marquess of Stratton's decision to leave the running of the hall in their hands.

Eva clambered out of the car, ran a hand down her grey woollen pencil skirt, another through her long dark hair and, on too-high heels, made her way to the Estate Management Office.

4

'OK, can we get started, we've a lot to get through?' Hannah Quinn, the third of the late Bill Astley's natural daughters and newly elected Chair of the Estate Management Committee at Heatherly Hall, tapped determinedly with a pencil on the pad in front of her. 'You're late, Eva.'

'And *you're* getting bossy,' Eva hissed crossly. '*And*,' she whispered in Hannah's ear as she pulled out the chair to her sister's left, 'looking absolutely *shagged*. Ben Pennington been keeping you up all night again?'

'Do you mind?' Hannah hissed back, glaring at Eva before smiling a polite benevolence she wasn't feeling at the others gathered around the long office desk. She'd been there much earlier than was necessary, putting out bottles of Harrogate spring water and little dishes of Heatherly Hall wrapped chocolate mints in the hope that she'd be taken a little more seriously as chair than at previous meetings. She'd even eschewed her usual jeans and Timberlands for the smart little navy suit she'd treated herself to last week in Leeds, and spent what seemed like hours putting up her hair in a business-like chignon. Which was now starting to hurt like hell.

'You're new to all this,' Rosa had advised after the very first formal get-together when Rosa had put forward Hannah as chair and Eva had seconded the motion. 'Don't go in all guns blazing; think what Bill would have wanted, what plans – if any – he had in mind.'

'But we *know* what Bill had in mind,' Hannah had snapped,

upset when the first meeting back in January hadn't gone quite as she'd hoped. 'He wanted us three in charge of the place, with me as chair.'

'He never actually mentioned you as chair… you know, in so many words,' Rosa had soothed.

'Well, *you* do it then.' Hannah had flounced off back to the apartment at the top of the east wing of the hall where Bill had lived for years and where both she, and now Eva, having separated from Rayan, spent several nights of the week. It wasn't like her to flounce, and she felt a bit daft once the little hissy fit had evaporated, leaving her not quite sure where to go from there. She was just so eager to get it all right, so desperate not to let Bill down after he'd left the responsibility of running the place to the three of them.

It was Lachlan Buchanan, the estate manager down from Scotland, employed by Bill only weeks before his death, who appeared determined to thwart her at every step until Hannah, red-faced and upset, had reminded him at the last meeting just who it was that carried fifty-one per cent shares in the running of the place.

'Yes,' Rosa, ever the peacemaker, had soothed once more when yet another meeting had concluded without them getting through half the items on Hannah's agenda. 'But there are others, Hannah, who together hold a forty-nine per cent share, who've been at this game much longer than us and who have an almost equal say in what goes on.'

'I just want to get it right,' Hannah had actually wept tears – she was premenstrual at the time which, Eva said, in the world of business was absolutely no excuse: you didn't pull the hormone card, in a world run too often by men who *didn't have* a period every month, if you wanted to have people not only listen to you but also give you what you wanted.

And now, on this beautiful late April morning, several months and more than several meetings on, Lachlan Buchanan continued to be a thorn in her side. He raised a sardonic eye (Lachlan, Hannah had soon come to realise, was exceptionally well versed in sardonicism) and leaned back in his chair.

'Can we get on?' he asked pointedly as Hannah and Eva continued to glare crossly at each other. 'Where's the village vicar? I hear she was in some confrontation with Jack Eastwood's cows last week?'

'Rosa has a funeral that couldn't wait.' Hannah smiled, trying her best to present a calm, cool, business-like exterior. 'At least Mr Grundy – the deceased – couldn't. What with Easter and, apparently an abundance of deaths and a dearth of slots at the crem for some reason, he's been hanging around for…'

'So, one down?' Lachlan interrupted.

'Who? Mr Grundy? Oh, sorry, Rosa, you mean.' Hannah felt herself redden. What was it about this man that made her appear like a bumbling idiot? 'She's coming as soon as she can,' Hannah went on, finding sanctuary in her glass of water. This taking the chair, with bolshie blokes like Buchanan trying to get his own way, was so much harder than she'd ever anticipated when, practising what she had to say in her bathroom mirror, she'd envisaged the other members nodding benignly to all matters on her list before she'd ask prettily, *So? Any other business?* 'And, while we can discuss plans for the hall without Rosa, we certainly can't be making any major decisions.'

'Well, let's make a start on the discussion then. I'm already behind with the annual end-of-year land survey.'

'End-of-year?' Hannah stared. 'It's April.'

'Exactly.' Lachlan Buchanan raised an eyebrow. 'The financial year ends and begins in April, although you don't appear to be aware of that and all the financial implications that go with it. Do you need Anthony here to take you through it again?' Lachlan's tone was condescending as he nodded towards the estate accountant who appeared to be heavily involved in the day's Wordle rather than ready with up-to-date figures of the hall's financial situation. 'And, without the extra help that Bill promised me would be on the way, I'm way behind. So, if we could just get on?'

Would Lachlan ever take her seriously, Hannah wondered? OK, as a trained youth offending officer previously working in the local youth courts, Hannah had had little – no, to be honest, absolutely no – experience of running any business, especially one as complex as Heatherly Hall PLC. Rosa, with all her business acumen should, in all fairness, have been elected chair, but it was the last thing she'd wanted, having only been at the helm of All Hallows Church down in Westenbury village since the previous autumn. Rosa, however, was her absolutely right-hand woman when it came to financial expertise and Hannah looked at the door hoping Mr Grundy (deceased) was well and truly on the way to his maker and Rosa would come to the rescue.

'Certainly, we can get on.' Hannah patted her chignon, pulled the sleeves of her suit jacket down over the cuffs of her white shirt and flashed what she hoped was a superior on/off smile in Lachlan's direction before turning to Anthony Watkins, the hall's chief accountant who was always on her side whenever she felt sides were being taken. 'OK, welcome all. If we can start with Anthony's presentation re Heatherly Hall's financial position? I believe, Anthony, the books are looking pretty healthy?'

'The *books*?' Lachlan interjected. 'This isn't the church accounts we're looking at.' Lachlan frowned, shook his head but said nothing further as Anthony launched into a fifty-minute monologue pointing out red lines and black lines, peaks and troughs on pie charts and graphs which, Hannah, not being the best of mathematicians, tried her best to follow in the beautifully presented folder Anthony had placed in front of her. Eva, being mathematically as well as artistically gifted, appeared to understand exactly what was going on, giving little nods of approval or a slight shake of the head where appropriate, as she followed the accountant's presentation. As far as Hannah could see, there appeared to be more black spikes than red and that, surely, had to be a good thing?

The door opened as Anthony was still in full flow and, mouthing apologies, Rosa slipped into the vacant seat on the other side of Hannah, poured herself water and immediately began to scrutinise the figures in the folder.

'Better than I expected,' Rosa eventually said, and Hannah gave her a grateful kick under the table while simultaneously raising a triumphant glance in Lachlan's direction. 'Looks like opening Tea and Cake a couple of evenings a week as Astley's Champagne Bar and Grill is beginning to take off, Anthony?'

'Early days, yet, Vicar…'

'Rosa, please,' Rosa murmured.

'…but yes, Hannah's idea for the café might just turn out to be one of you ladies' better ideas.' He smiled across at Hannah with puppy-dog eyes and, this time, smiling slightly, Rosa nudged Hannah while Hannah flashed another superior smile across at Lachlan.

Lachlan simply appeared bored, glancing at the office wall clock before prodding a finger at the itinerary in front of him. While she might have won this particular battle, Hannah knew the war for the best way forward for Heatherly Hall was only beginning. 'So,' Hannah went on, 'item two on the agenda.'

'*Westenbury?*' Lachlan said, reading out the single word in disdain and shaking his head. 'Really?'

'Really,' Eva and Hannah spoke as one. 'Bill had rock groups performing in the grounds previously,' Eva went on. 'The Screaming Eagles, if you remember them? Biggest rock band of the Eighties. It was a great success apparently. Before our time obviously, but…'

'You're going back over thirty years,' Lachlan interrupted. 'Before Bill went into breeding Angus beef cattle and the Blue-faced Leicester sheep on the estate. Having a festival to rival Glastonbury here in *Westenbury* is perfectly ludicrous.'

'As I said,' Eva went on, now complicit with Hannah, 'obviously before our time, but a great success.'

'And,' Hannah added, 'with the revenue from that concert, Bill was able to get a loan to refurbish part of the hall and eventually start the wedding venue. So I reckon, with a hell of a lot of planning, *Westenbury* is certainly on the cards. Look at Leeds Festival…'

'Exactly. Look at it.'

'And did you?' Hannah narrowed her eyes at Lachlan.

'Did I what?'

'Ever look at Leeds?'

'Certainly not.'

'No, I bet you didn't,' Hannah snapped. 'I bet at seventeen you were in your kilt up some heather-strewn Scottish mountain, tossing your…'

Eva started to laugh.

'…caber. Or blowing your…'

More titters from Eva.

'…bagpipes.'

'Bit of stereotyping there, Hannah,' Rosa murmured while Hannah, fed up with Lachlan's attempts at dissing their ideas, and now well into her stride, went on: 'Well *we* did.' Hannah looked at Rosa and Eva as the three of them remembered that fabulous summer of 2002 when they were seventeen and experiencing their first rock festival.

'Prodigy,' Eva said excitedly. 'Do you remember?'

'Foo Fighters,' Hannah responded. 'The Strokes. God they were good. And do you remember? There was a big rumour that the Backstreet Boys were going to turn up?'

'And did they?' Anthony Watkins was almost as excited as the triplets.

''Fraid not.' Eva pulled a disappointed face, seemingly as put out now as she had been twenty years earlier. 'Mind you,' she brightened up at the memory, 'there was Pulp and Muse…'

'Ash,' Hannah contributed.

'*Joe Rosavina*,' Rosa added dreamily and then, as Anthony Watkins frowned and said, 'Don't think I remember him, Vicar. What band was he in, then?' the other two started to laugh at Rosa's red-faced embarrassment as she realised what she'd said.

'Rosa's first boyfriend,' Hannah explained kindly. 'She met him *here*, in the llama pen, when we were sixteen and actually *rescued* him, last week, apparently, from a bunch of marauding...'

'I'm sorry, can we get on rather than hearing an extended litany of boy bands and first boyfriends you three have known, loved and latterly rescued?' Lachlan Buchanan interrupted, a weary look on his – Hannah had to admit – rather handsome face. 'I've another meeting in an hour or so. I've said I'll talk to some American who is supposedly writing a potted history of England's ancestral homes.'

'By yourself?' Hannah coloured slightly. 'You've not mentioned this before. Do you not think it might be a good idea if myself or Rosa or Eva is there with you? I mean, it is Heatherly Hall business.'

Lachlan brought up both hands and made to rise from his chair. 'You're more than welcome to meet with him instead of me and then I can get on with the real business of running this estate. You know, Bill and old Jim Mitchell left a lot to be desired when they were both in charge. I'm finding all sorts of things that should have been attended to: bills not paid, seed not ordered; a clear plan for where the lambs are headed in a couple of months' time...'

'Oh, they're not off to the... you know... the...?' Hannah, a vegetarian, was clearly distressed.

'The abattoir? For the chop?' Lachlan pulled a knife across his own throat and Hannah winced. 'What did you think was going to happen to them?'

'I just thought we could, you know, keep them as pets in the petting zoo.'

'Cute bouncy little lambs grow into ugly great sheep with ticks and foot rot, eating every bit of grass on the estate and weighed down with a fleece no one wants to buy any more seeing how everyone now wears Lycra and polyester.'

'Suppose.' Hannah nodded in agreement.

'So, is that what you want?'

'What? *Westenbury* festival?'

Lachlan sighed impatiently. 'No, Hannah, I'm asking if you want to meet this American instead of me and then I can get on and do what I'm actually paid to do instead of listening to yet more half-baked ideas that more than likely will come to nothing?' He glanced at his watch. 'He'll be here soon.'

'Hang on,' Eva protested. 'Before you go, I'd like some discussion around my art retreat idea.'

'Art retreat?' Lachlan sighed irritably. 'Go on then.'

'Right, OK.' Eva glanced round at both Rosa and Hannah and they nodded encouragingly. 'So, as I'm sure you're all fully aware, as well as Bill Astley being our birth father, our birth mother was – is – Alice Parkes.'

'The three of you conceived up in the rooms adjacent to the bell tower,' Anthony Watkins interrupted almost excitedly, his left leg doing a strange involuntary little jig under the table as he spoke. 'What was Alice actually *doing* up there?' he added, his eyes wide in anticipation of a bit of soft-porn gossip.

'Having sex with the twelfth Marquess of Stratton I would imagine,' Lachlan said drily.

'Admiring Bill's own artwork I believe,' Eva retorted hotly. 'They were both, as you know very gifted artists.'

'Well, yes, obviously.' Lachlan leaned back, seemingly bored with the way the conversation was going. 'You don't become the UK's – possibly the world's – most feted female artist by completing a W H Smith's Painting by Numbers.' Lachlan glanced at his watch once more.

'So, what an absolutely fabulous opportunity then to turn those attic rooms where Bill's art murals beguiled Alice into…'

'Into having sex with him?' Anthony interrupted helpfully

(and hopefully), his leg accelerating into a steady tantivy on the wooden floor.

'As you say, Anthony.' Eva nodded dismissively in his direction. 'This would be a total missed opportunity to not only open those rooms to the paying public, but to hold three- and four-day art retreats up there as well. We can work around the conference centre and wedding venue guest rooms so that after a day's painting, the delegates – the artists – will have a lovely room and a fabulous dinner to look forward to.'

'And who are you thinking of getting to teach on these retreats?' Paul Osborne, Heatherly Hall's banking representative, spoke for the first time. 'They won't come cheap, you know. For a good teacher.'

'Ah well, that's where you're wrong,' Eva said with some pride. 'I myself, having inherited something of my parents' artistic talents, will be artist in charge. And I *won't* charge to begin with.' Eva gave a little laugh. 'But…' she paused for effect '…Alice Parkes herself has discussed with me being artist in residence every now and again.'

'Alice has?' Hannah and Rosa turned in surprise. 'When did she agree to that? She's back in New York.'

'No, she's not. She's actually in Paris at the moment.'

'Alice is? Back in Paris?'

'You've kept that to yourself.' Rosa and Hannah spoke as one, both put out that Eva had been making arrangements with their birth mother without consulting them.

'Well, I'll believe that when I see it,' Lachlan sniffed. 'Mind you,' he added, relenting and smiling in Eva's direction, 'if you can pull that off, Eva, you'll be onto a winner.'

Hannah, even more put out that Lachlan was actually smiling at Eva's idea when he'd done nothing but diss anything she, Hannah, had put forward, snapped, 'You'll never get her here, Eva. She's notoriously unreliable.'

'Not only that,' Eva added, ignoring Hannah as well as Rosa

who had raised a hand to speak, 'I'm going to persuade Yves Dufort to come over for guest appearances as well.' Her face was suffused with excitement.

'Yves Dufort?' A cumulative shocked silence went round the room.

'You may as well suggest Leonardo da Vinci turn up to give lessons in how to hold a paintbrush.' Paul Osborne finally broke the silence, smiling condescendingly while screwing the top onto his expensive-looking fountain pen.

'Ooh, I like *him*.' Mrs Sykes, Bill's former part-time housekeeper, had come unnoticed into the room bearing a tray heavy with coffee and biscuits. Without Bill to cook for and look after, Hannah had, only last month, made the decision to 'let her go' and yet here she was, appearing to think she was still employed in the private apartments of Heatherly Hall. '*Titanic*'s my all-time favourite film.' She beamed, hanging on to the tray as if it were the doomed ship itself.

'Wrong Leonardo,' Paul Osborne murmured, while Lachlan jumped up to relieve Mrs Sykes of the tray.

He wouldn't do that for me, Hannah thought crossly. She couldn't for the life of her think what she might have done to make him so tetchy with her. She supposed it was her constantly coming up with ideas for the hall that Lachlan thought ridiculous or extravagant or downright unworkable. Or maybe it was just that he recognised a total amateur when he saw one. She really was trying her best with it all. Had been more than happy to give up her job as youth worker in the local juvenile courts in order to put everything into this fabulous new and exciting opportunity the three of them had been given.

But everything seemed to be getting out of control: Mrs Sykes was still coming in to work; Lachlan Buchanan was being pleasant to everyone but herself, and bloody Eva had gone off and arranged all this art retreat stuff with Alice without consulting her as chair first.

'Actually…' Eva smiled round at the meeting while Rosa

poured coffee and passed on a plate of rather lovely flapjack and tiffin Mrs Sykes had baked that morning '...the three of us are heading to Paris at some stage to meet up with Yves Dufort to discuss arrangements.'

'We are?' Hannah's head came up in surprise. 'Does he know about this? Did *you* know about this, Rosa?'

Rosa nodded. 'Eva and I chatted about it a couple of days ago.'

'And you didn't think to tell me?' Hannah was getting fed up with everyone now. What was the point of being elected chair of the estate committee if she wasn't kept in the loop on what was going on?

'This is, you know, *personal stuff*, Hannah,' Rosa soothed, 'rather than Heatherly Hall business. You know...?' She broke off as Eva gave them both a warning look.

'Right, everyone.' Hannah was determined to bring the meeting to heel. 'I think we've enough to be thinking about.' She turned to her sisters. 'I suggest we three reconvene this evening in my – Bill's – apartment to discuss this alleged trip to Paris – 7pm?' She glared meaningfully at Eva and Rosa before standing, shuffling and picking up papers like a BBC newsreader and, without a backward glance at anyone, exited as imperiously as she could.

There, that would show them who was in charge round here.

5

Would Lachlan Buchanan ever give her any credit? Hannah wondered as she left the main building and made her way over to Tea and Cake, the hall's thriving café (prefixed, latterly, with the loftily superior adjective *organic.*) Bar and restaurant, really, Hannah thought proudly, now that the rebranding of the place as Astley's three evenings a week at the weekend was, at her instigation, not only up and running but had, according to Anthony the accountant, a definite potential for profit.

The daytime café was much improved since the triplets had themselves worked there in their school holidays when they were in their teens, when a cheese-and-beetroot-filled teacake was probably the most exotic thing on the menu. Now, Hannah scanned the menu on the blackboard outside, there was a Cannellini Bean and Chocolate Chilli Casserole, Feta-and-Spinach-Stuffed Sweet Potato, and Roasted Pepper and Leek Tart.

Hannah had already set on a team of gorgeous young things from Midhope University eager to work in what she (and they) hoped would be the place to be seen, as well as pay off their student loans. 'Bit better than the Co-op's polyester overall,' she'd heard one say to another as they were issued their newly designed black logoed T-shirts and red aprons – Heatherly Hall's coat of arms colours – before Hannah had taken them through what would be expected of them.

'I was keen to get across to the new staff that, while we want Astley's to be upmarket, young and vibrant,' Hannah had explained importantly to Rosa and Eva, 'they must remember that this is a former historic stately home with all that that implies…'

'If they're young and vibrant, they'll still be vomiting behind the historic English oaks after too much fizz, no matter how upmarket you're hoping the customers will be,' Eva had remarked drily. 'You can up your prices and pretend you're on a par with London or Harrogate, Hannah, but when the gals from Goole or the lads from Leeds are on their hen and stag dos…'

'Hen dos? Stag dos? I don't *think* so…' Hannah had replied. 'This is Heatherly Hall and not an excuse for an almighty piss-up. I tell you, Eva, people come from miles around to get a table at Clementine's down in the village. I want them to consider coming out here to Astley's for a glass of fizz first. Or coming on here after they've eaten.'

'Talk to her, Rosa,' Eva had said, shaking her head. 'She needs to sit down with the rest of us, and particularly you, with all your business experience and acumen, and come up with a proper business plan. Or we'll be bankrupt and calling in the creditors before we've even started.'

But while the rest of the trustees – the accountants, the senior estate workers, the bank and the lawyers who made up the committee – had sat down with Hannah and eventually listened to and approved what she wanted in this, the very first plan of action in taking Heatherly Hall forward after Bill's death, it was Lachlan who had continued to question not only her ideas, but also appeared to find great pleasure – amusement even – in questioning her actual authority.

She wished Bill was here to help her.

Hannah picked up her coffee and made her way across the grounds to the main part of the hall where she knew Nicola, the conference centre manager, as well as Tiffany and her team of wedding planners, would now be back from the meeting, hard at work. Tiffany Peterson, in charge of the wedding venue for many years, was superb at her job and the member of staff Hannah trusted and relied on more than any other. This was one area of Heatherly Hall into which Bill had insisted on pouring money and resources fifteen years previously and, while it had taken a while getting there, it was, as a result, now one of the North of England's most sought-after venues both for weddings and up to three-day business conferences. It was, Hannah knew, what kept Heatherly Hall healthily in the black and she had the sense to defer to those who had been running the place for years and knew what they were doing.

Things weren't going that badly, Hannah reassured herself, apart from Lachlan Buchanan constantly sticking in his bloody long – and Scottish – nose where it wasn't wanted. She wondered if she had the power to sack him. As she walked, waving hello to the ground staff who all appeared involved in tying back the mass of dead and dying daffodils whose annual carpet of yellow was one of Heatherly Hall's spring attractions, she acted out the little scenario in which she would stand at the long table and say: "Mr Buchanan, you don't appear happy in your work here at Heatherly Hall. Please don't let myself and the rest of the trustees keep you from handing in your resignation and buggering off back to bloody Balmoral where you belong. I'm sure His Majesty would be happy to have you back."

Or not, Hannah thought grimly as she picked up a couple of pieces of litter and continued walking, rueing the fact that Lachlan Buchanan, having previously being employed at the Queen's Scottish estate, had been poached by Bill from his position across the border just a few weeks before Bill had died.

Hannah turned as the sound of a speeding vehicle had her stepping off of the tarmacked snaking driveway up to the hall and onto the verge.

'Going my way, darling?' The car pulled up at her side and a hand reached out of the driver's window to stroke her behind lasciviously.

'Ben!' Hannah beamed in delight. 'I thought you were in theatre all this afternoon – and evening?'

'Some bug going round, apparently. My op had to be cancelled. So, I thought, what could I be doing instead? And I thought: Hannah, that's what I could be doing.'

'I've a ton of stuff still to do.' Hannah frowned. 'There's a mountain of work I have to get through.'

'Hannah, give yourself a break. Give *me* a break.' Ben Pennington smiled winningly, stroking her bottom through the tight-fitted navy skirt with such expertise she thought her legs might buckle and she'd end up on the grass amongst the newly tied-back daffs. 'Get in. Come on. I don't have to be back at the hospital until this evening.'

'I really shouldn't...'

'You really should.' Ben's hand moved (an amazingly consummate and practised manoeuvre through a car window, Hannah thought, but of course he was a neurosurgeon and had hands that were skilled in clever and dextrous movements) his fingers gently inching their way beneath her skirt.

'OK, OK,' Hannah finally said. 'OhhhhhKaaaaay.' She turned, adjusting her clothing before making her way round to the passenger door of Ben's beautiful car. She was about to lower herself in when some instinct had her glancing over her shoulder. Lachlan Buchanan was standing talking to another man several yards behind her under one of the ancient oaks. He raised a hand in her direction, the customary sardonic smile on his face.

Bugger, Hannah thought, totally embarrassed. That was all she needed, for Buchanan to catch her being goosed by some man's hand through a car window in the middle of the day when she should be working.

6

Eva glanced round at the room, previously the grandiose east wing of Heatherly Hall in its glory days, which Bill had turned into his personal living quarters once the hall was taken over by the management committee, and he no longer had full run of the place. The April evening sunshine poured in through the tall south-west-facing windows, lighting up the expensively swagged drapes and the beautifully corniced and gilded ceilings. The fire in the sumptuous fireplace, lit earlier that afternoon with sweet-smelling estate logs to stave off the chill that rarely released its pernicious hold on the hall even in summer, was almost out. A quite magnificent vase of tulips and daffodils filched by Hannah from the grounds stood on an antique French polished table to one side of the fire. Hannah's red cardigan was thrown carelessly over one end of the Victorian sofa.

But there was, Eva thought as she continued to take in the contents of the room, evidence of a more masculine presence: Ben Pennington's navy Crombie, his large leather briefcase and pile of hardback John Grisham novels had set up residence on one of the Queen Anne chairs at the back of the room, exuding a sense of maleness, an almost indefinable *virile masculinity* that always makes its presence felt once a man moves his things into a previously very much female domain.

It was Rayan's turn to have his two days in the family home with her girls – alright, *their* girls – and Eva resented, but had to accept, her two days out of the house up at Heath Green and without her daughters, Laila and Nora. Thank goodness Jodie, their Australian nanny, had been persuaded to continue her job with them. She'd been about to fly home to Sydney, but had agreed to put her trip off for six months in order to give some degree of continuity to the children since seven-year-old Laila, particularly, had taken the split so badly.

Eva sighed. *Get a grip, girl*, she censured herself. Wasn't this freedom that she now had exactly what she'd wanted after meeting, marrying and working alongside Rayan for the past fifteen years or so? She supposed that not only had she been found wanting as a wife but – much, much more unbearable to contemplate – she possibly hadn't been, and obviously now wasn't, a terribly good mother.

Did she, Eva, have too many of her, Rosa and Hannah's birth mother's genes? She knew Alice Parkes had been more than willing, no *insistent*, on giving up the three of them for adoption once she'd realised, too late for termination, that her one-night stand with Bill Astley had led to their conception. Thank heavens for Susan, Alice's elder sister, who had apparently swooped down on their pregnant birth mother in Paris like some avenging angel and carried a pregnant Alice (not literally, obviously – Eva smiled at the very idea although, knowing Susan, if that had been the only way to get her pregnant sister to Westenbury in order to give birth to English, rather than French babies, she'd have hoisted Alice on her shoulder and done just that) back to Yorkshire.

'Hi, Eva. How're you doing?' Ben Pennington, the navy towel wrapped around his waist only accentuating his charismatic good looks and downright feral sexiness, headed for the kitchen and the kettle. Despite Eva's disapproval of Hannah's continued relationship with the handsome neurosurgeon (albeit, now separated from his wife, Alexandra) she couldn't help her eyes from wandering to, and taking in, the broad, tanned back and, as he turned, the matt of black hair rising from the towel slung carelessly low around his hips, the notion of what was hidden in its dark blue depths...

'Oy.' Hannah grinned, appearing silently at Eva's side and following her sister's gaze. 'Hands off.'

'My hands are nowhere near,' Eva sniffed drily, executing jazz hands in Hannah's direction as proof.

'Well, put your eyes back then.' Hannah actually laughed now, obviously relaxed and suffused with sex after a couple of hours of Afternoon Delight. 'They're out on stalks.'

Ben, evidently enjoying being under scrutiny, strolled leisurely towards them, a mug of coffee in hand. He kissed Hannah's cheek before giving them both the benefit of his retreating broad shoulders once more and, despite the towel, evidence of a tight, well-muscled bum and well-shaped thighs as he headed for the shower.

'So, it's definitely all on, then? Big time?' Eva asked. 'He's finally left his wife and kids?'

'Yep.' Hannah's tone was slightly triumphant. 'And don't go all holier-than-thou on me, Eva. Especially now that *you've* left Rayan and the girls.'

'I think you'll find, Hannah,' Eva snapped, 'that Rayan and I have left *each other*. I most certainly have *not* left Laila and Nora.' Tears welled and Eva dashed them away impatiently. 'This is what happens when a marriage breaks up,' she went on. 'There are winners…' Eva poked Hannah crossly in the arm '…and losers. And while, at the moment, you might be feeling particularly victorious, there is a broken-hearted wife and devastated children missing their daddy.'

'Alright, alright, Eva, don't go on. I tried, you know I did, to send Ben back to Alexandra. But he couldn't be without me…'

'Ah,' Eva interrupted Hannah, 'finally *thrown him out*, has she?'

'…and in the end, he just had to leave to be with me.' Hannah explained the situation patiently as if speaking to an irritating child. 'It's all very civilised. Very grown up. These things happen.'

'I bet those kids of his don't feel "very grown up".' Eva air-quoted the words.

'Give it a rest, Eva,' Hannah said, losing patience. She paused meaningfully then changed the subject. 'Right, Ben's back at the hospital this evening and you, Rosa and I have a lot to get organised for this trip to Paris you're insisting we go on.' Hannah patted Eva's arm. 'Come on, stop getting at me. Let's order a takeout curry once Rosa gets here and fetch a bottle – or two – of something from Bill's wine cellar.'

'Isn't it *our* wine cellar now?' Eva smiled.

'It is.' Hannah grinned. 'Absolutely.'

'So, Paris. *I love Paris in the springtime*,' Hannah sang, lowering her voice and aping a throaty Ella Fitzgerald.

'In the springtime?' Eva laughed. 'You've never been to Paris in *any* season.' She frowned in Hannah's direction. 'Have you?'

'Ben's promised he'll take me…' Hannah began.

'Well, *I* have,' Rosa interrupted quietly. 'And it *was* springtime. Joe took me to Montmartre for my birthday one year…' She trailed off, remembering how she and Joe Rosavina had spent their nights making Parisian love in a ravishing hotel across from the Sacré-Coeur, and their days wandering the Place du Tertre exploring the historic buildings in the cobbled square. She'd been particularly taken with *Le mur des je t'aime* situated on the square at Place des Abbesses where 'I Love You' had been declared and inscribed into the wall three hundred and eleven times (allegedly – Rosa hadn't counted) in two hundred and fifty languages. Joe had wanted to buy a piece of chalk or a chisel and make it three hundred and twelve but, instead, Rosa had told him that saying it that number of times in the next hour would suffice.

And he had. And it did.

'Come back, Rosa!' Hannah, in the process of decanting chicken tikka masala onto Bill's vintage Wedgewood plates – despite Eva impatiently saying she was starving and why not just eat it straight from the tinfoil container as they usually did?

– glanced across at her sister who was now mentally sipping cognac on the streets of Montmartre. 'Still hurting over Joe, Rosa?' Hannah went on, ignoring Eva who was now pouring a rather grand-sounding and expensive French wine.

'Of course she isn't still hurting over Joe bloody Rosavina.' Eva laughed. 'When she's got Sam Burrows in her vicarage and presumably between her sheets?' She gave a sideways glance in Rosa's direction but, when there was no reaction from her, went on. 'There,' she said, knocking back half a glass of red wine in one. 'That should get us in the mood for Gay Paree.'

'I think Rosa's already there.' Hannah grinned, laying cutlery and napkins. 'And don't even think about eating straight from that container, Eva,' she warned. 'We're the Marquess of Stratton's daughters and should act with some decorum.'

'God, you've changed your tune, Hans. Living here and taking on the role of chair of the board has obviously given your ideas above your station. It wasn't so long ago you were happy with a bag of chips smothered in ketchup and eaten with your fingers.'

'We all get where we want to be eventually,' Hannah retorted cheerfully. 'So, how is Joe, Rosa? Do you know? Has he been in touch since you rescued him?'

'You should have left him to be trampled into the mud,' Eva sniffed. 'Where he belongs, after what he did to you all those years ago.'

'Oh, give it a rest, Eva.' Rosa scowled. 'It was over six years ago he had a one-night stand with Carys Powell. Move on. Forgive and forget.' Rosa reached for her wine, feeling defeated. She *wanted* to move on. She *had* forgiven Joe. She just didn't appear to be able to *forget*. 'Joe's dad, Roberto, was in church with Chiara last week. Apparently, he's been exceptionally lucky: two cracked ribs, concussion, a broken wrist and a hell of a lot of cuts and bruising to just about every bit of him. I think Rhys, with his broken ankle, which he walked on when he managed to get Chiara out of the field, has come out almost worse. He's wanting to go out to Australia to be with Carys. She's in Sydney with her new man.'

'Best place for her,' Eva said. 'Twelve thousand miles out of your way.'

Hannah passed the dish of pilau rice in Rosa's direction. 'And Sam, Rosa? Everything OK there?'

'I hear he was really helpful with Joe?' Eva smiled. 'Sam was telling me in the surgery how he went to hospital with him in the ambulance. You see, now *he* really is a nice bloke. Dependable, kind and jolly good-looking. I tell you, Rosa, if *you* hadn't got in there first…'

Rosa hesitated. 'He's taking me over to Sheffield for lunch with his parents on Sunday,' Rosa said, grimacing slightly.

'Why the face?' Eva asked through a mouthful of food. 'God this naan bread's good.' She swallowed and wiped at her mouth with the back of her hand, ignoring the linen napkin Hannah pushed across the table in her direction. 'Have to say, I'm amazed you've not met them before. You've been seeing him almost six months now.'

'They've been away since February.'

'Hell of a long holiday.' Hannah frowned, pouring more wine.

'Australia,' Rosa said. 'Sam's sister lives in Melbourne. They'd not seen her for quite a few years apparently. I get the impression there was some sort of falling-out. Anyway, with Sam's son, you know, being killed in that avalanche, they appear to have decided to try and make it up with his sister so they can have some contact with the grandchildren over there who they've never seen. Now they don't have Ollie, Sam's son, any longer.'

'Right.' Eva polished off her glass of wine and reached for the bottle. 'I might as well take advantage of not having to drive tonight,' she went on as Rosa covered her own glass with her hand. 'So, what's the latest with the eggs, Rosa?'

'My frozen eggs are where they've been for the last nine years, safely – I hope – in their tanks of liquid nitrogen in the clinic in Wimbledon where I had my cancer treatment.'

'What do you mean "I hope?"' Eva stopped wiping round her plate with the last piece of bread and glanced across at Rosa.

'Well, just that.' Rosa frowned. 'You know, I lie awake some nights and worry that, unbeknown to the people in charge at the laboratory, there might have been a power cut or something and the freezer might have started to defrost. And then the power comes on again and my poor eggs are refrozen again. I mean, what sort of human being would I…'

'A bit like that time when Mum and Dad's freezer went on the blink?' Hannah interrupted nodding sagely. 'And we helped Mum clear out all that defrosted food, and found pork pies and prawns with a sell-by date seven years earlier? And she *still* wanted to refreeze it and hang on to it all. Couldn't *thoil* the idea, being a dyed-in-the-wool Yorkshire lass, of wasting good food.'

'Oh, for the love of God, you two.' Eva burst out laughing. 'You're supposed to be intelligent human beings. You can't equate an eight-year-old Co-op frozen pork pie with Rosa's beautiful eggs, which are just waiting patiently for the chance to become her beautiful babies.' Eva stroked Rosa's hand. 'And it will happen for you, Rosie Posie. It *will*, you know.'

Rosa ran a hand through her dark hair before sighing deeply. 'Yes, but it may have escaped your notice that a) those beautiful eggs are heading towards their ten-year sell-by date and b) I need a lovely man who not only wants to donate the… you know… the necessary in order to have children with me because c) it may *also* have escaped your notice, I am the village vicar and I'm not convinced the boss would approve of my going it alone if I'm unable to find said lovely man.' Rosa looked glum and reached for her glass. 'Oh, sod it, pour me some more wine, Eva. I can always bunk down in your bed with you tonight.'

'So, by "the boss" are you referring to the Bishop of Pontefract, the Archbishop of Canterbury or the Main Man Above?'

'All three really, I guess.'

'And do you really only have another year or so to rescue

those eggs from the freezer? To make the big decision on what you're going to do with them? That's a bit scary.' Eva frowned at the thought.

'To be fair, there used to be a ten-year limit on how long you could keep them in storage but, apparently, now, women like me who've made the decision to freeze their eggs prior to chemotherapy can advise the clinic that they want to extend the time.'

'Oh? For how long?' Hannah and Eva both leaned forwards.

'Fifty-five years.'

'Fifty-five years?' Hannah and Eva stared and Rosa could see the pair of them mentally doing the sums. 'What, you can have a baby when you're ninety-three?' Eva looked aghast.

Rosa began to laugh. '*I* don't know. Where they've plucked the idea of fifty-five years from is anyone's guess. But, you know,' she went on, no longer amused at the thought, 'the three of us *are* all forty in a couple of years.'

'God, don't remind me.' Eva's face was gloomy. 'I need to start living again while I'm young and up for it.' Eva sighed. 'Although, to be honest, I don't have a clue where to start.'

'Lots of women have their first child at forty and later,' Hannah said. 'It's quite the done thing these days; *I* fully intend waiting until my fourth decade.'

Eva turned back to Rosa. 'So, what do you think of putting Sam forward for the job?'

'The *job*?' Rosa frowned. 'You don't half have a turn of phrase, Eva.'

Eva grinned. 'Sorry. But, you know, *would* Sam be up for it?'

'I've really tried to avoid the question; although, I'm certain it's what Sam wants. He's desperate to have more children after losing Ollie.' Rosa paused. 'And to be honest, you have children with someone because you love them, not because you've been seeing someone and they might be *up for the job*.'

'So, Rosa, are you saying you *don't* love Sam?' Hannah's tone was gentle.

Rosa finished her glass of wine. 'Oh, sod it,' she sniffed before pouring more. She shook her head. 'I don't know. I just *don't know*. One minute I think, yep, this is it, Sam's the man for me, he loves me, would never hurt me, and would be happy to settle here with me.'

'You knew when you loved *Joe*,' Hannah coaxed. 'No doubt there, whatsoever.'

'I was sixteen,' Rosa reminded the others. 'And he looked like Nick from the Backstreet Boys.'

'You were with him until you were thirty,' Eva prompted Rosa.

As if she needed any reminder that she'd lived with the man she'd adored for almost fifteen years. Rosa shook her head slightly to rid herself of more pictures of herself and Joe together: of the terrible evening he'd returned to their apartment in Wandsworth – when they were both flying high with their respective businesses in the City – after a week's business trip in Chicago, his face white and desolate, to tell her Carys Powell was pregnant with his child. In the same week she'd received the shocking diagnosis she was ill with Stage Two Hodgkin's lymphoma.

'Irrelevant who he looked like,' Eva was saying. 'Joe could have looked like... like *Boris Johnson* and the chemistry would have still been there for Rosa.'

'Oh, I don't think so, Eva.' Hannah actually shuddered. 'Boris Johnson?'

'You know what I'm saying,' Eva replied impatiently. 'It's the chemistry. You know when you know. And, despite Sam being one hot dentist – I tell you now, they queue around the block to see him at the surgery...'

'Isn't that because he's the only dentist for miles taking on new NHS patients?' Hannah asked doubtfully.

'No, it's because he's one very hot, sexy man. And, I guess,' Eva conceded, 'a bloody good dentist to boot.'

'Will you stop talking about me and Sam as if I wasn't here?' Rosa said crossly, dragging herself back into the present.

'So, do you think Sam might be taking you to meet his parents *for a reason*?' Hannah leaned in to Rosa, eyes wide.

'A reason?' Rosa pulled a face.

'You know exactly what I'm saying, so don't act the innocent with us.' Hannah elbowed Rosa. 'I think we might be looking at a summer wedding, don't you, Eva?'

'I hope not,' Eva retorted, eyebrows raised. 'The surgery's so busy at the moment. With me cutting my days down there to spend more time running this place, we just can't afford Sam trolling off for two weeks' honeymoon and…'

'Look, I thought we were here this evening to plan the trip to Paris?' Rosa interrupted Eva in some exasperation. 'Can we do that instead of you trying to get me married off and pregnant?' Rosa had had the same thoughts as Hannah as to why Sam was making what appeared to be a big move in taking her over to meet his parents. And those thoughts, Rosa admitted only to herself, weren't exactly comfortable ones. 'Paris?' she repeated. 'I need to know when you're thinking of going, Eva, so I can organise my diary.'

7

The following Sunday, once Rosa had brought the morning service to a conclusion with a rather jolly rendition of 'At the Name of Jesus' followed by a final prayer and blessing, she'd accompanied the verger and choir down the aisle to Daphne Merton's thumping out of some tune she'd apparently been practising at the organ all week. Daphne was literally pulling out all the stops, totally going for it and, while Rosa couldn't quite work out what on earth it was – an off-the-wall version of an old favourite hymn or, much more likely, something Daphne had concocted herself – it was certainly tuneful, if a little jazzy. The organist brought the performance to a triumphant climax that rattled the vaulted wooden rafters of the church as Rosa stood at the heavy oak door, shaking hands before sending the parishioners home to their Sunday dinners.

It had been a full house this particular Sunday as there'd been not one, but two christenings during the service. Two gorgeous bouncing babies that Rosa had held in her arms, walking down the aisle to introduce to the congregation in turn: Portia Hyacinth Bradbury (someone had been watching Season Two of *Bridgerton*, Rosa thought to herself with a grin) and (much more down to earth and in keeping with his Yorkshire roots) Alfie John Openshaw from one of the dairy farms up near Norman's Meadow. After she'd managed to wet both babies' heads without their resorting to tears, Portia offered up a cross-eyed, somewhat drunken grin in her direction, belying any aristocratic leanings her parents might have hoped to bestow with the name, and Alfie continued to sleep throughout the whole service.

Now, as she finally finished shaking hands and smiling at grannies and cousins, aunts, uncles and friends of the two new recruits she'd latterly welcomed into God's arms, her own arms felt empty and she was unable to quash the longing that seemed to be hitting her with some regularity these days, for a baby of her own.

'Are you coming back home with us for your dinner, Rosa?' Richard Quinn, her dad, was helping Susan collect the hymn books and reposition the beautifully embroidered hassocks along the pews. While Susan – brought up as a churchgoer by her father, the Reverend Cecil Parkes, who had ruled the village with his particular brand of hell and damnation sermons during his thirty years' incumbency – was a regular attendee in Rosa's congregation, Richard most definitely wasn't. A very much lapsed Catholic Scouser, Richard Quinn rarely accompanied Susan and their other daughter, the triplets' eldest sister, Virginia, to church.

'Nice to see you here on a Sunday morning, Dad.' Rosa smiled and gave him a kiss. 'What's up? Come to confess something?'

'You C of E lot *don't* confess your sins, do you?' Richard frowned. 'Not that I've been up to anything sinful,' he added hastily. 'I just thought I'd not seen you for ages and I knew I'd be able to pin you down here.'

'Pin me down?'

'It's this trip over to Paris that Eva's planning. I did say I'd go over there with her. You know, to meet up with that Dufort artist chap. Give her some moral support as it were. But I reckon you and Hannah should be the ones to go with her, especially if Alice is going to be over in Paris as well.' Richard frowned. 'Eva needs to actually meet up with her father.'

'Dad, *you're* Eva's father. Our *dad*.'

'But Eva's desperate to meet up with her *biological* father.

And you can't blame her, Rosa: it came as a complete shock to all of us, but obviously utterly floored Eva, that those DNA tests Jonny Astley insisted on to make sure you three really were Bill Astley's biological daughters ended up proving Eva actually *wasn't* his. I don't think I'll ever get over the shock of finding that out. And to be honest, I still *don't get it*. I mean, I'm an intelligent bloke – well, I like to think I am – but how Eva can have a different biological father from you and Hannah when all three of you were together in the...' Richard paused, slightly embarrassed '...you know, in the womb together, is beyond me.' Richard rubbed somewhat wearily at his forehead.

'Pretty straightforward, Dad,' Rosa said patiently, stroking Richard's hand. 'You know the story: Alice had sex with Yves Dufort in Paris, was caught *in flagrante* by his wife, hopped on the next plane back to Manchester airport where she found herself sitting next to Bill Astley who invited her up to see his etchings and where they—' Rosa broke off and placed a warning hand on her father's arm as Susan Quinn walked towards them with Hilary Makepiece and Virginia. She lowered her voice. 'Eva's biological father being Yves Dufort really isn't common knowledge you know, Dad...' she said in a whisper. It certainly wasn't for the ears of Hilary Makepiece, the churchwarden, who would not only totally relish being apprised of this little nugget of information, but would have it round the village like a chickenpox outbreak by the time the congregation was tucking into its Sunday dinner Yorkshire puddings.

'Great sermon, darling,' Susan Quinn greeted Rosa warmly. 'And you managed those babies like a true pro. Your grandfather Cecil never enjoyed christenings when he was in charge here. I seem to recall he wasn't averse to giving any bawling baby a good dunking in the font to shut them up if they were making too much racket.'

'If we're talking *racket*, Rosa,' Virginia said with a sniff, after kissing her sister somewhat perfunctorily on the cheek, 'I do think you might exert a little more control over what Daphne

Merton comes up with on that organ of hers. Grandpa Cecil would *never* have sanctioned such excessive showing off. It sounded like something The Beach Boys might have come up with. You need to keep her in line, remind her this is God's house and not a... not a bawdy house.'

'Didn't know they *had* organs in a bawdy house.' Rosa laughed at Virginia's ridiculous verbosity.

'Oh, I think you'll find there's a hell of a lot of...' Hilary dug Rosa in the ribs '*...organs* in a brothel. Organs aplenty, I'd have said.' She went off into peals of laughter and Rosa joined in. Virginia didn't.

'Are you coming back for lunch, Rosa?' Virginia asked, ignoring Hilary who appeared unable to catch her breath she was so suffused with giggles. 'I've a nice bit of brisket been simmering all yesterday morning – it's pressed into a bowl ready for carving.'

Rosa inwardly shuddered. She loathed cold brisket when it had been left to cook for hours and pressed into a pudding bowl with a weight on top, resulting in overcooked grey meat ringed with white fat. Susan had often produced the dish when they were girls; all three of them would turn up their noses declaring that, when they were grown-ups, they would never – ever, ever – eat brisket *ever* again. But Virginia, the eldest Quinn daughter, had loved it then and obviously loved it now, offering it up as some sort of prize at the altar of her Sunday lunch. Rosa bet anything there'd be rice pudding as well.

'Sorry, Virginia, I've actually been invited over to Sam's parents' for lunch.'

'Oh?' Virginia was obviously piqued. 'There's my famous rice pudding as well, to follow.'

Famous? How the hell could anyone's rice pudding be *famous*? Rosa disliked milky puddings almost as much as cold sliced brisket.

'Wahey.' Hilary grinned, ignoring Virginia and still wiping at her eyes as images of organs in brothels continued to amuse. 'I reckon it'll be a summer wedding, Vicar.'

'Oh?' Virginia said once again. This time her ears pricked at the mention of a wedding. 'Is Sam Burrows about to make an honest woman of you then, Rosa? I have to say, I've never thought a single woman the best person to be a village vicar. Especially, if...'

'Especially if?' Rosa raised an eyebrow.

'You know, especially if you're having... you know... *men* staying over at the vicarage.'

'Men?'

Hilary started singing an out-of-tune parody of O C Smith's 'Son of Hickory Holler's Tramp', before dissolving into laughter once more.

Rosa stared: had her church warden been at the communion wine? She kissed Richard on the cheek, frowned at both Hilary and Virginia who, despite being her sister, continued to get right up her nose, and set off back towards the vicarage to change into the new flowery dress she'd bought for a special occasion but never actually worn. Was Sunday lunch with Mr and Mrs Burrows deemed a special occasion? And if it wasn't, Rosa asked herself, why wasn't it? She'd been with Sam almost six months now, and neither of them was getting any younger.

'For God's sake – sorry God,' Rosa said crossly to herself as she pulled off her vicaring togs and went to find said dress in the large wardrobe that had been in situ in the bedroom since Grandfather Cecil's day. 'I'm not even forty. Years ahead of me yet.'

'To have babies?' God reminded her.

'Yes, God, to have babies,' she replied defiantly.

Rosa sighed and headed for the shower.

'Oh, Rosa – may I call you Rosa...?' Sam's mother, Janet Burrows, appeared to have been hovering behind the front door of the neat semi-detached bungalow on the outskirts of Sheffield, ready to fling it open the moment she heard Sam's car pull up on the drive. Rosa wondered if she'd been on guard duty at the lounge window, or actually peering through the letterbox, agitatedly awaiting the arrival of her only son bringing home this new woman for Sunday lunch.

'Well, it is my name…' Rosa started, as a hand shot out in her direction, shaking her own limply with cold fingers before she and Sam were ushered down the hallway.

'I didn't know if I should be calling you *Reverend*,' Janet almost twittered, glancing behind her at Rosa who found she was being propelled gently along the heavily patterned carpet by Sam's hand at her waist.

'Oh, please don't…' Rosa started again, but the older woman wasn't listening.

'Stuart, they're here,' Janet Burrows called towards the kitchen before directing them into the small overheated, over-furnished room on the left. She was quite tiny, her blonde hair efficiently bobbed, her M and S shirtwaister dress buttoned to the neck and as neat as the bungalow she'd obviously cleaned and tidied to perfection in readiness for her visitors.

'They're *here*,' she called once more, her voice now steely. '*Stuart*.'

An extremely tall, almost lugubrious man in his late sixties appeared at Janet's side, his shoulders stooping slightly perhaps from years of bending down to his wife's much lesser height. Gosh, what a mismatched couple, height wise, Rosa thought, glancing back at Sam's broad-shouldered, six-foot stature. Sam had obviously averaged out his parents' heights to perfection.

Stuart Burrows held out his own hand to Rosa before patting his son on the back, somewhat awkwardly, Rosa noticed. 'Good to meet you, Reverend.' He smiled.

'Rosa, please,' Rosa almost pleaded. 'I've taken off my dog collar for the day.'

'Oh?' Janet frowned. 'Are you allowed to do that, then?'

'Mum, of course she is. Right, Dad, shall we have a beer?' Sam raised an eyebrow at his father.

Stuart Burrows glanced at Janet as if asking permission and she gave an almost imperceptible nod in his direction. 'I bought a couple of bottles – they're in the cupboard under the sink, Stuart. Now, Rosa, would you like a nice cup of tea?'

More tea, Vicar? Rosa almost replied but, instead, smiled and said, 'Do you know, I'd love a beer myself. Been thirsty work christening two new babies this morning.'

'A beer?' Janet's eyebrows shot up. 'You're allowed alcohol then?'

Rosa laughed out loud at that. '*Go, eat your food with gladness, and drink your wine with a joyful heart, for God has already approved of what you do…*' Ecclesiastes 9:7, I believe, but don't actually hold me to that, Janet. I'm never very good at remembering bits from the Bible unless it's like this one…' Rosa trailed off as Janet smiled a tight little on-off movement of her narrow, Max-Factored pink lips in her direction. 'Get a bottle for Rosa,' Janet called after Stuart and Sam's departing backs. 'And get a glass for her…'

'Oh, I'm fine drinking from the bottle.' Rosa smiled. 'Years of practice with my sisters.'

'Right.' Janet didn't seem to know how to reply to that. 'Do come and sit down, Rosa, and tell me all about these babies you've been christening. We miss our baby Ollie so badly…' Janet fished a little embroidered hanky from up her sleeve before scrunching it up in her hand. 'Sam will have told you what happened to our grandson?'

'Yes of course. You must have gone through a terrible time when it happened? I'm so sorry.'

She broke off as Sam came back into the room, passed a bottled beer in her direction with a: 'You OK? I'm just off to give my dad a hand with his car,' before leaving the two women alone once more.

'Terrible,' Janet said, lowering her voice, although Sam was well out of earshot. 'Quite dreadful. He was the love of my life, the little chap. We lived for him.'

'I'm sure you did. He was twelve or so when the accident happened, I believe?'

'Still my *baby*,' Janet sniffed. 'Well, obviously not *my* baby, but we grannies do become terribly emotionally attached to our grandchildren. Does your mother have them?'

'Them?' Migraines? Haemorrhoids? Nits? For a second Rosa couldn't quite grasp what Susan might be a martyr to. 'Oh, grandchildren?'

Janet looked at her strangely. 'Yes, grandchildren?'

'Oh, right, yes. My eldest sister, Virginia, has two children and my sister Eva also has two.'

'Four? Oh, what a joy they must be to her? And to your father?'

'Do you know, I've never really thought about it. I reckon my mum and dad spent so much time, effort and expense bringing up the four of us girls – as well as the trauma of three very bolshie teenaged girls hitting adolescence the same time Mum hit the menopause – they're quite happy to take a back seat with other people's kids.' Rosa laughed. 'They'll babysit occasionally for my sisters' kids, of course, but if Mum can ever persuade my dad to go up in an aeroplane again, I reckon she'd rather be off to Italy or Paris or somewhere than running round after grandkids.'

'Right.' Janet gave Rosa the benefit of another of her looks. 'Of course,' she went on confidentially, lowering her voice as Sam and his father walked past the sitting room door and then out into the front garden, 'if Sam's *wife*...' she paused to sniff accusingly '...hadn't taken Ollie off skiing with her new *man*, then he'd be here with us now, living with Sam back in his house in Sheffield, and coming over for his Sunday dinner every week.'

'I'm sorry,' Rosa said once more. 'It can't be easy for you.' She smiled. 'But Sam tells me you have grandchildren in Melbourne? You've just been out to Australia to actually meet them?'

'Yes.' Janet pulled at a large red photograph album she'd obviously placed strategically on the arm of the pink Draylon sofa specifically to show off these new grandchildren as soon as she could. 'Amy is three and Vivien just one.' She sniffed once more and Rosa wondered if she had a cold and moved away slightly: if she was off to Paris soon, a cold was the last thing she wanted to take with her. 'I always thought Vivien was a girl's name,' Janet went on slightly disparagingly, 'but my new grandson is a boy. What do I know? My daughter, Sam's sister Ruth, is married to someone with, you know... *indigenous* blood.' She paused. 'I'm not convinced mixed marriages ever work.'

'Mixed marriages?'

'You know, different views on life, different ideas and culture, different *colour*...'

'Oh, how exciting to have grandchildren with Aboriginal heritage.' Rosa beamed.

'Exciting?'

'Yes, absolutely. My sister Eva is married to someone with Pakistani heritage.'

'A Pakistani?' For a few seconds, Janet Burrows looked quite horrified before she rearranged her face. 'But of course, how silly of me – that's how you and Sam met. I forget that Rayan, Sam's partner at the surgery, is from Pakistan.'

Rosa stared. Was Sam an actual *partner* at Rayan and Eva's dental surgery in Westenbury? She didn't think so. 'Well, Bradford actually.' Rosa smiled, referring to Rayan's place of birth. 'I don't think Rayan's ever stepped out of Yorkshire.' Apart from when he was off to Leicester every Sunday, secretly meeting up with the psychosexual counsellor he'd turned to when Eva was scaring the pants off him – literally – demanding they try every position (and, knowing Eva, some that weren't) in *The Joy of Sex*.

'He met my sister, Eva, when they were both studying dentistry together here at the university in Sheffield,' Rosa went on, 'and then they decided to return to the village we girls grew up in, where Sam now lives. Have you been over to see Sam's place in Westenbury, Janet? He's managed to find the most divine cottage that luckily came back up for rent just as Rayan offered him the post at the surgery.'

'Renting?' Janet's next sniff was derisive. 'He shouldn't be *renting* at his age. If that wife of his hadn't gone off… Right, Rosa, you enjoy your… drink…' Janet glanced towards the beer bottle Rosa had just about drained '…and we'll be ready to eat PDQ.'

'Can I help?' Rosa made to stand, but Janet put up a hand. 'No, no, I know what you single girls are like when it comes to cooking. A bit of salad and a tub of cottage cheese every night, I'll bet.' She smiled knowingly. 'I've always maintained, you don't learn how to budget and cook until you've a hubby and a couple of kiddies to look after.' Janet glanced towards Rosa's middle (was the woman sizing her up in the child-bearing hips' stakes?) before collecting the now-empty beer bottle, straightening a couple of pale green cushions and heading for the kitchen.

8

'Now, Rosa, I do hope you're not a *vegetarian*?' Janet Burrows put as much disdain into that one word as though asking if Rosa was a drug dealer. She turned away from the kitchen sink where both Sam and his dad were washing oil from their hands and lowered her voice at Rosa, whispering, 'Penny, Sam's wife, went down that route and was encouraging my Ollie not to eat meat either. Growing young lads, especially those jumping and leaping around dancing like Ollie was, need meat. Did Sam tell you what a talented dancer Ollie was, Rosa?' Janet indicated a framed photograph on the mantelpiece, which had caught a young boy of around twelve leaping apparently effortlessly through the air in a most amazing jeté, and Rosa gasped in genuine admiration.

'Wonderful, isn't it? Mind you, I did think it a bit, you know, a bit *strange* when he started doing ballet stuff. Did hope he wasn't going to become a bit of a nancy boy. Can I say that these days without being hauled out for being a bigot?' Janet sniffed once more. It was becoming truly irritating. 'It's the protein, you know.' Janet winked conspiratorially.

'Is it?' Rosa was a bit lost at what Janet was insinuating: was the woman trying to say protein made you gay? Or bigoted?

'*I* made sure he had his meat when he came here,' Sam's mother continued, smirking a little at her obvious pride in getting one over on her former daughter-in-law. 'If God hadn't wanted us to eat meat, he wouldn't have given us Morrisons' butchery department, would he? Young lads – talented lads like Ollie – need meat. Now, I do hope you like brisket?'

'Love it,' Rosa said faintly, sending a silent prayer to her boss up above that there wouldn't be too much fat on it. She looked longingly both at Sam and her wine glass. With a glass of the red wine she'd carefully chosen and brought as a present from Bill's still-ample wine cellar, inside her, she could eat anything.

'Stuart, pour Rosa a glass of that wine I brought home from Morrisons yesterday. Now we know she's a drinker, we'd better keep her glass filled.' Janet tinkled a little laugh that didn't quite meet her eyes.

'Golly.' Rosa smiled, embarrassed. 'I'm more than happy with a glass of water. Really.' She looked beseechingly towards Sam who winked in her direction before taking the bottle from his father's hands and filling all their glasses with a white wine.

The wine glasses were tiny, doll's-house-sized, and Rosa knew she could have knocked down the contents in one. Instead, she praised, 'What pretty glasses, Janet.'

'A wedding present from Stuart's boss at the Coal Board,' Janet said proudly.

'Goodness, you've managed to keep them in pristine condition,' Rosa said admiringly, fingering the cut crystal of the glass. Obviously, not used half enough, she almost added. Instead, she said, turning to Stuart as he helped Janet bring dishes of boiled potatoes and greens to the table. 'The Coal Board, Stuart? You were a miner?'

'Goodness me, no,' Janet was straight in before her husband could reply. 'A miner? No, no, Stuart was *management* at the colliery in Grimethorpe and then moved to work for the NCB.'

'What Mum's dying to tell you, Rosa, is that these glasses were a present from Ian MacGregor and his wife. Dad actually worked for him.' Sam grinned across at Janet who was preening slightly as she poured an insubstantial-looking gravy onto Sam's plate. Needs a full-bodied red wine in that gravy, Rosa thought, simultaneously racking her brains to think who the hell Ian MacGregor was.

'Oh, *the* Ian Macgregor?' It suddenly came to her. 'Appointed and approved by Margaret Thatcher in the Eighties, and seen as the man behind the destruction of the mining community round here?'

'Ian Macgregor destroyed the mining community?' Janet stopped helping her menfolk to peas and carrots and stood up straight. 'I don't *think* so. I think you'll find it was the miners themselves, along with Arthur Scargill, who finally finished off the coal industry in this neck of the woods. In the whole country actually.'

'Oh?' Rosa didn't quite know what to say. After all, here she was, a guest in Sam's family home: not the best time to be provoking a political argument. Instead, she picked up her knife and fork and went for the watery-looking cauliflower on her plate, devoid – she saw – of any cheese sauce that would surely have enhanced both its insipid colour and boiled-out flavour.

Janet Burrows obviously had no compunction about showing her hand when it came to her political leanings. 'Margaret Thatcher tried every which way to help and accommodate those bolshie striking miners,' Janet said, attacking her cold sliced brisket with zeal. 'But would they listen? Would they let her and Ian modernise the pits in this country? In this area? No, they *would not.*' She shook her head crossly. 'They just came out on strike for more and more money.'

'I don't think it was money…' Rosa started.

'If they'd listened, just listened to what Mrs Thatcher was planning for them instead of following Scargill onto the picket line. Three years, Rosa, that my husband—' Janet spoke as if the man himself wasn't sitting across from her, starting his Sunday dinner with a somewhat gloomy air '—was out of employment because of what the miners did to the whole industry, coming out on strike.'

'The thing is, Janet…' Rosa smiled placatingly '…I'm not

convinced anything could have saved those mines. They were in need of huge modernisation as well as up against cheaper foreign imports of coal.'

'You appear to know quite a bit about it, dear?' Janet's tone was condescending.

'Well, just a little.' Rosa realised she was probably on dangerous ground here, but went for it anyway. 'As part of one of my business degree modules up at Durham, we were asked to consider the business model and subsequent failure of a British industry. I did think I'd like to look at British steel – my grandmother's family were actually all from Sheffield and had a long tradition of working in the steel foundries – but I opted for the coal industry instead. I found it all quite fascinating.'

'Fascinating? Really?' Janet sniffed. 'And you were at Durham? Doing business?'

'Mum, Rosa ran a very successful business in London – Rosa Quinn Investments – before deciding to go into the church.' Sam smiled proudly across at Rosa and she smiled back, thankful that he'd come to her rescue. 'More wine, Rosa?' Sam nudged her elbow and she accepted gratefully. Thank goodness she wasn't driving – she was beginning to think she'd never get through this lunch without several glasses inside her.

'Oops, serviettes. What will Rosa think?' Janet jumped up and left the dining room and Stuart Burrows spoke, almost for the first time.

'So, Sam's just told me you're on the management committee of Heatherly Hall now, Rosa?'

Rosa swallowed a mouthful of the overcooked greens, (a touch of garlic and rosemary would have improved them considerably) and put down her cutlery. 'That's right. We're hoping, once my sister, Eva has her planned art retreat up and running, and Alice Parkes can be persuaded to be around…'

'Alice Parkes? What's *she* got to do with anything?' Janet Burrows, bustling back into the room, mid conversation, handed round white paper napkins. 'Bit of a trollop, I've always thought.

She's as bad as that Tracey Emin as far as I can see: you know, calling her dirty, unmade bed *art*? And I...'

'Mum,' Sam warned, interrupting, 'Alice Parkes is Rosa's biological mother. I told Dad the whole story while we were trying to sort that gasket.'

'Alice Parkes? She's your *mother*?' Janet stared. 'But you're a vicar...'

'Well, I'm proof that vicars can be born the wrong side of the tracks.' Rosa smiled. 'And I can understand why some people might find Alice's artwork somewhat avant-garde.'

'Avant-garde? Mucky stuff, I'd have said.' Janet sat back down, cut a small piece of carrot and popped it primly into her equally small mouth. 'All those naked bodies she paints. Pornographic, I'd say. I like a nice Constable myself. You know? *The Hay Wain?* Mind you, once our Ollie got into ballet, I really began to favour Degas. Do you know him?'

'Er, no, I'm afraid I don't?' Rosa smiled encouragingly before forcing a boiled potato, bereft of any salt or butter, into her mouth.

'Edgar Degas?' Janet pulled a superior face. 'And you with a degree from Durham, dear? Does the most beautiful paintings of ballet dancers. Every time I see one—' and here Janet waved a hand in the direction of the far wall of the stuffy little dining room which, Rosa now saw, was covered with framed prints '—I find much solace, remembering Ollie.'

'That's so good that they bring comfort to you.' Rosa smiled again at Janet before glancing longingly at the wine bottle that had been moved onto the sideboard alongside the 1970s hostess trolley. She turned to Stuart who was methodically making his way through his food. 'And how do you spend your time, now you're retired, Stuart?'

'Oh, he spends his time with his head stuck in history books,' Janet interrupted, obviously put out that the conversation had moved both from herself, her lost grandson and Edgar Degas. 'And, you have some connection with Heatherly Hall, I believe?

Are you the vicar in residence or something, up there?' Without waiting for Rosa's response, Janet went on, 'Stuart and I spent a couple of hours there one afternoon a few years back, didn't we, Stuart? Not a patch on Chatsworth House of course, but then, where is? And that old chap in charge – Bill Astley, is it? Well, I think we bumped into him in the café there. We *thought* it was him, didn't we, Stuart? Scruffy-looking article with that grey ponytail and wearing *jeans*. At his age too. You wouldn't get the Duke of Devonshire having a cuppa with the public, like that.'

'Well, if you were to visit Heatherly Hall again, you wouldn't see him now,' Rosa said gently. 'I'm afraid my father died last year.'

'Oh, I'm so sorry, dear.' Janet patted Rosa's hand. 'Your father's just passed?'

'Mum.' Sam frowned. 'Bill Astley is – was – Rosa's father. Together with her sisters, Hannah and Eva…'

'Well, my biological father,' Rosa explained. 'My dad is Richard. We were adopted at birth by Alice's sister, Susan, and my dad, Richard.'

'Goodness me.' Janet put down her knife and fork and stared at Rosa. 'Some right goings-on there, then? And you knew all this when you were little girls?'

'Oh, yes. We were brought up knowing that, basically, we had two dads.'

'Right. And two mothers as well then?'

'Not really. While Bill was just up the road at the hall and we saw him regularly and always knew he was our biological father, we didn't really have much to do with Alice, despite her being our biological mother and our mum's little sister, because she's always lived in the States.'

'Goodness,' Janet repeated. 'So, it's this Bill Astley that's passed?'

'Bill's dead, yes.'

'And do you still have some connection with the hall?'

'Mum, I've just been telling Dad, Bill Astley left Heatherly Hall to Rosa and her sisters.' Sam sounded proud.

'Well, not really left the whole place to us...' Rosa frowned. 'OK, so the three of us have been left Bill's shares in the management committee of Heatherly Hall. We basically, along with the other trustees, now run the place.'

'So,' Stuart Burrows said, 'you must know quite a bit of its history then, Rosa, I would have thought? Always fascinated me, has local history. Any history really.'

'Very little really, I'm afraid, Stuart.' Rosa smiled, placing her knife and fork together on her plate with some relief.

'Dad retrained as a history teacher,' Sam explained, helping to clear the dishes. 'Once there was no future for the mines round here, he went back to college as a mature student and did a teaching qualification.'

'Despite my telling him he'd be better off doing accountancy or law,' Janet cut in. 'But no, no one listened to me.'

'Did you enjoy it?' Rosa asked, turning to Stuart. 'Teaching, I mean?'

'Loved it.' Stuart smiled. 'Talking about history all day? What could be better?'

'A job that brought a bit more money in at the end of the week?' Janet sniffed. 'Thank goodness Samuel had the brains to train to be a dentist. *He* won't have to scrape a living together.'

Hell, Rosa thought, what a victim this woman was. 'And you, Janet? Did you have a career?'

'Me?' Janet reacted as if Rosa had asked if she'd been on the game. 'I was a shorthand typist at the colliery in my day. That's where I met Samuel's father. And then, once I was married, had a home and two kiddies to look after, I made sure I wasn't foisting them off on anyone. I made sure I stayed at home and brought them up properly. I don't believe in working mothers.' She stood, gathering up the remains of the meal, almost crossly.

'So, Heatherly Hall is now in your hands?' Stuart Burrows'

eyes gleamed with interest and excitement. 'You own an historic hall?'

Rosa laughed at his animation. 'Not really. We're just looking after it for the trust. Deciding the best way forward to make it pay for itself.'

'If you give me your email address, Rosa, I'll look into some of the history of the place for you, and send you what I find out. Although,' he added, almost apologetically, 'I'm assuming you've done some of your own research?'

'What are you sending Rosa?' Janet Burrows' tone was sharp as she came back into the dining room with pudding. 'Oh, don't bore the girl with your dry old history, Stuart. I'm sure she's not a bit interested. Now, I've got rice pudding – Samuel's favourite – and then, Rosa, I'll show you my Ollie's ballet videos.'

'Sorry. My mum can be a bit full on, Rosa. She took Ollie's death particularly badly.' Sam turned to Rosa as they drove back towards Westenbury, flashing her an apologetic smile. The country roads from South to West Yorkshire, through the beautiful countryside of Cawthorne and Silkstone were Sunday-evening quiet and Sam drove quickly. Too quickly. The stolidly heavy rice pudding, jam and cream were beginning to churn uncomfortably in Rosa's stomach and she just wanted to get home. Thank goodness evensong – never very well attended, particularly after a full house in the morning – was being taken by All Hallows' verger Denis Butterworth who was always more than happy to step into Rosa's size 4s if she asked him. She bet he'd been practising all day.

'Of course she did,' Rosa soothed. 'What granny wouldn't?'

'Trouble is, she's becoming quite bitter about the whole thing. She blames Penny for taking Ollie off skiing with her new man.'

'Again, that's understandable.' Rosa patted Sam's hand. She was desperate to take off her tight-fitting dress (which, after a large Sunday lunch of wind-inducing soggy vegetables, was now measurably tighter than when she'd put it on), get into her pyjamas and spend some time just curled up by herself in her favourite armchair. She didn't even want to read or watch TV. Just to sit and listen to some Backstreet Boys music and be by herself.

'Rosa?'

'Hmm?'

'Hang on.' Sam pulled into the lay-by of a country lane, killed the engine and turned to her, taking her hand. 'Look, I know we've only been seeing each other six months or so, but you must know how I feel about you. You must know… Oh hell, I'm not very good at this. Look, I wanted my parents to meet you.'

'Yes, and I met them. Thank you. They were lovely.' Liar, liar, pants on fire. You'll never get past St Peter telling porkies like this, Rosa.

'Mum really likes you.'

Rosa raised an eyebrow.

'Look, Rosa, we're both nearly forty. I'd really like more children. I'd love to have children with you. Love to make babies with you. You will make such a wonderful mum.' Sam was gabbling now and Rosa knew that, despite the confident veneer he wore, he was nervous, embarrassed even.

'Oh, Sam, you know I'm not sure I can ever have children.'

'Rosa, there are ten of your eggs just waiting for someone to bring them to life. To turn them into babies.'

Rosa stared across at Sam whose handsome face was animated. Turn them into babies? All ten of them? As though in a magician's trick? Ta da, drum roll together with a big round of applause from the audience: and now those eggs are babies!! That didn't sound quite right somehow and Rosa felt embarrassed in turn. 'Sam, what exactly are you asking me?'

'You know! Alright, Rosa, will you marry me?'

'Oh gosh, Sam, this is a bit sudden.'

'Sudden? No, it isn't, Rosa. You must have known where I was heading, asking you to meet my parents.'

'I thought we were heading for Sunday lunch in Sheffield, not marriage, babies and galloping off into the sunset.'

'Are you turning me down?' Sam laughed, but Rosa could see the hurt in his eyes. When she didn't say anything, wasn't quite sure *what* to say, Sam turned the key, indicated and set off at speed.

'Could you just slow down a bit, Sam? I'm feeling slightly sick.' Rosa wasn't convinced it was just travel sickness that was making her want to get out of the car.

'Nearly there,' Sam said almost brusquely but, five minutes later, the car was forced to a standstill when the temporary village traffic lights had them waiting outside The Jolly Sailor – Westenbury village's main pub.

Rosa turned to Sam, placing a hand on his arm and wanting to explain how she felt but, even though he must have known she was willing him to look at her, smile at her, he stared straight ahead. Rosa glanced to her left, disconsolately watching several groups enjoying the last of the warm evening sunshine in the pub's beer garden. *We could have sat outside this afternoon*, Rosa thought; sat in Janet and Stuart's Garden and had coffee, instead of trooping back into the overheated lounge where they'd sat on the pink Dralon, the curtains drawn to shield the TV from the May sunshine.

Rosa was suddenly aware of a blonde-haired little girl waving shyly at her, before drawing the attention of those she was with to the car. Roberto Rosavina, Joe's father, turned first, waving madly and blowing kisses in a way that only someone born in Sicily can blow kisses. One by one, the others turned and waved: Rhys, Joe's fifteen-year-old stepson, grinning and holding up his leg in its plaster cast while waving a crutch in her direction; Michelle Rosavina, Joe's mum, who Rosa adored and finally, Joe himself.

After the quite terrifying cow drama, Rosa had taken Chiara home to the vicarage, travelling together in the police car, sitting her down in the vicarage kitchen and feeding her beans on toast and ice cream (comfort food, she'd explained to Roberto once he'd arrived to pick up the little girl). And, in the three weeks since, Chiara had greeted her in school, and in church, like a long-lost friend. Or a substitute mother now that Joe's ex-wife, Carys, was far away in Sydney? Rosa knew she was only setting herself up for heartache if she was to become too attached to Joe's daughter, but it wasn't easy stopping herself from falling in love with the gorgeous little thing.

Joe was turning to see who the others were all waving at. He raised the plaster cast on his right hand and rubbed ruefully at his head before mouthing, 'thank you' in her direction.' He appeared to be about to make his way across to the still-stationary car, but then must have seen she was with Sam and thought better of it.

Rosa stared across at the group through the open car window, wanting to be with, and a part of, Joe and the whole Rosavina family so much it actually hurt. She felt such a sense of loss, it was manifesting itself as a deep-down pain. Knowing that Sam was totally in tune to anything she might be feeling, Rosa plastered on a smile and offered up a simple wave towards the group in return.

And then she felt her heart pound and the blood drain from her face.

An elegantly tall, blonde-haired woman had now joined the others in the beer garden, linking her arm through Joe's and kissing his mouth long and hard before turning slightly to see who her companions were waving and blowing kisses at.

The traffic lights turned green and Sam's car moved off.

9

The following morning, a Monday, Eva climbed several flights of narrow stone stairs towards what had been Bill Astley's private art gallery at the very apex of Heatherly Hall. Private, in as much as the artwork was purely that of one artist – Bill Astley – and private in that it was up here, so Eva's biological mother, Alice Parkes – who'd never been afraid to tell it as it was – had recounted that, overcome with both amazement and lust (as well as a surfeit of gin) on viewing these incredible, almost pornographic, images, she'd been more than happy to be seduced by the artist in residence, nearly forty years previously.

Eva opened the heavy wooden door at the top of the stairs leading to a long gallery, which stretched seamlessly in front of her. She and Hannah and Rosa had been up into what Bill called 'the gods' of Heatherly Hall on many previous occasions (it had been a thrillingly scandalous place to discover when playing hide-and-seek as kids) but now, standing alone, taking in the somewhat salacious images of men and women (as well as animals) in various stages of undress and sexual contortions, Eva could only stare in wonder at Bill Astley's professionalism and talent while pondering anew on the man from whom she'd always assumed she'd inherited half her own artistic capacity.

Until one DNA test had proved conclusively that, while the triplets patently and undeniably all shared Alice Parkes's genes, she – Eva – was now the odd triplet out having apparently been conceived twelve hours or so earlier in Paris. Before Alice, in panic, so the story went, had fled back to Yorkshire when the wife of her lover – Yves Dufort – had forced her at knifepoint from his bed.

Was it any wonder, Eva asked herself, that she was so mixed up about her own relationship with her husband Rayan, after facing such life-altering proof that the twelfth Marquess of Stratton was not her biological father after all? Eva sighed, conveniently forgetting that her marriage had begun to sour long before being told the truth by the DNA test – and then confirmed by Alice – about her parentage.

She wondered, not for the first time, if Alice had ever considered the possibility of *all three of them* being Yves Dufort's daughters? Surely, she must have done? Falling pregnant after having sex with two different men within twenty-four hours of each other, albeit on either side of the English Channel, must have raised the question in Alice's mind of who had actually fathered these babies? But Alice, head in a cloud, interested only in herself and her own artwork, probably never gave it another thought. And certainly, like everyone else, could never have considered that one of the three triplets might have been fathered by one of the men, while the remaining two girls had been fathered by the other.

Eva hated the idea of being only *half*-sisters with Rosa and Hannah, but had kept these feelings to herself, instead saying she'd always known she was different, special, set apart from the other two. Wasn't it she, Eva, who was the eldest triplet? The first to be pulled out of Alice (first in, first out?) and handed immediately over to Susan and Richard? Hadn't she always been the more outgoing, the more academic, with her love of science and maths as well as the art gene all three had inherited? (Yves Dufort must have had a good brain pool.)

And yet, she just felt miserable, the odd one out, not, as she'd always thought, a fully paid-up member of the Quinn triplets. And, now it had been proved she had, in reality, absolutely no genuine connection to Bill Astley, she was suffering hugely from imposter syndrome. What was she even doing up here, assessing the rooms and attics for the Heatherly Hall Art Retreat she'd set her heart on for years when, in reality, she had no right to her share of the inheritance Bill had left the three of them?

Eva shook herself. 'For heaven's sake, woman,' she said out loud, feeling immediately silly at vocalising her thoughts to the figures on the wall who now appeared to turn and look down at her with interest from their lofty height. 'Bill loved you, knew you as his daughter. He wouldn't have allowed Yves Dufort's newly unmasked fast-racing little sperm to come between us. Would he?' Eva looked directly into the eyes of a beautifully created image of a man and a woman now in front of her as she moved down the gallery. The semi-naked man, his thigh wrapped expertly around a woman dressed only in a thin, transparent shift, was patently too busy seducing his lover to answer Eva's question and, berating herself for talking to a painting, she set off purposefully towards the rooms beyond the gallery, which she and Hannah had pinpointed as the possible main area for the retreat.

In one of the rooms, to her left, she'd set up her own easel, brushes and paints. A couple of years earlier, after Nora was born, Eva had had such an absolute *longing* for some time to herself that Bill had allocated her this room all for herself, clearing out long-abandoned chests, tables and chairs, old boxes, newspapers, crockery, broken umbrellas, hatstands and hatboxes. Bill had thrown them all out, building a bonfire and consigning them all to the flames, before telling Eva if she was serious about rekindling the artistic talent she'd shut away since A-level Art, in order to pursue her career in dentistry, then here was her chance. He, Bill, and Mrs Sykes his housekeeper, would look after Nora on the afternoons Eva still had left of her maternity leave before returning to Malik and Malik a few months later.

As Eva approached the huge canvas she'd been working on seemingly aeons earlier – since the break-up of her marriage she'd had little time or appetite to carry on with it – she thanked God that Bill had never known she wasn't actually his biological daughter after all. She also wondered idly, as she picked up a couple of badly cleaned brushes stiff with paint and lack of use, why Jonny Astley, Bill's legitimate son and his quite dreadful wife, the American Billy-Jo, hadn't done as they'd threatened and tried to overturn the terms of Bill's will now that it had been scientifically and conclusively proved she, Eva, had no connection whatsoever to Bill Astley.

Having said that, Rodney Bowman, the lawyer in charge of Bill's estate and will, had confirmed that Eva's parentage was largely irrelevant: Bill Astley had had every right to leave his shares of the management committee as well as his own personal wealth to whomsoever he wished. The title, of course, had to be handed down to both Jonny and Billy-Jo but, unless the pair of them wanted to take it further, at the end of the day, that's all they were to end up with.

Eva sat at the canvas, the afternoon light flooding through the magnificent domed windows above her, as well as directly from the long bank of windows to her right, and felt a surge of excitement knowing that this was what she wanted to do. She'd ask Rayan to allow her to work just two days a week at the surgery in order to keep her hand in – and to earn the money she needed to keep herself and the girls when it was her turn to have them – but the rest of the time she'd be up here, teaching, painting, putting Heatherly Hall Art Retreat firmly on the map.

She stood with the paintbrushes and a bottle of turps, intending to take them to the sink in the next room but, instead, moved over to the window that looked down onto the formal gardens and lake, open to the public, and beyond to the Stratton farmland and woodland over which Lachlan Buchanan was now in charge. Buchanan wasn't really her type – and certainly not Hannah's. (After sixteen years with Rayan, she wasn't exactly sure what *was* her type.) She grinned as the man himself came into view below, walking purposely towards the hall. She recalled the many arguments and differences of opinion between the estate manager and Hannah. But, Eva conceded, and she would never admit this to Rosa, and particularly not to Hannah, there was definitely something very lust-making about the sardonic, auburn-haired man from across the border.

Eva's lustful thoughts – surveying Bill's immodestly lewd artwork must have got her in the mood – were broken by her phone ringing.

'Mrs Malik?' Eva didn't at first recognise the woman's voice.

'Yes?'

'Mrs Beresford, head teacher at Little Acorns.'

'Oh, right? Is everything alright?'

'Just wondered, if you were picking up Laila this afternoon, whether you could pop into my office for a few minutes for a little chat?'

'Well, I wasn't. My nanny, Jodie, is picking her up as usual. And a little chat?' Eva gave an involuntary nervous titter. 'That sounds ominous.'

'Just a little problem Laila is having at the moment.'

'A problem? Has my husband not done her reading homework with her? This is what happens when…'

'Miss Worthington – Laila's teacher – says Mr Malik is always conscientious about Laila's reading, Mrs Malik.'

'Right.' Was this a dig at her then? Was the school ringing to say *she* was the problem re homework?

'So, shall we say three o'clock then, Mrs Malik?'

'Yes, fine, no problem. Could you give me some idea…?' but the head teacher had gone, no doubt to sort out other pressing matters.

'What are you doing up here all by yourself?' Hannah was at Eva's side before she realised she was no longer alone.

'Oh, God, you made me jump, creeping up on me like that,' Eva said crossly, taking the irritation she felt at Laila's head teacher not being more forthcoming out on Hannah.

'I wasn't creeping anywhere,' Hannah replied mildly. 'I

thought you were supposed to be sorting this Paris trip out? I thought I'd find you up here rather than on the computer in the office.'

'I keep putting it off,' Eva admitted. 'I'm terrified of meeting the man who is my dad. I might not like him one bit. He might not like me.'

'He's not your dad. Richard is. Yves Dufort is merely the sperm donor to Alice's eggs.'

'Do you have to be so clinical... so biological?'

'Well, this man *is* your biological father. Jesus, another father to add to the mix: Richard, Bill and now Yves. Good job Mum and Dad never divorced and remarried or you could have ended up with four fathers. Bloody expensive at Christmas.' Hannah started to laugh.

'It's not funny, Hans. You know, leaving my marriage, I thought I'd be filled with a new zest for life, a new confidence to take on exciting things: this art retreat, a new father in Paris, lots of new men, sex...'

'I thought you'd have been swiping left and right the minute Rayan moved out,' Hannah said, still laughing.

'It's not funny, Hannah,' Eva said once more. 'I seem to have lost all my confidence.'

'Of course, you have.' Hannah nodded, now with some degree of sympathy. 'No one leaves sixteen years of marriage, and the next day strips off their pants and gets down and dirty with someone else.'

'Are you sure?'

'Well, OK, I'm sure some are doing it actually *before* their other half has packed up their share of the DVDs and filched their favourite pillow from the marital bed.'

'Like Ben you mean?' Eva raised an eyebrow in Hannah's direction.

Hannah merely patted Eva's arm, ignoring any implications about her own affair with Ben Pennington. 'You've had a lot thrown at you, all at once, Eva: inheriting this place; discovering you're not, you know, who you thought you were; moving in here with me two days a week; having to share the girls; realising you're now a free agent to find yourself sexually – which, forgive me for bringing it up, was the main reason for you and Rayan actually splitting up, wasn't it?'

Eva nodded sadly. 'Nearly two years without sex, Hans. And, despite Rayan off to his psychosexual counsellor every week, and the pair of us trying hard to make a go of it, especially for the girls, we just seemed unable to.'

'Maybe this separation is exactly what you need? A little break before realising you can't be without each other?'

'You know, Hannah, I was just wondering – in fact, to be honest I've been wondering this for a while…'

'Whether Rayan isn't a latent homosexual?' Hannah finished Eva's sentence for her.

'Gay, you mean?'

Hannah nodded and they both looked at each other.

'To be honest, I've never seen him eyeing up other men. Or other women come to that.' Eva sighed. 'But maybe it's just me he doesn't fancy anymore.'

'I suppose he could be gay,' Hannah said doubtfully. 'You know, it would have been hard for him, coming from a Muslim family where, perhaps, homosexuality is frowned upon?'

'Oh, *I* don't know, Hannah.' Eva was irritable. 'When your husband doesn't want to have sex with you anymore, and is actually, you know, *unable* to have sex with you anymore and ends up secretly taking himself off to a psychosexual counsellor every Sunday when he's supposed to be off on his bike…' Eva paused. 'And now, apparently, there's a problem with Laila too.'

'Laila?' Hannah frowned. 'What, she's gay as well?'

'Oh, don't be so facile,' Eva snapped crossly. 'I don't know what's up. I've just been summoned to the Great White Chief's office.' Eva looked at her watch. 'I'd better get going. I'm just wondering if Rayan should be with me?'

'You get off, it's probably nothing. Maybe she's fallen in the playground and the TA has put neat Dettol on the graze or something. It's probably something like that, or Laila's had one of her plaits cut off by the classroom bully and the head wants to apologise before you go to the local paper?' Hannah laughed. 'Anyway, I've got an hour or so spare now before I've a meeting with Tiffany across at the wedding venue. Don't you just love being in charge of all this, Eva?' Hannah beamed. 'I don't think I've ever been as happy as I am right now. Look, I'm going to get our tickets booked on Eurostar and a nice hotel. Montmartre do you think? Week after next? Rosa's free then.'

'The train, rather than flying?' Eva asked doubtfully.

'Yes, new experience for all of us.' Hannah smiled. 'And you, Eva, get yourself on a few dating sites and find what you were missing with Rayan.'

'What I was missing?' Eva pulled on her jacket, hunting for car keys.

'A satisfactory sex life, I believe, Eva,' Hannah retorted. 'Sex? Wasn't that what the separation was all about?'

'Do go straight in to Mrs Beresford's office, Mrs Malik. She's waiting for you.' Jean Barlow, Little Acorns school secretary, ushered Eva through the open door before retreating back to her own office.

'Ah, Mrs Malik, come in.' Cassie Beresford stood, inviting Eva to sit in the chair opposite. 'We've not seen you for a while. How are you?'

Was this a criticism of Eva not spending enough time in school? Had the playground Mafia reported her to the head for not pulling her weight? Should she be on the PTA? Making flapjacks and millionaire's shortbread for the upcoming Summer Fair? (It was only May, for heaven's sake, wasn't it?) Coming into the classroom and taking her turn at hearing readers like Rosa, in her role as governor, did every week?

'I've been exceptionally busy,' Eva said almost defensively.

'And I'm sure you're aware that Laila's father and I have separated? I did write and let you know.'

'Of course you did. Thank you for that.' Mrs Beresford paused. 'How do you think Laila is coping with it all?'

'Well, she's not wetting the bed or having nightmares,' Eva said, still in defence mode. 'And her father and I are obviously at great pains to make sure she knows she's loved and none of this is her fault.' Eva relented. 'Are you seeing a different story here? Is that why you've asked me in?'

'Laila is an exceptionally bright little girl as you well know.' The head paused again. 'And there appears to be a bullying issue in Laila's class.'

'Laila's being bullied?' Eva felt her heart miss a beat. 'Just when she's going through her parents separating? Who is it exactly who is doing this bullying? Have you had the child's parents in? Been able to nip it in the bud?'

'I've asked you in now, Mrs Malik,' Cassie Beresford said gently. 'Because, as you say, we need to stop Laila from doing the things she's doing to other children.'

10

'It's my daughter who's the bully?' Eva stared. 'Is that what you're saying?'

'According to Miss Worthington, yes. And to be honest, Mrs Malik, I've seen Laila in action as well.'

'In action?' Eva felt herself go cold and then hot. 'What exactly has she been doing?'

'Sometimes kids torment others because that's the way they've been treated themselves…'

'I beg your pardon?' Eva felt her pulse race now. 'Are you saying my husband and I torment our kids at home? Because if that's…'

'No, I'm not saying that at all.' Cassie Beresford was calm. This head teacher had obviously dealt with a bully's parents before and, distraught though she was, Eva herself tried to remain in control of the situation. 'Children may think their behaviour is normal because they come from families or other settings where everyone regularly gets angry and shouts or calls each other names.'

'I can assure you, Mrs Beresford, there have been many occasions when I've wanted to get *very* angry and shout in the past few months, but, as a dental surgeon—' there, that would show this woman with her accusations, that she was *a professional* and not some fishwife yelling at her kids in the middle of Tesco '—I am well able to present a veneer of calm when required… I mean, I have patients terrified of my drill…' Eva broke off, realising she was perhaps digging a hole for herself. 'I mean…'

'Mrs Malik,' Cassie Beresford, interrupted calmly, 'it's always upsetting when we're told something we didn't realise about our children.'

'Oh.' Eva felt herself grow even crosser. 'And you've been told upsetting things about *your* children, have you?'

'Yes, in the past.' Mrs Beresford smiled. 'But we're not here to talk about me. Or you…'

'You appear to be doing quite a bit of talking about me.' Eva glared at the woman.

'We're here to talk about Laila, and what's going on in *her* life, not ours. Although, whatever is going on in your life at the moment, must surely reflect Laila's behaviour.' Mrs Beresford offered a smile, but whether it was one of encouragement, accusation or sympathy, Eva couldn't tell, so didn't respond. Instead, the head went on, 'Most kids get teased by a sibling or a friend at some point. And it's not usually harmful when done in a playful, friendly, and mutual way, and both kids find it funny. But when teasing becomes hurtful, unkind, and constant, it crosses the line into bullying and needs to stop. Bullying is intentional tormenting in physical, verbal, or psychological ways. It can range from hitting, shoving, name-calling, threats, and mocking to extorting money and possessions. Some kids bully by shunning others and spreading rumours about them. Others use social media or electronic messaging to taunt others or hurt their feelings.'

'Mrs Beresford, Laila is only seven years old,' Eva now said. 'I can assure you she doesn't have a Twitter or Instagram account. Just yet.'

'I didn't say she had. I was merely pointing out what the face of bullying might actually look like.'

'And extorting money?' Eva folded her arms.

'Yes.'

'Yes? Laila has been demanding money with menaces?'

'Laila has been taking money, as well as sweets and biscuits from her classmates.'

'But Laila is rarely allowed sweets and biscuits. As dentists, we don't generally allow them in the house.'

'Neither do we, in school. Maybe that's why she's been ordering her classmates to bring some in for her?'

Eva shook her head in disbelief. She wanted to cry: she was a failure as a daughter (she wasn't Bill's daughter after all), as a wife (Rayan didn't want sex with her), as a sister (Hannah and Rosa were only her half-sisters, and Virginia had never thought much of her, as Susan had once pointed out after an awful argument when, as a thirteen-year-old, Eva had gone into her big sister's bedroom and nicked her new Max Factor mascara. And now she was a failure as a mother.

She pulled herself together and managed to speak. 'So, Mrs Beresford, could you tell me just what Laila has been up to?' Then, remembering Hannah's words, attempted levity. 'Not cut off another little girl's plaits, has she?'

'Almost.'

'Sorry?' Eva felt herself go cold once more.

'I think that was probably Laila's intention with the scissors. She cut the little girl's ear instead.'

'Oh my God. Assault?'

Mrs Beresford smiled slightly at that. 'I've already spoken to the girl's mother. Don't worry, she's not pressing charges.'

'What?'

'Sorry, that didn't come out right.' Mrs Beresford smiled again. 'What she did say was that she was thankful it wasn't her own daughter wielding the scissors. Would prefer her daughter to be the victim rather than the perpetrator.'

'Right. Yes, I can see that.'

'The little girl in question is one who will always hold her own with Laila. They both want to be Queen Bee in Y2. However, there are children who are unable to stand up to Laila. They're frightened of her.'

Eva paused. 'To be honest, Mrs Beresford, there are times when I find her pretty frightening myself. She's always needed a firm hand… Not that I've ever laid a hand on her… goodness that came out wrongly.'

'It's a couple of these children whose parents have already had a word with me about Laila. She's been teasing and saying quite unpleasant things to the less able kids. I was going to have a word with you about all this today anyway. This cutting incident is the icing on the cake.'

'Cutting incident?' Eva briefly closed her eyes against the awful image of her seven-year-old daughter in *Peaky Blinders*' mode, flat cap pulled down over her beautiful brown eyes, razor blade to hand.

'Look, while we have to take this at its highest level, try not to worry too much. My daughter, Freya, was quite ghastly at the age of seven. Like Laila, she was exceptionally bright. The problem is, very bright kids can become bored in the classroom and if, like Laila, there are things going on at home she can't control, she can try to exercise that control over those weaker than herself.'

'She's taken money you say?'

'The little boy she sits next to had brought 20p for a charity sticker. Laila took it from him because she wanted a sticker herself and hadn't the money.'

'But I'd have given her the money,' Eva protested. 'I didn't know anything about it.'

'The children were asked to write it down in their homework journals. The information was also on the school's website.' Mrs Beresford's tone was gentle, understanding, rather than accusatory. 'You and your husband have probably had other things on your minds, Mrs Malik. I've been there. I understand.'

Eva's head came up. 'It's not easy going through a separation.'

'No. But not easy for our kids either. We have this idea that children are resilient. Probably better to say that they learn to put up with whatever's thrown at them, but sometimes their way of coping is trying to prove that they are still important people, despite changes at home. And, maybe, one way of doing that, for a seven-year-old, is to pick on other kids because they need a victim – someone who seems emotionally or physically weaker, or just acts or appears different in some way – to feel more important, popular, or in control of what's going on in their lives.'

'So, where do we go from here?'

'Well, to begin with, we'll have her in for a chat. Tell her that what she's been up to must stop. Right now.'

Eva found herself glancing round at the head's study. 'I don't know if what I'm going to say now makes this any better or any worse.' Eva hesitated and Cassie Beresford's eyes were questioning. 'I've sat in this seat before. When I was probably Laila's age or a bit older – Y5, I think it was. With Susan, my mum, who'd been called in. I was a horror at school: full of myself, very confident, like Laila; not overly pleasant to either the other kids or to the teachers. I worried my mum daft.'

'And Rosa and Hannah?' The head smiled. 'I can't imagine our village vicar giving her teachers hell.'

'No, it was just me. Genes will out.'

'But you and Rosa and Hannah surely have the same gene pool? I'm sure...'

'Nope.' Eva brushed away a furious tear. She felt so angry, so lost. 'Long, long story, and I know you'll keep this to yourself and I don't know why on earth I'm telling you this *anyway*, but I've recently found out I have a different biological father from the other two. And I think it must be his genes that have made me into the selfish, arrogant person I am today. Why my marriage has ended. Why my daughter is a bully... Sorry, sorry, this isn't what you want to hear. Really sorry...' Eva stood up, tried to smile. 'I'm sorry. OK. So Laila...'

'Of course, Laila. Shall we have her in?'

Once Jodie – Laila and Nora's Australian nanny – had left for the evening and Eva had fed the girls and put Nora to bed early, Eva waited for Rayan to arrive from the other end of town where he was renting a rather upmarket apartment so, together, they could talk to Laila about the events of the afternoon.

'Daddy, my *daddy*.' Laila flung herself at Rayan the second he arrived, and Eva instantly regretted encouraging her daughter to watch Jenny Agutter's outpourings in the original version of *The Railway Children* the previous week. She'd promised to take Laila to the new, follow-up version, showing at the village's one remaining cinema, after enjoying watching the original once more with both her girls on TV. She'd bet any money Laila had been practising the immortal lines in front of the bathroom mirror, ready to execute them when she next saw Rayan. 'I've missed you,' Laila added, looking sideways under her lashes for Eva's reaction.

'We've all missed Daddy.' Eva smiled a smile she wasn't really feeling.

'Well, if we're all missing Daddy, and Daddy is missing us, then why isn't Daddy coming back home to live with us again?'

'Laila.' Rayan for once spoke firmly. 'So, I hear you've been up to something you shouldn't at school?' He took Laila on his knee and the three of them sat at the kitchen table before Eva jumped up in search of wine. After the day she'd had today, she needed the help of alcohol.

Laila pouted. 'I only tried to cut Florence's plait off because she was saying mean things.'

'What sort of mean things?' Eva and Rayan both paused in lifting a glass to their lips.

'She said *my* hair was black and dirty, not blonde and clean like hers.'

'Your hair's not dirty, Laila.' Eva leant over and sniffed at her daughter's head. 'There, I can still smell shampoo and conditioner from washing it last night.'

'She said I was a half-caste.'

'She said *what*?' Eva raised her eyes at Rayan.

'What's a half-caste, Mummy?'

'Not a very nice word at all, darling. You're not half of anything. Did you tell Miss Worthington or Mrs Beresford she'd said that to you? And that's what had made you cross?'

Laila shook her head. 'And she said: "your daddy's a black man," Daddy.'

'I am a black man, darling. And very proud to be a black man too.'

'I think you're brown, not black.' Laila gazed up at Rayan, scanning his features for confirmation.

'Darling, it doesn't matter what colour someone is.' Rayan smiled. 'It doesn't matter what colour you are. It doesn't matter if you're brown, blue, pink or green…'

He trailed off as Eva shook her head furiously at him. The blue, pink or green story might have been fine several years ago, but now, with Black Lives Matter, brown lives *did* matter. Mattered just as much. Blue and pink was just trivialising.

'What had you said to this Florence girl to make her say mean things to you?' Eva asked, still frowning at Rayan.

Laila pouted once more but said nothing.

'Laila?'

'I didn't say anything.'

'Laila!'

'I said that everyone hated her and no one wanted to play with her. And that she was a bastard no-hoper drongo.'

'What?'

'It's what Jodie shouted down the phone to her boyfriend when he went off and had sexy with Marnie Bell's nanny last week.'

'Laila, you can't say horrible words like that to people.' Eva looked across at Rayan.

'Jodie does. All the time. And she's a grown-up.' Laila pouted once more. 'And *you* say horrid things about Daddy.'

'No, I *don't*,' Eva said in exasperation as Rayan raised an eyebrow. Oh hell, had Laila been listening when she was talking to Hannah about the state of her marriage.

'Yes, you do. You say he doesn't want to do sexy anymore. Jodie's boyfriend wants to do sexy with *everyone*, Jodie says. Why don't you try Jodie's boyfriend, Mummy? You know, if you want sexy?'

Jesus. Embarrassed at having been outed by her daughter, Eva drained her glass and said, 'I need to tell Mrs Beresford what Florence said to Laila, Rayan. I'm assuming the school has a safeguarding policy about racist comments? I'm also assuming it's Florence's mother who has bandied the… you know, the *h-c* word about in front of her daughter? I'm going to get straight on the phone now, and have it out with her.' Eva made to stand, the burning fury she was feeling at the woman's careless, unpleasant choice of words overcoming the more rational decision to speak with Florence's mother when she was calm.

'Eva, don't be silly.' Rayan placed a restraining hand on Eva's arm as Laila, quiet now, looked up at the pair of them. 'Do you even know this woman's number? You know what you're like when you lose your temper. And you don't *know* that it's Florence's mother who's put these words into her daughter's head. You've no idea. And,' he added, 'while I think it's a sensible way forward that you have a word with her, *not* when you've all guns blazing, for heaven's sake.'

'Guns?' For a second Laila looked fearful and then she laughed. 'Mummy's not going to shoot Florence's mummy, is she?'

'Oh, don't be ridiculous, Laila,' Eva snapped. 'Right, your bath time. We'll sort all this out tomorrow.'

'Daddy, I don't want to go to school anymore.' Laila pouted, forcing out a couple of tears and snuggling up to Rayan who had, it appeared, now assumed the mantle of good cop while she, Eva, was obviously bad. 'Miss Worthington and Mrs Beresford were cross with me.'

'I'm not surprised if you go round trying to cut off people's ears,' Eva said in exasperation.

'It was her plait – her *blonde* plait – I was trying to cut off, not her ear.' Laila was sulky. 'Anyway, Vincent Van Gogh cut off an ear and *he's* an artist like you, Mummy.'

'He cut off his own ear, Laila, not someone else's when trying to get at their plait.' Eva was feeling irritable once more: Laila didn't appear a bit sorry for what she'd done.

'Maybe we should send Laila down to the vicarage to live with Rosa for a while,' Eva said, attempting levity. Rayan had returned downstairs after sitting and reading Harry Potter with Laila, and Eva had got through another glass of wine. 'Indoctrinate her with a few good Christian values. You do know she's more than capable of reading by herself now?' she added.

'Who? Rosa?' Rayan looked momentarily startled and then tutted. 'Of course I know Laila is a capable reader, Eva. She's a very clever girl.' Rayan was irritable himself. 'That's not the point though, is it?' Rayan hesitated, folded his arms and then, glaring across at Eva said, 'Maybe I should have the girls live with *me*. Permanently. You've so much on with working at the surgery two days a week and now with Heatherly Hall and this setting up of an art retreat you're so keen on. You could move into Heatherly Hall on a permanent basis, and let me move back here with my girls.'

'What?' Eva was incensed. 'Are you trying to say I'm not a good mother? That it's my fault Laila is going round cutting off other kids' ears?'

'Oh, don't be so bloody dramatic, Eva. Laila's unpleasant behaviour is obviously a direct result of our separating. Of *you* wanting to do your own thing. She says she doesn't want to be given away to an orphanage like, and I quote, "Mummy's real Mummy, Alice Parkes, gave *her* babies away to Granny Susan so she could become a famous artist."'

'What!' Eva felt herself explode. 'Have *you* told her about Alice? Because I most certainly haven't.'

Rayan shook his head, rubbing at his beard before running

a hand through his thick dark hair. 'This Florence girl again, it seems. Most people round here know the story of your birth, Eva. How can they not, when Alice Parkes is a village legend? She also told Laila, now that we're divorcing, that Laila will have to go and live in an orphanage like Oliver Twist in the Victorian workhouse and have to share a bedroom with ten other children and eat gruel.'

'Bloody Victorians *again*,' Eva snapped, recalling Laila's class assembly about life in the workhouse. 'About time Y2 moved on to the Egyptians.'

'Pulling brains down noses before mummification?' Rayan made his own attempt at levity after throwing out the car crash of a suggestion that Laila and Nora should live with him.

'What? Brains down noses?' Eva shook her head in exasperation. 'Rayan, I'm going in to school to have it out with Mrs Beresford and this Florence girl's mother tomorrow. And,' she snarled, 'there is *no way* that I'm letting the girls live with you. Here. On a permanent basis. They're *my* daughters.' Eva, suddenly finding she was crying, sat down at the table, burying her head in her arms.

'Mine too,' Rayan said gently, crossing over and pulling her to him. 'How've we come to this, Eva?'

It felt so wonderful to have Rayan's arms round her, to feel his solid, safe *goodness*, and Eva moved automatically into his chest, her head underneath his chin where it had always rested in the seventeen years or so since she'd met him in her third year at university. Eva breathed in this husband of hers, taking in the citrus tang of the aftershave he always used despite having a beard; his lovely Rayan smell. Eva reached up a hand to stroke his face and he kissed the top of her head.

She stepped back slightly before snaking one arm around his neck and, with the other, made to unbutton his shirt. She had three buttons freed from their repository, and one hand reaching into the matt of black hair on his chest. He was in bloody good shape for a man of almost forty. The thought that he was going to celebrate his fortieth birthday without her flashed through her mind, and she realised she'd probably drunk far too much wine far too quickly. Slowly, she removed her hand from inside Rayan's shirt (who was ironing his shirts so beautifully?) and moved it downwards towards his groin, feeling him immediately stiffen. Unfortunately, not where she'd intended.

Rayan's whole body tensed and he removed Eva's hand with a 'Don't, Eva. Not here.'

'Not here? Where then?' Eva smiled up at this lovely man of hers and, while she saw love for her in his beautiful brown eyes, she also saw regret. Pity even.

'I need to go, Eva.' Rayan's voice was matter-of-fact as he gently, but firmly, unhooked her body from his own before turning away from her to button his shirt. 'If you want me to come with you when you go back into school to try and sort Laila, just let me know. And, give me the dates you and the others are off to Paris and I'll be here for the girls.'

He took his jacket from the back of the kitchen chair where he'd left it, picked up his car keys and headed for the front door.

11

'Rats. You've got Rats, Vicar.' Denis Butterworth, the verger, appeared almost gleeful, surreptitiously repositioning the sandy-coloured toupee, which had slipped slightly from its customary position on his balding pate.

'Rats?' Rosa stared. 'Are you sure? Sure they're not mice?'

'Bloody big mice, if they are, love; you want to see the droppings.'

'I'd rather not.' Rosa sighed heavily. The vicarage was already in a mess because, in a fit of not being able to stand the gloomy hallway and stairs décor a minute longer, she'd set to, several weeks earlier, and started to rip off the peeling, nicotine-stained Anaglypta that must have been up since Methuselah was a lad. The same grungy brown wallpaper and paint had certainly been in situ when she, Hannah and Eva were kids and playing hide-and-seek in the vicarage when visiting the Rev Cecil Parkes with Susan and their big sister, Virginia. Virginia, who, for some reason the others could never fathom, had adored that cantankerous and irascible old man, had been happy to sit on the sofa while their grandfather puffed relentlessly on his Benson and Hedges, always ranting about something or other. The state of the government, his dwindling congregation, the lack of morals of villagers cohabiting rather than being married in his church were favourite topics and, once he was on a roll, the triplets would inevitably leave him to it, slipping upstairs to play in the huge bedrooms and even bigger attics.

Now, bereft of wallpaper and the faded, threadbare stair carpet, the hallway appeared even more depressingly sombre than before, the bare wooden stairs creaking and echoing Rosa's every footstep when she went upstairs to bed. Once she'd stripped the area bare and got Denis and her dad to help her pull up the quite disgusting ancient stair carpet, she couldn't face decorating the stairs and hallway herself. She and fifteen-year-old Rhys Johnson, Joe Rosavina's stepson, had decorated the kitchen and sitting room together when she'd moved into the vicarage last October.

She didn't suppose, now that Rhys was still sporting a pot on his ankle, she was able to ask him if he fancied earning a few quid getting stuck in with a paintbrush again, even though both Eva and Hannah said they'd seen him still helping out at Roberto Rosavina's pizza restaurant down in Midhope at the weekend. Rosa missed Rhys coming round, as he'd done fairly regularly after school back in the autumn, but was really pleased he appeared to finally be forming some sort of relationship with Joe's father, Roberto. And, at least not seeing Rhys meant he wasn't able to tell her what Joe was up to and with whom.

And now, not only did Rosa have a hallway in need of decoration and carpeting, she apparently had bloody rats into the bargain. She'd heard what sounded like a herd of elephants racing above her bedroom from the attics a couple of nights previously. They'd been noisy and industrious enough to waken her but she'd assumed it was the usual field mice having a, well, a *field day*. A mousy knees-up, perhaps? A murine wedding, maybe; a rodent rave? The thought had amused her and, not being in the least frightened of the tiny, brown country mice, she'd smiled at the thought, turned over and gone immediately back to sleep.

Last night, however, had been very different. The thundering overhead had intensified and, sitting up in bed, looking upwards, she'd have sworn she could hear gnawing and chattering. There was something big up there. She'd wished Sam was with her. No, that was a lie – she didn't. And that was worrying her too. To be honest (and, after all, wasn't that what vicars were paid to be?) she'd longed for Joe Rosavina to be with her. He'd have laughed, made some joke, sorted it out for her, whereas Sam would have gently, but condescendingly, berated her for insisting on living in this dump of a vicarage when she could have been staying with him over at his lovely Holly Close Farm cottage.

'Yep,' the verger was reiterating his original conclusion regarding Rosa's new upstairs neighbours, 'definitely rats, love. You'll need to be careful: they'll chew through all your electrics and then where will you be?'

'In the dark, I reckon, Denis.'

'Right, I'll have a word with Cliff.'

'Cliff?' All she could bring to mind was Cliff Richard. 'We're all going on a… *summer holiday*,' she sang, grinning in Denis's direction.

'Well, yes, I know you're off to Paris fairly soon, Vicar. And don't you worry about leaving us all here while you're off gallivanting. Sandra and me'll be keeping an eye on the church. But you need to get them there rats sorted afore you go. Or they'll have chewed through the timbers and be raining down on you while you're asleep.' Denis sniffed. 'Cliff's the man to ring when you've got rats. He'll send in his terrier, flush 'em out and then he puts 'em in a barrel with the dog. Goes for their throats…'

'Oh, no!' Rosa was quite horrified. 'They're God's creatures; they didn't ask to be reviled for being rats.'

'Reviled?' Denis looked puzzled. 'They're bloody rats, love, and we don't want the buggers spreading into the actual church. 'I bet you've been feeding the birds, haven't you?'

'Well yes…'

'Rats'll reckon there's a new eating place in town once you start doing that.' Denis raised an eye, wanting to know more. 'So, have you still got that dentist fellow in tow?'

'In tow?' Rosa wanted to smile at that. 'Yes, I'm still seeing

Sam.' *But not for much longer*, Rosa was shocked to hear her inner voice telling herself.

'Get *him* up in your attic then if you don't want Cliff on the job.' Denis was obviously put out that she wasn't taking up his offer of the Village Rat Catcher.

'I'll ring Rentokil.'

'Get yourself a cat, love. Ben Carey, the last vicar, had two of 'em and never had rats. I'd let you borrow our Jess, but she's a homebird. Wouldn't be happy in the vicarage without me and Sandra.'

'Funnily enough, Denis, I *was* thinking of getting a cat. I'd prefer a dog really – you know, to take out for walks – but Sam…'

'Sam?'

'The dentist *I have in tow*? Sam hates cats,' Rosa continued, 'and, come to think about it, dogs as well actually.'

Another reason to kick him into touch?

'Well, he'll hate rats more when they're dropping on his head from above.' Denis glanced across at Rosa. 'You know, when he's *staying over* with you?' When Rosa didn't react, he went on, 'Actually Vicar, just had a thought.'

'Oh?'

'Nancy Parker – and a right nosy parker she is as well – has gone into Almast Haven.'

'The care home?'

Denis nodded. 'Don't know who's looking after Elvis.'

'Elvis? Is that her husband?'

'Her cat. Big – 'scuse the language, Vicar – son of a bitch is Elvis. I'll find out. He'd be ideal.'

'Right.' Rosa hesitated. Did she really want a cat? Didn't they pee everywhere and leave hair? Sam didn't like cats one bit. And this Elvis sounded to be a handful. 'Right,' she repeated. 'I'll leave it with you and I'll try and get Rentokil in as well.' And a decorator, she mentally added. 'Got to go, Denis; meeting Nigel over in the church.'

'Nigel?'

'Cartwright. He's taken over from Pandora Boothroyd in charge of the church choir. Wants a quick word about acoustics or something.'

'Oh?' Denis pulled a face. 'You want to watch that one, Vicar.'

'Watch him?'

'He's as leet geen as a billy goat.'

'Gosh, I've not heard that expression for years.' Rosa laughed.

'Well, you wouldn't, would you? Living *dahn sarth*.' Denis affected an atrocious cockney accent. 'Now he's in charge of the choir, he'll be even more up himself.' Denis sniffed. 'Right, can't stop here gossiping all day with you, Vicar.' Denis made to move back down the garden. 'I'll make enquiries as to whether Elvis can be persuaded to make a comeback.'

'Like Take That?'

'Take *what*?' Denis frowned and Rosa started to laugh.

'Lovely,' she called over her shoulder as, glancing at her watch, she set off, racing down and round the path leading to the church. Catching sight of Nigel Cartwright waiting in front of the huge wooden door, she waved her key in his direction. 'Sorry, Nigel, on my way.'

'Not to worry, Rosa. Here now.' Nigel put out a hand to slow her down as she belted past him, the hand remaining on her jeaned backside, even as she came to a standstill at the locked door. 'Here let me.' He reached for the huge metal door key and his hand seemed to be attached now to her own.

'Not a problem, Nigel.' Rosa extracted her hand from his, holding up the key. 'I'm a strong healthy woman.'

'I can see that, Rosa.' Nigel winked somewhat lasciviously.

'Been turning church keys for years,' she went on, hurriedly. 'All part of the job spec.'

Nigel stood directly behind her, breathing heavily down her neck as she struggled with the key until, with some relief, she managed to unlock the door, pushing the heavy wood and metal back on itself and allowing the May sunshine to stream into the vestibule.

Oh, she loved her church: loved opening up the building; loved watching the dust motes dancing in the light coming in through the glass-stained windows; the feeling of calm and peace, of coming home every time she walked down the nave towards the sanctuary. *Her* sanctuary.

Remembering Nigel, she turned back towards him. 'How come you're not at work, Nigel? On a Wednesday morning?'

'Taken a few days off from the office. Now I've the responsibility of the choir—' Nigel almost preened '—I want to get some things sorted.' He moved towards her. 'I hope we'll see *you* at choir practice, Rosa?' Nigel stroked her arm invitingly but whether it was an invitation to exercise her tonsils or something else, she wasn't prepared to hang around to find out.

'Me? Can't hold a note to save my life, Nigel.' Rosa glanced down at the man's jeans and shiny brogues. Both appeared brand new – and worryingly tight – and she extricated herself from the pew he seemed to have backed her into. 'Right, need to get on. You do what you have to do, Nigel, and I'll be back in, what? Twenty minutes?'

'Actually, Rosa, it isn't Nigel.'

'What isn't?' Rosa stared.

'Always hated my name. Nigel? Duh! Whoever would call a baby *Nigel*?'

'Well, presumably your mum?' Rosa smiled.

'Yes, and I've had to live with it nearly fifty years. Anyway, I've tried Nige and Nig – but you know, in these days of PC...' Nigel trailed off, sighing.

'I think Nigel is a very nice name,' Rosa said stoutly.

'You *don't*!' Nigel looked almost affronted.

She didn't.

'So, I've taken out the middle G.'

'I thought it was middle C?' Rosa was confused. 'You know, when you're singing?'

'No, I've taken the G from Nigel.'

'Right?'

'So now I'm Ni-el.'

'*Ni-el?*' Rosa repeated the two syllables.

'Well Nile actually.'

'Ah, you've decided to *identify as* a river.' Rosa began to laugh. 'You're in *de Nile* about your name?' She was helpless with laughter.

Nigel was beginning to look hurt and, rearranging her face, she went on, 'That's great, er *Nile*. Really great. Like Nile Rodgers? I *love* Nile Rodgers,' she gushed. 'You know, Ah, *freak out*,' she sang, waving her hands in the air and really going for it, 'du du du du du du, *c'est chic!*'

'I wouldn't know about that. Hmm, I can see what you mean about hitting those notes, Rosa. Now, might you be interested in having some private singing lessons? One to one?' Nile – formerly known as Nigel – smiled wolfishly and reached out a hand to her arm once more. 'I have a couple of pupils on my books at the moment, but could always fit you in.'

'Not me, I don't think, *Nile*,' Rosa said hurriedly. 'Right, I'm off. I'll leave you to your acoustics.' She managed to slide past him without a goosing, and was about to head back up the nave when she realised a woman had come in while she was doing her impression of the great Nile Rodgers and was sitting, head bent, at the front of the nave. Rosa walked quietly down towards her.

'Hello? Are you alright?' When the woman didn't say anything, Rosa went on, 'You want a bit of peace and quiet? That's no problem: I'm going to leave the door unlocked all day. You know, for praying and peeping?' Rosa started to walk back up the nave where Nigel was now limbering up, clearing his throat and singing scales, when she realised the woman was crying. She walked back. 'You OK? Can I help?'

The woman shook her head but Rosa slipped into the pew beside her. 'OK if I just sit here? Or would you rather be alone?'

The woman nodded and Rosa made to rise but sat once more as the woman shook her head. She was probably about Rosa's own age and Rosa wondered if they'd been at school together. She did sort of recognise her. 'Weren't we at Midhope Sixth-Form College together?'

The woman nodded but said nothing further for a few minutes and Rosa made the decision to stay with her. Eventually she asked gently, 'What is it that's making you so upset?'

'Five times now and I can't do it again. I can't go through it again. And this time… this time I held her.'

Rosa put out a hand and the woman let it stay there. Gemma, that was it. Rosa racked her brain. 'Gemma Drinkwater. We were in the same A-level Economics class?'

Gemma nodded. 'Roebuck now.'

'Can you tell me what's wrong, Gemma?'

The woman turned, unstoppable tears rolling down her face. 'I've just had my fifth miscarriage, Rosa. *Five* babies. All *gone*. I don't know why I'm *here*,' she spat. 'Your god is a cruel, spiteful god.'

'I know he can appear so,' Rosa said. She certainly wasn't going to serve up the platitude that everything was for a reason; that this was God's will. There could be no *reason* for this poor woman to have lost five babies. Five pregnancies coming to nothing: no new babies in that lovingly prepared upstairs nursery; no vanilla-smelling new-borns in her arms.

'I thought everything was going to be OK this time. I was twenty-two weeks' pregnant. Can you imagine? I was over halfway there. Out of the danger period. And I'd been feeling really well. You know? Blooming? I thought, this is it: this is what all the books are on about.' She paused, unable to go on. Rosa waited. 'And I was at work, just sitting down, when I began to feel unwell. Wondered if I had a cold. Didn't dare take any paracetamol – you know, I've not had one drink for years while I've been trying to get pregnant, and then when I've been pregnant. And I seem to have been pregnant *for ever*. I tell you now, Rosa, I'm going home after this and I'm going to get legless.'

'I can understand that, but you'll only feel worse tomorrow.'

'Anyway, I stood up at my desk and woosh, my waters went and they had to call an ambulance. Two paramedics all the way up into the office with the rest of the staff trying not to look as if I was about to give birth on the office floor. They just continued with their calls; eating their tuna sandwiches from their Tupperware boxes.' Gemma shuddered. 'I'll never be able to open a can of tuna again without remembering. But I held her, Rosa.'

'You were a mum. You *are* a mum.' Rosa felt her own tears well.

'She died in my arms. Her lungs just weren't developed enough.'

'What was she called?' Rosa asked gently.

'Heather.'

'That's such a lovely name.' Rosa suddenly found she was crying too. They didn't tell you what to do at vicar training school when you were listening to someone's grief and were feeling that same grief yourself. Grief for her own frozen eggs that were unlikely to come to anything. Grief for the little girl, her own little boy, that she'd never hold in her arms.

'Rosa?' Gemma wiped at her eyes and turned in surprise towards Rosa who was now openly sobbing along with her. 'I'm really sorry to have upset you like this. Have you been through it as well? Is that what it is?' When Rosa didn't reply, Gemma patted her hand and they sat in silence for several minutes.

'Can I light a candle for Heather?' Rosa asked eventually, glaring down the nave towards Nigel Cartwright whose humming and lip trills, fricatives and descending nasal consonants were beginning to get right up her own nose.

'Thank you, I'd like that,' Gemma said. 'But for God's sake, don't pray over me, Rosa. I'm not speaking to your boss.'

They wiped their eyes and Rosa led the way to the front of the church, where she lit fifteen candles.

'Fifteen, Rosa?' Gemma managed a smile. 'Don't set the place on fire on my account.'

'One for each of your five babies, Gemma and one for each of my ten frozen eggs.'

'I'm sorry, Rosa, I didn't realise.'

Rosa smiled. 'Why would you?' She squeezed the other woman's arm and, instead of running the gauntlet of Nigel's wandering hands and ascending scales, walked through into the vestry, letting herself out through the back door.

Unsettled by Gemma's sad story and her own embarrassing reaction to it, Rosa felt an overwhelming urge to hide away for an hour somewhere she wouldn't be obliged to put on her jolly vicar front. Instead of dropping in on the weekly mother and toddlers' club in the church hall – which she usually really enjoyed – she decided the comfort of home baking was needed. Maybe she could take what she ended up baking with her when did her visiting of the sick and elderly she'd pencilled in for that afternoon? Although, she reminded herself, past history told her it would probably mean she'd end up comfort *eating* and wolfing most of it herself, but it was the only thing she could think of to shake off her despondency.

She knew the feeling of depression was probably down to three things: her poor old frozen eggs that were, in reality heading towards the end of their shelf life; the growing realisation that she really couldn't see any future for herself with Sam; missing Joe Rosavina so much it was an actual physical pain.

'Sort yourself, Rosa,' she chastised herself. 'Thank God for all the blessings in your life.' And with that, Rosa actually bowed her head and closed her eyes, finding comfort in her faith, in her calling to God. 'And, dear Father,' she finished, as she sat at the kitchen table, 'thank you so much in advance for next week's trip to Paris; for the chance to be with my sisters and have them to myself for a couple of days. Please make Eva happy and like this new father of hers.' Here Rosa opened her eyes before closing them once more and concluding, 'and, if you think it a good thing, Lord, let there be croissants, macarons, tarte Tatin and millefeuille over there.' Feeling that God was with her once more, she felt slightly better and, with that, found flour, eggs, butter and chocolate and set to.

She was in the middle of folding sifted flour and cocoa into the whisked batter in the bowl when there was a knock on the door. Always it went through her mind, as she walked down the stripped-walled and gloomy corridor to the front door, that it could be Joe. Joe who'd come to see her, to tell her he couldn't be without her, to tell her he loved her still. She unconsciously fluffed up her hair, rubbed at the flour on her cheek and reached for the lipstick she kept on the hall table. *Vanity, thy name is woman.*

It wasn't Joe. It was Denis. And a present.

'Right, here y'are love,' Denis beamed proudly. 'Elvis.'

'Oh, Denis.' Rosa frowned. Did she really want a cat? And what was she supposed to do with it when she was off to France the following week?

'He's a champion mouser.' Denis was eager to extol the cat's virtues. 'He'd been taken in by Nancy's neighbour – I had to knock on a few doors to find where he was hanging out these days – and she was more than happy to let you have him for as long as it takes.'

'Hanging out? He sounds like some gangster.'

'Wait until you see him in action, Vicar. He'll be running them rats out of town like Reggie Kray himself.' The big black bundle of fur in Denis's arms didn't look as if it could run the skin off a rice pudding. It yawned widely, looked round at Rosa with benevolent orangey-green eyes and settled once more against the verger's Fair Isle tank top. 'Hang on, you take him, love, and I'll nip back across home for our Jess's spare cat bed and a couple of tins of Whiskas to get you going.' He handed the cat over.

'Denis, I'm in the middle of making brownies,' Rosa tutted, almost staggering under the weight of the animal. It was the size of a small donkey.

'Oh, a cat hair or two won't matter. Ooh, don't mind if I do,' he continued, eyeing the still-warm blueberry muffins she'd just taken out of the oven. 'Lovely,' he said through a mouthful of muffin. 'Nearly as good as our Sandra's. Now, just make sure the cat flap the last vicar's cats had is still working and open, and you're up and running, love.'

By ten that evening, Rosa felt exhausted. After falling sick with cancer and undergoing chemotherapy treatment seven years previously, she was totally aware when she'd been doing too much and needed to take herself off to bed. The bare wooden stairs echoed ponderously and slightly eerily as she took herself, a scandalous plate of muffins and flapjacks, a huge mug of chamomile tea and her Kindle, up to bed. *You wouldn't be able to do this if you had some man in tow*, she told herself, remembering Denis's words about Sam.

She caught sight of herself in the landing mirror, her white winceyette nightie billowing out around her in the harsh light of the unshaded lightbulb, her long dark hair, out of its usual plait, hanging past her shoulders. Hell, she looked like some bag lady – or cat lady: she was a spinster cat lady whose only friends were a plate of cakes and a huge lazy lump of a cat called Elvis who'd already wolfed down two tins of Whiskas before eying her muffins with interest. Maybe she should really go for it and get stuck into the cherry brandy a parishioner had given her at Christmas. An alcoholic, unloved cat lady no less.

Rosa frowned. Where *was* the cat? Wasn't he supposed to be on rat duty? She made herself comfortable in the big king-sized bed, ears alert for any rat movement above her, eyes moving occasionally to the bedroom door she'd left ajar for Elvis once he came home from wherever he'd gone off to. She did hope he was seeing off some rats. She'd only managed one chocolate brownie and two pages of the D H Lawrence she was rereading, before her eyes were closing with fatigue. The racing and clawing of tiny feet above her head had her sitting bolt upright against the pillow, heart racing. She'd have to move out – go and stay with Hannah up at the hall until Rentokil had been to do their job.

And then all was quiet. Dear God, where had the varmints gone now? Rosa clutched at the duvet, straining to listen. Nothing. She began to relax. And then came a *pad, pad, pad, creak creak, creak*… Then silence. Please don't say the rats were coming up the wooden stairs for her? There it was again. Dear God, not burglars again? She'd done the burglars breaking in bit before Christmas. Not again, surely? She was just a poor country vicar woman. What were they after? There it was again: *pad, pad, pad, creak creak* on the uncarpeted stairs. And then she smiled with relief. Elvis obviously. *Pad, pad, creak creak*. But no, hang on, Elvis had obviously come home and was actually here, across from her, snoozing on a nest of clean sheets and pillowcases she'd intended for the airing cupboard.

Pad, pad, pad. Creak, creak creak. The noise came nearer; the slightly ajar bedroom door began to open further. This was it then: a rat or a burglar in her bedroom. Just as she was trying to work out which she'd prefer, which would be the better option, a furry ginger head poked its way tentatively round the door. Oh, the relief, the utter relief to see Jess – Denis and Sandra's own big ginger mog – instead of an effing great rat or burglar.

The two cats eyed each other and then, raised tails stiff as toilet brushes and fur flying, launched at each other, yowling and screeching in a cats' chorus loud enough to wake the dead while the rats continued to thunder overhead like bison on the Serengeti.

Who was nearest? Her mum and dad, Eva or Hannah up at the hall? Stopping only to text Hannah with:

Cat and rat problem. Tell Security to let me in.

Rosa grabbed jeans, sweater and trainers, phone and car keys and headed for the door. Where was Joe Rosavina when she needed him so badly?

12

'Right, I think that's it, then. Paris here we come.' Hannah turned to Rosa, flapping the Eurostar tickets she'd just downloaded in her sister's direction. 'I have to say, Rosa, Eva's doing very little to help organise this trip. I mean, we're going for her benefit after all.'

'You're not bothered about going then?' Rosa drained her cup of coffee and took up the tickets, feeling excited at the thought of a trip across the channel, just the three of them.

'No, no, I am.'

'You just don't want to leave Ben? Is that it?'

'No, no…' Hannah trailed off. 'Well, in a way. His wife's constantly ringing him up on some pretext or the other. Wants him round to fix a plug. Or sort out the garden. Or it's one of the children who's not well.' She frowned. 'I've never known two kids have so many illnesses. Or accidents.'

'They're children,' Rosa said gently. 'Children have accidents and get sick. And they'll be missing their daddy.'

'Suppose.'

'So, when do you get to be stepmum?'

'Stepmum?' Hannah stared. 'Oh, I'm not sure I'm ready for all that. What if they don't like me?'

'They probably won't.' Rosa laughed. 'But, Hannah, if you're in a more solid relationship with Ben – which, now that he's left Alexandra for you, you appear to be – then obviously he'll want you to be a part of his children's lives.'

'Not convinced Alexandra will allow that,' Hannah said slightly gloomily. 'And I'm not sure I'll be any good in the role.'

'Why on earth wouldn't you be?'

'I know I'm OK with bolshie teens. I mean I wasn't too bad as a youth worker, even though I say it myself.' Hannah turned back to her computer, scrolling through Booking.Com where she was looking for a decent hotel to stay in Paris. 'I do hope we haven't left it a bit too late to book a good hotel, Rosa. But,' she went on, pulling a face, 'you know, *little* kids? I know what to say to skunk-smoking fifteen-year-olds with a machete down their undercrackers, but a two- and a six-year-old who see me as the enemy?'

'But you're great with Laila and Nora. Laila's seven and Nora's three and you're brilliant with them.'

'Yes, but they're my *family*. I'm related to them. They love me.'

'Well, if you end up with Ben,' Rosa went on, jabbing a finger towards a particularly nice-looking hotel in Montmartre that had just come up on the screen, 'now that you've got him to yourself, his kids will become your family.'

'Hang on a minute.' Hannah moved towards the open office door where a gentle breeze was wafting in the late spring scents of sweet woodruff, nicotiana and honeysuckle from Heatherly Hall's private cottage garden, previously tended to assiduously by Bill Astley, and which was now looking somewhat unloved.

'You need to do something with these lisianthus and ranunculus.' Daisy Maddison, the village's trainee vet was bent, examining the plants with a critical eye.

'I thought you were a vet, not a horticultural expert.' Hannah smiled as Rosa joined the pair of them outside in the sunshine.

'Trained as a landscape gardener after my biology degree,' Daisy said. 'Botrytis can develop on the leaves, flowers, stems, and pedicels if they're packed too tightly. And these are: there's not a good airflow here and there's some mechanical damage as well; damaged tissue is an entrance for botrytis.'

'Right, if you say so. I thought you were coming to tell me about a problem with one of the animals in the petting zoo,' Hannah said. 'Is everything OK up there?'

'You've obviously let a pretty randy boar in with the pigs,' Daisy said, matter-of-factly. 'Most of the six sows are pregnant and should farrow by early July.'

'Right, isn't that good then?'

'Well, you'll have to decide what you're doing with them once they're weaned, or you'll be overrun with piglets. Five sows, on average ten piglets each. That's fifty piglets to sort out. Who's supposed to be in charge up there?'

Hannah looked slightly shame-faced. 'I told Lachlan Buchanan I'd take over…'

'Hannah, you're joking.' Rosa stared at Hannah. 'You can't do *everything* here at the hall: the wedding venue, this cottage garden, the conference centre, Tea and Cake and now the new wine bar? I didn't think you were running the petting zoo as well, for heaven's sake! You've *got* to start delegating. What's happened to Barry Dewar who was in charge at the zoo?'

'Left a few weeks ago. Said he could earn more working for Amazon. And his new girlfriend couldn't stand the smell of pig on him.'

'Surely, it's Lachlan's job to find someone to take over? He *is* estate manager, not you.'

'We had a bit of an argument over it. He said I didn't know what I was talking about. I said we three had all worked in the pigs when we were kids.'

'Yes, when we were *kids*. We didn't know what we were doing when we were Saturday girls; in fact, we hated it when it was our turn to be in the pigs, Hannah.' Rosa shook her head.

'I'm interviewing someone next week,' Hannah said hotly, embarrassed at being told off by both the vet and the vicar. (*The Vet and The Vicar*: sounded remotely pornographic and Hannah wanted to giggle…) 'Meanwhile, I'll have you know I've been in there every morning at 5am.'

'Bet Ben's overjoyed at that.' Rosa raised an eyebrow. 'I *thought* you were a bit whiffy when I was standing next to you in the office, but I didn't like to say anything.'

'Never stopped you before. As I say, they're sending a couple of interviewees over from the job centre next week.'

'I thought we were going to Paris next week?' Rosa reminded Hannah.

'Look, is this anyone's argument or can I pitch in?' Daisy smiled. 'Hannah, the pigs are fine. They're happy and well looked after…'

Hannah gave a little triumphant thumbs up in Rosa's direction.

'…but I can't see anyone wanting to work in the pigs from the job centre. You need someone who knows what they're doing. Because, come July, Hannah, you're going to have a lot of piglets to care for and you'll have to make some decision about where they're going.'

'Don't people eat bacon and eggs anymore?'

Daisy sighed and looked at her watch. 'I'm going to have to get off.' She turned to leave. 'Hannah, you need to get Lachlan on board. He's a good guy – knows what he's doing. He can appear a bit narky, but, honestly, let him do the job he knows best. Let *him* interview people for the pigs – he knows what he's looking for.'

'OK, OK, I will. Hell, fifty piglets in two months' time?' Hannah closed her eyes. She felt knackered and wished she could just lie down in the May sunshine and sleep.

'Right, I'm off.' Daisy made to leave and then turned back. 'Blimey, I'd forgotten the real reason I'm here.'

'Not the alpacas?'

'Alpacas?'

'Don't tell me they're all up the duff as well?'

'Well, unless it's another immaculate conception – sorry, Rosa – then no: they're all girls.'

'I knew that,' Hannah said sagely.

'No, you didn't!' Daisy started to laugh and Rosa joined in.

'There's a distinct lack of dangly bits in the alpaca pen. No, I came to tell Rosa that I was talking to Sam this morning – you know it's my sister Charlie's cottage at Holly Close farm he's renting? And mine is the adjoining cottage? I'd like you both to come for supper on Saturday night if you're free, and Sam said to confirm with you. And then I thought, why not ask Hannah as well?'

'Can I bring my partner?' (How wonderful that sounded, Hannah thought, almost smugly: 'my partner'.)

'Yes, course you can. I'll have done my exams for this module and I'm determined to crack open a few bottles. Now, I can't cook…'

'Rosa's a brilliant cook,' Hannah said nudging her sister. 'She'll bring a pud.'

'No, it's fine, honestly. I was just warning you. I always invite my best mate Frankie, who *is* a brilliant cook. I drink and she cooks. Lovely. Seven-thirty? See you then.'

Saturday evening and, while Rosa was really looking forward to the supper do at Daisy's place, she was still feeling distinctly more ambivalent about her relationship with Sam. Was it having lunch with the depressingly awful Janet Burrows the previous week that had done it, or was it seeing Joe Rosavina, hurt and quite possibly dead in the cow field? Or, much more likely, seeing Joe in The Jolly Sailor's pub garden, his arm linked possessively by the tall attractive blonde?

Sam had appeared, moving into Rayan and Eva's expanding dental practice; into the rented cottage belonging to Daisy Maddison's sister over at Holly Close Farm, and into her life at the same time she'd moved back into the village herself. She'd fancied him, of course. How could anyone *not* fancy such a good-looking, personable and intelligent bloke as Sam Burrows? He'd apparently gone through so much when his marriage broke down and then, just months after that, losing his twelve-year-old son in a freak avalanche in Italy. And surely, now, he had to be the answer to her constant longings to have a child of her own? Sam wanted to marry her; he wanted to have a child with her. Here was her chance.

So why wasn't she grabbing this chance with both hands? Saying yes, she'd marry Sam and try for that baby with one of those frozen eggs of hers, just waiting for her – and Sam – to take the next step in starting a new life? Literally, a new life. Was marriage – and procreation – something you did when the time was right, or when – as in her case – time was running out?

Since the previous Sunday lunch over in Sheffield, Rosa had been so busy with several funerals, two weekday weddings, plus all her regular services as well as supporting Hannah in her role as chair of the management committee, that she'd had little time for any social life with Sam. He'd been away at some three-day dental conference in Harrogate (Dental Trauma in the Paediatric Population), standing in for Rayan when he hadn't wanted to be away from home and miss his set child custody days with Laila and Nora. And for that Rosa, although she certainly didn't acknowledge it to Hannah and Eva – barely liked to admit it even to herself – felt some relief.

Sam had rung her from Harrogate and sent a couple of texts, but neither had referred to the previous Sunday's drive home from Sheffield. And then, this Saturday afternoon, after yet another morning wedding at which, as always, she'd officiated, smiled and congratulated, there'd been a massive bunch of over-the-top flowers from Sam with the message:

To my favourite vicar
Love you
Hope you've made up your mind to marry me!

which had sent her into such a state of panic she'd had to spend the rest of the day in the vicarage garden, hacking and hewing away at the bloody yew as if her (and the hedge's) life depended on it. She needed time to work out just how she felt about Sam: he'd asked her to marry him, for heaven's sake. Maybe she'd immediately know the answer the minute he opened the door on her when she drove over to Holly Close Farm cottages that evening? She hoped so anyway.

So it was, by 7pm, Rosa found herself showered and dressed in her favourite cream shift dress, nursing a gin and tonic and waiting for the taxi to take her the five miles or so through the village and out to the glorious countryside where Sam was renting the cottage next to Daisy the vet. After an afternoon in the garden, she was bearing the battle scars of the recalcitrant yew hedge, but also a rather becoming blush to her face and arms from several hours out in the May sunshine. She'd made up her face carefully, blow-dried her long dark hair until it bounced and shone, knowing that, if she was going to accept Sam's proposal, at least she'd be looking good for the occasion. Hearing the metronome tick tick of the black cab, Rosa downed the gin, grateful for the surge of Dutch courage it offered, and set off down the vicarage path.

Rosa adored this part of the village, and was, without fail, always awestruck at the wonder of God's good gifts (*All good gifts around us are sent from heaven above, so thank the Lord, oh, thank the Lord for aw aw all his love*) every time she came over to stay with Sam and simply gazed at the view down the valley beyond the cottages that sisters Charlie and Daisy Maddison had renovated.

Rosa took a deep breath and was about to knock on Sam's door when he opened it before she could make contact with the polished brass knocker. Had he been waiting (like his mother, Janet, the previous Sunday) for her arrival? He obviously had because, within seconds, despite her suggesting they might go straight round next door to Daisy's place (safety in numbers, no proffered white leather jewellery box) Sam was doing exactly that.

He ushered her through the door, handed her a glass of fizz and actually went down on one knee (it had to be just *one*, Rosa thought somewhat wildly glancing down in panic, because if he was down on two, wouldn't he just fall over…?) before reaching for a black (she'd obviously got the colour wrong) leather box containing the biggest emerald she'd ever seen.

'Rosa, you've come into my life and I… I need you to stay there.'

Stay there? *Where?* At the vicarage? In front of him, unable to speak? Where, for God's sake? Sorry, God…

'Marry me!' It appeared a command rather than a proposal.

Ah, in his life then. As his wife.

Without waiting for an answer (she could neither get a word in or out, but instead uttered a bizarre little mewling sound, which he obviously took as consent) Sam took her left hand and, with some difficulty, slid the ring onto her third finger.

'Sam, I…' Rosa looked down at the huge emerald. She hated emeralds.

'I know, I know, Rosa, I've probably rushed this, but I also know that, like me, you've been terribly hurt and don't feel you can trust anyone again. I just feel that, together, we can…'

'Come on, you two, we're waiting.' Daisy Maddison was at the open door to the cottage shouting at them to get a move on. 'We're in the garden. Champagne's on ice.'

'Champagne?' Rosa said faintly, twisting without success at the huge green rock on her finger.

'Yep, exams over. I can get lashed now… Oh… oh…' Daisy stopped as she saw the glasses of untouched champagne on the hallway by the open front door and then the flash of green on Rosa's hand. 'Is this what I think it is?'

Sam nodded, taking Rosa's hand. 'Rosa's still to say yes, but we're trying the ring out for size.'

'Sam, just let me take this off…'

'Come on. They're all waiting for us.' Sam put a protective arm around Rosa's shoulders (what did he think she needed protection from? Him?) and ushered her out of the open door, picking up and draining his glass of champagne as he passed. The bottle, now almost empty, was obviously testament to Sam's nerves while he'd waited for her to arrive; Rosa closed her eyes slightly, took a deep steadying breath and downed her own glass. If she couldn't beat him, she needed to join him: she'd sort out the bigger problem later.

13

'Righto, everyone.' Daisy was obviously dying to be the one to break the news that the new village dentist had just become engaged to the new village vicar. 'We appear to have some more celebrating in hand...' She trailed off as Rosa shook her head furiously at their host, glaring and elbowing Daisy in a most unvicarly manner. Rosa shook her head once more. This was ridiculous; surreal even. She had a church service to take in the morning and the last thing she wanted was any rumour going round the village before matins was even off the ground, together with the accompanying shower of congratulations.

'So,' Daisy went on gamely, obviously unsure where to go next. 'So, erm, let's raise our glasses and celebrate the fact that Rosa and Sam have erm actually... erm... made it over the garden fence.'

'They've come through the gate, not over the fence.' Hannah laughed. 'Come on, you two, you're wasting valuable drinking time.' She shifted herself and Ben down the long wooden bench attached to the garden table at which they were seated and proffered the bottle of wine in the ice bucket in front of them. 'You're not driving, are you, Rosa? You're staying at Sam's place tonight? Get your Holyhead – no, hang on, that's the place you get the ferry across to Ireland – *holy head* off for once, and get stuck in.'

Holy head? Oh, hell, Rosa thought, Hannah was obviously well stuck into the alcohol herself.

'Right, who doesn't know who?' Daisy asked, laughing at

Hannah's pronunciation. 'So, I don't know if you know Jude, Rosa?'

'Ah, our local MP I believe?' Rosa made to shake hands, ensuring she placed her left hand with the rock on it into her jacket pocket first. 'How's it going in office?'

'Bloody hard work,' Jude replied, 'but I'm loving every minute. We've been in opposition long enough,' he added. 'Our turn soon for glory.'

'Really?' Sam gave a knowing little smirk before turning back to Rosa and placing a hand possessively on her arm as she continued to question Jude about his agenda as a backbencher.

'It sounds fascinating.' Rosa smiled, easing her arm casually from Sam's hand.

'Have you never been round the Houses of Parliament?' Jude asked, filling Rosa's glass. She was about to put a warning hand over the top of the glass but, again, remembered the ring and kept it where it was in her pocket so that the wine poured right to the top and was in danger of overflowing on to her fingers.

'No.' She smiled. 'I…'

'Too busy running your own empire, Rosa,' Sam interrupted proudly. 'You may have heard of Rosa Quinn Investments, Jude? A bit of a filthy capitalist was our Rosa before she turned to God.'

'I don't think I was ever that.' Rosa frowned. 'I paid my taxes and gave to those less well off. In fact, my company had a foundation for…'

'I'm teasing, Rosa. Teasing you.' Sam patted her arm somewhat condescendingly.

'Oh, Frankie. Sorry, I was just coming into the kitchen to give you a hand.' Daisy turned to help the dark-haired woman manoeuvring her way around the guests and garden table. 'You shouldn't be carrying that tray.'

'Don't be daft, Daisy, I'm pregnant, not disabled.'

'Rosa and Sam, do you know Frankie? Frankie Dosanjh? Daler, come and help your wife with this tray of goodies.'

Rosa saw the man turn – heavens, he was the image of Dev Patel – and hurry to his wife's side to take the tray of delicious-looking canapés. 'Gosh, these look a bit professional.' Rosa smiled, peeling herself off, and moving away from Sam who appeared to be wanting to stick to her like Velcro.

'Frankie's a brilliant cook,' Daisy said proudly. 'I invite her to all our supper dos.' She laughed, taking a whipped blue cheese and pear crostini in one hand and a celeriac remoulade with chorizo in the other. 'Come on, dig in. We're waiting for our friend Melissa to arrive. She said she'd be a bit late – so we won't actually be eating for a while, and we need to mop up some of this alcohol.' Daisy chewed, swallowed and, turning to Rosa, lowered her voice. 'Am I picking up some vibes that you're not totally happy about that great green rock sitting on your ring finger?' Daisy's tone was sympathetic.

Rosa looked at her in despair. 'Oh, Daisy, I thought it was what I wanted. Sam is so lovely…'

'He is. He's a great neighbour and tenant. Charlie said she'd never seen the toilet looking so clean when she called in to see him last week to ask if Sam wanted to rent for another six months.'

'And did he?' Rosa held her breath.

'Did he what? Keep the toilet clean?'

'No, want to stay here another six months?'

'Probably not. Said he'd let us know asap. Said he was hoping to *buy* somewhere pretty soon: a family-sized house. I've talked to him a lot about what happened to his son Ollie. I guess he's hoping to start again? You know, another family?' Daisy finished her canapé, brushed crumbs from her T-shirt and looked questioningly at Rosa. 'He's one hell of a catch, Rosa.'

'You make it sound like I've landed an enormous haddock.' Rosa pulled a face.

'Always preferred cod myself.' Daisy began to laugh. 'And Hannah's man is pretty tasty too. First time I've actually met him. The pair of you have done well for yourselves: Ben the brain surgeon and Sam the dentist? And inheriting Heatherly Hall into the bargain?' Daisy spoke without a hint of rancour.

'And you've got the lovely Jude and are on the way to being a fully qualified vet.'

'Hope so.' Daisy laughed but then frowned. 'Not sure the exam paper went my way yesterday.'

'Well, if Jude continues the way he's doing, you might find yourself in Number 10?'

'Not convinced there's much call for a farm vet – which I'm specialising in – in the city. God, I'm starving. I wish Melissa'd hurry up – she's bringing her new man and we're all dying to meet him. She's kissed a few frogs in the past, but says this one's a keeper.'

Rosa laughed at that and glanced across to where Sam was in serious conversation with Hannah and Ben before her sister stood, a little unsteadily, kissed Ben as if marking her territory and then made her way over.

'Rosa!'

'Hannah?'

'Don't give me that innocent look, Rosa. That vicarly, saintly look you plaster on when you're hiding something.' Hannah slurred her words.

'How much have you had to drink?' Rosa asked.

'There you go again: *vicarly*.' Hannah belched slightly and, tittering, brought a hand up to her mouth. '*Beg your pardon, Reverend Ardon, how're the cabbages in your garden*? Had quite a bit actually.' She giggled again. 'We've been in bed all afternoon with a bottle of wine. Several bottles actually.'

'Too much information.' Rosa smiled.

'Maybe, but it was jolly good.' Hannah squinted across at Rosa, lifting her hand to shade the setting evening sunshine from her eyes. 'Now, when were you going to tell me and Eva?'

'Tell you?'

'Don't play the innocent with me, Rosie Posie. I've known you since we were feet...'

'Feet?'

'*Feet us us*,' Hannah got out grandly before frowning. '*Feeti?* So, when were you going to tell us, you were planning on marrying Sam?'

'Has Sam just told you?' Rosa glanced across to where Sam and Ben were deep in conversation.

Hannah nodded. 'This is great. We can have a double wedding.'

'I thought Ben had to get divorced first?' Rosa raised an eyebrow.

'A mere formality.' Hannah laughed. 'Weird, isn't it? The minute you and I are about to get married, Eva's on the point of divorce.'

'And has he asked you?'

'Asked me what? Oh, to marry him? As I say, a mere formality.' Hannah frowned. 'Actually, as a vicar are you allowed to marry a divorcee? That might scupper your plans.'

'Hannah, I'm not marrying Sam.'

'You're not? Oh? Why did he say you were then? And what's that sodding great green thing doing on your finger if you're not engaged? I thought you didn't like emeralds?'

'I don't.'

'Ah, is *that* why you're not marrying him?' Hannah laughed. 'If he'd produced diamonds, would you now be heading down the aisle? I think Sam's lovely. *I'd* marry him tomorrow… you know, if I wasn't going to marry Ben…'

'Hannah, go and sit down before you fall down.'

'Rosa, you're not my mother. Off for a pee… Oh… for fuck's sake…' Hannah trailed off as Daisy leapt forward to welcome the two newcomers who were in the throes of apologising for their lateness.

Rosa placed her half-drunk glass of wine on the garden table and turned to where Hannah was staring across at the garden gate. She felt her heart pound, the blood drain from her face and her hands – the left, with its unwanted appendage, still firmly ensconced in her jacket pocket – grow sticky with sweat.

'Sorry we're late, Daisy.' The tall, attractive blonde accepted a glass of wine gratefully. 'Florence took some persuading to stay with the babysitter; wanted to come with us – you know what seven-year-olds are like.' The woman drew a tanned, manicured hand through her short blonde hair, moved her sunglasses to the top of her head and pulled the man she was with to her side, before placing her arm through his. 'This is Joe, Daisy. Joe Rosavina.'

Now that the latecomers had finally arrived, Frankie Dosanjh almost immediately ushered the party inside.

'Come on, food's ready,' she called. 'Bring your drinks and sit where you want.'

'No seating plan, Frankie?' her husband asked, rounding up guests and half-filled glasses with the expertise of a no-nonsense sheepdog. 'OK, sit where you like: boy, girl, boy, girl.'

Oh, where to sit? Rosa felt sick, thought she might be in the throes of a panic attack and, instead of sitting at the table where a basket of warm home-baked bread was already in the process of being handed round, headed for the upstairs bathroom. Once in there, she laid her burning forehead against the cold mirror and splashed water over her wrists. She tried to wrench off the damned emerald, which had now taken on the mantle of some sort of claustrophobic chastity belt, but it was mulishly going absolutely nowhere. Great stuff. Was she going to have to take a trip up to A and E and have it cut off like her mum once had to do after fracturing her ring finger?

Rosa reached for a bar of soap, ferociously rubbing and twisting until, miraculously, it was off, shooting like some sort of latter-day Apollo 11 into orbit through the bathroom and disappearing somewhere behind the soil pipe of the lavatory cistern.

'Jesus. Fuckity fuck. Sorry, Jesus, for the profanity. So sorry. But you know how it is. And don't pretend *you* never got to swore – don't forget how you turned over those tables in the temple on Palm Sunday.' Rosa heard herself muttering and wondered if she was going mad. She got down on her knees, scrabbling round on the wooden floor, searching with her hands for the ring. 'Come on, God, please, give us a hand…'

'Rosa?' Rosa froze and sat up as a loud knocking came at the bathroom door. 'Are you OK? Who are you talking to?'

Rosa stood up, and unlocked the door.

'What are you *doing*?' Hannah slid through the narrow gap Rosa had allowed, before closing and locking the door once more. 'Who are you talking to?'

'God.' Rosa closed her eyes briefly and got back down on her knees.

'Rosa, I know you take this calling of yours very seriously – and that's good – but for heaven's sake, the food's on the table: you don't need to be praying to your boss, especially in *the lavatory*, for what we're about to eat. Mind you, I'm not convinced Daisy would be wanting you to take grace back in the dining room; always a bit awkward when a couple of people have already dived in to the starter and then they have to put down their forks, bow their heads and look repentant…' When Rosa didn't say anything, but continued to scrabble about desperately behind the pipes, Hannah went on, 'Joe, I suppose? Praying for the courage to face him? Come on, you're going to have to come out and face him with this new girlfriend of his. She's very attractive, isn't she?'

'Got it!' Rosa's fingers met something round and metallic and she pulled it in triumph towards her together with a ball of hair, fluff and a used tissue; it was pretty obvious Daisy Maddison didn't rank alongside Sam in the high echelons of toilet cleaning. 'Hell, that's not it.' Rosa fished out a large clip-on earring from the detritus in her palm.

'What's not it?'

'Hannah, I've lost the ring.'

'Which ring? Not your *engaged-for-just-five-minutes* ring? Not your *I'm-not-really-engaged-sodding-great-emerald* ring? Bloody hell, Rosa. Bit careless that, isn't it? Looked to be worth a few bob too. Here, let me have a look. Shift over.'

Thirty seconds later, Hannah surfaced. 'It must have gone down that hole.'

'What hole?'

'There's a sort of huge mousehole in the floorboard right next to the pipe.'

'You are joking!'

'No, I'm not. Unbelievable you actually got it down the hole: you were always pathetic at Crazy Golf when Mum and Dad used to take us to that place in Filey.'

'Rosa?' Sam's voice was at the other side of the bathroom door. 'You OK?'

'Just helping Hannah. She's had a bit too much to drink.'

'No, I *haven't*,' Hannah hissed crossly. 'Don't make out I can't hold my drink. You're supposed to be *a vicar* and not tell lies.'

'I *am* a vicar,' Rosa hissed back. 'Won't be a minute, Sam. Honest.'

'Your ex is obviously wondering where you are.' Rosa could almost see the pleasant, questioning smile Sam always adopted whenever Joe Rosavina was mentioned – she and Hannah pulled scary faces at each other from the safety of their position on the wooden bathroom floor, behind the locked door. 'And actually, Rosa, I wanted to say you appear to be hiding the ring I gave you. Look, if it's a problem, if you don't want to wear it, just hand it back and I'll put it somewhere safe. Really, not a problem, darling. It's just that it was actually my grandmother's and probably worth quite a bit...'

'Shit!' Hannah mouthed.

'*Holy* shit,' Rosa mouthed back.

'Passive-aggressive,' Hannah mouthed sagely.

'What?' Rosa mouthed back.

'I said, "he's obviously a passive-aggressive."' This time Hannah said the words out loud and she clamped a hand over her mouth.

'Sam, I'm just helping Hannah. Won't be a minute.'

'Do you want me to get Ben?'

'No, Sam, I'm fine, really. All tickety-boo,' Hannah sang gaily. There was silence. 'Has he gone?' Hannah mouthed.

'Dunno. Right, I'm going to have to confess what's happened.' Rosa rubbed tiredly at her face. 'We'll have to get a plumber in or something.'

'Or a joiner? It's not the pipes, it's down the floorboards.'

Rosa saw, with relief, that she was seated down the other end of the table from Sam, but totally aware his eyes were following her every move while trying to make contact with her own, now that it was pretty obvious her ring finger no longer carried the huge emerald. Daler Dosanjh to her left, and Jude Mansell on her right had finished eating and were turned away from her, both fully engaged in conversation with people at their other side. Trying to calm her racing heart, while knowing her mouth was dry with anxiety and the prospect of eating anything was a Herculean task, Rosa sank a glass of water before giving her undivided attention to the starter of scallops with charred leek, onion broth and pink purslane. She gamely concentrated on the divine earthy flavour of the raw purslane, which brought out the fishy taste and texture of the scallops to perfection.

She could have been eating cardboard.

14

When she finally worked up the courage to put down her cutlery and reach for her glass of wine in order to take a surreptitious glance across the table at Joe Rosavina, as well as at the woman he was with, Rosa found the pair of them sitting next to each other and laughing together over something obviously very funny Frankie Dosanjh was in the process of telling them.

When Joe did deign to look across at her he simply smiled and said, 'Hi, Rosa, how are you?' before turning back to the woman he'd brought to the party and making introductions. 'Rosa, this is Melissa McClean. Melissa, this is Rosa, our village vicar, who was so helpful in sorting Rhys when he was in such a bad place last year and driving me and my parents to distraction. As well as, of course, together with Sam here, saving my life after my encounter with the herd of cows from hell.' Joe held up his hand, still encased in a now somewhat grubby – if colourful – cast, adorned with Chiara's felt-tip drawings of unicorns and rainbows.

Rosa stared: our village vicar? Was she being introduced simply as the woman in charge of the village church? The do-gooder to whom Joe had turned when Rhys, Carys's son, had ended up in the youth courts? Not: *Melissa, this is Rosa, whom I promised to love for ever; Rosa, with whom I fell in love at sixteen before spending fifteen years of my life with, here in Westenbury, at Durham University and then in London? Before having a one-night stand with Rosa's PA, and best friend, Carys?*

'Hello, Melissa, how lovely to meet you.' Who was this

speaking? Apparently, herself. Rosa almost shook her head in surprise as the calm, polite, friendly words of welcome rolled glibly off her tongue. 'Are you new to the area?'

'You're a vicar? Goodness, you don't look like one. So, if you call being here almost a year, *new*, Reverend? And I'm so sorry, apart from introducing myself and my daughter Florence to the previous vicar when we first arrived, I'm afraid – which is *not* like me – I've not had any involvement with the village church.' Melissa gave a little tinkle of laughter which only emphasised she appeared to know little of Joe's past relationship with Rosa. 'Now, I can see I must rectify that immediately, Rosa – may I call you Rosa? We'll be down to church and on our knees in the morning.' She laughed the strange, affected little noise again, but accompanied, this time, with a slow seductive stroke of Joe's good arm. 'If I can tear myself away from this gorgeous man here, that is.'

'So, how do you two know each other?' Rosa asked, at which point Joe now looked across at Rosa and opened his mouth to speak. 'You and Daisy, I mean, Melissa?' Rosa went on, ignoring Joe and smiling at the new woman in Joe's life. She wasn't going to give Joe the satisfaction of meeting his eye or showing any interest in his new relationship. Ignoring both Joe and Sam – for very different reasons – was bloody hard work and Rosa suddenly longed to be back at the vicarage in her PJs with a giant Toblerone and the pirate copy of *Top Gun: Maverick* which Denis, the verger, had, with a wink and a tap of his nose, pressed on her the previous week under cover of a *King's Singers' Collection (1976)* DVD.

'Through Jude,' Melissa replied, sitting back as Daisy stood and started to clear plates.

'Melissa is a bit of a party activist.' Daisy nodded. 'Have to say, she's been brilliant helping Jude with all his political stuff – you know leafletting, organising coffee mornings to raise money and volunteering to help man his Saturday morning surgeries.'

'MPs hold surgeries in their constituency to give people an

opportunity to meet them and discuss matters of concern, Rosa,' Melissa said importantly. 'I wanted to do my bit to help. Being still fairly new to the area means I get to know the locals, as well as putting my weight behind the push to get Jude's party into government at the next election.'

'Right. Lovely.' Rosa didn't quite know how to reply to all this.

She obviously wasn't being given the chance, because Melissa launched once more. 'My daughter is at the village school, so I do my bit there as well. You know, PTA? Fundraising? I know Mrs Beresford and the classroom teachers appreciate me giving my time as a parent helper.'

'Right.' Rosa reached for her glass of wine. 'And as a school governor? We're always looking for new…'

'Oh yes, that's my next step. Most definitely. I want to be at the chalk-face as it were; helping the head to make decisions re the school. I do have some experience of being in charge in a school: I was head girl at my own high school.' Melissa actually paused to allow Rosa to take this in. 'And, to be frank, Reverend, there appears to be some bullying going on at Little Acorns. My daughter was actually attacked by another girl in her class with a pair of scissors recently. Of course, I made light of it, didn't want to be seen as an overanxious parent, but Florence, my little girl, has been extremely upset over the whole affair. Luckily—' and here Melissa stroked Joe's hand possessively '—this lovely man has an equally lovely daughter, Chiara, who is in the class below, who's taken Florence under her wing somewhat. They're such good pals.'

'Bullying? Right. Lovely. And…' Rosa felt quite dazed at the onslaught of Melissa's non-stop soliloquy.

'Lovely?' Melissa's eyes narrowed. 'I don't feel any aspect of intimidation and persecution amongst seven-year-olds can ever be *lovely*, Rosa.'

'Of course not. I…'

'And I do a stint volunteering at the village library. I'm sure you're aware, Rosa, we nearly lost our little library almost a year ago and I worked tirelessly, as soon as I arrived in the village, campaigning to keep the place open. We won,' she added smugly. 'I'm now very much involved in a scheme *I* actually instigated at the library – you might be interested in this, Rosa, as the village vicar: to get volunteers – grannies and the like, as well as folk like yourself without their own kiddies – to read to the children who come in. Can you believe, Rosa, there are some children in this village, in the local school, whose parents just don't take the time to sit with them to hear them read?'

'Really?' Rosa smiled, ignoring Joe, Sam and now Hannah who were all taking in the conversation. 'I can't believe you have time, Melissa, with all this volunteering, to actually hold down a proper job as well?' Oh hell, did that come over as a bit bitchy? Hannah obviously thought so from the faux look of disapproval and shaking of her head that she now countenanced.

'Oh, Rosa, *of course* I work.' Melissa gave another little tinkle of laughter. The tinkle, along with the overuse of the *Rosa* handle in every sentence, was really beginning to grate. I own my own business in Leeds...'

'Really?' Rosa glanced across at Hannah who, listening to Melissa's litany of volunteering, pulled another of her scary faces at Rosa from behind her raised glass.

'Yes, I own and run Oui! Oui!'

'Wee wee?' This was too much for Hannah who started to laugh. 'Wee wee? Incontinence pads and big knickers and the like for old ladies?'

'*Ah, non, maintenant, tu es ridicule*,' Melissa said in perfect French before shooting an on-off smile across Hannah's bows who, well and truly chastised, winked somewhat haphazardly at Rosa before retreating behind her glass of wine once more. Obviously bored with this Melissa woman's boasting, Hannah's eyes searched out Ben who was deep in conversation with Frankie Dosanjh.

'Oui! Oui! is Melissa's dress shop in the Victorian Arcade,

Hannah.' Joe spoke and, for the first time that evening, Rosa turned and looked at him full on while he was endeavouring to make conversation with her sister. Rosa raked his face almost hungrily, taking in every one of the features she'd so fallen in love with the minute she'd set eyes on him when they were both just sixteen and working in the school holidays for Bill up at Heatherly Hall. Oh, but he was still so lovely. Embarrassed at her longing for him, and knowing that Sam's whole attention was on herself and any reaction, any *feelings* she might still be harbouring for Joe, Rosa dropped her eyes to the table.

Melissa was still speaking.

'I lived and worked in Paris for many years,' Melissa was saying rather prettily. 'Hence the name Oui! Oui! It means Yes! Yes!' Melissa uttered the words as if in the throes of a particularly good orgasm and Hannah started to laugh once again. Ben, alerted to Melissa's thrown-back head and slightly parted lips, opened his eyes in surprise and obvious admiration. With what Rosa estimated to be her five-foot-ten height, blonde cropped hair, quite startling almond-shaped dark eyes and olive skin, Melissa McLean was one exceptionally striking woman.

'Really?' Hannah asked, kicking out under the table in the direction of an open-mouthed Ben. '*Fermez la bouche*, Benjamin,' she added in a stage-whispered broad Yorkshire accent, before standing somewhat unsteadily to help Daisy and Frankie bring in the main course. 'Or *vous attraperez beaucoup de* flies.'

'Frankie, you simply *must* come and pay me a visit!' Melissa was now saying, Hannah's words apparently going completely over her head. 'I'm awaiting the new summer stock for my Oui! Oui! Bébé! range. All new mummies should pay my shop a visit. And, as a trained neonatal counsellor – I trained in England after giving birth to my daughter in Paris where, I have to be more than honest, Parisians have a quite different outlook to pregnancy and childbirth than here in the UK…'

'Another Brexit reality?' Hannah drawled, coming back to the table ladened with food.

'… and one I most certainly wasn't expecting or prepared for…'

'We'll have to make sure none of us are about to give birth when we're in Paris next week, then, Rosie Posie,' Hannah warned, shooting a dish of glazed carrots unceremoniously across the polished table top and making both Ben and Joe jump back in alarm.

Melissa gave scant regard to the out-of-control vegetables as, fully in her stride, she continued to warn all the women at the table, but particularly Frankie, who was looking slightly worried, about her experience of what she felt to be the *laissez-faire* attitude to giving birth in France.

'Parisian women seem to feel they can give birth without making any radical or extravagant changes to their belief system or life stance. Which, I'm sure, those of us lucky enough to have been, or about to go through…' Melissa patted Frankie's arm empathetically '…the life-affirming experience of giving birth to a *new* life, would have to disagree. It would appear, to our Parisian sisters, giving birth is just a matter of…'

'OK, spuds anyone?' Hannah cut Melissa off mid-sentence. 'These look absolutely ravishing, Frankie. You are so clever.' Hannah was herself interrupted by Ben's mobile going off.

'Sorry, sorry, everyone.' He jumped up, immediately moving towards the open kitchen door to take the call where, after only a minute or so, he returned the mobile to his trouser pocket. 'Apologies. An emergency at Midhope General. I've been drafted in to help.' He turned to Daisy and Jude. 'So sorry, I'm afraid this is the way it goes.'

'But you've been drinking,' Daisy said. 'You can't be opening up someone's head after drinking all day. Can you?' She looked decidedly worried.

Ben smiled. 'Not me. I knew I was on call all day and I've not had a drop. Probably why Hannah's somewhat worse for wear – she's had my share as well as her own.' He dropped a kiss on Hannah's head, whispered, 'Sorry, sweetie, don't wait up, I'll see you back at home at some point tomorrow,' shook Jude's hand, kissed Daisy and, with a brief wave at the other guests, found his jacket and his keys and left.

'What a *hero*,' Melissa breathed. 'Our marvellous NHS springs into action once again. You must be *very proud* of your husband, Hannah.'

'Unfortunately, he's not my husband,' Hannah replied, obviously fed up that Ben had had to leave. 'He's someone else's. And I'd say I'm more pissed off than proud at his leaving.'

'Not overly supportive, Hannah,' Melissa admonished, eschewing the potatoes – *I do try to be carb-free wherever possible* – 'I mean, where would we be without brain surgeons like your husband?'

'He's not my husband,' Hannah repeated. 'He's someone's *else's* husband. And, I guess, Melissa, to answer your question, without brain surgeons, people wouldn't be able to change their minds.' Hannah laughed at her own wit and then, looking directly at Joe while still addressing Melissa asked, 'Do you know the one about the brain surgeon, Melissa? I bet Joe does.'

Rosa's head came up and she gave a warning glance towards Hannah who, she knew, had never forgiven Joe for his mistake with Carys. With too much alcohol inside her, Hannah could be just as caustic, and as irreverent, as Eva.

'So,' Hannah went on, 'this neurosurgeon is preparing his patient for a brain transplant and he asks the patient: "Would you like a woman's brain or a man's brain?"

'"Why are there options?" the patient asks.

'"Well," replies the surgeon, "the woman's brain is actually half the price of the man's!"

'"Oh really? Half price? Why's that then?" asks the man.

'"Because it's used!"'

Hannah smiled sweetly in Joe's direction, piled too much dauphinoise potato onto her plate and started to eat.

'Somewhat contemptuous belittling half the human race, do you not think, Hannah?' Melissa asked. 'I really do feel, in this day and age, sexist jokes like the one you've just told, demean not only…'

'So, how are you, Joe?' Hannah asked, wiping her mouth methodically on her napkin while making a show of deliberately ignoring Melissa. 'I bet you didn't think, after it all blew up in London, you'd ever be sitting next to me and Rosa again? You know, back in Westenbury? At the same table?'

'Hannah, leave it out.' Rosa put a warning hand on Hannah's arm. 'I'm sorry, Melissa. My sister's had too much to drink. Drink some water, for heaven's sake, Hannah.' Rosa was embarrassed, felt her face flush and didn't dare look across the table at Joe.

Melissa glanced at Hannah, before reaching for Joe's hand. 'I didn't realise there was some history between Joe and your sister, Rosa. Mind you, all in the past now I guess.' It was a statement rather than a question and, ignoring both Rosa and Hannah, Melissa moved closer to Joe, turning her back on the pair of them.

'Shall we all move round a bit before we fill our plates?' Frankie asked, feeling the tension at one end of the table and standing up. 'I'm going to come and sit next to you, Hannah, because I'm dying to know about your plans for Heatherly Hall.'

'Great idea,' Jude said, also standing. Within minutes, Jude and Frankie had rearranged the table, Sam immediately taking the opportunity to move down the table to sit on Rosa's left.

'Quite an evening, all this,' Sam said, lowering his voice. 'Are you OK?'

'Bit of a headache actually.'

'Do you want to go?'

'It would be rude to do that. Listen, Sam…'

'The ring is safe, isn't it?'

'The thing is…'

'I'm sorry. I badgered you into wearing it.'

'Yes, Sam, you did.' Rosa started eating the food on her plate, not quite taking in exactly what it was. Duck or chicken? Turkey even? Being a total foodie, she was ashamed that she felt unable to give her full attention to what she was eating. She glanced across at Hannah who appeared to be drooping over her plate.

'Delicious pheasant, Frankie,' Jude was saying.

Ah, pheasant then.

'But you know how good we are together, Rosa. What we both want.' Sam was cutting into his own plate, loading the delicious food onto his fork, but Rosa could feel the tension emanating from him, his back rigid, his fingers clenched around his cutlery. 'You know how much we both want to have children; to start a family.' They both gazed across at Frankie's beautiful bump, swelling almost majestically under her long cotton sweater as she stood, stretched and rubbed lovingly at her abdomen, before finding a more comfortable position on her chair next to Hannah.

'Not here, Sam,' Rosa almost pleaded. 'Look, I'm a bit concerned about Hannah. She's had far too much to drink. I think I need to get her home.'

'Not the first time, is it?' Sam replied caustically, and Rosa heard his mother's voice: berating the striking miners, dismissing her husband's love of history, lambasting Sam's first wife, Penny. 'You're not your sister's keeper.'

'Well, I think I am.' Rosa looked across at Hannah who was looking pale and hadn't touched much of the food on her plate. 'And listen, Sam, I'm sorry. You might as well know: a mouse has got your emerald.'

'Pardon?' Sam stopped chewing and replaced his knife and fork on his plate. 'Sorry, obviously bitten off more than I can chew,' he went on, placing a hand to his mouth while continuing to masticate and then swallow, his Adam's apple bobbing almost comically as he did so. Rosa wondered if he meant in more ways than one. 'A *mouse*?' he finally managed to get out.

'I was washing my hands in the bathroom and the ring came off and, according to Hannah, it's gone down a mouse hole at the back of the toilet. Which surprised us both as I'm absolutely rubbish at Pitch and Putt.'

'You *are* joking?' Sam made to stand, but Rosa pressed him

back into his seat. He tried to smile, although Rosa could see he was upset. Cross even.

'It's fine. It really is, I promise. Tomorrow I'll…' She broke off, glancing towards Hannah who after her attack on Joe, was continuing to quietly drink. What on earth was matter with her sister? Surely not just Ben's having to leave for work so unexpectedly? Having a relationship with a gifted neurosurgeon, constantly on call, Hannah would know, would expect, she'd be deserted on a fairly regular basis.

'…and being a member of the opposition party…' Jude was deep in conversation with Daler and Joe.

'I love a good party,' Hannah drawled, raising her glass and spilling some of its contents onto the polished table. 'Not sure about the opposition bit though. And, unfortunately, I reckon I have some. That Lachlan Buchanan at the hall is a bloody nightmare.' Hannah wiped at the spilled wine with her sleeve and Rosa decided, once Jude finished what he was explaining re his position at Westminster, she was going to ring for a taxi and take Hannah and herself back to the vicarage for the night.

'…I knew absolutely nothing about it until I was chatting to a bloke called Roy Newsome the other day. He's a retired miner – was actually at the Battle of Orgreave…' Jude's words were drifting down the table.

'Not exactly the Battle of Hastings, Jude,' Sam offered, his tone slightly mocking, and again Rosa heard the same sneering tones she'd first heard in Sam's mother's cynical voice.

'Well, I'd slightly disagree with you there, Sam.' Jude's tone was pleasant. 'The Battle of Orgreave was a violent confrontation in 1984 between the striking pickets and local and national police. Probably a defining moment that changed, for ever, the conduct of industrial relations and how this country functions as an economy and as a democracy…'

'Get on with it, Jude.' Daisy laughed affectionately, handing round dishes of trifle. 'You don't half know how to spin a tale out.'

'Spin doctoring. He's an MP.' Sam raised an eyebrow. 'He's had plenty of practice.'

Rosa was beginning to realise that she might have been with Sam six months or so, but his politics were perhaps not what he'd led her to believe.

'OK, OK,' Jude said with a laugh, reaching up to grab and kiss Daisy's hand as she placed an enormous mountain of jelly, custard and cream in front of him. 'Blimey, Daisy, do we eat or climb this?'

'You'll find it on your head in a minute,' Daisy said pointedly. 'It's my contribution to the meal; you know it's the only pudding I can do.'

'Get *on with it*, Jude,' the rest of the guests were now laughing.

'So, while I was chatting to Roy about how dreadful the whole Miners' Strike of 1984 had been for him and the mining community here in Yorkshire, he then went on to tell me about his father, Frank, and how *he'd* been involved in the Battle of Cable Street back in October 1936.'

'Battle of Cable Street?' The others shrugged and looked lost.

'The violent anti-fascist demonstration in London where communists and trade unionists met to protest and fight against Mosley's Black Shirts.' Jude's eyes gleamed with the excitement of relating the story.

'Communists and trade unionists?' Sam's tone was mocking. 'Bit of a motley crew that lot, weren't they, Jude?'

'No more so than the damned fascists they were up against, Sam.' Jude smiled, his tone still pleasant, but his eyes narrowing slightly.

'Right, Jude, enough of the politics already. Eat your pud.' Daisy glanced at Sam who was shaking his head almost contemptuously. 'Coffee anyone?'

15

Rosa realised Hannah had fallen asleep over her pudding, the remains of her almost untouched trifle collecting in her long dark hair.

'Sorry, Daisy, so sorry, everyone,' Rosa apologised, embarrassed. 'I think I'd better get my sister home.'

'You see, Jude, you're boring everyone witless with your political rhetoric.' Daisy, standing up and moving behind Jude's chair to wrap her arms round him, dropped a kiss on his head. 'Give it a rest now and let's bring on the Northern Soul, roll back the carpet and dance instead.'

'Sorry, I do get a bit carried away.' Jude laughed. 'Do you want a hand with Hannah, Rosa? Daisy, it's your blinking trifle that's finished the poor girl off. How much sherry did you put in it?'

'Half a bottle or so.' Daisy frowned. 'You know, the usual amount?'

'Come on, Rosa.' Sam stood up, moving towards Hannah who opened one eye sleepily. 'Let's get Hannah to bed in my spare room. Looks like she needs to sleep it all off.'

'Sorry, so sorry,' Hannah murmured, trying to smile. 'Let myself down a bit here.'

'As we can all see, Hannah,' Sam said, smiling but sounding, Rosa thought, like a judgemental head teacher. 'Come on, you're being a bit embarrassing.'

Or, a parent? Would this be what it'd be like in fifteen or sixteen years' time if they had children together? She supposed it would. A shiver of misgiving went through her, adding to those she'd manfully tried to ignore, to actually discard, but which, she realised, she'd stored away, ready to mull over when trying to make up her mind about any future she might have with Sam. They were all there, dancing before her, determined to raise their irritating little heads when she so much wanted to ignore them. She'd so wanted her relationship with Sam to work.

'Actually, Sam,' she said, 'I think it best if I take Hannah back home with me down to the vicarage. I'll ring for a taxi.' Rosa reached for her bag and her phone, shaking Hannah gently. 'Come on, Sleeping Beauty, we're nearer my place – better than taking you back to the hall.'

'I do hope Hannah isn't going to vomit in the taxi,' Melissa said, frowning. 'You'll have to pay cleaning expenses. In fact, the driver will probably take one look at her and refuse to take her.'

'Melissa's right, Rosa.' Sam nodded his approval towards Joe's girlfriend who, in turn, smiled back at him before reaching for Joe's hand, plainly determined to show they were the perfect dinner party guests and nothing like this drunken sister of the village vicar who obviously couldn't hold her drink and was making such a show of herself. 'She'd be far better, sleeping it off next door at my place.'

'I don't seem to be able to get a signal in here,' Rosa said, ignoring Sam. She wanted fresh air and to be away from him. And from Joe also, she realised. Sitting across from the man she'd loved, with whom she'd spent so much of her life, while trying to be interested and friendly with this new woman of his, had been such hard work and now, with Melissa stroking Joe's arm while being condescendingly contemptuous of Hannah, it was suddenly all too much for her to bear.

'I'll make Hannah some coffee.' Jude smiled, moving to the kitchen. 'You go and ring for a taxi, Rosa. You'll get a better signal in the garden.'

'Make it a double gin.' Hannah slurred the words, giggling. She yawned, smiling beatifically, before winking at Jude.

'I do hope she's not going to vomit here.' Melissa's voice drifted down the hallway after her as Rosa made her way through the front door and out into the garden. 'I mean, we're not teenagers anymore, are we?'

The surprisingly warm May day with its clear blue sky had ended in cloud as it so often did up here in Yorkshire, and the cool night air, with its promise of rain, felt wonderfully refreshing after the somewhat cloying, almost claustrophobic atmosphere back inside Daisy's cottage. Rosa quickly pressed for an Uber, surprised as she always was that the taxi service had made its way to this part of the world, before breathing in the reviving sweet-smelling air drifting up and across from Daisy's wonderful garden.

'Nicotiana,' Daisy said knowledgably, as she joined Rosa who, with closed eyes, was breathing in the delicate smell of the night-scented flower. 'Fabulous, isn't it?' She passed Rosa a mug of coffee, which Rosa took gratefully, drinking deeply of its contents. 'Listen, Rosa, I'm really sorry.'

'Sorry?'

'I'd no idea you and Joe had past history.'

Rosa smiled at that. 'Past history? Well, yes, I suppose it is *history* now. Gone down into *the annals of history* like the Battle of Hastings…'

'The six wives of Henry the Eighth.'

'Captain Cook "discovers" America.'

'Wasn't that Columbus?'

'Dunno. I never was much good at history.'

'Or letting go of past loves?' Daisy nudged Rosa meaningfully. 'Look, Rosa, I'm not the best person to give advice on relationships – God knows, it's taken me a hell of a lot of kissing damp squibs before I've finally found my firework…' Daisy started to laugh. 'Quite poetic that analogy, don't you think? Sorry, I've had too much to drink, otherwise I wouldn't dream of commenting on your past – or present – relationships. Or start spouting rubbish about fireworks.'

She laughed again. 'And, as you're a wise vicar, with full access to God's ear, I'm probably the last person to be adding my two-penneth of advice. Sorry... Jude was right... too much bloody sherry in that horrible trifle...' Daisy trailed off. 'It's just, Rosa, you Quinn triplets have always been village icons. I mean, not only that you're triplets – and bloody gorgeous to boot – but, you know, being Alice Parkes's and the Marquess of Stratton's natural daughters? We kids, in our first year at Westenbury Comp, spent every morning assembly turning to catch a glimpse of you at the back of the hall when we should have been concentrating on *Fight the Good Fight* and the Lord's Prayer.' Daisy laughed again.

'Oh, gosh, really?' Rosa was touched.

'Absolutely really. So, all I'm saying now – and tomorrow I'll wish I'd kept my big mouth shut – much as I like having Sam as my neighbour and tenant next door, I'm not sure he's the man for you. If I've offended you, I'm sorry... Look, I'd better shut up – he's here now, looking for you.' Both of them turned as Sam appeared, silhouetted in the light of the front door, while obviously searching for Rosa down the garden.

'Right. OK.'

'Rosa, I'm sorry, it's not my business, nothing to do with me.'

'It's fine, really. You've just confirmed what I've been realising for the past couple of weeks, Daisy.' Rosa made to hug the other woman.

'Oh,' Daisy replied, the warm contact with Rosa clearly giving her renewed confidence to speak what was really on her mind. 'And, while we're at it, don't give up on Joe. I know what happened there – Frankie filled me in while we were in the kitchen. I can't believe I didn't know all this. We all make mistakes, Rosa. And, as a vicar, you should know there's a time to forgive and forget. Right, bloody sermon's over. Uber's here, let's go and get your sister. She's going to have one hell of a head in the morning.'

'Thanks, Daisy.' Rosa hugged her once more.

'Not a problem. All part of the Daisy Maddison Dinner Party Experience. Oh, and one more thing…'

'Yes?'

'I believe I've to wrestle a damned great emerald from the finger of some ring-nicking mouse in the morning?'

'Do mice have fingers?' Rosa started to laugh as the Uber driver peeped his horn and a bedraggled-looking Hannah appeared at the front door with Jude.

'Dunno, but better the ring on the mouse's finger than yours, I reckon.'

'So, what was all that about?' Rosa gave instructions to the taxi driver before prodding at Hannah who now appeared to be back in the land of the living and was gazing out of the car window.

'All what about?' Hannah asked somewhat sulkily.

'Hannah, you'd been drinking all afternoon, you said, and then this evening you put away enough to sink a ship.'

'So, point me in the direction of the nearest AA.'

'They hold a session in the church hall every second Tuesday evening.' Rosa smiled.

Hannah didn't.

'Hannah?'

'I'm such a fool,' Hannah almost snarled. She turned back to the window, sinking further into the seat but refusing to say anything else.

'Well, we all drink too much sometimes,' Rosa said cheerfully. 'Mind you, you really went for it tonight.' She started to laugh. 'Good job you fell asleep in your trifle instead of eating it or you'd have been under the table instead of with your head down on top of it.'

Hannah didn't reply, clearly not amused by Rosa's trying to downplay how bloody embarrassing she'd been. Instead, she continued to gaze out of the taxi window. Suddenly, she sat up, knocking loudly on the glass partition separating the driver from themselves on the back seat. 'Go down here,' she shouted. 'Turn left. Down here.' Hannah pointed almost wildly.

'Down here, lady?' The driver, who'd introduced himself as Girma from Eritrea, turned slightly. 'Not way to Westenbury village.'

'Just go down here,' she insisted crossly.

'Hannah, what are you *doing*? This doesn't take us back home.' Rosa stared.

'OK, now down here,' Hannah instructed Girma. 'Yep, that's right… and take a left… no, no, sorry… right… and…' Hannah was almost glued to the window '…just down here…'

'Hannah!' Rosa grabbed at Hannah's hand but she shook it off.

'Well, there you go.' Hannah's voice was strangely triumphant. 'Stop, Girma, just stop here. So, Rosa, do you see what I see?'

'What, Hannah? What?'

'The car? There? Whose car do you think that is?'

'I've really no idea, Hannah.'

'The registration? Do you want to take a look?'

'I haven't got my glasses. Hang on.' Rosa moved across Hannah, nearer to the side window, peering out at the rather upmarket sports job parked outside the terraced house to her left. 'NSBP 300,' she read. 'Somebody who's got National Savings with a petrol company…? Oh, Hannah…'

'Yep, Ben's car: Neurosurgeon, Ben Pennington. And I can tell you now, there's no emergency brain surgery going on in there.'

'No, I can see that. Maybe, there's some reason…'

'Yes, the reason is Tiffany. Probably in stockings and suspenders and having a whale of a time with the randy, cheating brain-mender.'

'Tiffany Peterson? The wedding planner from the hall?'

'Yep. Got it in one. As *she's* obviously getting it right now. I once gave her a lift home so I knew she lived down here.'

'But what on earth made you think Ben would be *here*, Hannah?' Rosa felt absolute shock. And pity for her sister.

'Got a quick glimpse of a text that came through on his phone from her. Twenty minutes before he made his excuse to say he had to go over to Midhope General.'

'And you didn't say anything to him? There and then, I mean?'

'I was too shellshocked. Didn't want to make a scene in front of everybody.' Hannah laughed mirthlessly. 'Which seems a bit daft seeing I ended up with my head in the custard.'

'I'm so sorry, Hannah.'

'That's why I just carried on drinking. By myself. Wanted to drink myself into oblivion. He was all I ever wanted, Rosa. And now, I'm just furious. *Wild*.'

'Fury's good, I would imagine.'

'Well, I'm not going to turn into Alexandra, his wife, and find a potty full of pee to throw over Tiffany, like Alexandra did to me.'

'We go now, lady?' Girma turned, obviously impatient to be off.

'We go now, Girma. And thank you for stopping.'

'Bad mans?' Girma asked, shaking his head as he indicated and pulled out into the deserted street. 'Been up to no goods?'

'Very bad mans, Girma.' Hannah shook her head in reply. 'Constantly up to no goods with gullible womens. Women.'

'What are you going to do, Hannah?' Rosa turned to her sister and took her hand, wishing she could take away her pain.

'Well and truly got my comeuppance, haven't I?' Hannah grimaced, one tear rolling down her cheek. She brushed it away angrily. 'The mistress becomes the wife. And so it goes on. And on.' She started to laugh, a raw, hiccupping noise that had Girma turning from the wheel and Rosa turning to take her hand once again. 'Maybe Alexandra Pennington and I should start the Ben Pennington's Survivors' Club?'

'We're here. Come on.' Rosa opened the door once the taxi pulled up at the vicarage gate.

'But this is church,' Girma said. 'You sure I leave you here? In churchyard? By graves?'

'My sister is the Westenbury village vicar, Girma. And a jolly good one too,' Hannah, sobering up fast, said proudly.

'But you woman?'

'I was last time I looked.' Rosa laughed, closing the taxi door. 'Right, Hannah, I'm going to tuck you up in bed with a hot water bottle, a pint of water and a bucket – just in case. No more discussion tonight. Stay in bed in the morning. Once I'm back from Sunday morning service, we'll get Eva round and work out your plan of action.'

'I thought your lot all turned the other cheek?'

'Maybe at times there's another way…' Rosa unlocked the heavy vicarage door and they went in together. 'An eye for an eye, maybe?'

Another beautiful May morning and, walking back to the vicarage after the Sunday morning service, Rosa was glad she'd insisted on the congregation singing Hymn number 342: 'All Things Bright and Beautiful', despite Hilary Makepiece saying they needed to move with the times and shouldn't be churning out stuff that had gone out with the ark. Which had made Rosa not only laugh, but extend her prepared sermon by going off at a tangent, asking those present to join in with her to choose their all-time Top Ten Hymn hits.

It had all got rather heated, and she was beginning to feel a bit like Tony Blackburn announcing the Top Forty while Daphne the organist thoroughly enjoyed herself thumping out the first few chords of each suggested hymn in order remind the congregation of their choices. It was eventually whittled down to 'I Vow to Thee, My Country', 'Rock of Ages' and 'Jerusalem' and the service extended in order to sing all three finalists.

Rosa had been delighted to see Girma the Uber driver in church, valiantly doing his best to join in with the singing but, guiltily, *not* so pleased to see Sam, sitting in the very front pew with her mum, Susan, and big sister, Virginia, as he valiantly tried *his* best to make eye contact with her throughout the service.

'Bit *happy-clappy* your sermon this morning, do you not think, Rosa?' Virginia volunteered with a slight smirk. 'It'll be *jazz hands* next week.'

'Great idea, Virginia,' Rosa deadpanned. 'I'll practise "All that Jazz"—' Rosa sang the words while executing perfect jazz hands toward her big sister '—from *Chicago*, for my sermon next week. Brilliant thinking, thank you.' She turned to Sam who had appeared, and was now hovering, at her side. 'I'm going to have to love you and leave you, Sam,' Rosa said, hurrying off in the direction of the vicarage. 'Church business, I'm afraid,' she lied (sorry, God) before relenting and suggesting he come round to eat with her in the evening. She knew she not only had to make sure the ring had been returned to its rightful owner (sorry, Mouse) but also needed to let Sam down carefully and tell him the truth about how she was feeling.

Letting down a man when you were in your late thirties was a lot more difficult than when you were thirteen and dumping (adolescent parlance) the red-faced, sticky-out-eared youth you'd snogged at the youth club and who assumed he was now your boyfriend. A quiet word to his sniggering mate, or a note passed surreptitiously along the bench and down the Bunsen burners in the science lab had been more than sufficient to curtail any further progress *then*.

Now, it was going to take a lot more than a quick 'It's not you, it's me' to let Sam down and Rosa's heart plummeted at the thought of what she had to do later that day.

Meanwhile, Eva and Hannah were waiting over at the vicarage for her.

16

Eva was already sat eating toast and drinking tea at the long wooden table when Rosa walked into the vicarage kitchen.

'Sorry, made myself at home,' she said through a mouthful of toast and honey.' She raised an eyebrow in Rosa's direction while waiting for the next batch of toast to pop up. 'So, good do then, was it, last night? I feel a bit left out not being invited, to be honest. I'm a girl in need of a social life now I don't have a husband any longer.'

'Not sure you could actually call it *good*.' Rosa felt at the large brown teapot, decided its contents were warm enough and poured herself a cup. 'I mean, the food was out of this world – Frankie Dosanjh certainly knows how to cook. And the local MP was there.'

'MP? Really?'

'Jude Mansell. Really nice bloke; hope his lot get in next time. And then Hannah fell in the pudding and I thought I'd better bring her back home with me.'

Eva stopped chewing. 'Home? Hannah's *here*?'

Rosa nodded. 'She had rather a lot to drink.'

'Do you not think she's, you know—' Eva lowered her voice '—drinking rather too much at the moment?'

'Depends what you mean by *too much*?' Rosa smiled. 'She's not been at the communion wine while she's been here. Well, at least I don't think so.'

'I'd have thought, now that she's got Ben to herself after months of being his mistress, she'd have no reason to drink,' Eve said. 'Mind you, I don't think she's coping too well with all the responsibility up at the hall…'

'D'you mind not talking about me behind my back?' Hannah had appeared in the kitchen without the other two noticing. 'Any tea in that pot? My mouth thinks something's died in it. And all I can smell is sweet stuff up my nose.' She took hold of a chunk of her long dark hair and sniffed. 'Blimey.'

'Trifle.' Rosa reminded her. 'Had you forgotten?'

'Where's Ben?' Eva indicated upstairs. 'Did he come back with you as well?'

'Ben, I would imagine, will still be in Tiffany Peterson's bed.' Hannah sipped at her tea.

'Tiffany?' Eva stared. 'Tiffany, the wedding planner?'

'The very one.' Hannah closed her eyes, drinking long and noisily. 'Whoever invented tea deserves to be canonised; mention it to your boss, would you, Rosa? And yes, Eva, Ben Pennington has moved on. The mistress – me – has become the boring partner and he's off looking for excitement – and sex – elsewhere.'

'Already?' Eva stared. 'But he only left Alexandra, what, two or three months ago? The bastard, the absolute fuckwit.'

Hannah nodded.

'You OK, Hans?' Eva took Hannah's hand but she shook it off crossly before upending the dregs from the teapot into her mug.

'Listen, Eva, I'm telling you now, I'm not going to sit and cry over the pillock.' Hannah dashed away a furious tear, rubbing it into the previous night's still-in-situ eye make-up. 'I stole him from his wife…'

'Rubbish, Hannah. People only get stolen if they *want* to be stolen.' Eva sat back and folded her arms.

'…I stole him from Alexandra and now he's moved on once more. And if you think I'm going to sit and cry over him, you're absolutely mistaken.'

'What about sitting and *drinking*? We'd rather you cry, than be up there at the hall making your way through Bill's wine cellar by yourself every evening.' Rosa's voice was gentle.

'Will you stop making out I'm some sort of alcoholic, the pair of you?' Hannah was cross.

'Don't forget Dad's from Liverpool,' Eva reminded Hannah.

'What the hell has Dad's being from Liverpool got to do with anything?' Hannah threw up her hands in despair.

'Well, Liverpool is across the sea from Ireland. And with a name like Quinn? We must have Irish blood, d'you not think? The Irish have always drunk a shedload.'

'Oh, for heaven's sake, Eva, that's the biggest load of bullshit stereotyping I've ever heard.' Hannah thumped her mug down onto the table. 'And, if you've forgotten, Richard may be our dad, but he's not our *birth father*. And, as such, we can't have inherited *any* of his genes.'

'OK, OK, OK.' Eva put up her hands in defence. 'But Alice is our birth mother and *she's* always knocked it back a bit, you know. Hannah, we're just worried about you, that's all.'

When Hannah continued to glare, was about to stand and leave the kitchen, Eva put out a placating hand and hurriedly went on. 'So, good, good then. Moving on, you need to kick the bastard Ben out of your life…'

'He's out,' Hannah growled.

'…and decide what you're going to do about Tiffany.'

'Sack her.'

'No, you're *not*,' Eva replied crossly. 'Understandable though that may be. She's a bloody good wedding planner, Hans. Bill always said he couldn't be without her. You're going to have to just put your personal life behind you. You know, for the good of the hall.'

'I think she's right, Hannah.' Rosa crossed to the open kitchen door, staring up at the sky where a couple of thuggish-looking clouds were threatening to block out the May sunshine. 'You have to rise above this and move on. You're making such good progress with Heatherly Hall, after just six months; you can't start to throw it all away now because of one man…'

'Who apparently,' Eva interrupted crossly, 'is a serial cheater who can't keep his dick in his pants. I tell you now, Hannah, if ever I need a brain transplant, I'll be shopping around before going to *him*. Hell, you wouldn't know *where* his hands had been. Right, OK, moving on, anything else happen at this do last night?'

'Rosa got engaged.'

'*What?*' Eva stared. 'Sam actually proposed? Well, it's been on the cards for ages, I suppose.'

'Is that supposed to be: *Congratulations, Rosa, I'm so happy for you*, Eva?' Hannah said crossly. 'Because, if it is, you need to put a bit more effort and enthusiasm into it.'

'I'm sorry, Rosa.' Eva turned to Rosa who was still standing at the door, and went over to hug her. 'Congratulations. Honestly. I might be off men myself at the moment, but it's wonderful for you. And where is he? Sam, I mean?' She looked round the open door, peering down the garden. 'Have you got him outside, gardening? Will you stay here at the vicarage or look for somewhere new together?'

When Rosa didn't say anything, didn't seem able to but, instead, continued to watch the gathering clouds, Hannah sighed and said, 'Apparently, our sister got herself engaged and, er, *unengaged*, all within the space of ten minutes. And then threw the emerald – bloody big thing it was as well – down Daisy Maddison's toilet.'

'You threw Sam's ring down the lav?' Eva stared and then started to laugh. 'Not an overly Christian act of kindness, I wouldn't have thought, Rosa?' Eva was shaking her head. 'OK, tell all.'

'That's hilarious,' Eva guffawed, ten minutes later, once Rosa, with interjections from Hannah, retold the tale of the misplaced emerald.

'Sam didn't think so,' Rosa replied ruefully. 'I'm afraid I've hurt him very badly and that was never my intention.'

'I don't suppose it was.' Eva patted Rosa's arm through her white surplice. 'And you a woman of God, too.'

'Thanks for that Eva.' Rosa shook her head. 'I should have broken it off weeks ago. I knew Sam wasn't right for me; I just kept on hoping and hoping that he *was*. You know, I so *wanted* him to be. So wanted to be married with my own children, my own family.'

'Not all it's cracked up to be,' Eva said gloomily. 'You know, having a husband.'

'So why do we spend a good percentage of our lives looking for one?' Hannah asked crossly.

'I think, Hannah, that if I'd accepted Sam's proposal, said yes, I'd marry him and try for the family we both would love to have, then it would have been a compromise.'

'Are we not allowed to compromise when we're pushing forty?' Hannah replied, still cross.

'And end up actively disliking the compromise five years down the road? The thing is, after meeting Sam's mother the other week, I just keep seeing more and more of her coming out in Sam. And I can't bear it.'

'Nothing to do with Joe Rosavina being sat opposite you at the do?' Hannah asked, eyebrows raised.

'Joe? Joe Rosavina was there as well? Bloody hell, you two, you kept that quiet. And is he OK now? Concussion gone? Back in the land of the living – worse luck? You should have snuck those cows a couple of quid to finish him off completely.' Eva sat down, shaking her head before turning to Rosa once again. 'Please don't say you turned Sam down because Joe Rosavina was looking at you with those big blue eyes of his once again?'

'I don't think Joe looked in my direction for more than two seconds,' Rosa said ruefully. 'Too busy with his new woman.'

'New woman? Joe's got a new woman? Who is she?' Eva's eyes widened. 'Anyone we know?'

'Melissa somebody.' Rosa smiled. 'Moved from Paris into the village about a year ago.'

'Paris to Westenbury?' Eva pulled a face. 'Why would *anyone* leave Paris to come and live in a backwater like this? So, what's she like? How did you feel, Rosa? Does this Melissa woman know about you and Joe?'

'McLean,' Hannah said suddenly with some degree of triumph.

'Sorry?' Rosa and Eva turned as one.

'Melissa McLean, that's what she's called. I remember because she has the same surname as AJ McLean in the Backstreet Boys. And,' Hannah went on, 'I kept wanting to laugh – I suppose because of my drunken state,' she added ruefully. 'I just kept looking at her neck.'

'Her *neck*?'

'She has incredibly short hair – suits her; gamine I suppose you'd call it – and I just kept thinking what a clean neck Melissa *McLean* had.' Hannah laughed.

'You are joking?' Eva was staring.

'No, really, incredibly clean. Quite pink and shiny actually.'

'She's called McLean?'

'Yep, definitely. *I* remember now as well,' Rosa added. 'Was going to google her once I got home.'

'Are vicars allowed to stalk people?' Hannah asked, frowning across at Rosa.

'Did she mention having any kids at Little Acorns?' Eva asked.

'Yes, she did actually,' Rosa nodded. 'Because she goes in to hear readers, like I do.'

'Florence?' Eva leaned forward. 'Did she mention Florence?'

'No, Paris, not Florence. She'd been living in *Paris*. Was going on and on – and on – about giving birth in Paris. Poor Frankie Dosanjh was beginning to look a bit green.' Rosa tutted at the memory.

'Florence McLean. Ha!'

'No, really, Eva, she's called *Melissa* McLean.'

'Her daughter is called Florence McLean,' Eva said, 'and Laila tried to cut her ear off at school.

'Whose ear? Melissa's ear?'

'No. For heaven's sake, Hannah, you're obviously still under the influence.'

'Think I am actually.' Hannah rubbed at her eyes and the back of her own neck.

'Laila was aiming for the daughter Florence's plait with a pair of scissors and ended up cutting her ear.'

'Good for Laila. If she's anything like her mother, she probably needs a good roughing up.' Hannah laughed as she remembered the woman.

'Well, I've a meeting with Cassie Beresford – the head – and this Melissa McLean woman tomorrow,' Eva said grimly. 'I'll let you know what I think of her then, Rosa.' Eva patted Rosa's hand. 'You OK? You know, seeing Joe with this new woman?'

'Not really,' Rosa admitted. 'Knocked me back a bit actually. I just thought, you know, Sam and I were actually getting it together: that I might actually be able to find a father for my poor old frozen eggs… And now…'

'And now?'

'I'm back to square one with it all.'

'So,' Eva reminded the other two, 'good job the three of us are off to Paris next week then, I reckon. I think we all need to get away and put some space between ourselves and what's going on here in the village.'

Once the other two had left for Heatherly Hall and the many jobs involved in the running of the place, Rosa went upstairs, took off her surplice and replaced it with jeans and sweatshirt. She needed to cook and garden – two things that would help take her mind off the coming meeting with Sam – but didn't want to lull him into any false sense of hope about their relationship by cooking up something fabulous. Instead, she found the ingredients for a simple vegetarian lasagne – pasta, home-made ratatouille, and kidney beans, blanketing the layers in a thick, creamy Bechamel sauce and finishing with a ton of Parmesan. She assembled a quick green salad and laid the kitchen table simply with cutlery and paper napkins while eschewing any flowers or candles.

Then, desperate to get into the garden – she always felt that bit nearer to God with a spade beneath her booted foot and the smell of newly turned, wet earth in her nose – Rosa opened the kitchen door and went out.

Three hours later, a sheen of sweat on her face and the start of an ache in her back, Rosa sat back on her haunches to survey her handiwork. The yew was finally pruned into some sort of submission (although one bit down the far side of the vicarage garden now had an appendage that looked particularly phallic) and the last of the spring daffodils were bent over and tied with a rubber band to ensure their blooming once again the following spring.

Every time she'd paused to rest, or reached for her bottled water, her heart gave a little lurch as she rehearsed the two-way dialogue she knew she'd have to have, in reality, once Sam arrived. She waved at Denis, the verger, and his wife, Sandra, making their way towards the main entrance of the church in order to unlock and prepare the building for the six-thirty evensong service. With its customary expected handful of attendees, Denis had volunteered to take the service as he so often did, leaving Rosa to collect up her gardening tools and head back to the vicarage.

Sam was standing at the vicarage door, arms folded, watching her.

'Goodness, you made me jump.' Rosa laughed slightly nervously. 'How long have you been standing there?'

'Ten minutes or so. I was just enjoying watching you.'

'Right. Hang on.' Divesting herself of boots and gloves, she straightened up, ran a hand through her hair and opened the door. 'Come in, I've made a lasagne.'

'Oh, not pushing the boat out then?' Sam looked towards the simply-laid kitchen table and gave a somewhat condescending smile. 'I guess not.'

'I'll just stick it in the oven.' Rosa took the dish from the fridge and placed it on the top shelf of the oven, her back to Sam. Why on earth was she feeling so nervous? This was Sam, the man she'd been in a relationship with for the last six months. The man she'd truly thought she was going to end up with. Be with. Have children with.

'So, must have been a bit of a shock coming face to face with your ex like that last night, Rosa?'

'A shock? Not really.' Rosa smiled pleasantly, wondering if a glass of wine might ease her nerves.

'You didn't seem able to take your eyes off him.'

'Erm, I don't think that was the case at all. I was more concerned with making sure Hannah was OK.'

'You're being a bit argumentative, Rosa.' Sam gave a little smile and then, when she didn't react, asked, 'Aren't you going to offer me a drink?'

'Of course. There's a beer in the fridge. Help yourself.'

'I've brought champagne.'

'Look, Sam, I'm sorry…'

'I got the ring back.'

'Oh, thank goodness for that.' Rosa turned from the fridge where she was searching for the couple of bottles of lager she knew were in there somewhere.

'Had to take up the floorboards.' Sam was smiling, but his eyes were unfriendly.

'But it was there?'

'I had to get Jimmy Dobson in.'

'Jimmy Dobson?'

'Joiner and handyman. He wasn't overly pleased at being called out on a Sunday morning.'

'No, I can see that.'

'Disturbed Daisy and Jude as well. You know, Sunday morning and all that?'

'I'll apologise. Take some flowers round.'

'Expensive as well. You know, Sunday morning call-out.'

'Let me know what it cost, Sam, and I'll pay. Happy to pay – it was my fault.'

'Oh, I don't want your money, Rosa.' Sam took the bottled beer and, when there didn't appear to be any opener to hand, used his teeth.

'Ooh, and you a dentist.' Rosa winced, sensing it was an act of aggression rather than impatience.

Sam said nothing but drank deeply from the bottle before placing it onto the kitchen table, folding his arms and holding Rosa's eye. 'I thought, after I'd met you, Rosa, you'd be the one to help me move on. Help me come to terms with the failure of my marriage and losing my son.'

'You've been through a lot, Sam – I know that…'

'But you're not being helpful *at the moment*, are you? In fact, you seem to be hell-bent on making me feel worse now, Rosa.'

'Hell-bent? Oh, don't be silly, Sam. Look, I'm sorry…'

'Will you stop saying sorry?'

'But I *am* sorry,' Rosa said. 'I'm *so sorry* that this hasn't worked out for us after all.'

'I don't know why you're doing this. Is it deliberate?'

'Deliberate? I don't know what you mean.'

'Getting your own back?'

'My own back?' Rosa stared.

'I think this is your way of getting your own back after what that ex of yours did to you with your best friend.'

'What? What *are* you talking about? I most certainly…'

'I think you've led me on. And now you're turning me down. Does it give you some pleasure to know you've the upper hand this time in your relationship?'

'This time…?'

'I think your turning me down is some sort of warped revenge against men in general.'

'Why would I…?'

'Yes,' Sam sneered, not listening at all to what Rosa was attempting to say. 'Probably the reason you went into the church as well.'

'I went into the church, Sam—' Rosa was trying her best to remain calm '—because God called me.'

'Oh, on the phone, was it?' Sam's tone was pleasant but there was an underlying sneer to it that made Rosa's pulse race. 'Rosa.' He seemed to relent, reaching for her hand. 'I've been through so much, losing Ollie… I can't bear to lose you too.'

'I think you should go, Sam.'

'Go? I'm not going anywhere. We need to sort this out. Make you see that you can't *do this* to us. To *me*.'

Rosa felt an inkling of fear but knew she needed to remain calm. 'I don't think it's a good idea if we sit down and eat together after all.'

'Not breaking bread together then?' The sneery tone was back.

'You're upset.'

'Of course, I'm upset. You tried to throw my grandmother's ring down Daisy's toilet.'

'Oh, don't be ridiculous, Sam.' Rosa actually started to laugh.

'Please don't laugh at me, Rosa.' Sam's voice was harsh.

'I'm not laughing *at you*. I'm laughing that you seem to think I deliberately tried to throw your granny's ring down the lav. And obviously missed! I was never much good at netball at school, but, honestly, Sam, come on…' The whole thing was becoming ludicrous.

'Just try the ring on again, Rosa. Please. You'll see that it's just made for you.' Sam took the ring from his pocket and moved towards her and she backed up.

'Enough, Sam, now. I'd like you to go...' Rosa broke off as a knock came at the kitchen door followed by its opening and a cheery voice.

'Rosa, love, you left your cardi in the vestry.' Sandra Butterworth waved Rosa's best navy cardigan in her direction. 'Cashmere an' all; you don't want anyone walking off with this. I saw Daphne Merton eyeing it up earlier. Mind you, she'd never get those arms of hers anywhere near it...' Sandra paused, taking in the tension in the kitchen, which could have been cut with a knife. 'Sorry, love, you've visitors.' She put the cardigan on the worktop. 'I'll be off.'

'No, Sandra,' Rosa said firmly. 'Sam is just leaving. And there's something I need to discuss with *you*,' Rosa lied. She turned back to Sam. 'Right, have you got everything you came with? Hmm? Lovely. Thank you for dropping in, Sam. I'll see you sometime.'

In bed, later that evening, Rosa tossed and turned, unable to get the image of Sam's desperately sad face from her mind when she closed her eyes. She *had* genuinely liked him very much, enjoyed his company, tried very hard to convince herself that she was in love with him. Wanted to marry him and have children with him, even. Would it have been so wrong to go along with it all? To have the home and children they both so yearned for?

At 2am, Rosa put on the bedside lamp and reached for her go-to comfort book: Hardy's *Far From the Madding Crowd*. She opened the paperback, reading some of her favourite bits, wanting a Gabriel Oak of her own, until one sentence, spoken by Oak to Bathsheba had her nodding in agreement:

'*The real sin, ma'am, in my mind, lies in thinking of ever wedding wi' a man you don't love honest and true.*'

Rosa closed the book and slept.

17

While Rosa had been in the vicarage garden that afternoon, working out the best way to break it off with Sam once he arrived at the vicarage, Hannah was back at the hall and packing up her lover's things.

'Hannah? What's going on?' Ben Pennington stood in the doorway as she sat at the computer on the long oak table of Heatherly Hall's boardroom. 'I've been looking for you up in the flat. I couldn't find you. Or half my things? What are doing in here all by yourself? Why are you working? Up here on a Sunday afternoon?'

'Like you, Ben, I often have to work at strange hours of the day. I've a lot to do; I'm way behind with everything.' She turned to look at him, taking in the longish dark hair, the blue eyes not quite able to meet her own and holding, she could see, something akin to panic; fear even? The clothes he'd been wearing the previous evening were now slightly crumpled and he was, Hannah thought with some satisfaction, looking decidedly seedy. 'Your things are all packed up and ready for you down in the porter's lodge. Much as I wanted to chuck all your Paul Smith shirts, Brunello Cucinelli suits and ties out of the window, I had to think of all the visitors to the hall: didn't want reviews up on TripAdvisor commenting on the Ralph Lauren boxers blooming in the formal gardens when they were expecting larkspur and hydrangea.'

'Hannah…' Ben started, moving towards her, reaching for her

shoulder as she sat in the chair. She stood before he could make contact with any part of her and he was left, foolishly standing, one hand raised and redundant in the air. 'Hannah, I've had a hard time over at the hospital...'

'No, Buster, you've had a *hard* time over in Tiffany's bed. Now, as I say, your things are in the porter's lodge. You'll find an Aldi carrier bag with the dirty pants and socks you left in my linen basket; I didn't want you deprived of those. I'm sure Tiffany will switch on her washing machine for you.'

'Hannah...'

'No, Ben, absolutely NOT.' Hannah put up her hands, her thumping head testament not only to the alcohol she'd put away the previous evening, but also to the unbelievable betrayal of the man she'd adored for the past year. Apart from the splitting headache – maybe she should see a neurosurgeon? – Hannah realised she was feeling only a strange numbness, as if the painkillers she'd downed that day had bypassed her head where they were needed most, swathing the rest of her in an icy calm. No doubt the real pain would hit her like a ten-tonne truck pretty soon.

'Hannah, listen to me; it's not what you think. Tiffany had told me earlier she was having problems sleeping.'

'Well obviously. I'm sure sleep was the last thing on her mind when she was in bed with you.'

'*In bed* with me? *Tiffany?* Where on earth have you got that from? I knew she was having problems sleeping so, on the way back here from the hospital, I called in and posted something to help through her letter box. Something strong I'd picked up for her from the hospital. She obviously thought she was being burgled, because she came down and then just... you know... invited me in and then, I had a quick drink with her while I explained the medication to her. It must have knocked me out – don't forget I'd been up half the night...'

'Only *half* the night? You're losing your touch, Benjamin.'

'…and when I woke up, I was on her sofa with a blanket over me.'

'Right.' Hannah glanced up at the clock on the boardroom wall. 'It's four in the afternoon.'

'Yes, and I've been to see my children. I told you I'd arranged with Alexandra to do that.'

That at least was true.

Hannah actually started to laugh. 'Well, at least you'll be able to make a living writing fantasy if ever your lying, cheating hands let you down. Off you go, Ben, out of my hall, out of my life. No,' she shouted, as he moved once again towards her. 'Fuck off, Ben. Fuck right off. Right out of my life.'

'Has he gone?' Eva came into the boardroom an hour later, standing behind Hannah at the computer.

'I believe so.'

'You OK?'

'At the moment yes. The thing is, Eva, I'm not going to wail and cry and ask myself where it all went wrong: I backed the wrong horse. I'm actually thoroughly ashamed that the three of us have been given this chance to take over and expand Heatherly Hall and I've not pulled my weight. Even though I'm chair of the board.'

'Oh, come on, Hannah, you've not stopped since you moved into Bill's apartment here and took over at the helm.' Eva folded her arms. 'Stop beating yourself up – you've been up at five every morning with those pigs.'

'Which isn't my job, I know. So, I'm calling a meeting in the morning.'

'I've an appointment with Laila's teachers and…' Eva started to laugh '…your McLean Neck woman in the morning.'

'Good luck with that.' Hannah smiled. 'Nine o'clock meeting here. That should give you time to fit in both if Jodie's around to take Laila to school? Let's hope Rosa doesn't have a funeral or anything else to be at. I'm in the middle of sending emails out to everyone now.'

'Bit last-minute, isn't it? Do people even look at their work emails on a Sunday afternoon?'

'They do if they've anything about them.'

'What's it all about?'

'I can't do everything here.'

'We've been telling you that, Hannah.'

'OK, I'm listening now. I've been *playing* at this job, running off with Ben when things got tough, when bloody Lachlan Buchanan was horrible to me. So, I've had a sort of epiphany while I've been sitting here this afternoon: we need someone with management experience to help run the place. I'm going to put it to the board tomorrow. Advertise for someone.'

'Fine. Good, that's good. I'll back you every way if Lachlan and the others are not for it; say we haven't got the money.'

'Oh, and one more thing and then I'm off back to the flat for a cheese and tomato sandwich, a big mug of tea and a very early night: I'm off the booze as from now.'

'What about the lovely wines we were going to sample in Paris?'

'Nope, I'm on a mission. All I care about is this place and making a success of it. Are you staying here tonight with me or heading back home to your place?'

'I'm going to spend another couple of hours up in the gallery where the Heatherly Hall Art Retreat is going to be. I need to take photos and measurements and make lists of what we need to set it up. Actually, if I go up there now and get started, I can report back to this extra meeting you've called. Tell the accountant how much money I need. Then I'm heading off home; Rayan's bringing the girls back at seven.' Eva made for the door.

'D'you miss him, Eva?'

'Rayan?'

Hannah nodded.

'All the time. Seeing you with that bastard Ben, and Sam who hasn't quite turned out to be the lovely bloke we all thought he was…'

'He really isn't, Eva. I saw him in action at Daisy's place. I went quite off him. Can you imagine? Forcing that ring on Rosa's finger? Horrible thing it was as well. Absolutely tasteless. He obviously doesn't know Rosa if he thought she'd appreciate that monstrosity.'

'Anyway, hearing how possessive Sam has turned out to be – not sure how I'm going to be able to have a normal conversation with him when I'm on the same shift as him on Tuesday and Wednesday at the surgery next week – as well as Ben being the total bastard he is, has made me realise just how lovely Rayan is.'

'Of course he is, Eva.' Hannah nodded, pleased that things might be looking up for Eva and the brother-in-law she'd always loved. 'Rayan's always been my favourite brother-in-law.'

'Your *only* brother-in-law. And looks like staying that way, now that Sam appears to be out of the framework.'

They both were silent as they mulled this over for a few seconds.

'I just didn't appreciate Rayan when I had him,' Eva eventually said with a sigh. 'But I don't half miss him. And I absolutely hate not having the girls with me all the time.'

'Wasn't there the little problem of sexual incompatibility?' Hannah raised an eyebrow in Eva's direction.

'You mean I wanted sex and Rayan didn't? I know, I know. Well, hopefully all those sessions he's been having with the Leicestershire psychosexual therapist will have sorted all that out. You know, made him feel he's a real man.'

'Instead of the terrified mouse you turned him into, demanding sex every two minutes in every conceivable position while dressed to kill in your slit-crotch panties? I saw you eyeing up that huge hall chandelier the other day.' Hannah started to laugh.

Eva tutted. 'I wish I'd never told you all this.'

'You tell me and Rosa everything,' Hannah said comfortably,

wandering over to the window and surveying the beautiful gardens where a good number of visitors continued to walk, sit and admire the late spring blooms and foliage. There was still a gratifyingly long queue outside Tea and Cake café and every outside table – with their mint-green and cream striped umbrellas – was taken.

'Yes, but it doesn't put me in a very good light, does it? You know, how he says I frightened him into... you know... not being able to... you know...?'

'Just talk to him, Eva, tell him you miss him, tell him you'll go along to the counsellor with him. Tell him you love him. Save your marriage, for heaven's sake.'

'I was thinking, maybe another baby?' Eva flushed slightly pink as she said the words. 'Just a thought, you know? Maybe to help get my family back on track. To show Rayan I'm serious about us being together and working it all out?'

'Really?' Hannah pulled a surprised face. 'Don't they say never have a baby to save a marriage?'

'Who says?'

'Oh, I don't know – those in the know...' Hannah broke off, walking quickly away from the window and over to the door. 'Right, I'll see you at nine in the morning. Bring all your art retreat stuff and be prepared to fight your corner. Give Rayan a kiss from me. Tell him Rosa and I miss him and to get himself back to you and the girls where he belongs.'

'Where are you going?'

'Tiffany,' Hannah said grimly. 'Just going to have a quick word.'

Tiffany Peterson, the pretty wedding planner who had been taken on by Bill Astley as assistant wedding planner almost eight years earlier, and who had now risen, like cream on a bottle of milk, to the top position of managing the entire Heatherly Hall wedding venue, was several yards in front of Hannah. Her blonde ponytail swung like a pendulum as she walked briskly towards her office, her neat little behind taut and high in the tight black suit she wore for work.

'Tiffany!' Hannah called.

The girl stopped dead before turning, her face pink.

'Hannah.'

'Can I have a word?'

'You can have several – including my notice.' Tiffany was obviously coming out fighting.

'Your notice?'

'Absolutely. I don't come to work to be sexually harassed.'

'Sexually harassed?'

'You heard, Hannah.' Tiffany turned back towards the wedding venue main door.

'Hang on. It's Sunday. There are no weddings on today.'

'No, but we have three next week and I like to be prepared.' Tiffany looked Hannah directly in the eye. 'I'm coming in to update my CV as well. I'd have been in earlier this morning, but I didn't leave here until eleven last night and I was up quite a bit of the night.' She looked at Hannah meaningfully.

'Right, come on. Coffee. You and I need to chat.'

Hannah led the way to the wedding venue, using her lanyard to let them both in. Inside was quiet and immaculately tidy, considering the large wedding that had been held in the beautiful old rooms only the day before. She made her way to the catering kitchen, using the upmarket and recently installed machine to prepare coffee for them both.

'So what, or who, kept you up, Tiffany?'

'Just let me give my notice in, Hannah. I think it best all round.'

'So, you can continue to sleep with my boyfriend without feeling guilty?'

'Sleep with him? Hannah, I wouldn't touch that creepy brain surgeon of yours with a bargepole.'

'You texted him last night, Tiffany. I saw his phone.'

'He'd been texting *me*. Several times. I'd been chatting to him on Friday when he called in here.'

'He called in *here*? While you were at work? For what reason?'

'To chat me up, Hannah.' Tiffany was cross. 'And not for the first time. I've given him no reason to believe I've ever wanted that. He said I looked pale. I told him I wasn't sleeping – running this place can be very stressful – and he said he could give me something to help.'

'Right.'

'And all said while he had his hand on my bum, Hannah.'

'What!' Hannah stared, shocked to the core.

'And just so you know, I did *not* lead him on. I don't fancy him, Hannah. Never have done. Anyway, he said he'd be more than happy to put something through my letter box. To be honest, I didn't know if that was some sort of metaphor for – you know...' Tiffany, who'd always seemed fairly shy, broke off embarrassed and, despite the totally dreadful onslaught of stuff about Ben hitting every part of her, Hannah had to supress an utterly irreverent, and uncalled for, nervous giggle. 'I said fine, and gave him my address just to get rid of him. Realised it was a *big mistake* as soon as I did it. And then, last night he knocked on my door just as I got home. I thought it was the police or something. Anyway, he had a bottle of champagne with him, and, despite my telling him absolutely not to, proceeded to pour us both a glass and then, when I didn't join in, drank the whole bottle and passed out cold on the sofa.'

'I'm so sorry,' Hannah repeated, feeling so shocked she wanted to vomit. Or at least sit down. She looked around for the nearest chair and did just that, head in her hands.

'Yes, well, he was pretty embarrassed this morning. Took himself off to see his kids as far as I know. So, how did you know about him spending the night on my sofa?'

'I saw you'd texted him...'

'Only replying to say I was absolutely fine and totally didn't need his medication. He must have found my number in your contacts, Hannah.'

'He told me he was needed at the hospital. An emergency.'

'That much was true: car accident on the M62. Apparently, the poor kid died – terrible head injuries – just as Ben got there. He was no longer needed. And, instead of going back to your dinner party or coming back here to the hall, he thought he'd have another crack at me.'

'I'd had a lot to drink myself,' Hannah confided ruefully.

'Well, absolutely no excuse for him stopping off at my place and trying his luck. The arrogance of the man.' Tiffany sipped at her coffee. 'What are you going to do?'

'Already done.'

'Oh?'

'Thrown his stuff out.'

'Blimey.' Tiffany stared. 'And are you, you know, hurting?'

'Yep.'

'Well don't be. Never understood what you saw in him. Men who think they're God's gift usually aren't. Anyway, Hannah, I'm handing in my notice.'

'Not because of Ben?'

'No.' Tiffany raised an eyebrow. 'Despite what I said – and I did say it to get over to you just what a tosser that boyfriend of yours actually is – it'd take more than one pillock with wandering hands to shift me from a job I love. Particularly now you've thrown him off the premises. The thing is, Hannah, I feel as if I've done as much as I can here: I love it, but I need to move on. I miss Bill a lot – we started the wedding venue together. There's a job going at Castle Howard – you know, promotion, more money. I need the challenge.'

'How about joining the management team here?'

'I thought I already *was* part of it?' Tiffany raised an eyebrow once again.

'No, I mean on the management committee of the whole Heatherly Hall estate. Not just the wedding venue.'

Tiffany stared. 'Really? As what exactly?'

'As my deputy. I've come to realise, six months on, I just can't do it all.' Hannah breathed out and thought she might be in danger of crying. 'I've *tried* but I can't get my head round it all. I get up earlier and go to bed later to try and fit it all in, and I'm so *tired*. I need to deputise, need to delegate.'

'I could have told you that.' Tiffany smiled and then frowned. 'Hang on, you're not having me in the pigs at 5am? And what about the wedding venue? Who's going to run that if I'm doing *your* stuff?'

'I would have thought Felicity more than able to take over,' Hannah mused. 'She's been your second in command for a couple of years now. We could just move everyone up?'

'She's more than capable.' Tiffany was beginning to show some excitement at the prospect of promotion.

'I can't tell you how tired I feel, Tiffany. How I'm beginning to think it was all a mistake us three taking over at the helm. And with me as chair. I'm not up to it; I can't do this anymore.'

'Imposter syndrome, Hannah,' Tiffany said almost crossly. 'Right, have you discussed me coming in as your deputy with the others? It's not just a knee-jerk reaction to Ben Pennington messing you around?'

'I've called a meeting for 9am to put forward the idea of taking on a new deputy manager. Need to get it past the accountant and the bank. And Lachlan.'

'Lachlan's not a problem.' Tiffany's eyes went dreamy. 'He's a total sweetie.'

'A sweetie? Lachlan Buchanan?' Hannah stared and then shook her head. 'So, are you with me in theory? Would you like the job?'

Tiffany laughed. 'Depends what you're paying me. As well as giving me a guarantee that Ben-bloody-brain-surgeon is off the premises and won't be bothering me anymore.'

Hannah heart gave a little lurch as she remembered: realised once again her affair with Ben Pennington was over. Had to be over. 'I promise.' She nodded grimly. 'Leave it with me: I'm going to put the idea forward in the morning. This is day one of a new, independent – and manless – me, as well as a way forward for Heatherly Hall.'

18

'Hello, my darling girls.' Eva, back at the house in Heath Green and waiting impatiently for Laila and Nora to be brought back from visiting Azra, Rayan's widowed mother in Bradford, ran down the garden path to welcome them home and usher them back inside where they belonged.

'We've had party,' Nora shouted in excitement, desperate to impart the news before Laila could.

'A party?' Eva smiled. 'How lovely. A birthday party?'

'No,' Laila tutted knowingly. 'It was Eid-al-Fitr.'

'Oh,' Eva smiled again. 'I thought that was last month?'

'Of course it was, Mummy,' Laila agreed condescendingly. 'But Nanni Azra said seeing you hadn't let Nora and me celebrate it when it was really on, she'd invite everyone over to her house and do it all over again.'

'Not let you? I—' Eva broke off when Laila waved an imperious hand in her direction as they walked up the path towards the house and Eva saw both of her daughters' hands were decorated in henna.

'That's beautiful, Laila.' Eva admired the mehndi tattoo. 'And you have one too, Nora? How lovely. I want one.'

'Florence McLean is going to be so jealous when I show her,' Laila crowed. 'And, Mummy, you *can't* have one. Nanni Azra said so. You are *kafir*.'

'I *beg* your pardon?' Eva glanced at Rayan who had joined them, laden down with cardigans, jackets, school book bags and sweets.

'I made moons like bananas,' Nora said happily. 'And blew up big yellow balloons. And I've had lots of cake.'

'Crescents, Nora,' Laila corrected her three-year-old sister. 'The *crescent* moon is the beginning and ending of Ramadan.'

'*Kafir?*' Eva hissed in Rayan's ear as the girls ran into the house to reunite with the two goldfish Eva had bought for them the previous month. 'Did your mother call me *kafir*? That is a really rude term to use, isn't it?'

'Leave it out, Eva,' Rayan said almost tiredly. 'She didn't mean anything by it. She just can't get used to the situation.'

'Neither can I, Rayan.' Eva grabbed at his hand. 'Come on, let's get the girls ready for bed together and then… you know… at least talk.'

'It's only seven o'clock,' Laila interrupted crossly, coming back into the kitchen and glancing at the huge clock on the wall. 'Put Nora to bed, *Ammi*, not me.'

'Ammi?' Eva stared at her elder daughter and then across at Rayan.

'It's what Sharjeel and Usaid call Aunty Hadhira,' Laila explained, looking up at Eva from under her lashes.

'OK, Laila, *Mummy*'s going to put Nora to bed and then I'm going to hear you read.' Eva spoke firmly.

'Daddy's already heard me,' Laila replied. 'I read all the last three chapters of Harry Potter to Daddy and Nora in the car coming back from Bradford.'

'Without feeling carsick?'

'I'm never carsick,' Laila said pointedly. 'Not like Nora. We had to stop when we got into Westenbury. Just by Aunty Rosa's church where the road is bendy.'

'Nora was sick?' Eva looked across at Rayan who was filling the kettle.

'Only a bit.' He looked tired. Appeared defensive.

'Too much cake,' Laila crowed. 'I told Nanni *you* wouldn't let her have three slices, Mummy.'

'Right, OK, well it was a party after all.' Eva smiled, heading for the sitting room where Nora was stirring the water in the goldfish bowl with her finger.

'Nora, don't do that, you'll make them dizzy and sick.'

'*I* was sick,' Nora said proudly. 'Just a bit. By Aunty Wosa's church.'

Eva sniffed at her daughter. 'Hmm, I can tell. You OK now? Come on, bath time.' She hugged her daughter, unable to put her down, so desperate was she to have her back home. Where she belonged. 'You smell of cake and sick.'

'Mummy, I don't want to go to school tomorrow.' Laila's swaggering bravado at being at a party, from which her mother had patently been ostracised, appeared to melt into the ether. She pushed Nora from Eva's arms, wanting to insert herself into Eva's embrace. 'Miss Worthington will be cross with me. And Mrs Beresford will be too.'

'Laila, I'm going to come into school with you early tomorrow morning.' Eva mentally arranged how she'd take her elder daughter in to school for eight-fifteen and then rush up to the hall for nine. 'I'll have a word with Miss Worthington and then go back to see Mrs Beresford and Florence's mummy later on.' The bitch, Eva added mentally and illogically, going off with Joe Rosavina in front of Rosa. 'It will all be alright. I promise. OK, both of you in the bath together. And I'll put in lots of bubbles. And then, bed.'

'What are we *doing* to our girls, Rayan?' Eva found Rayan at the kitchen table reading the sports section of *The Sunday Times*. When he didn't answer but, instead, drained his mug of coffee, she went on, 'Quite a weekend.'

'Yes, it has been. The girls need to know their cousins more.'

'I actually meant here.'

'Oh?' Rayan looked up.

'Ben Pennington's been messing around again.'

'Doesn't surprise me. Once a cheat, always a cheat.'

'And Rosa got engaged to Sam.'

'Oh?' Rayan said once more and, for the first time that evening, his eyes lit up. 'Well, *that's* good news. Means he'll stay in the area. And stay at Malik and Malik. He's very popular with the patients. Particularly since you've gone down to two days at the surgery,' Rayan added pointedly.

'Unfortunately, she broke it off ten minutes later.'

'What? What *is it* with you and your sisters?'

'What do you mean, what *is it* with us?' Eva stared.

'All three of you seem incapable of maintaining lasting relationships.'

'What rubbish,' Eva replied hotly. 'Rosa was with Joe for fifteen years before they broke up. And you and I have been together seventeen.'

'Had.'

'Sorry?'

'We *had* been together, Eva.'

'Rayan, we need to sort this. I don't want to carry on like this. It's not doing the girls any good.'

'It's not doing *me* much good either.' Rayan pulled a hand through his thick black hair and, for the first time, Eva noticed the start of grey at his temple. It only added to his good looks, and Eva felt a frisson of love for her husband. Of lust.

'OK, let's sort this, Rayan. Before it goes any further. I don't want to lose you.' Eva reached out a hand to his face but Rayan stilled it before it could make contact.

'Eva, the girls will be fine.'

'You won't even try?'

'I've been trying for years, Eva. I've tried to make you love me.'

'I do love you.' Eva felt tears start.

'But not enough,' Rayan said gently. 'I loved you from the minute I saw you at university. You were always so bold, so exuberant, so… so *exciting*. Alice Parkes's daughter for heaven's sake.'

'What's Alice got to do with it?'

'You were almost an icon at Sheffield. A triplet? And the natural daughter of the Marquess of Stratton and Alice Parkes? I wanted to get to know you. *Everyone* did.'

'But you *did* get to know me.' Eva stared. 'You married me.'

'But did you ever marry *me*?'

'What? What are you talking about, Rayan? Do you want me to go and find the marriage certificate?'

'I loved you, Eva. Adored you, even. But I was never enough for you. I felt like I was trapping – imprisoning – a colourful exotic butterfly…'

'What utter bollocks, Rayan.'

'Oh, you loved me – love me – in your own way. But never in that all-consuming way I loved you. The way Joe loved Rosa. And Rosa loved him back.'

'I hate to remind you this, Rayan, but Joe slept with Rosa's best friend.'

'A drunken mistake. A one-off. One he says he'll regret for ever.'

'You seem to know a lot about my sister's relationship with her ex?' Eva felt as though she couldn't breathe. Why was Rayan coming out with all this stuff now? Just as she was desperately trying to mend her marriage to him?

'Joe's been having treatment for a root canal.'

'Good job he didn't go to Sam then. Sam would have probably knocked his teeth *out*, he's so jealous of Joe, from what I can see.'

'I went out for a beer with Joe afterwards. We talked for a long time.'

'Rayan, never mind Rosa and Joe. It's *us* we need to put right. For the sake of the girls.'

Rayan smiled and, moving Eva's hand from his knee where she'd placed it, said sadly, 'For the sake of the girls, Eva? Not for *my* sake?'

'Of course, for *your* sake, Rayan. I…'

Rayan stood, gathering up his keys and jacket. 'I'm sorry, Eva, you need to know before the girls tell you.'

'Know? Know what?' Eva felt an invisible icy hand veer towards her chest.

'I'm seeing someone.'

'*Seeing* someone? Eva felt the hand clutch and squeeze mercilessly at her heart. 'As in, you're having hallucinations?' She spat. 'Seeing apparitions? Or, *having sex* with someone.'

'You know exactly what I mean, Eva. Don't make this any harder than it is already.'

'Oh, so it is *hard*, is it?' Eva heard herself sneer. 'You can get it up for some other woman, when you couldn't for me?' Eva thought the blood rushing round her head might just explode its way out. Would she need to call on Ben Pennington to put her brain back together again? she thought wildly.

'I'm going, Eva.'

'Who *is* she?' Eva grabbed hold of Rayan's arm but he gently replaced it back in her direction.

'I'm going.'

'And why would *the girls* tell me? What do they have to do with it?'

Rayan hesitated, said nothing, just looked at Eva steadily.

'Rayan?'

'Because I'd very much like Laila and Nora to meet her soon.'

'No way! No way, Rayan, is some other woman having anything to do with my girls.'

'Jodie, I did ask you to get here early.' After a sleepless night, Eva had found herself downstairs in the kitchen at 5am, sorting washing, cleaning the fridge, hunting for Laila's lost library book; anything to take away the picture of Rayan with another woman while Laila and Nora smiled on adoringly. No way was this happening.

'Sorry, Boss.' Jodie went to fill the kettle. 'Hell, I need coffee; had a bit of a wing-dinger of a night.'

'On a Sunday?' Eva asked disapprovingly. 'When you had work the next morning?'

'You never had a session the night before you were in the surgery pulling teeth?' Jodie looked across at Eva as she spooned coffee into the machine.

'I most certainly have never gone to work smelling of booze. We have standards to maintain as dentists. As do *you*, as nanny to my children, Jodie.'

'Who mentioned booze?' Jodie grinned. 'I had one small glass of wine just to break the ice.'

'The ice?'

'Hot date.'

'What happened to the *bastard no-hoper drongo*? Who, incidentally, Laila overheard you talking about. She stored it up to insult the kid she sits next to at school with.'

'*No!*' Jodie's eyes danced with merriment and, not for the first time, Eva realised it was probably a good thing her nanny would soon be heading back to Sydney. Having said that, the girls loved her and Eva dreaded the idea of starting all over again looking for another. 'Good for her.'

'Good for her? Jodie, *I* have to go and pick up the pieces once she's come out with stuff like this to another seven-year-old. Just be careful, will you? You know, what you're saying on the phone? Who's listening?'

'No problem, Boss.' Jodie moved to the adjacent utility room, emptying the washing machine, feeding in another load, hunting for pegs. Eva knew, despite her predilection for discussing – and dissing – her many men on the phone to other nannies in the area, Jodie was a jolly good, competent nanny and her being ten minutes late was no excuse for Eva taking her own misery out on her.

'Sorry,' Eva apologised as Jodie came back into the kitchen

with a basketful of wet washing and a still-pyjamaed Nora in tow. 'I didn't mean to imply you came to work drunk.'

'Well, you probably *did*.' Jodie, never one to bear a grudge, grinned once more. 'But *you* know, as *I* know, I never have. So, it's obviously something else that's getting to you?' When Eva didn't speak – didn't trust herself to speak – but, instead poured herself yet another cup of coffee, Jodie went on, 'Rayan?'

Eva nodded and then warned, 'Shhh,' as Laila walked into the kitchen, hair unbrushed, eyes full of sleep, her arms wrapped round Wolfie Wolf, the cuddly fox she'd refused to be parted from when she was tiny, but which had been disdainfully abandoned for more grown-up toys years ago.

'Wolfie Wolf?' Eva asked gently. 'I've not seen him for a while.'

'Don't want to go to school,' Laila muttered. 'Want to stay here with you and Wolfie.'

Heavens, Eva thought, now she's even talking like a two-year-old. 'Laila, is it OK if Jodie takes you to school because I've a meeting up at the hall…' Eva glanced at the clock '…in exactly an hour and a half.'

'But you said you'd take me. And come with me to see Miss Worthington. Want *you* to take me,' Laila said mulishly.

Images of another woman – this new woman of Rayan's – escorting a smiling Laila into school, bending down and hugging her daughter, handing her home-made cookies (when was the last time that she, Eva, had baked with her girls?) had Eva making rapid calculations and new decisions.

'No problem, Laila. You go upstairs, wash your face properly and clean your teeth and then I'll come up and plait your hair. Breakfast, yes? And *I'll* take you into school.'

'You'll be late for your meeting,' Jodie warned.

'So be it,' Eva breathed. 'There's more important things at stake here. And, girls, how about we bake this evening?'

'Kahk?' Laila asked excitedly.

'Kahk!' Nora shouted, joining in and jumping up and down, her pyjama bottoms falling and hiding her bare feet.

'Kahk?' Eva and Jodie shrugged shoulders at each other.

'Eid cake. Eid cookies,' the girls chorused as one.

'Well alright, girls,' Eva said, a rictus of a smile on her face. 'Absolutely we'll do that. But how about a nice Victoria sponge, as well? OK, Laila, half an hour and we're off.'

'Which one's Florence?' Eva asked as she escorted Laila across the playground towards her classroom. She'd made the decision to accompany Laila all the way in, and have a word with the class teacher, Miss Worthington, now, as well as during the meeting with the head later that morning.

'I don't think she's here yet,' Laila said, her eyes scanning the sea of kids in the yard. 'Will you come in to see Miss Worthington and tell her not to be cross with me anymore?'

'I am doing,' Eva said grimly, her hand in Laila's. 'Come on.'

'Hello, Laila. Hello, Mrs Malik?' The teacher's voice was questioning. She looked up from the display she was attending to and smiled in their direction.

'I know we have a meeting with Mrs Beresford later on this morning, but I just wanted to come in and have a quick chat now?' Eva returned the smile. There was absolutely no point in her coming in all guns blazing – after all, it was *her* daughter, Laila, who'd attempted ABH on this Florence girl. 'The thing is, Miss Worthington, Laila has got herself into a bit of a state and didn't want to come to school this morning. She knows she's in trouble.'

'Laila, we have talked about this, haven't we?' Miss Worthington patted Laila's head and Laila visibly melted. Just about eating out of the teacher's hand, Eva could see. Was that what she needed to do, Eva thought? Pat Laila's head when she was being obstreperous at home? The teacher glanced towards Eva. 'Why don't you pop over to the reading corner and make yourself comfy? Put your feet up and enjoy sitting down and reading all by yourself?'

For a split second, Eva thought the teacher was talking to her instead of Laila. Oh, the bliss of lying down in the reading corner on the beanbags and losing herself in a good book; not having to think about her shattered marriage; Rayan with another woman; going off to Paris to come face to face with the man who was actually her birth father, when she missed Bill Astley so much.

Laila trotted off obediently and Eva was relieved to see her daughter reach for headphones and an audio book. Golly, the wonders of modern classrooms: in her day here, there was a chalk-covered blackboard and a metal cage holding the kids' black rubber-smelling pumps. And that was about it. Eva turned back to the teacher. She was young – must only have been in her mid-twenties – with swishy blonde hair, a full mouth and huge grey eyes. *I bet there's never any lack of fathers sitting in front of* her *at parents' evening*, Eva thought, feeling old, tired and sort of bashed about. It had been a long time since she'd looked as young, energetic and dewy as this lovely teacher in front of her. No wonder Laila was in love with her, reluctant to come to school this morning because this classroom goddess had been so cross with her before the weekend.

Eva found herself sitting on a tiny red plastic chair in front of the teacher and wanting to cry. 'The thing is, Miss Worthington, Laila's father and I are in the process of a trial separation.' Would she be saying *a permanent separation* in a few weeks' time? *Divorcing*, after that? Eva swallowed and found she could go no further. The teacher pushed a box of tissues towards her, but Eva waved them away. She was Eva Quinn, the strong, bolshie triplet: she'd never cried when she was a pupil here herself and often in trouble. She wasn't about to start now.

Eva cleared her throat, sniffed, and said, 'I think what's happening at home is probably influencing Laila's behaviour here at school.'

'Of course, and we are very much mindful of that.'

'I don't know if you're also aware, but the reason Laila launched at Florence – and I'm really not one of those mothers who think their child can do no wrong: I know Laila is more than capable of giving out as much as she gets – was that she was being called…' Eva lowered her voice '…a half-caste; that her daddy is a black man…'

'I *am* aware of that, Mrs Malik, and that is why Mrs Beresford is handling this. We don't tolerate *any* racial slurs here at Little Acorns.' Miss Worthington was obviously very proud of the fact. She smiled benignly but then hesitated. 'Apparently, the victim here…'

'The *victim*?'

'The *casualty*,' Miss Worthington amended, 'retaliated with this after Laila told Florence her father was…' she hesitated once more, lowered her voice '…a horrid frog.'

'I'm sorry?' Eva stared.

'A horrid frog.' Miss Worthington whispered the words in the way Eva remembered her Granny Glenys talking about anything remotely gynaecological, and Eva wanted to laugh.

'And is he?' Eva had to swallow a titter.

'Is he what?' There was no sign of humour on the young teacher's earnest face and Eva immediately realised she and this young professional were poles apart. Miss Worthington relented slightly. 'Florence's father is a Parisian and she is *very* proud of the fact; enjoys sharing with the class the many French words that she knows…'

I bet she does, the little show-off, Eva thought.

'You know: *Je m'appelle; Quelle heure-est-il?*' The teacher smiled, almost dreamily, obviously recalling previous conversations with Florence McLean *en français*, and Eva began to glean Miss Worthington might not be the unbiased referee she'd first imagined her to be. 'Where Laila has learned the stereotypical racist slur that is sometimes applied to the

French…' of course, Eva thought as Miss Worthington hesitated, unwilling – or unable – to repeat the insult; weren't all kids in their twenties *woke*? '…you know… is anyone's guess.' The teacher glanced slightly accusingly in Eva's direction and Eva came out fighting.

'Miss Worthington, I'd never even *heard* of Florence McLean until the end of last week. And, as such, was certainly not aware her father was French. And, if I *had* been made aware of her French heritage, I most certainly would not be bandying it around as a racist insult. Especially as…' Eva found her heart pounding and heard herself telling herself to *shut it, Eva, while you can* '…my own birth father is a Parisian.'

Miss Worthington frowned. 'I didn't realise the previous Marquess of Stratton was French.'

'Bill Astley isn't – wasn't – *French*,' Eva managed to get out through gritted teeth.

'Right. OK.' Miss Worthington frowned, totally lost. She glanced at her wristwatch, obviously wanting Eva gone: children were lining up outside the classroom. 'The thing is, Mrs Malik, I know Mrs Beresford was a little concerned that any bad feeling between yourself and Mrs McLean might have spilled over and been taken out on Florence by Laila.'

'Bad feeling?' Eva shook her head. 'Between myself and Florence's mother?'

'You know, with… you know…'

'With what?' Eva demanded and the teacher went very pink, her pretty face suffused with embarrassment.

'Well, you know… with Laila's daddy involved with Florence's mummy?'

'This Melissa McLean woman is having an affair with *my husband*? *She's* the one?' Eva stood in fury. Then, remembering Laila at the back of the room who, seeing the other children with their noses pressed against the window separating the corridor from the Y2 classroom, was replacing the headphones neatly,

Eva knew she needed to be calm. 'Laila, sweetie, the bell's gone. All is OK. Miss Worthington isn't *a bit* cross anymore. I'll see you this afternoon.'

With that, Eva Malik kissed her daughter, left the classroom and, scattering kids and teachers alike, strode across the schoolyard, the busy main road and into Malik and Malik Dental Surgery.

19

'Oh, brilliant, Eva, you're here.' Tamsin, one of the growing fleet of receptionists and nurses needed to man the seemingly ever-expanding village surgery, looked up as Eva marched meaningfully into the beautifully decorated reception area of Malik and Malik. A much-coveted George Smith sofa, a rack of bang-up-to-date glossy magazines and an upmarket coffee machine stood between herself and the main reception desk where Tamsin, dressed in the surgery's green and gold livery, was now replacing the phone. 'Mrs Williams is waiting for you.'

'Here? Waiting for *me*? It's not Wednesday or Thursday, is it?' There was so much stuff buzzing round her brain at the moment that if Tamsin had told her, it was *Christmas* Day, Eva wouldn't have felt able to argue the toss.

'I assumed you'd got the message? Rayan has had to dash off.'

'Dash off? Where to?'

'Dunno, he didn't say. Just asked me – *told* me – to ring you and get you in. Sam has taken Rayan's first two appointments, but he's got a hell of a list himself.' Tamsin indicated with her pen the number of patients waiting – some of them not so patiently – in the waiting area. And, I don't know what's matter with him, but he's in a foul temper. We're seeing a quite different side to him at the moment.'

'Who? Rayan?'

'No, *Sam*. Rayan just seemed a bit not quite with it. Actually, a lot not with it when I think about it. Other things on his mind. Didn't say where he was going. Not convinced I'd have been happy with his drill in *my* mouth today,' she added and then laughed. 'Good job he's not got a Botox clinic today: he'd have ended up *drilling* the stuff into women's foreheads thinking he was filling a back molar rather than the wrinkles of women-with-more-money-than-sense…'

'Tamsin!' Eva lowered her voice and glared across the desk at the receptionist who was now in full throttle. 'D'you mind?' She turned her back on the patients behind her who, obviously bored and frustrated with their wait, began to prick up their ears and look with interest in their direction. 'Patient files please.'

'Already up in Rayan's surgery,' Tamsin said sulkily, affronted at being called out in front of clients. 'Ellie's waiting for you up there.'

Well, that was a blessing, Eva thought, smiling in what she hoped was a winning, if not totally placatory, manner at the waiting patients: Ellie was one of their best dental nurses. 'Sorry to keep you all waiting,' she trilled, her professional head replacing the angry wife head she'd been wearing since leaving Laila's classroom. She *was* a professional, she reminded herself; half of Malik and Malik Dental Surgeons and with a reputation to uphold. The last thing she wanted was either their NHS or private patients writing bad reviews on the surgery website.

Eva hurried up to Rayan's spacious modern consulting room in the new extension of what had previously been the former Freeman, Hardy and Willis shoe shop, grabbing freshly laundered scrubs en route and, after a quick consultation with Ellie, called for Rayan's first patient. She'd have preferred to be in her own little consulting room where she knew just where everything was, but she had a job to do. She *was* a professional she reminded herself once more and, five minutes later, was preparing the elderly woman for a root canal, talking her through the process and reassuring her as to the procedure as well as the outcome.

'Any idea where Rayan had to go?' Eva asked Ellie after they'd dealt with the root canal, four inspections and a filling and were having a ten-minute break. Mrs Williams' root canal – always a tricky procedure – had taken a lot longer than anticipated and, glancing at her watch, she saw it was now going on eleven. She felt the caffeine hit from the strong black coffee Tamsin had brought them reach her brain – no time, Tamsin had warned, still slightly sullen at Eva's earlier reproach of her, to retire to the rest room – and realised she'd totally missed the meeting Hannah had called up at Heatherly Hall. Damn it: she'd so wanted to be there to support Hannah, and just hoped Rosa had been able to make it.

'No, I'm afraid I don't know where he suddenly had to go,' Ellie replied sipping daintily at her coffee. 'One minute we were preparing the surgery for Mrs W's endodontic procedure—' *alright, Ellie, you don't need to impress me with the correct terminology*, Eva thought irritably 'and the next he was off, pulling off his scrubs and telling Tamsin to ring you to take over.'

'Right.' Eva suddenly had a thought. 'It wasn't Nora, was it?'

'Nora?'

'Well, I was with Laila across at Little Acorns and I know *she* was OK.' Had she been OK, though, once she, Eva, had left Laila to face Miss Worthington and Mrs Beresford alone?

'No, he didn't say anything about Nora…'

'Oh *hell*,' Eva interrupted, glancing at her wristwatch and putting the mug of coffee down too quickly and spilling much of its contents down her scrubs. 'I've a meeting with Mrs Beresford in five minutes.'

'Mrs Beresford?'

'Head teacher.'

'Ooh, you'll have a ruler across your knuckles,' Ellie said, eyes wide.

'Shit.' Eva looked at the clock once more with a wild look. Which to deal with next: her unhappy eldest child? Her sisters up at Heatherly Hall? Her errant husband? Sorting out this Melissa McLean woman who was not only having an affair with her husband, but whose daughter was racially abusing Laila? Or Mr Wood's back molar?

'Ellie, go down to reception and tell Tamsin to ring Little Acorns and send apologies; I'll be ten minutes late.' Eva ran a feverish hand through her hair. 'Sam will just have to take over Rayan's list while I run over there... Oh... Sam?' Spotting Sam Burrows through the open consulting room door as he walked back to his own room, she dashed over towards him.

'Sam, I've *got* to go back across to the school. Got a meeting with the head,' Eva gabbled. 'Can you just fit in a couple from Rayan's list while I run over there?'

'No, I can't.'

'Sam, I'm not asking,' Eva said crossly, 'I'm *telling* you. I'm one half of Malik and Malik and...'

'Presumably for not much longer,' Sam interrupted, obviously put out that Eva was pulling rank.

'I beg your pardon?'

Sam shrugged and put up two hands but said nothing further.

'Do *you* know where Rayan's gone?' Eva demanded.

Sam remained silent but raised an eyebrow in her direction. A condescending, somewhat arrogant eyebrow, Eva would later relate to Rosa.

'You *do* know, don't you? He's having a thing with Melissa McLean, isn't he?'

'Melissa McLean?'

Ellie's head moved perceptibly from Sam and back to Eva as though she were watching finalists thrashing it out on centre court at Wimbledon.

'Ah, is that who it is?' Sam went on, leaning against the open door, arms now folded, a knowing smile on his face. 'Well, *she* doesn't half get around. She was with Rosa's ex on Saturday night. Well, well, well...'

'So, you knew?'

'I knew he was seeing *someone*. Been seeing someone for quite a while from what I can make out.'

'And you never thought to tell Rosa? So she could tell *me*?' Eva felt her pulse race.

'Not my place.' Sam raised his hands once more.

Passive-aggressive, Eva concluded, echoing Hannah's verdict of the man now standing in front of her with a sardonic smile on his handsome face.

Ellie's well-exercised neck muscles swivelled back to Eva who, instead of replying, was rummaging in her bag for her lipstick. No way was she about to have a meeting with the head teacher and this McLean woman without her Crimson Dawn in place: a girl had to uphold some standards in the face of adversity.

'Is owt 'appening up 'ere?' a voice from behind Sam asked crossly. 'This tooth of mine's hurting to buggery and I want one of you lot to tek it out. Can't stand t'pain much longer.'

'Ah, Mr Wood?' Eva said kindly, rubbing her newly painted lips together. 'Sorry to keep you waiting. My colleague here,' Eva indicated, with a nod, Sam, who was now glaring in her direction, 'will deal with that tooth of yours.'

She swept down the stairs and into reception, calling out to Tamsin as she went. 'Will be back in twenty minutes – have to go – emergency…' and made to exit by the front door before the receptionist could argue.

'First Rayan and now Eva,' Eva heard the junior receptionist say in hushed undertones to Tamsin. 'Do you reckon someone's died? Someone been told they've got cancer? You know, only a few months to live?' There was a thrilled excitement in the young girl's voice.

'Someone's been told *someone else* is up to no good,' Tamsin replied drily as Eva let the door close behind her. 'Mrs Washington-Brown? On your marks, love, it'll be you in ten minutes.'

'Just a moment, Mrs Malik, I'll see if Mrs Beresford's ready for you now.' Jean Barlow, school secretary at Little Acorns, pressed a button. 'She's actually got Mrs McLean…'

'Fine, fine, it's fine, I'll go straight in, she's expecting me.' Eva moved to the head's office door.'

'Yes, but if you just…'

Eva knocked sharply, opened the door and went straight in.

'Ah, sorry, I was just having a chat with Mrs McLean here first…' Cassie Beresford stood as Eva marched in. 'Maybe if you…'

'Apologies for my tardiness.' The smile plastered on Eva's Crimson Dawn lips was saccharin sweet. 'As you can see,' Eva indicated her coffee-stained scrubs and pulled a hand through her hair, 'I'm up to my ears in root canals, fillings… and… and coffee…'

'You seem a bit frazzled. Would you like more coffee? A glass of water…?'

'What I *would* like, Mrs Beresford, is to know how long, exactly, Florence's mother here, has been having an affair with my husband?' Eva turned to the strikingly attractive woman seated to the left of the head teacher, taking in the short cropped (very French) blonde hair, the endlessly long bare and tanned legs (it was only the end of May, for heaven's sake) crossed neatly at slim ankles and ending in stylish trainers, the elegantly up-to-the-minute short skirt and obviously expensive shirt.

'You're Joe's wife?' Melissa McLean blanched slightly but immediately regained her composure, standing to offer a slim tanned hand in Eva's direction which Eva ignored. 'I thought you were in Australia?' She stared at Eva. 'I didn't think you were a dentist either?' She glanced across at Cassie Beresford for help. 'I thought we were waiting for Laila's mummy…?'

'I *am* Laila's *mummy*,' Eva snapped, any pretence at a smile now gone into the ether. 'And I'd like to know why you think you can have an affair with Laila's *daddy*?'

'Joe is Laila's father? I didn't know that.' Melissa McLean looked shocked. 'Goodness, this *is* small-town goings-on. I might have expected it living in Paris, but here? In a Yorkshire backwater? Mind you, I sometimes think you lot are all interbred…'

'…I believe the correct term, Mrs McLean, is *consanguinity…*' Cassie Beresford attempted to put in, but was beaten back by the other woman, obviously on a roll.

'…interbred,' Melissa repeated. 'I can quite imagine some of you in this village have never even been as far as Sheffield or… or even *Halifax*.'

'I'm not talking about Joe *Rosavina*.' Eva spat the words. 'Although, what you've just said is confirmation that you're knocking off my sister's ex as well as my husband.'

'*Knocking off*? I can assure you, I'm not in the habit of *knocking* anyone *off*…'

'One man not sufficient for you?' Eva sneered. 'It's obviously *de rigueur* to have two lovers? Hmm, Hmm? Very French…' Eva thought she might actually explode, unable to clear, or even navigate through, the red mist that had descended in front of her eyes, and through which, although she was fully aware she was embarrassing herself, she couldn't stop herself from blundering like an out-of-control carthorse.

'Mrs Malik,' Cassandra Beresford pleaded, putting a consoling hand on to Eva's (coffee-stained) arm. 'Can you try to calm down? Just for a moment?'

'I think it fairly obvious where Laila gets her anger issues?' Melissa McLean turned away from Eva towards the head teacher and Eva saw that the woman did indeed have the squeakily clean neck Hannah had described. She turned back to Eva. 'And why on earth you think I'm having some sort of *aventure*, some *liaison…*' both words said in a perfect French accent '…with your husband, Mrs Malik, I really have no idea.'

'Oh, Oh?' Eva began to actually see through the red mist, but it was still there. 'Are you trying to say you *wouldn't* have an affair with my husband then? And, is that because he's *a black man*, Mrs McLean?'

'No, Mrs Malik, it's because I've never met your husband and, as such, wouldn't know *what* colour or heritage he was.'

'I'm sure you know which is my daughter and, as such, are *exactly* aware of my husband's heritage. Derogatory, racist remarks – *half-caste* – have been bandied around by your daughter.'

'*Slimy frog* used to describe *Florence's* father?' Melissa McLean came straight back at Eva. 'Just as derogatory? Just as racist?'

'Mrs McLean, Mrs Malik!' Cassie Beresford, red-faced and obviously extremely embarrassed, came between the two. 'Please calm down. This is my *office*, not *The Jeremy Kyle Show*.' The head teacher pulled a hand across her forehead. 'The thing is…' she hesitated '…there's been gossip…'

'Gossip?' Eva and Melissa McLean spoke as one.

'Gossip in the staffroom.' Cassie Beresford was now scarlet. 'And, I'm ashamed to say, I listened to it.'

'And the gossip?' Again, the two other women spoke in unison.

The head teacher hesitated once more. 'That Mrs McLean here was involved with one of the Quinn triplet's exes. I knew nothing about our village vicar's previous relationship with Mr Rosavina; only knew that you, Mrs Malik, after writing to inform us of the fact, were no longer with your husband.'

'And you put two and two together, Mrs Beresford,' Eva said softly, 'and came up with five?'

'I can only apologise for getting the wrong end of the stick.'

'Well,' Eva sniffed, 'if your own maths is so bad, Mrs Beresford, I worry for your pupils' SATs results in a couple of months' time.'

Cassie Beresford continued to shake her head in acute embarrassment. 'I can only apologise profusely to both you ladies about my error of judgement in this matter.' Then, appearing to pull herself together, she went on, addressing Melissa McLean: 'As Florence and Laila appear to be constantly at loggerheads at the moment, I assumed it was because of a perceived relationship between yourself, Mrs McLean, and *Mr* Malik. As such, I felt

Miss Worthington, as Laila's and Florence's teacher, should be made aware of the facts. It was passed on purely in your daughters' interests. I hope you will both accept mine and the school's apologies and I can quite understand that, if either of you feel you need to take the matter further, I will inform our chair of governors.'

'David Henderson, I believe?' Eva raised an eyebrow. She was experiencing such relief that this woman, this Melissa McLean, wasn't going to end up as Laila and Nora's stepmother after all, that she was prepared to be magnanimous. 'I have no desire to take this any further, Mrs Beresford. I certainly don't want uncorroborated tittle-tattle about my personal life flying round the school and the village. Mrs McLean?'

'At the end of the day we're here this morning to discuss the girls' behaviour, I believe, not ours? We've not even discussed the potential plait-cutting-off incident…' The raucous clanging of the school dinner bell finished the sentence for her and Melissa McLean smiled slightly in Eva's direction.

Eva gave a barely imperceptible smile back, wondering if it wouldn't be out of order to ask just where that skirt and top the other woman was wearing with such *élan* actually came from.

'Look, shall we try and draw a line under all this? Miss Worthington and I have spoken to both your girls, separately and together.' Cassie Beresford, a relieved smile on her face, nodded towards the window where children were streaming onto the playground for their lunchtime break, and Eva and Melissa McLean turned together to where she was looking. Laila Malik and Florence McLean were walking across the yard together, arms wrapped around each other, laughing and giggling in unison with one another while a little band of lesser mortals followed hopefully in their wake.

Hurrying back across the school playground and then the busy main road through the village towards Malik and Malik, Eva felt the start of a headache. She really was going to have to try to be a little more restrained, keep herself a bit calmer about what was happening in her life if she wasn't going to end up blowing a gasket. Neither Rosa nor Hannah would ever have just barged their way into the head's office when there was already a meeting underway; would never have lost their temper and accused another woman of having an affair with their husband. If they'd had one: but wasn't that the whole point? – those two had never *had* husbands; didn't have two little girls to protect from a broken home; from becoming a dysfunctional family.

When Joe Rosavina had confessed to Rosa that he'd had a drunken one-night stand with Rosa's best friend and PA, Carys Powell, when they were living and working in London, Rosa hadn't taken a kitchen knife to either of them, hadn't ripped Joe's suits from their hangers in that fabulous apartment in Wandsworth or emptied his wine collection down the sink. Rosa, completely broken and distressed, especially as she'd just been diagnosed with Stage Two Hodgkin's lymphoma, had simply packed a few things and come home to Susan and Richard, to Bill, Hannah and herself. Back home to Westenbury and to those who loved her.

Not that Eva believed Joe Rosavina had ever stopped loving Rosa. She, Eva, might have ranted and raved at what Joe had done to Rosa when he'd had too much to drink and been seduced, yes, seduced – Carys Powell, whom they'd all adored and been taken in by, had the capacity to seduce the birds from the trees – but she'd never for one minute thought he'd ever stopped loving Rosa. Funny how they'd all gone their separate ways but, like spawning salmon using all their energy to return to their home stream, were all now back here in Westenbury village. Strange too that, despite their children being at the same village school, she and Joe Rosavina had not bumped into each other on the school playground or at school events. Which was probably her fault, letting Jodie or Susan and Richard take and pick up Laila from Little Acorns.

Bad mother.

I need to calm down, she censured herself; *need to be more of a hands-on mother, need to take a leaf out of Rosa's book*. It must be this birth father of hers, Yves Dufort, from whom she'd received more than her fair share of some anger gene: the need to fly off the handle and explode with fury when faced with anything she seemed unable to cope with.

All these thoughts were whizzing manically through Eva's head as she used her lanyard to re-enter Malik and Malik from the back garden of the surgery rather than through the front door. Rayan's car was still not in its usual parking spot and Eva made the decision to be more adult, more proactive in all this. Instead of spending the afternoon on her own artwork – she was desperate to get back to the canvas she was working on – and sorting out her ideas for the new art retreat about which she'd promised both Hannah and the management committee she'd address them at the next meeting (now missed) at Heatherly Hall, she'd stay here at the surgery where she was needed. She'd stay here until Rayan returned from wherever he'd rushed off to, and then become that hands-on mother she'd failed to be, and go back to school at the end of the school day to pick up Laila herself.

Once she'd found out where Rayan had been of course. And with whom.

20

While Eva was divesting herself of the coffee-stained scrubs, exchanging them for a clean pair before making her way back to Rayan's consulting room, Rosa and Hannah were still buzzing from the morning's meeting that had gone on for hours, and from which they were now released.

'That went really well, Hannah. You're getting so good at chairing these meetings.'

They were sitting outside Tea and Cake in the late May sunshine having treated themselves to coffee and Eccles cakes from the hall's cafe rather than a mug of instant and a custard cream back up in the flat. For a Monday lunchtime, the place was gratifyingly busy and Hannah had suggested the two of them shouldn't sit at the umbrellaed table Rosa had found but move to sit on the grass to free up space for paying customers.

'Not sure whether to take that as a compliment or not.' Hannah frowned. 'If you reckon I'm *getting better* at handling Lachlan and the rest of them, then I must have been pretty rubbish to begin with, when I first took over.'

'Of course, you're getting better.' Rosa smiled, taking a bite of the cake and closing her eyes against the deliciousness of its flaking pastry and juicy currants. 'And yes, no one is saying it was easy to begin with. But honestly, you've only been doing this these five months or so and you were thrown right into the lion's den without any experience of taking meetings, or how to handle bolshie hecklers – and there's always at least one – determined to have a say and put a spanner in the works.'

'I don't think we should be selling Eccles cakes,' Hannah mused, pulling out a couple of raisins and nibbling them before pushing her plate in Rosa's direction. 'Eccles is in Lancashire, not Yorkshire.'

'Is that the reason you're not eating it?' Rosa laughed, stuffing the last glorious piece of her own bun into her mouth while eyeing the almost untouched one of Hannah's. 'Or just not hungry?'

Hannah shook her head.

'Ben?'

'Of course, Ben.' Hannah sighed. 'I really loved him, Rosa.'

'He's not worth losing your appetite over.' Rosa patted Hannah's hand. 'And you know that.'

'Of course I know that,' Hannah said crossly. 'But that doesn't make how I'm feeling any better. Probably worse, really. I've been such an idiot.'

'Learn from it and move on.'

'I was telling Eva, yesterday,' Hannah said, 'that all I'm bothered about now is *this place*. I want to put it on the map: want it to be the place to visit, put it up there with Chatsworth and Castle Howard. I'm already thinking about Christmas.'

'You'll have to be.' Rosa smiled. 'Can I have that bun if you're not eating it?' She took a bite from the pastry, wiped her mouth and sticky fingers on the paper napkin and went on. 'You have to be well ahead with your seasonal plans: you know, Christmas in spring? Summer in January? That's how it works or you miss the boat.'

'I realise that now.'

'And Lachlan was pretty much on board with all your suggestions today, don't you think? He was practically purring when you said you wanted to bring Tiffany across from managing the wedding venue to being your deputy and working with you.'

'Must have a thing about her,' Hannah said almost sourly.

'Well, she's certainly got a thing about *him*.' Rosa laughed. 'Once it was all agreed and you went across to the wedding venue to ask her to join us at the meeting, she couldn't keep her eyes off him.'

'Don't know what she sees in him.' Hannah pulled a face.

'Oh, come off it, Hannah. Six foot two with that gorgeous auburn hair and brown eyes? And that wonderful Scottish burr?' Rosa uttered a most unvicarly *phwoarr* before taking another bite of Hannah's Eccles cake.

'Fancy him yourself, do you?' Hannah felt cross for some reason. 'You seem pretty perky this morning? Considering you saw Joe Rosavina with his new woman on Saturday? And you appear to have blown Sam into touch. Have you? Did you?'

Rosa nodded sadly. 'It wasn't working. I didn't want what he wanted.' She paused and frowned. 'No, that's not true; I did want what he wanted. *Do* want it.' Rosa's face fell and she pushed away the cake. 'Sorry, God: *thou shalt not pig out on thy sister's unwanted bun*.'

'That the eleventh commandment?' Hannah laughed and Rosa was pleased to see some sort of humour return to her sister's face.

'Probably.'

'So, you did want, *do want*, what Sam also wants, but just not with him?'

'Yep.'

'Have to say, I saw a very different side to Sam Burrows on Saturday night.' Hannah pulled a scary face.

'Didn't think you were capable of taking note of *anything* on Saturday night.' Rosa pulled her own face and they both chortled, almost evilly, remembering the tasteless monstrosity of a ring disappearing down behind Daisy's toilet.

'Hell, Rosa, I hadn't half knocked some back, even before we got to Daisy's place. Anyway, as I told Eva yesterday, I'm totally not drinking anymore. For the moment anyway. Ben and I had got into the habit of drinking at least a bottle of wine a night with our meal. And sometimes not even with a meal. I never used to drink so much, until I met him.'

'Don't they say doctors and consultants drink more than average? You know, because of the stress? Can you imagine how stressed and pressurised Ben must have been every time he was faced with opening up another head and examining yet another brain? The responsibility of playing God? You know, deciding who will live and who he has to close back up, knowing there's nothing he can do to help?' Rosa pulled a face. 'No wonder a swift gin and tonic's a welcome relief from all that.'

'Or sex with other women?' Hannah raised an eyebrow. 'You're not defending Ben Pennington, are you?'

'No, not defending. Maybe just understanding.' Rosa smiled and fingered her dog collar.

'For me, the glass of wine helped blur the edges when, even though Ben had moved into the flat with me, I still couldn't totally relax and trust him.'

'Really?' Rosa looked at Hannah in surprise. 'I thought once he'd left Alexandra, you felt pretty sure of him? Felt he'd left his wife and children for you?'

'I'm fairly certain he left his wife and children only because Alexandra had seen the light and actually thrown him out. Probably the reason I was drinking so much was, as I say, to blur the edges of knowing that he was with me because he didn't have a home to go back to.'

'I'm sorry, Hannah. I didn't realise.'

'So, you and me, Rosie Posie, are footloose and fancy free as we begin to approach our fortieth birthdays.'

'Bit scary that, isn't it?' Rosa tried to smile. 'You know, time running out…'

'Running out? Rosa, we're thirty-eight, not eighty-eight.'

'I know, I know, but you know…?'

'Those frozen eggs of yours?' It was Hannah's turn to comfort and then, to cheer Rosa up, added, 'When was the last time the three of us went away together? Now I know I can leave some of this Heatherly Hall stuff to Tiffany, I'm really looking forward to it all.'

'I'm not convinced Eva is,' Rosa said frowning. 'In fact, I reckon she'll do anything to get out of it.'

'Even though we're all booked and it was her idea in the first place to go over to Paris to meet up with Yves Dufort?' Hannah shook her head. 'Even though Alice has actually done all the groundwork and apparently prepared him to meet his new daughter?'

'She's frightened of coming face to face, after all these years, with the man who fathered her. You can understand that, Hannah, can't you?'

'No, I don't see why, to be honest. Richard's our dad and always has been. This Yves Dufort's rogue sperm just got in the way of Bill's, and Eva was the result. And,' Hannah went on, 'to be honest, I think she needs some time away from Rayan.'

'Really?' Rosa frowned. 'I think you're being somewhat cavalier about all this, Hans. If I was meeting up with the man I'd only just been told had fathered me, I'd be feeling exactly the same. And, as regards Rayan, I'd have thought she needed to spend *more* time with him. Sort out her marriage; work out what's broken, *why* it's broken and attempt to mend it.'

'Maybe. Right,' Hannah said, standing, 'got a ton of stuff to do, including sorting out Tiffany's new job description and what we're going to be paying her. If she's going to be my deputy, I need to sort the package out with Elspeth.'

'Elspeth as in personnel?'

Hannah laughed at that. 'Elspeth as in "*I do everything round here and need more help to run this bloody HR department.*"' Hannah did an excellent take off of Elspeth Harrington who'd been in situ in the little office, along with two part-time secretaries, next to the estate management office, seemingly for ever. 'She's probably right,' Hannah added. 'This place is getting bigger and more complicated every week.'

*

Back in the centre of Westenbury, at Malik and Malik, Eva was taking in a huge breath, expelling it in one long drawn-out sigh and glancing at the upmarket TV screen Rayan had insisted installing into his consulting room, as well as downstairs in the waiting room. Each of Rayan's patients – but particularly his private clients – was now offered a choice of radio, TV, or music piped through the Bose headphones as they gave themselves up to his ministrations. Fine, Eva thought, if it was a long-drawn-out operation such as the removal of wisdom teeth or the surgical implants for which Malik and Malik was becoming well known, but she was getting fed up of standing around while Ellie fiddled about with the technology for a simple inspection.

She was just about to put her thoughts into words and tell Ellie they needed to get on before Mrs Daniels got stuck into the past episode of *First Dates* she'd requested (thank the Lord it wasn't *Naked Attraction*) when Rayan reappeared, in scrubs and apparently ready to take over.

Concentrating on confirming the numbers reflecting the depth of Mrs Daniels' gum pockets to Ellie, Eva could only glance in Rayan's direction with raised eyebrows.

'Ah, Mrs Daniels?' Rayan was all professional bonhomie and hail-fellow-well-met. 'How are we this afternoon? Do you want me take over, Eva?'

No, Rayan, I want you to tell me where the fuck you've been and why you're now standing in front of me looking pale and terrified.

Instead, she smiled, the professional in her coming to the fore and said, 'We're nearly finished, Mrs Daniels, aren't we? You've been taking great care of these gums. Fabulous. No problem.' Eva replaced the dental probe and mirror and adjusted the chair so that Mrs Daniels shot upwards at speed. 'Oops a daisy,' she sang, a rictus of a smile on her face, 'bit of a fairground ride there. Ellie will see you out. Rayan?'

Once Ellie had followed Mrs Daniels through the door and

down the stairs, Eva closed it firmly behind her and, folding her arms, faced Rayan who was looking deathly white.

'Well?' she asked.

'Not now, Eva. I've at least six more people to see before I can leave this afternoon.'

'Yes, Rayan, *now*.'

'No, Eva, I'm telling you *no*. I'll explain when there's just the two of us.'

'You're scaring me.' Eva felt her pulse race. 'Are you ill?'

Ignoring her last question, Rayan attempted levity. 'And I've spent all this money trying to make sure, as a dentist, I'm *not* scary.'

'Maybe, but you've not succeeded as a husband.'

'Not succeeded?' Rayan glared across at Eva. 'Well, I think that just about sums up what you think of me, Eva.'

'I meant, as my husband, you're coming across as about to tell me something scary – not… not that you'd not *succeeded as a husband*.' Eva tutted, falling over her words to assure him she wasn't putting him down as she so often had in the past. 'You know what I meant, Rayan.'

'Mr Taylor, Rayan.' Ellie bobbed her head round the consulting room door. 'Are you ready?'

'I'm ready.' Rayan moved to wash his hands. 'I'll come round this evening, Eva. Once the girls are in bed. Ah, Mr Taylor? Do come in. Two tiny fillings, I believe?'

By nine o'clock that evening, Eva was pacing.

She'd picked up Laila from school, her daughter emerging, while chattering ten to the dozen, from the Victorian doorway, still wrapped round Florence McLean.

'Mummy!' Laila, who'd been expecting Jodie and Nora to be waiting for her, flew across the playground beaming. 'Mummy, Mummy, Florence says I can go for tea. Can I?'

'Well, I'm sure she doesn't mean right now, sweetie.'

'Oh, she *does*.' Laila had hopped from one foot to the other in excitement as Florence ran to the other side of the gate where the tall, willowy Melissa McLean was standing, engrossed in a phone call.

Eva had taken Laila's hand and started to make her way over, to smile and show there were no hard feelings after their meeting that morning (and maybe glean the origin of that skirt and top the other woman had been wearing) when she saw Melissa turn and, laughing, begin talking to the man who'd joined her. Eva stopped. She'd not actually seen Joe Rosavina for years. The *last thing* she wanted to do was go over and make small talk; pretend there was no fifteen-year history between Joe and Rosa, see Joe playing seemingly happy families with Melissa McLean, Florence, and Joe's daughter with Carys Powell, Chiara.

'Come on, Mummy, Come *on*.' Laila pulled at her hand but, as they approached the other four, she saw Melissa kiss Joe's cheek and, taking hold of both Florence and Chiara's hands, hurriedly cross the road, followed by a laughing Joe, attempting to keep pace with them.

Laila stopped and her little face dropped.

'Not a problem, Laila.' Eva smiled, feeling slightly foolish that they'd dashed halfway across the yard for no reason. 'Tell you what, I'll ring Florence's mummy this evening—' she'd get the number from somewhere '—and invite Florence to tea. Maybe for a sleepover at the weekend?' How could that work, she censured herself when she, herself, was heading off to Paris on Friday?

Eva had turned a slightly mollified Laila back towards the surgery where her own car was parked. For some reason, seeing Joe with Melissa McLean and the two girls had left Eva feeling ridiculously let down and, like Laila, left out.

And now, it was after 9pm, the girls were fast asleep (she'd not told them Rayan was coming round or they'd never have gone off) and she was showered, made up and dressed in the chocolate-coloured shift dress Rayan had always loved. She was even wearing heels: dark chocolate brown suede that hadn't seen the light of day since God knows when.

She started, almost guiltily for some reason, as she heard Rayan's key in the lock and moved into the hall to greet him.

'Come in,' she said softly, determined not to descend into the raucous fishwife she knew she'd often resembled in the past. She loved this man: needed to persuade him to come home where he belonged; to start afresh with her and his girls. 'Would you like a glass of wine?'

Rayan shook his head.

'Have you eaten?' she asked.

'I made a sandwich when I got home.'

'You need more than a sandwich, Rayan. Let me make you something?'

He shook his head once more. 'It's fine, really.'

'You managed to get home then? From the surgery, I mean?'

'For an hour or so. I had patients until almost seven.'

'You work too hard.'

'Thank you for covering today, Eva.'

'Why wouldn't I?' She smiled in his direction, yearning to go up to him, put her hand in his, just sit with him while he told her there was no one else and assured her that, if there was, he'd finish the relationship and come back to her and the girls. They'd find help; have counselling. As he already had done at the end of the previous year with regards his seeming inability – his not wanting – to make love to her.

'So,' Eva finally asked, when she'd returned from the kitchen with mugs of tea that, Rayan – she could tell – didn't really want. 'Where did you have to go to in such a hurry this morning? It wasn't Azra, was it?'

'No, Mum's fine as far as I know.' Rayan sipped at the hot tea, being careful not to make a slurping noise for which, so often over the years, she'd irritably called him out.

'So?'

'Leicester. '

'Leicester?'

'To see Yasmin.'

'Yasmin?' Eva's heart began to race.

'Dr Yasmin Amir, my psychosexual counsellor.'

'Oh *her*.' Relief poured over her like a warm shower. 'I never did get to know her name. So, you still have sessions with her?' Maybe this was good? It *was* good, surely? Rayan racing off to see this woman in order to sort out the problems he'd had with his wife? 'And, has it helped seeing her? Can we try again?' Eva reached for Rayan's hand and he reached for her other.

'Eva, I've been seeing Yasmin.'

'Yes, I know, Rayan. And if it helps, I'll come with you. She can see us together.'

'Eva.' Rayan's voice was firm. 'I've been *seeing* Yasmin.'

And then she understood. 'As in *seeing* her?' she whispered, trying to swallow something hard in her throat. 'And is it serious? Actually, are you allowed to have a relationship with your counsellor? Isn't it against the Hippocratic oath or something…?' She trailed off. There was such pity in Rayan's eyes. 'And why were you *rushing off*?' The fishwife was making her comeback. 'Had a surprise hard-on and needed to show the teacher how well her counselling had worked?'

'Yasmin was in hospital.'

'Hospital?' Eva saw a light at the end of her tunnel of despair: was there Hope after all? Had she escaped Pandora's box and found her way here to 16 Heath Green Gardens? A car crash maybe from which this Yasmin hadn't recovered? A suicide attempt because Rayan had attempted to break it off with her in order to come back home to herself and the girls?

'Hospital?' Eva repeated, her fists clenched in Rayan's own.

'Yasmin was rushed in at nine this morning with a suspected miscarriage.'

The woman was messing around with Rayan, her husband,

even though she was pregnant to someone else? As the penny finally dropped, Hope winked sneerily in Eva's direction before making a quick exit through the sitting room door.

'She's pregnant?'

'Yes. The pregnancy is still valid. She was able to leave the hospital.'

'And the baby is yours, Rayan?'

'Yes.'

'And are you happy about this?'

'Very.'

'Right.'

'I'm so sorry, Eva. You know you and I have been washed up for months, years even. I really need you to divorce me.'

'So, you can marry this Yasmin?'

'Yes.'

'What if I won't divorce you?'

'That's your prerogative, Eva, but I hope you will.'

'And this is the woman you want my daughters to meet and see as their stepmother? With a new brother or sister into the bargain?'

'Yes.'

'OK.' An icy calm took hold of Eva as she turned and said, 'Can you go now, Rayan, please? I need my sisters.'

21

Eva Malik was in turmoil.

Always the strong, independent, and yes, let's face it, contrary – truculent even – one of the Quinn triplets, it had always been her who led, while Rosa and Hannah followed in her wake. She was their self-appointed leader, the one who did the least work at school but came out with the best results; the first to start her periods, be almost expelled from Westenbury Comp, the first to snog a boy, have a fag, get drunk and be ill on alcopops; the first to have a joint, to lose her virginity; the first (the only one) to marry; the first to return to Westenbury, to have children.

And now she was a failure. She was being pushed aside and would have to share her beautiful, precious girls with another woman. And they'd have another sibling who had absolutely nothing to do with her – Eva. She closed her eyes against this panic-inducing realisation, leaning back against the rather upmarket blue headrest while trying desperately hard to dispel the images of Laila and Nora with their new family.

'You OK, Eva? We'll be going under the sea soon.' Rosa patted at her sister's arm. 'Can you believe we're racing along at 186 MPH?'

'The scariest bit is the thought of all those gallons of water pressing down on our heads.' Hannah pulled a face. 'What if the tunnel springs a leak? And whose idea was it to come by Eurostar rather than flying from Manchester, anyway?'

'I think you'll find it was yours, Hannah.' Eva spoke for the first time since boarding the train at St Pancras. 'You said you didn't want to get to forty and never have experienced Eurostar.'

'We should have flown,' Hannah tutted. 'At least planes don't leak and we've another two years before we hit the big 4-0.'

'We'll be a long way under the seabed.' Rosa laughed as the train began its thirty-minute journey through the actual Channel Tunnel and the Kent countryside quickly slipped from view. 'I read it's the equivalent height of 107 baguettes balanced on top of each other.'

'Is that supposed to make me feel better?' Hannah frowned. 'Actually, it's just making me feel hungry. I could murder a massive baguette full of pâté.'

'And you a supposed vegetarian?' Eva gave Hannah one of her looks.

'You're not hungry, Eva?' Rosa asked, eyes wandering down the train in search of any indication of the presence of food and drink, her own stomach rumbling. She'd actually managed to stop thinking of Joe Rosavina for a while, her thoughts instead turning to cassoulet, croque monsieur, concombre à la menthe…

'I feel sick,' Eva said, eyes closed once again.

'Understandable,' Rosa soothed. 'We'll get a good night's sleep and then be ready to collect Alice in the morning to meet up with Yves. We'll have to get Le Taxi: Mum says Alice is really struggling with her arthritis.'

Hannah flexed her fingers, looking worried. 'It's hereditary, isn't it?'

'What? Pulling at your fingers like that?' Eva was irritable.

'You're stressed, Eva,' Rosa soothed again.

'No, I'm bloody *nervous* actually,' Eva snapped. 'We're not just waltzing in, saying *bonjour*, hoovering up *boeuf bourguignon* and then waltzing back out again. We're going to be introduced to France's most famous artist who, you may recall, just also happens to be *my father*.'

'He's not your father,' Hannah said mildly. 'Dad is. *Richard* is.'

'Oh, don't start all that again, Hannah. I've come from this man's… this man's *loins*…'

'Bit biblical that, Eva.' Rosa smiled.

'Well, you should know!'

'Do you want to go home, Eva?' Hannah was getting irritable in turn. 'Because if you do, once we land… sorry, disembark…'

'Pull in?' Rosa offered.

'Once we *pull in* you can find the train back home and Rosa and me will enjoy Paris without you.' Hannah looked down the aisle. 'Could do with a drink.'

'Thought you'd sworn off the demon drink.' Eva frowned. 'No bacon or sausages, no lovely glass of wine. What's left?'

'Paris in the springtime.' Rosa sighed, remembering. 'But a glass of vino would go down very nicely while we're waiting.'

Rosa had been up, dressed and off before the other two were even awake. Excited at being back in Paris, she'd left the hotel on the Boulevard de Rochechouart, walking the steep cobbled streets right into the heart of Montmartre, breathing in the early morning French air (she didn't care what anyone said – French air had to be more exotic, more alluring, more enchanting than British air) stopping at a pavement café for coffee, happy just to sit and stare and take it all in. The bittersweet memory of being on these same streets with Joe. Once back at the hotel, she was impatient to be off out once more.

'Come on, Eva, up you get.' Rosa pulled at the duvet.

Eva scowled from its depths. 'I didn't sleep a wink. You try sharing a bed with Hannah next time: she makes funny popping noises with her mouth all night.'

'I do not make funny popping noises.' Hannah was cross. '*You* just kick out all night and hog the duvet.'

'I was merely trying to stop you *popping*.'

'This is just like being back at home with you two again.' Rosa laughed. 'Come on, get showered and dressed. Look fabulous for your new dad, Eva.' She dug out the black leather trousers and silky top Eva had brought with her and passed them in her direction. 'We need to get a move on if we're picking Alice up from her apartment before we meet Yves.'

'I never thought Alice would come back to live in Paris,' Rosa mused once they were in the taxi and driving along the Rue de Miromesnil. 'You know, after spending almost forty years in New York?'

'She's always said the damp winter air here in Europe plays havoc with her fingers.' Hannah frowned, examining her own fingers. 'Can't hold a paintbrush from October onwards, she says.'

'She's here for the spring and summer anyway,' Rosa explained. 'Wanted to get in touch with Yves Dufort again and explain his role in all this. Right, OK, she's renting a place on the Rue de Grenelle on the Left Bank.' Rosa pressed her nose against the taxi window, loving the hustle and bustle, the whole heady experience of being in the capital.

'Frog Street?' Hannah frowned. 'Sounds pretty damp *there* to me.'

'That's *grenouille*, you idiot.' Eva started to laugh. 'You were always hopeless at French.'

'Right.' Hannah was put out. 'I'll have my teeth whitened *and* some Botox for that little jibe.'

'Well, she must have made a fair penny if she's staying here,' Eva said once they were out on the pavement below the address Alice had emailed to Rosa. 'Look at these fabulous buildings. Right, this is it.' Eva led the way to the elevator in the lobby of the apartment located on the Quai de Grenelle in the 15th arrondissement. Alice was apparently on the twenty-fourth floor of the twentieth-century building and, as the elevator shot skywards, all three wondered at her choice of accommodation, considering her arthritic hips and knees.

'Girls, *my* girls.' Alice Parkes's husky New York accent, tinged with West Yorkshire, could be heard behind the closed door as the older woman appeared to fumble with the locks. 'Hang on, darlings, I'm coming.'

Alice, Eva thought, looked a hell of a lot better than when they'd last seen her, just before Christmas at Bill Astley's funeral. And since when had their birth mother ever claimed any maternal possessiveness as she appeared to be doing now? Had *she* been watching *The Railway Children* as well? The thought made her smile for the first time since Rayan had dropped his bombshell about this Yasmin woman and she glanced across at Hannah and Rosa, who seemed to be thinking exactly the same.

'You're looking well, Alice,' Rosa said as she bent to kiss and then follow the woman down a beautiful sunlit hallway and into a light and airy sitting room. 'Oh,' she cried. 'The Eiffel Tower! Right outside your window. How wonderful is that?' Rosa gazed across the cyan-green Parisian rooftops towards the iconic structure, transfixed.

'Too many bloody tourists,' Alice grumbled, lighting up a Gauloise before sucking the acrid smoke deep into her lungs.

Why was it, Rosa wondered, that stale cigarette smoke hanging around in buildings and on people's clothes and breath was so foul and yet the smell of a newly lit French cigarette had an almost erotic thrill? She was very tempted to ask for one herself, but Alice had turned to the window, frowning.

'I wouldn't have *chosen* to live up here...' she almost scowled '...but, you know, one must never look a gift *cheval* in the mouth.'

'Whose apartment is it?' Hannah asked, joining Alice at the window.

'Oh, darling, just someone I used to know in the village.'

'The village?' Hannah looked surprised. 'Westenbury?'

'Greenwich, you daft thing.' Eva grinned. 'You know, in New York?'

'Being in Paris always gives me a little *joie de vivre*,' Alice was saying as Hannah and Eva joined Rosa at the window. 'And of course, there's my connection with Yves.'

'Look, Alice, I don't wish to be cynical here...' Eva was obviously determined to be just that, and Rosa shot her a warning glance. 'But, you know, apart from an affair you had with him almost forty years ago, how well do you know Yves Dufort now?'

'Well, Eva, to be honest, apart from acknowledging his talent as an artist – and the man does have some, I concede, although what he produces isn't really up my street – I'd had little contact with him over the years. But, once the DNA tests proved you couldn't be Bill's child, that you had to be Yves', then I came straight back over to Paris after Bill's funeral and explained the situation to him.'

'Alice, I'm going to ask you this now...' Eva broke off, obviously nervous.

'Was I having sex with *anyone else*?' Alice raised an eyebrow at Eva.

'Well apart from Yves and obviously Bill Astley, then yes, that's what I need to know. Before I meet *yet another* father and find out that, after all, oh sorry, Eva, yes, there was...' Eva threw up her hands '...Pierre or Guillaume or Henri... or... or even another member of the British aristocracy thrown in for good measure?'

'Eva...' Rosa put out a warning hand.

'I can assure you, Eva darling, I never fucked Prince Charles... King Charles, I suppose he is now?'

Rosa winced at her crude words. How on earth was Alice ever Susan's sister? Or her own birth mother?

Alice relented. 'Eva, I promise you, at the time I was very much involved with Yves Dufort. We were both trying desperately to make our names in the art world. When his wife found out and came after me with that knife, I decided to hop it back to Westenbury for a few days. You know the rest of the story: I fled Dufort's bed that morning, and ended up in Bill's that same evening.' Alice laughed at the memory which segued into a bout of protracted coughing. She took a long final drag on the cigarette before grinding the tab into a saucer. 'Not that there ever was any *bed* in Bill's case. I'm afraid it was a quick – but very erotic – fu… *coupling* after being utterly seduced by Bill's own artwork up in the attics of Heatherly Hall. Bill Astley,' she went on, 'was an exceptionally gifted artist in his own right.' She smiled. 'You three girls have all come from an amazingly talented artistic gene pool.'

'And you can tell, Alice, that Eva is definitely Yves Dufort's daughter?' Hannah asked.

'Yes.' Alice stopped and stared at all three of them before resting her gaze on Eva. 'You know, when you girls came out to New York with Susan and Richard and that niece of mine…'

'Virginia?'

'Sorry, I always forget her name: want to call her Valerie, Veronica or Vera…' Alice started to laugh once more.

'Alice, that's dreadful.' Rosa felt quite put out on Virginia's behalf. 'She's your *niece*.'

'When you all came out to see me in New York,' Alice went on, ignoring Rosa and continuing to look hard at Eva, 'I knew you were different from these other two, Eva.'

'Did you? Why?' Eva looked suspicious.

'You had the most artistic flair, you were the most determined, you knew what you wanted.' Alice took Eva's face in her hands, turning it this way and that. 'Why the hell you threw it all away to become a dentist is beyond me,' she added softly.

'Right, shall we go?' Eva said, extracting herself from Alice's bony grasp, embarrassed.

*

'I'm beginning to think I don't know who I am anymore,' Eva whispered, once they were back in the taxi. 'I thought I was Bill's daughter and then I find out I'm not. I thought I was you two's full sister, and then I find out I'm only half; I wanted to be an artist, but ended up being a damned dentist; I wanted lots of lovers, but ended up married to one man at the ridiculously young age of twenty-four. I didn't want children and now I adore my two girls and wish they were here with me right now instead of with some other woman...' Eva broke off unable to go on, and Rosa and Hannah each took one of her hands. 'The thing is, I've always been confused as to who I actually am.' Eva wiped away a tear. 'And now I'm absolutely *terrified* of meeting this new father of mine...'

The taxi pulled up right in front of the Palais-Royal on the Galerie de Valois and, with much sighing and complaining from Alice, the others managed to manhandle the internationally famous artist out of the vehicle. 'Don't get old, my darlings, it takes away all the fun of life and living.'

'You're only just over seventy.' Eva frowned. 'That's no age. Mind you, Alice, you *have* lived life to the full: knocked back the gin and smoked like a chimney.'

'And had my fair share of *amour*.' Alice dug Eva in the ribs. 'Eva, I fully expect you'll be out there looking for the same, now that you're no longer shackled to one man.'

'I loved being *shackled*,' Eva hit back crossly.

'Really?' Alice gave Eva a long hard stare. 'Darling, if you say so.'

'Come on, you two.' Rosa, ever the peacemaker, took Eva's arm and was surprised to find that her sister, who was never afraid of anything, was actually shaking.

'It's all a bit much,' Eva finally got out in a stilted whisper to Rosa as Hannah and Alice led the way through the entrance of the magnificently located Palais-Royal restaurant beneath the arcades of the former royal palace. 'I'd feel a bit better if we were just meeting up in Starbucks for a quick latte and a blueberry muffin.'

Rosa laughed at that. 'Come on, look, this place is fabulous. Just remember to use your napkin and your knife and fork properly. Show this new father of yours you've been well brought up.'

A tall silver-haired man in his seventies was already seated at the white-clothed table to which the maître d' led them, and he immediately stood, kissing Alice on both cheeks before releasing her to look hard at Rosa, Hannah and Eva in turn. '*Mais, de si belles filles*,' he breathed almost reverentially. 'What beautiful girls you have, Alice.' He spoke a heavily accented, but perfect English, seemingly unable to take his eyes from Eva who, embarrassed, anxious, appeared rooted to the spot.

'*Asseyez-vous, asseyez-vous*.' Yves Dufort waved a hand towards the chairs. 'Please, sit. And please, Eva, you must sit with me.'

Rosa and Hannah exchanged glances. How the hell did this man know which of the three of them was his biological daughter? Had Alice shown him photographs? Had she subtly pointed out which was Eva as they'd walked in? They both turned to Eva who still seemed unable to speak or move, but continued to stare at the man.

'Eva?' Rosa came to her sister's rescue, pressing her down on to the vacant chair at Yves' side.

'You are my sister.' Yves smiled, patting Eva's arm once she sat beside him.

'I thought I was your *daughter*?' Eva replied, still seemingly in some sort of daze.

'You are… how you say… *the spit* of my sister, Arlette. *Mon Dieu*, you are she. I knew you as soon as you walk in, Eva.' He turned to Alice who was sitting, with an almost smug expression on her face, across from him. 'Why you keep these girls from me, Alice? Why it take almost forty years to know them? To know my own daughter?'

'Yves, darling, I've explained the circumstances.' Alice waved arthritic fingers in the direction of the hovering waiter whose toned physique and incredibly chiselled face Alice was admiring quite blatantly. 'We need a little drink to celebrate this reunion. How about absinthe?' she almost purred, stroking the waiter's arm.

'Champagne.' Yves smiled. 'It's not every day I meet my daughter for the first time.' His eyes came back to Eva, drinking in her every feature once more.

'Lovely,' Alice concurred. 'As long as you're paying, darling.'

'It never occurred to me that my daughter might look anything like me or my family, but Eva…' Yves broke off, simply staring.

'Do you have other children?' Hannah asked, trying to break the spell.

'I 'ave 'ad three wives…'

'Blimey.' Hannah was shocked. 'I don't appear to be able to get one. Husband, I mean. I'm not wanting a wife,' she added hurriedly.

Yves smiled at Hannah. 'But unfortunately, none of them want *ze bébés*. *Hélas*, I have no one.'

'*I* didn't want *ze bébés* either.' Alice cackled. 'But look what *I* ended up with!'

'You didn't *end up* with us,' Eva snapped. 'I hate to remind you, Alice, but you gave us away. And,' she went on, 'you don't think it strange, Yves, that you've had all these wives and probably lots of partners, but no other children? And yet Alice is trying to tell us that you must have fathered *me*?'

'Ah, Eva, my wives were either models or *artistes* – all very much concerned with their work, I'm afraid – and made sure, despite my wanting, indeed begging for them to come off the pill, that there would be no children. My partner now is long past child-bearing age.'

'Hmm, seems a bit fishy to me.' Eva was not to be won over. 'I'm not convinced at all about this, Alice.'

'Eva.' Alice's voice was steely. 'I can absolutely assure you that there were only ever two options for who your father might be.

You've told me that the DNA proved beyond doubt that Bill Astley was not your father. If Bill isn't, then Yves most certainly *is*.' Two spots of pink were visible in Alice's cheeks and, for the first time ever, the girls saw their birth mother begin to lose some of her customary sangfroid.

'Eva, I think this might help convince you.' Yves reached into his jacket pocket and retrieved an expensive-looking leather wallet from which he took a photograph, passing it over to Eva.

'Oh,' she said, confused. 'You had a picture of me all along? All that guff about me looking like your sister...'

'That *is* my sister, Eva. That is Arlette when she was a little younger than you are now.'

Rosa and Hannah both leaned across to look, taking in the dark-haired pretty woman seated at an easel while smiling into the camera. 'Bloody hell, Eva, that's *you*.' Hannah continued to stare repeatedly from the photo and back to Eva.

'Arlette was a very good artist in her own right,' Yves said with a smile.

'Was?' Rosa asked.

'Tragically, she died.' Yves face reflected the pain of losing a dearly beloved, only sibling. 'She was *ma jumelle*.'

'*Jumelle?*' Hannah shook her head, not understanding.

'His *twin*,' Eva confirmed, gazing at Yves.

'*C'est vrai*. Arlette was my twin. She die in a fire. She was pregnant at the time.'

Rosa put out a hand to the man as he tried to contain his emotion. 'I'm so sorry, Yves. How terrible for you.'

'She was the only woman I ever really love. You know?'

'Not even *moi*, darling?' Alice cackled once again and the others were relieved when the waiter arrived with their champagne and lunch menus.

'*Santé*. To my beautiful new daughter, Eva.' Yves raised his glass and the others – apart from Alice who had already downed her champagne in one thirsty gulp – joined in the toast. 'And to my *other daughters* as well.' He smiled across at Rosa and Hannah who, both beginning to fall under the spell of this charismatic famous artist, grinned back. 'I want to get to know you all. May this be the start of a very long and very beautiful relationship.'

22

'Now girls, we must order. We must have lovely food to celebrate.' Yves Dufort raised a questioning eye. 'The food here tries to convey emotions through flavours and textures and aromas that combine to bring nature's beauty and wonder.'

'Gosh.' Rosa grinned. She was absolutely starving, had been desperately trying to cover up her growling stomach and would have eaten anything put in front of her, including *un chien mort*. 'Said like a true artist,' she continued, while looking round in the hope that food was imminent.

'*Certainement.*' Yves patted Rosa's hand as she continued to take in the interior of the restaurant, which echoed the architecture of the exterior galleries. 'Now what would you enjoy?'

'A gin would be good,' Alice said hopefully and Yves gave her a look.

'Ah you English…'

'I think I'm American these days, darling,' Alice drawled.

In the end, while Alice drank absinthe and then went on to gin, the others shared a bottle of Guigal Condrieu, a crisp white wine from the Rhône Yves had suggested would complement the food.

'I love this place,' Yves confirmed. 'The food is quite striking. A refined cuisine with subtle Greek touches.'

'I don't think I've ever been in a Michelin-starred restaurant before,' Hannah said, wide-eyed, sipping at her wine. 'How difficult is it to get these stars?' she asked hopefully. 'Could we apply for one – or two – for Heatherly Hall?'

'It doesn't quite work like that, Hannah.' Rosa laughed. 'I'm afraid we've a long way to go with Astley's, and I didn't think a fine dining restaurant was ever on the cards for the hall?'

'You'd never compete with *Clementine*'s in the village,' Eva said shortly, shaking her head. 'And you've enough on with your pigs.'

'Pigs?' Yves looked startled. 'You have pigs, 'annah? You are farmer?' He broke off as the waiter placed a tiny dish of *feta avec herbes, Tiffanyma et oeuf* in front of them all.

'I sometimes think I am when I'm up with the pigs at 5am.' Hannah sighed. 'This looks heavenly,' she added, but her stare was one of suspicion. 'What exactly is it?'

'Sheep cheese, with Tiffanymasalata and an egg,' Yves said proudly. 'It is *exquis*.'

And it was. Rosa almost closed her eyes in ecstasy, enjoying every tiny morsel and, while Hannah, always the fussiest eater of the three of them, was somewhat more tentative, Alice happily hoovered up what was on her plate before taking her stick and pack of Gauloises outside for a smoke. Eva was quiet, draining her glass of wine but seemingly unable to eat.

'You not 'ungry, Eva?' Yves asked solicitously, patting at her hand. 'It all a bit much for you, meeting me?'

'Something like that.' Eva nodded. 'I've a lot going on in my life at the moment.'

'Oh?'

'I appear to have found my father in the same week as I've lost my husband.' Eva put down her knife and fork and, realising her napkin was linen and not paper and she certainly couldn't blow her nose on it, fumbled in her bag for a tissue.

'After we eat, Eva, you and I walk.' It was a statement rather than a question. 'Walk in the *jardins* here and you tell me all about it.'

'Oh no, you don't want to hear…'

'Eva, *cherie*, I want to know everything about you. And, Alice tell me you talented artist? Like me? Like Arlette? We talk, *oui*? Now eat – this too good not to eat.' Yves picked up Eva's fork and, for one awful moment, she thought he was going to try and feed her like a child refusing its food. Instead, he handed the fork to her, encouraging, pointing out everything on her plate, and Eva finally ate.

After a heavenly combination of *porc avec cerise, oignon et moutarde*, was set before them ('Is this pork with cherries?' Hannah asked) and devoured by both Rosa and Hannah, Yves, seeing Eva really couldn't finish her food, suggested he and she should walk, while Alice retreated for yet another cigarette and the other two continued eagerly to the *cours de desserts*.

The early June sunshine felt hot as Eva followed Yves Dufort out of the restaurant and into the gardens of the Palais-Royal.

'This is the only garden in Paris classified as a "Remarkable Garden,"' Yves said, air-quoting the phrase before taking Eva's arm in his own. Together they strolled through the verdant lushness. 'You would never believe we are so near l'Opéra and the Rue de Rivoli,' Yves continued, making conversation when Eva seemed reluctant to talk.

'It's beautiful,' Eva breathed. And it was. The oasis of serene calm in the vibrant capital city was helping to dispel the feelings of almost claustrophobic panic she'd been experiencing ever since Rayan had dropped his bombshell about his counsellor. The alarm and anxiety had intensified while on Eurostar and only slightly subsided in the hotel in Montmartre, before swooping back to return in the restaurant itself.

'Let's walk down here,' Yves advised, pointing to a double row of limes, their new acid-green foliage a welcome parasol against the afternoon heat. 'Now, Eva, tell me everything.'

And she did. At first, feeling slightly disloyal to her dad, Richard, as well as to the memory of Bill Astley who, until last year, she'd recognised and loved as her birth father, she hesitated, giving only the barest outline of her life so far. But, with Yves' subtle questioning, and an obviously genuine interest in knowing everything about this new daughter of his, Eva began to open up.

'But why a dentist?' Yves eventually asked when, uninterrupted, Eva had spoken for a good fifteen minutes. 'When you could, by the sound of it, have gone to art school and become as accomplished and as famous as Alice?'

'And yourself?' Eva smiled.

'I have had success, yes.' Yves returned the smile. 'It give me money to have very very good lifestyle; to have lovely *déjeuner* at expensive restaurants whenever I want. But, you know, *cherie*, fame and money are not everything. It is what is in 'ere…' Yves thumped his chest '…'ere, in the 'eart, that is what is important.'

'My *'eart* is broken,' Eva said bleakly.

'I 'ave loved and I 'ave lost that love. I get the feeling, Eva, you 'ave lost what wasn't really right?'

'Rayan was right for me.' Eva protested hotly. 'I love my little girls.' She stopped suddenly. 'Oh, of course, Laila and Nora are your granddaughters.'

'And I would very much desire to meet them.' Yves turned to look Eva in the eye. 'I'm not saying you don't love your little girls, Eva. They are your life and you will continue to do your very best for them; give your life for them. But you are not yet forty. There are other loves just waiting for you. And I think your artwork is what you should be concentrating on.'

'You've not seen any of my artwork.' Eva smiled. 'It might be rubbish.'

'No, I 'aven't, but Alice 'as.'

'Alice has?'

'When she was over for this Bill Astley's funeral?'

'She didn't say anything to me.' Eva frowned.

'She wouldn't. Alice rarely compliments the work of other artists. She 'as – what's the word you Brits and Americans use?

– *dissed*, that's it, she 'as dissed plenty of others' artwork. She was full of praise for yours. Said I should see it.'

'Alice did?'

'She did. I would like to see it, Eva.'

'Listen, Yves, I'm trying to get an art retreat up and running at Heatherly Hall.'

'I know all about Heatherly Hall.' Yves smiled. 'Alice 'as told me it all. And, I google it as well.'

'So, I'm hoping to turn the attics into a taught art retreat. If all goes to plan, you know, planning, insurance, getting it all past the management committee…'

'I believe you *are* the management committee?' Yves laughed. 'Alice tell me it all. Eva, just get on with it. Put all your energy into this, rather than trying to mend a marriage that is too far broken.'

'Rayan, my husband, is having a child with another woman. He wants to marry her.' Eva felt panic rise once more.

'Darling, Eva, let him. Accept it's over. Look into your own 'eart and accept it rather than fight it. And move on.'

'And, Yves – I can't call you *Papa*: Richard is my dad – Yves, would you consider…' Eva broke off, embarrassed.

'Would I consider?' Yves took Eva's hand.

She took a deep breath. 'Would you consider coming over to Yorkshire…'

'Yorkshire?' Yves frowned, but there was humour in his brown eyes. 'Isn't it all puddings and little whippety *chiens*, flat caps and bleak moorland?'

'…to open the art retreat?'

'Eva, *cherie*, I thought you'd never ask. *Du café, maintenant*?'

They spent the next two days sightseeing, having a wonderful, if thoroughly exhausting time discovering the highlights of Paris. Although both Eva and Rosa had previously done the Eiffel Tower, Hannah hadn't and they dutifully trooped all the way to the top, admiring the view, with Hannah wondering what it would be like to jump off. (Eva, who was missing her girls, and whose feet were already aching, suggested she might help Hannah over the safety barriers, so she could find out.)

From there they walked and walked, winding their way through the medieval courtyards and pretty streets of Le Marais, making time to stroll through the Jardin des Archives Nationales, a mesmerising hidden gem right in the heart of the 3rd arrondissement. Sitting in the warm sunshine, they flung off cardigans and tops and picnicked on huge crusty baguettes, smelly, runny cheese and shared yet more wine.

Finally, wanting only to lie down in the sunshine and sleep off lunch, Rosa determinedly roused the other two and they made their way to Place Georges Pompidou, stopping to watch and admire myriad street performers, mime artists, and caricature and sketch artists before moving across to Centre Pompidou – arguably a work of art in itself – and going inside to admire its modern art collection.

On their final morning *à Paris*, they set out exceptionally early from the hotel to meet up with Yves ('far too early for me,' Alice had protested) for breakfast at the Marché des Enfants Rouges in Le Marais. Rosa, whose fourth love after her sisters, her church and Joe Rosavina was food, insisted on her and Hannah continuing down the street to take in every bit of France's oldest covered food market, while Eva stayed to enjoy more coffee and talk with her new father.

With the market straining at the gills with stalls of wonderful food, heavenly cheeses, olives, Italian deli and Lebanese fare, and wondering if God had shown her her own personal heaven, Rosa ended up laden down with a ridiculous number of jars, packs of saucisson and cheese. From there, they picked up Eva once more, said their goodbyes to Yves, taxied back to the hotel to collect their bags and made their way to the Gare du Nord and the return Eurostar back to London St Pancras.

Eva, Rosa was pleased to see, appeared much less anxious than on their outward journey a couple of days earlier.

'How are you feeling now?' she asked, once they'd found their seats.

'Oh, Rosa, so much better. It was the not knowing. I mean it might have been that I disliked Yves Dufort on sight. How awful if Yves and I had not got on. Not liked each other.'

'But you did?' Rosa patted Eva's arm.

'Absolutely.' Eva turned. 'Didn't you? Like him I mean? After all, he is my father. I'd hate it if you two hadn't thought he was up to much.' She glanced hopefully at Rosa.

'Gosh yes.' Rosa rushed to reassure her sister. 'Both Hannah and I thought he was absolutely wonderful: intelligent, gifted, interesting. *Interested*...'

'Yes,' Hannah agreed, 'you appear to have won the lottery with Yves. But don't forget Bill, will you? Or Dad?'

'I loved Bill,' Eva said slightly huffily. 'And Richard will *always* be Dad.'

23

'I am knackered.' Eva breathed a huge sigh of relief as the three of them hurried through the spectacular domed concourse at King's Cross towards the last Leeds train, finding their seats with minutes to spare. 'Bollocking knackered,' she repeated closing her eyes.

'Worth it though, Eva?' Rosa asked gently.

'Totally. I'm not feeling anything like as panicked as when we set off. Mind you,' she added, frowning, 'I'm sure it'll be back as soon as we get near Wakefield when reality starts to set in again.'

'Hopefully not.' Rosa smiled. 'You've a hell of a lot to sort out, but I'm sure you'll fight your corner where the girls are concerned, once you're back home.'

'You coming back with me to the hall, Eva?' Hannah, sitting across from the other two, opened one eye.

'Going to have to: Rayan's at Heath Green with the girls.'

'That's good,' Hannah replied sleepily.

'What, that Rayan is in my house with my girls and I have to camp out with you?' Eva felt irritation mount.

'No, you daft thing. I meant good that you're coming back with me. I'd feel a bit lonely going back by myself.'

'Now that Ben's not there?' Rosa asked.

Hannah nodded. 'Well, not just that Ben's not there. Spending time with you two, it's like being back in the womb...'

'Is it? And you remember that, do you?' Eva's interjection was dripping with sarcasm.

'...and I'm not ready,' Hannah went on seriously, 'to be born again and split up from you both.'

'You do talk daft, Hannah,' Eva said, scrolling through her phone for messages.

'You coming back with us as well?' Hannah appealed to Rosa.

'The rats have gone,' Rosa said. 'I need to get back to the vicarage; I want to see what the decorators have achieved as well.'

'OK, OK.' Hannah closed her eyes but said nothing further.

'You alright, Hannah?'

'Just thinking of everything I have to do: all those pigs I need to help into the world; more arguments with Laird Lachlan about trying to get Westenbury Festival off the ground next year.' Hannah sighed deeply. 'And yes, I'm missing Ben.'

'Well don't.' Eva patted Hannah's arm. 'Let him go.'

'Either of you fancy a chunk of cheese?' Rosa asked hopefully, glancing upwards towards her case? 'A sliver of saucisson?'

Hannah shook her head. 'I just fancy beans on toast when I get back, to be honest.'

'Am totally garlicked out,' Eva agreed.

'Well, I'm not,' Rosa said cheerfully, pulling down her case, unzipping it and releasing an overpowering smell of sweaty feet and garlic into the carriage. She tore off a wedge of Munster, placing it untidily between a couple of thick slices of saucisson, and tucked in.

'God, that smells like Rayan's trainers after he's done a 10K run.' Eva pulled a face. 'For heaven's sake, Rosa, everyone's looking,' she hissed. 'You're a *vicar*.'

'They're not looking, they're *smelling*.' Hannah laughed.

'What's my being a vicar got to do with anything?' Rosa asked, genuinely surprised. 'You sound like Virginia. And I'm *hungry*.'

'Well just get on with it and stop making such a fuss,' Eva said irritably, which made Rosa want to laugh and take a bigger bite than she'd planned.

'OK, OK, I've finished,' Rosa said eventually, replacing her case and sniffing at her fingers which were orange and oily from the saucisson. 'I need to wash my hands. I could do with cleaning my teeth as well.'

'Do *not* get that case down again, for heaven's sake, Rosa,' Eva warned as other passengers started glancing in their direction. 'God, it's like being back on a school trip all over again.'

Laughing, Rosa made her way up the aisle towards the toilets, manoeuvring herself (rather deftly, she thought, considering the amount of food she'd put away the past few days) round the advancing buffet trolley, only to find both toilets engaged.

'One up there on the left, two carriages up, was free.' The buffet steward pointed a thumb over his shoulder. He sniffed suspiciously at the sandwiches on his trolley. 'These smell a bit garlicky,' he frowned. 'Or at least something does.'

'It'll keep the devil away,' Rosa tittered, heading in the direction the steward had indicated. He was wrong, she thought somewhat irritably once she got there, folding her arms and balancing herself against the swaying train as it shot through a long dark tunnel: both loos were occupied. Actually, he was right, she conceded, she really was giving off the most awful fumes.

The bolt of the loo to her left shot back and the door opened.

'Oh,' the man said, obviously startled. 'Rosa.'

'Joe.' Rosa was doubly startled. 'I...'

'What...?'

'Have you...?'

'Where...?'

Words tumbled out at speed from both of them; no sentences complete, no actual sense made.

Rosa was the first to gain some measure of equanimity. 'Your hand's healed? Your bruises gone?'

Joe nodded. 'I just get a lot of headaches, but they're better than they were. Oh, and I can't bear to have milk on my Rice Krispies now.'

Rosa stared. 'Really?'

'Joking, Rosa.'

'Right. So, you've been to London?' she asked.

Joe nodded. 'You?'

'Yes, London. This *is* the London train,' she gabbled. 'Well, no, Paris actually.'

'Paris? How lovely.' He paused. '*By yourself?*'

Rosa frowned, shaking her head. Why on earth would she be going to Paris by herself? She was a vicar, no longer a businesswoman constantly flying off abroad as she once had. And then she understood. 'No, Joe, I was with Eva and Hannah. We went out to meet—' She broke off remembering that only a handful of people knew the truth about Eva's parentage. 'We went for a few days to meet up with Alice.'

'Oh? She's not in New York?'

'No, we…'

She broke off as a large woman brushed past her. 'If you're not using this lav, love, I'm fair busting.'

'Oh, I'm so sorry.' Rosa moved to let the woman through to the lavatory.

'You're not going to stand there, listening, are you?' The woman looked at both Joc and Rosa with some suspicion. 'Only, I can't get, you know, *get golng*, if I think I'm being overheard.'

'I'm heading back to my seat.' Joe smiled, but didn't move. Instead, he simply stared at Rosa, scrutinising every bit of her face.

'Garlic,' she said, embarrassed. 'Tons of it. Need to wash my hands.'

'OK. Bye, Rosa.'

'Bye, Joe.' Rosa shot into the now vacant lavatory on her right, leaning her forehead on the cracked and tarnished mirror. When she did eventually stand back and take a look at herself, there was an almost feverish air about her. 'Feck,' she snarled at her reflection. 'You look like some bloody provincial traveller on her first trip out of Yorkshire, and you stink to high heaven into the bargain.' She raked a hand through her mass of dark curls, bared her teeth in the mirror and rinsed her mouth. She washed her hands and, finding no towels, dried them by shaking them in front of her. And behind her. And in front again. Jeeze, she was doing the hokey-cokey now. And someone was rattling at the door. Rosa wiped her still-damp hands down her jeans and took another deep breath. 'Oh God,' she implored, looking heavenwards, 'why've you made me *still love him*?'

Rosa eventually exited the loo, smiled apologetically at the long queue gathered there and headed back through the first carriage, her eyes straight ahead, not wanting to see Joe. She was halfway down, stepping over bags and feet, apologising for knocking into arms and elbows as the train lurched, moving round other standing passengers, when a hand snaked out, taking her own and pulling her none too gently down.

'Come and sit with me, Rosa. Talk to me. Please?'

'Is no one sitting here, Joe?' she asked, pulse racing. 'The train's really full.'

'I offered the bloke who was sitting here £50 to move.'

'You didn't!'

Joe nodded. 'He can use it to upgrade to first class. I checked with the guard. 'I just needed to talk to you, Rosa, need to know you're OK.'

'OK?' Rosa smiled. 'I'm fine.'

'And you're totally clear of the… of the…?'

'Cancer, Joe? It would all be a hell of a lot easier for people going through cancer, if other people could actually say the word. Cancer. There, said it. Not so scary, is it?'

'I'm sorry.'

'Don't be.'

'Rosa, I've never said thank you to your face for, you know, rescuing me and the kids the other week.'

'To my face?'

'Well, I wrote you that letter. Bit cowardly, I know, but every time I've tried to get you alone to talk to you, to say thank you, to tell you how I still feel…'

'Which letter?' Rosa stared. 'I've not had any letter?'

'Ah.'

'Ah, what?'

'Well, I came round to see you once I was out of hospital, but you weren't in. Sam said you were up at the hall.'

'Sam did?'

'He was just leaving.'

'Was he?'

'So, I put the letter I'd written – for if you weren't in – through your letter box.'

'And Sam saw you do that, did he?'

'Well, if you didn't get it…' Joe trailed off, frowning. 'I'm sorry, I shouldn't have come between you and him. I'm sorry… He seems like a good bloke.'

'You know, you could have always come to the vicarage or to my church.'

'After you telling me in the restaurant before Christmas that you wanted nothing to do with me? When I laid my cards on the table and told you I still… you know.' He trailed off, obviously embarrassed. 'Anyway, I have. Several times.'

'Have what?' Rosa stared.

'Sat at the back and just watched you while you take your Sunday service. You're very, very good, Rosa. Your becoming a minister really was a calling.'

'At the back?'

'Behind a pillar. There's a great big pillar at the back. Has the wooden thing with the hymn numbers on it.'

'The hymn board?' Joe *must* have sat there if he knew about that damned hymn board hanging there. Few of the gathered congregation could see it, and she'd been meaning to move it for ages. 'Right.'

'And I was determined I was going to talk to you at David

Henderson's wedding. You know, when Chiara was part of the yellow-metre-ruler guard of honour?' Joe laughed at the memory. 'It was a great excuse to talk to you. But then, suddenly, you were with your new man – Sam – so Chiara and I left. I didn't want to embarrass you, you know...'

'Right.'

'So many times, I've made my way into church, just sat there, hoping to catch you. I needed to know you were well; that you are happy?'

Happy? How on earth can I be happy without you, Joe?

Instead, she said, 'And then you find me in a train toilet?' Rosa smiled. 'Was it planned?' She started to laugh at the very thought that Joe might have been lying in wait for her.

Joe laughed as well. 'And *then* I catch sight of you in the pub. Or driving through the village in your car. Or talking with people in the village. Or, just missing you when I go to pick Chiara up from Little Acorns and you're running across the playground, a load of kids in tow, like some sort of modern-day Pied Piper.'

'Well, I've got bloody rats...' Rosa started to say, but Joe was on a roll.

'And I can see how much you love those kids. And they love you, Rosa.' Joe smiled at her, obviously proud of her success as the village vicar. 'Or, like the other week, at that dinner party. I was so desperately pleased to see you. Thought, at last, I can talk to you. But you were with the dentist.'

'And you were with someone...' Rosa started to say.

Sam glanced sideways at Rosa. 'Melissa is – was – just a friend, Rosa. And I didn't know how to handle seeing you with Sam. Rosa, I just didn't know how to handle it. Especially...' Joe paused '...especially when he told me you'd just agreed to marry him? That you were engaged? You're going to marry your dentist?'

When Rosa didn't respond to that, didn't feel ready to tell Joe that she'd failed at another relationship – she had some pride – Joe sighed, but said nothing further.

'So, you've been in London?' Rosa eventually asked.

'For two days.' Joe nodded.

'Work?'

'A series of interviews.'

'Oh?'

'I can't stay with Mum and Dad for ever. They've been brilliant helping with Chiara – and Rhys of course.'

Rosa felt an icy trickle down her back. 'Oh?' she said again, trying not to show the distress she was feeling that Joe might no longer be around. No longer in the village. 'Where are you off to? Back to London? Barnsley? Bradford? Somewhere else exotically exciting?'

Keep smiling, Rosa.

'If you count Australia as exotically exciting?'

'Australia?' The icy trickle became a frozen deluge. Joe was following Carys out to Australia? She was losing him again.

Rosa, get a grip, he isn't yours to lose.

'Rhys and Chiara – Chiara particularly – miss Carys terribly.' Joe shrugged, but didn't appear able to meet Rosa's eyes. 'I just thought taking the kids out to Sydney might be the solution. New job, get myself and the kids from under Mum and Dad's feet… new start…'

'From under your dad's feet? Come on, Joe, Roberto adores Chiara. He and your mum will be devastated if you leave the country.'

I need you to stay, Joe. Don't go again.

'Sydney and Melbourne are still in the top twenty of the Global Financial Centres Index,' Joe was saying. 'There's exciting stuff going on over there…' He trailed off and there was silence once more.

'So, are you hoping to get back with Carys?' There, she'd said it. The elephant in the room. 'She *is* your wife after all.'

'My wife?' Joe stared. 'Rosa, we've been divorced over three years.' He almost laughed. 'There's absolutely no love lost between us. You know that? You *must* know that? I just have to think what's best for the kids, but particularly Chiara.'

'Carys left them, Joe. Went off to Australia with some new man and didn't give a toss about Rhys. Or Chiara.' How could any woman, any *mother*, leave a devastated four-year-old and move 12,000 miles away?

'She wants them back. Wants them over with her in Australia.'

'Carys *wants* them now? Oh, Joe. And you as well?'

'Me?' Joe actually laughed out loud at that. 'Absolutely not!'

'Joe, you can't let her just swan off with Chiara.'

'Rosa, Chiara's her daughter.'

'She's *your* daughter as well,' Rosa burst out angrily.

'She's remarried, actually, married the very wealthy Australian she met in London and ran off with three years ago. She's got a huge estate in Manley… the big house, the pool, Sydney society… she now wants the children. She's going to fight for her children.'

'She can't have them. That's ridiculous. I hope you've got a solicitor? *Get* a solicitor, Joe.'

'Rhys isn't mine, Rosa – you know that. I have no legal right to him; he still has his father's name. And Chiara asks every day when can she go to Australia to see Mummy. When Chiara told her about the cow fiasco, she was on the phone telling me I was utterly irresponsible and she'd be using it against me to make sure Chiara was back safely with her, where she belonged. What do I do, Rosa?' Joe sighed heavily. 'It's all such a fucking mess.'

'Well, I…'

'Surely better for me to go there as well and we can have joint custody? And the job I've just been offered is a very *very* good one.'

'I…'

'And, Rosa, you've made it pretty obvious there's nothing for me here with you. You're about to marry the dentist… I don't want to fuck your life up again.'

'I don't… I'm not…'

'Well, if it isn't Joe Rosavina!' Eva was suddenly standing in the aisle next to them, arms folded, tone mocking. 'And how is Mrs McLean? Neck as clean and scrubbed as ever?'

'Sorry?' Joe stared.

'What the hell are you *doing*, Rosa?' Eva turned to her sister. 'We've been looking all over for you! It's been like something out of an Agatha Christie novel; up and down every damned carriage. Hannah was all for pulling the communication chord. We thought you'd been murdered…' she glared at Joe, daring him to look away '…or worse.'

'Worse than being murdered…?' Rosa began, but was cut off by Eva's strident tones.

'Come on, Rosa,' Eva said bossily. 'We've a coffee gone stone cold up there for you.'

When Rosa glared back, didn't appear to be moving, Eva added, '*And* a chocolate muffin.'

'Eva,' Rosa snapped, embarrassed, 'I'm not a dog you can tempt back to its basket with a treat.'

'Well, I've never known you turn down a muffin before. Especially a chocolate one. OK, OK.' Eva threw up her hands. 'On your head be it.'

She glared once more in Joe's direction before reversing to make her way back down the three crowded carriages to her seat.

'Sorry about that,' Rosa said, her cheeks flaming. 'She's very protective of me since… you know…'

'I know. And she's going through a hell of a lot with her marriage breaking up.' Joe's tone was sympathetic. 'It's the kids, isn't it? Always the kids who suffer from the grown-ups' cock-ups.'

'You know about Eva and Rayan?' Rosa was surprised.

'I had a late dental appointment with Rayan a couple of weeks ago. We went for a pint afterwards.' Joe smiled. 'I tried to get out of him what you were up to these days, but he didn't seem to know. Or he was just being protective of you and *your dentist*.'

'Rayan wouldn't know; I've not seen him since he moved out of Heath Green. And, the dentist is called Sam, Joe.'

'I know, I know. I'm sorry. I suppose my not giving him an actual name makes him less real. I can pretend he doesn't actually exist in your life.' Joe looked out of the window as the train pulled into a station. 'Doncaster,' he said. 'Soon be at Wakefield. Can I give you a lift back to Westenbury?' Joe looked directly at Rosa.

'Oh,' she said, flustered, 'Eva has her car parked there.'

'Right, OK.'

'So, when do you go?' Rosa found that her heart was pounding. She tried to drink in every bit of Joe; to be able to remember him when he was on the other side of the world.

'To Australia?'

Rosa nodded.

'They want me there at the beginning of August.'

'About six weeks then?'

It was Joe's turn to nod.

'And Mrs McLean?'

'Melissa?' Joe frowned.

Rosa nodded.

'I think she's actually read too much into the friendship.'

'Friendship?' *Not relationship then?* Rosa's heart beat faster.

'Chiara had teamed up with Florence, Melissa's daughter, at school, even though Florence is in the year above. I met Melissa in the playground and it sort of went from there, with the girls instigating more meetups. Chiara sort of idolises Florence.'

'As does Laila.'

'Laila?'

'Eva's eldest. Laila and Florence are in the same class and are either best buddies or belting seven bells out of each other.'

'Oh, it's *Eva's* daughter who's causing all the problems with Florence, is it? Well, if Laila's anything like her mother, that figures.'

'To be honest, Joe, I think it's six of one… you know.'

'Very likely.' Joe laughed. 'You certainly don't cross Florence and live. Or her mother.'

'So, you're happy to leave Mrs McLean behind and go off to Sydney?'

'As I said, Rosa, Melissa has read more into the friendship than I certainly ever intended it.'

A heavily tattooed, rather fat individual appeared in front of them, laughing. 'Was she worth it then? Was she worth 50 big ones?' He reached above Joe for a small case, pulling it down and narrowly missing Rosa's head. 'Sorry, mate, forgot this. And, anytime you fancy doing this again, I'm your man.' He laughed again. 'Great free smoked salmon sarnies.' He belched delicately. 'Pardon.' And he was off towards the exit as the train slowed and began to pull into Wakefield Westgate Station.

'Gosh, I need to get back down the train for my own stuff.' Rosa stood up. 'Bye, Joe.'

'And yes, Rosa…' Joe called after her. She stopped and turned back towards him, the line of exiting passengers tutting when they couldn't get past her and the aisle came to a standstill. 'It *was* worth £50. I'd have paid *£1000*.' A couple of passengers turned, frowning, and then the remaining, standing passengers turned, en masse, towards Joe as he shouted after Rosa's now-departing back, 'And no, Rosa, I'm *not* happy setting out for Australia, but I can't live in the same village as you and not be with you. I can't do it anymore, Rosa. I just can't do it.'

24

A week after their return from Paris, Eva was up in the Heatherly Hall attics making final notes on the initial plans she was due to present to the management committee later that day regarding the intended art retreat. Should it be called a retreat? A course? A haven? A sanctuary? A hideaway? She didn't want it to sound twee or cheesy – she envisaged some seriously good artists paying their way to spend three full days at the hall – but neither did she want to frighten off, or eliminate, the amateur artist who needed encouragement.

'You've managed to persuade Yves Dufort to be here then?' Eva turned, jumping slightly as Lachlan Buchanan appeared at her side.

Eva nodded. 'Yep. He's coming for the opening and then staying for at least a week.'

'That's amazing; you've done an incredible job.' Lachlan gazed up at the long bank of tall windows and skylights through which the June sunshine was now flooding. 'I know absolutely nothing about art, but I can appreciate you'll need a certain light. This is brilliant. What about in winter, though? When it's dark by 5pm?'

'All in the plans that I'm putting forward this morning. All the costings for everything to get this place up and running: extra lighting, tables and comfortable chairs, easels, materials, plus an advertising budget.

'You'll need more than just an advertising budget.' Lachlan frowned. 'You'll need marketing and PR.'

'Already spoken to our marketing people. Over the years

they've done an amazing job with the wedding venue and getting the wine bar up and running. We're going to need a whole load of glossy brochures to send out showing the hall and these rooms to their best advantage so I've asked Simeon and Lucy from marketing to join us later on this morning.'

'Stick Yves Dufort on the front of the brochure and you'll be sold out immediately.'

'Alice has promised to do a stint here as well.'

'Alice Parkes?' Lachlan whistled. 'You're aiming high.'

'The least she can do in return for handing the three of us over to my mum and dad to bring up.'

'And do you think you and your sisters would all have done as well as you have if she'd kept you?' Lachlan smiled. 'Seems to me you got a good deal when she gave you up for adoption. Can you imagine being dragged from pillar to post with Alice Parkes? From Paris to New York and back with a mother who was resentful of having to give up her time to bring you up?'

'You seem to know a lot about Alice?' Eva raised an eyebrow.

'Read that biography of hers that came out a couple of years ago. Great innovative artist – not so sure what kind of mother she'd have been.'

'You shouldn't believe everything you read.' Eva frowned. 'Right, I think we'd better get going. They'll be waiting in the boardroom.'

'OK, Eva, we're all ears.' As much as Hannah loved her sister, she was ashamed to be feeling a slight resentment that, while everyone here this morning – including Lachlan – appeared ready to listen to Eva, no one on the board had appeared at all interested in her, Hannah's, plans for Westenbury Festival next summer. She hadn't even dared moot the idea of a retreat for looked-after kids here at the hall. A week where maybe up to ten kids at a time would work in the hall's allotments and kitchen gardens, cook their own meals from the organically grown vegetables, go for long hikes over the Pennines… Hannah dragged herself back from the rather nice vision of herself leading a group of singing teenagers over the hills and far away, after a tiring but worthwhile morning digging up the Jersey potatoes, which would be transformed into supper later that day.

'…so, I've worked out some sort of initial budget,' Eva was saying, 'but of course, initial budgets, as we all know, do have a tendency to run away with themselves…'

Got them all eating out of her hand, Hannah thought somewhat sourly. And look at Laird Lachlan, nodding in agreement. What does *he* know about art? He's just a jumped-up farmer at the end of the day.

'…I intend teaching the watercolours and oil painting courses and I've done a fair amount of ceramics…'

'You'll be wanting a kiln up there then?' Anthony Watkins, the accountant, pursed his lips but didn't appear to object.

'And a reinforced floor,' Hannah put in. 'You can't have a bloody great heavy kiln crashing through from the attics.'

'I've already been out looking in the old outhouses.' Eva smiled. 'There's plenty of room for one there. And, I've approached Daisy Maddison…'

'Daisy the vet?' Hannah pulled a face. 'She an artist now as well as a landscape gardener and vet?'

'…I've already approached Daisy Maddison's mum, Kate,' Eva went on calmly, ignoring Hannah, 'who is an absolutely superb potter and ceramicist.'

'Ooh, I've seen some of her stuff.' Tiffany nodded enthusiastically. 'In fact, we already sell some in the gift shop. She's *very* talented.'

'Well, she's agreed to come and teach on a ceramics course here.'

'Really, really great.' Anthony Watkins almost clapped his pleasure and even the usually inscrutable Lachlan Buchanan smiled, nodding his agreement.

'While I'm going to be here overseeing the retreat, and actually teaching on the watercolours and oils courses, I'm in the process of searching out artists willing and able to teach other areas of art.'

'Such as?' Hannah asked.

'Textiles, acrylics, photography, screen-printing.' Eva smiled, reeling off a list. 'The potential's endless. And, we could do day courses for kids during the school holidays. Parents will pay a fortune to get their bored offspring out of their hair for a day or two.'

More nods of agreement until Hannah interrupted with: 'While we're on about courses for kids, it can't be all about the rich ones, surely?'

'Can't it?' Anthony, who was usually always on Hannah's side, looked puzzled. 'Why not? We're a business, Hannah. We have to bring in a huge income to keep this place going. The gas and electricity bill itself is enough to finish us off,' he added gloomily.

'What about the looked-after kids who have *nothing*? The ones I used to deal with when I was a youth worker?' When there was no response from the others, apart from heads down looking at Eva's plans in front of them, Hannah went on, hotly, 'I really, really want to do this.'

'Do what, Hannah?' Lachlan smiled politely. Or was it condescension?

'A retreat for kids who are pushed from pillar to post. Kids who live in London but who are sent to homes in Nottingham… and then Birmingham… and then Preston…'

'Preston?' Anthony Watkins smiled almost dreamily. 'I'm rather fond of Preston; there's a nice little restaurant…'

'Kids who are vulnerable to the county lines gangs.' Hannah felt her temper rising.

'Well, the last thing Heatherly Hall needs is a reputation for harbouring OCG,' Elspeth Harrington from human resources put in primly.

'OCG?' The others leaned forwards in Elspeth's direction and she went slightly pink.

'Organised crime groups,' Lachlan offered. 'I think you've been watching too much *Line of Duty*, Elspeth.'

'I'm sorry,' Eva tutted, looking at her watch, 'can we just get back to *this*?' She waved her file of plans impatiently. 'And, Hannah—' Eva held her sister's eye '—I'm afraid this idea of yours, where you see yourself as some sort of latter-day Julie Andrews yodelling through the Pennines with a set of skunk-smoking, machete-wielding delinquents, as an alternative to a DTO...'

'DTO?' Anthony leaned forwards.

'Detention and Training Order,' Hannah snapped. 'The *nick*.'

'...as an alternative to a DTO,' Eva went on, 'is just not viable. I'm so sorry, Hannah, really. I just don't think it would work. At the moment, anyway.'

'You said you *agreed* with me, Eva?' Hannah said hotly, glaring across at her sister. 'Said you'd help me put this forward.' When Eva said nothing, and an embarrassed silence descended on the meeting, Hannah went on, 'Bill would have been on my side – you know what *his* political stance was: he was always for the underdog. And Rosa would be on my side too, if she were here. You know she would.'

'Where *is* the village vicar?' Anthony Watkins interrupted. '*She's* always a sight for sore eyes.'

'Rosa sent her apologies... *my* apologies.' Hannah was embarrassed. 'I should have read them out when I opened the meeting.'

'That *is* the correct way of going about things, Hannah.' Elspeth sniffed her disapproval.

'Hannah is still getting to grips with all this,' Tiffany put in, eager to show whose side she was on now she'd been promoted to Hannah's deputy. 'It's not easy.'

Hannah shot Tiffany a grateful look.

'Eva,' Lachlan now said, ignoring Hannah and Elspeth, but

smiling at Tiffany before turning back to Eva, 'do you think it might be a good idea to take yourself off to some art retreat that's already up and running? Spend a few days at one of the best in the country? Find out what works and what doesn't?'

'A bit like a spy?' Anthony said, eyes gleaming in excitement.

'Exactly like a spy.' Eva grinned. 'You don't think Sainsbury's and Tesco haven't got their surveillance teams out in Waitrose, do you? So, already done.'

'What is?' The others leaned forwards across the huge oak desk.

'I'm off to the Lake District at the weekend. One of the oldest and most prestigious writers' and artists' retreats in the north. Well, in the country actually.'

'*Writing* retreat as well? Wow, that's a thought,' Tiffany said excitedly. 'We hadn't thought about that.'

'*I* had,' Eva said pointedly.

'We could get Ian Rankin, Joanne Harris – she's *very* local – and Joanna Cannon – she's just down the road in Doncaster.' Tiffany was already scribbling on a blank page in front of her. 'In fact, we could have an annual literary festival here: the *Heatherly Hall Literary Festival*.'

'What about *Westenbury Festival*...?' Hannah tried to put in, but no one was listening.

'Your trolling off up to the Lake District for a couple of days won't be cheap.' Anthony Watkins shook his head dolefully.

'No, it isn't,' Eva agreed. 'In fact, it's bloody expensive. But that's what we want here, isn't it? *Upmarket and expensive?* The last thing we want is cheap and cheerful; buy one get one free?' Eva's tone was scathing. 'This is Heatherly Hall. *Heatherly Hall*. We want to put it on the map, *don't we*?'

Bloody hell, Hannah thought, Eva was on a roll. She wouldn't have been out of place standing next to Churchill: *We shall fight them on the beaches* and all that. 'How can you go away again, Eva?' she blurted out, trying to dampen the envy of Eva she'd always felt as a child and a teen but which, as she grew older, she'd managed to repress. 'We've only just got back from Paris. What about *your girls*? What about Laila and Nora?'

'Hannah!' Eva shot her sister a look, before relenting and turning to the others once more. 'I think it appropriate, at this stage, to explain to the board that I shall be spending more time here.' Eva cleared her throat, picked up her glass of water, hesitated and seemed unable to go on. Eventually she said, 'I'm sure you're aware that my husband and I...'

Oh, now she thought she was the bloody Queen, Hannah thought petulantly. As kids, Eva'd always insisted on being the Queen while she and Rosa had had to put up with wearing the princess dresses from the dressing-up box.

'...my husband and I have separated,' Eva eventually managed to get out. 'We're now looking to divorce.'

'I'm sorry to hear that, Eva,' Lachlan said. 'Never easy for anyone. If there's anything we can do to help...?'

Hannah stared. Had the sardonic, cynical Laird Lachlan Buchanan just said that? He obviously fancied Eva.

Eva shot Lachlan a grateful look. 'And don't worry about the expense, Graham.' Eva turned to the accountant. 'I've been wanting to do an art retreat for years. I'm happy to pay for it myself – it doesn't have to come out of the hall's budget.'

'Oh, I'm sure we can make a contribution, Eva.' Anthony patted her hand.

'As you wish.' Eva smiled prettily, and Hannah wondered how many years one got these days for sororal murder.

'Hannah?' Lachlan Buchanan called as she made her way to the door in search of coffee and relief from the petulance she was feeling. Maybe a long walk in the woods would help? But she had so much to do. 'Can we have a word about these pigs at some point? What you intend doing with them all?'

25

On the Friday afternoon, just five days after the board meeting where she'd presented her plans to the others, Eva was heading up the M6 to Ullswater and the Dame Bryony Fisher art retreat.

Maybe that was the answer, Eva had mused, once she'd rung and been put on hold by someone at the other end of the phone at the retreat in the Lake District: the Alice Parkes art retreat? The Yves Dufort art retreat? Her musings on the handles for the new Heatherly Hall retreat had been rudely interrupted by the person at the retreat actually laughing at her request, informing her they were *totally* booked up until the middle of the following year.

While that was disappointing, at least she'd be able to report to the meeting the good news that expensive residential courses like this were not only popular, but obviously over-subscribed. Eva had begun to google other similar retreats a couple of hours' drive from Westenbury, when the same woman had almost immediately rung back to suggest, certainly in more inviting tones than previously that, if Eva was interested in a two-day pottery course, rather than the watercolours or oils she'd first suggested, then she was in luck: they'd just had a cancellation.

So it was that, while Eva had never seen herself as a potter, she'd been able to tell the others at the board meeting that she was already booked, and on her way, that coming weekend. After all, it wasn't the actual course she was particularly interested in, but the way the whole establishment was run. And why she was now, on this Friday afternoon, stuck on a gridlocked M6, rain beating down on her windscreen, with a good sixty miles still to go.

And homesick. She was feeling so homesick for Heath Green, her house, her home. Her girls. And while, after the trip to Paris the previous weekend, it was Eva's weekend to be back in the family home with the girls, it was Azra's seventieth birthday and Rayan and his sister, Hadhira, had organised a big birthday bash, taking their mother and all her family to some swish hotel up near Bolton Abbey for the weekend.

'Who's going to look after Nora?' Eva had objected. 'She's only three years old. You can't just take a little girl and put her in a hotel room with Laila overnight. How safe is the hotel? How safe are the rooms?' Images of quickly spreading fires and marauding paedophiles had swum before her eyes.

'Hadhira has booked a big family room for myself and the girls, Eva,' Rayan had said. 'And Jodie's said she's more than happy to come with us too. You know how well she and my mum get on.'

That much was true, anyway.

'And is your *girlfriend* going?'

'No, Eva.' Rayan had spoken calmly. 'Yasmin and I don't think it appropriate to be introducing her to my family and the girls at my mum's birthday do.'

Yasmin and I? The three little words hit her right between the eyes. 'But they know about her?'

'Who? The girls?' Rayan sighed and shook his head. 'No, not yet.'

Well, that was something anyway.

'But Mum and Hadhira *do* know.' Rayan had raised an almost defiant eye in her direction. '*Know everything*, Eva.' He'd relented slightly. 'Look, Eva, I know it's your weekend to have Laila and Nora, but they love Mum and Hadhira's lot and they can't wait to stay in a hotel. You can have the girls the next two weekends and I'll get them to ring you lots of times. Don't say they can't go,' Rayan pleaded. 'They've already made birthday cards and been out with me to buy Mum's presents.'

This pottery course then, was a godsend. She wouldn't be on her own at the house with just a bottle of wine, a takeaway and a catch-up of TV boxsets.

The traffic ahead started to move and Eva indicated, moved into the fast lane and put her foot down.

The rain was still belting down as it can only in the Lake District and, by the time she'd parked the Evoque, retrieved her case from the boot and followed the signs for reception, Eva was soaked, her lightweight summer mac doing little to protect her from the deluge. The Dame Bryony Fisher art retreat was housed in an elegant Georgian mansion and, according to the glossy brochure, which Eva had read from cover to cover in bed the previous evening, situated on a previously privately owned estate on the very shores of Ullswater, Cumbria's second largest lake after Windermere. The original owner (a mate of Wordsworth and Coleridge? Eva had idly wondered as she turned the pages) had grown rich, not only from tenant farmers working his land, but apparently dabbling in politics as well as investing in the railways and coalmines northwards towards Newcastle and south to industrial Yorkshire.

No wonder this place was popular, Eva thought, as she stood dripping on the polished wooden floor of a beautiful, high-ceilinged room waiting for someone to tell her where to go. There was an air of calm, relaxed benevolence about the place, and Eva began to feel the stress of the motorway journey, as well as the last few horrible months of the breakdown of her marriage, begin to ease from her neck and shoulders. She shook the tiny bell on a delicate, beeswaxed Queen Anne table and, when no one immediately came to her assistance, sat down on

– actually, fell into – a huge cushioned Knoll sofa, closing her eyes as the wonderful softness enveloped her, almost caressed her.

'Mrs Malik?' A young, very attractive blonde-haired woman appeared beside her. 'You made it up the motorway from Yorkshire?'

A very personal touch, Eva thought, mentally making notes. She'd certainly insist on a sofa like this in the Heatherly Hall retreat and make sure her staff welcomed guests by their name. She'd have a glass of prosecco on hand as well.

'I'm Alicia and if there's anything at all I can help you with, please, just let me know? Now, a glass of champagne?' The girl smiled.

Ah, actual champagne then.

'Or would you prefer wine? A spirit maybe? Or a soft drink? Dinner will be served in an hour. Give you chance to have a shower, settle in? You're booked in for your first pottery class after that, I believe?'

'Really? This evening?' The idea of imbibing a couple of glasses of wine, having dinner and doing little else had been looking a welcome prospect.

'Absolutely.' Alicia smiled. 'We want you to totally relax, take full advantage of the wonderful facilities here at Dame Bryony Fisher; but you're here for a reason and we don't want to waste any time, do we?

Don't we? *Actually, Alicia*, Eva wanted to say with a laugh, *the last thing I want is clay under my newly manicured nails*. (As a treat, and a heads up to her weekend away by herself, she'd booked in for a manicure for her paint-ingrained and broken nails – something she'd not had the patience or desire to do for years – and was now sporting a rather jaunty set of bright red ones.) *The only reason I'm here, is to nick all your best ideas; see how an upmarket art retreat like this has gained such a good reputation.*

Instead, she nodded, dutifully. 'Absolutely right, Alicia. Lead me to the wheel this very minute.'

'The wheel?' Alicia looked slightly startled. 'Oh, the potter's wheel? Of course. So, let me get you that drink and then I'll show you around, direct you to your room. Dinner in an hour.'

Did such opulent surroundings take away from any *real* artists coming to a retreat such as this? Eva wondered as she showered and dressed for dinner in the beautifully interior-designed room, blow-drying her still-damp long dark hair into some sort of submission before attempting to mend her make-up. Surely, proper artists didn't give a fig about posh designer curtains (Zoffany, at a guess), critically lighted mirrors and upmarket products (Molton Brown and Jo Malone) and a fully stocked minibar fridge? Wouldn't genuine, bona fide artists be simply stuck into their creations, a tub of pot noodles (when they remembered to eat) and black coffee the only thing in their paint-stained hands, apart from a paintbrush? She could see she had a lot to learn about the running of a place like this.

Eva went down for dinner. She'd assumed she'd have a table to herself and was looking forward to the prospect of not only a couple more glasses of wine and delicious food (she'd not had a proper meal since Paris, grazing on hunks of Cheddar and Hob Nobs once the girls were in bed) and not have to make conversation with strangers. She was slightly put on the back foot then, when, descending the elegant red-carpeted staircase (was she going to have to persuade the management committee to cough up funds to carpet those somewhat bleak stone stairs leading to the attics in Heatherly Hall?) she entered the equally elegant dining room to find just one huge oval table, set for dinner for at least – Eva did a quick calculation – twenty.

'Mrs Malik?' Alicia was back in charge. 'Do come and take a

seat and meet some of your fellow artists. Most have been here for several days—' wealthy, then, Eva surmised '—but we have a few guests, like yourself, here just for the weekend.'

Eva felt suddenly shy, lacking in confidence, aware the break-up with Rayan had carved a hole in her self-esteem. She made her way across to the seat pulled out by Alicia and sat down before eyeing up the other guests who were already stuck into dishes of olives and focaccia. Those around the table, Eva quickly surmised, were predominantly middle-aged white women and, she soon realised, listening to their conversation, the majority were American.

'Ah, you're a Brit,' the woman next to her said as Eva thanked her for the bread basket. 'You're a rare species here.'

'Oh?' Eva laughed. 'Even in Britain?'

'Aren't we in Scotland up here?' The woman frowned.

'Well even if we were, which we're *not*, we'd still be in Britain,' Eva pointed out, smiling.

'Right, OK.' The woman obviously didn't really understand or care. 'So, where you from, honey?' Her accent was pure Deep South. 'I'm Julie-Ann.' She extended a soft white hand adorned with rings and a heavy charm bracelet that clunked excessively with her every move.

'Yorkshire,' Eva said. 'Eva Quinn.' For a second, Eva's hand was arrested on its journey to the dish of oil and balsamic: Eva *Quinn*? Had she just said that? Ditched her married *name* now, as well as her actual marriage?

'Oh, York *Shire*.' The woman emphasised the two syllables. 'Have we done York *Shire*, Janey?' The woman referred to the woman to her right. 'D H Lawrence, right?'

'Nearer Nottingham, I would have thought,' Eva corrected. 'Maybe the Brontës? Sylvia Plath…?'

'Possibly, honey, possibly.' Julie-Ann was dismissive. 'What are you down for?'

'Down for?' Eva smiled. 'Oh, what course am I doing? Pottery. Just for the weekend.'

'Oh, you're in luck there, honey.' Julie-Ann nudged Eva almost suggestively.

'Oh? A good session, is it?'

Julie-Ann pointed a beringed finger in the direction of the door across the dining room from the table. A dark-haired man was making his way towards them, an artist's smock still in place over clay-spattered jeans. 'That's your teacher, honey.' She grinned but then lowered her voice. 'I love the way you Brits don't stand on ceremony. We'd never have the hired help at the same table as paying guests at home in South Carolina. Mind you, with a butt like that, I don't reckon anyone'd object to his parking it with us.'

He might have a butt to be revered, Eva thought, but the rest of him was nothing to write home about. Probably around her own age, the man had a mass of longish black curls tied up in a high ponytail, slight beard and moustache and olive skin. He glanced across at Eva, held her gaze with shrewd brown eyes and, obviously finding little to interest him, gave his attention to dipping his bread into the dish of oil and balsamic before demolishing the piece in two large careless bites while simultaneously reaching for another.

'Pretty hunky, huh?' Julie-Ann nudged her once more. 'Wish I'd enrolled in making pots instead of the watercolours.'

'And do you do these retreats often? I mean, do *a lot* of Americans come over to the UK in order to do artwork?' Eva knew she was probing, researching what people wanted from an art retreat and was aware that Alicia was hovering, listening. Julie-Ann, however, was willing to sing like a canary.

'We just love you Brits,' Julie-Ann was saying. 'We just love little old England. You have so much history. Mind you, we're catching up.'

'Oh?'

'You'd want to visit our old plantations. And Lou sitting across there with Andrea…'

'Andrea? Which one is she?'

'No,' Julie-Ann tutted. 'Andrea – An-*dreya* – is the hunky potter.' She waved across at Lou, an exceptionally blonde, but very tiny, wizened woman who was trying, but seemingly having little success, in making conversation with the dark-haired teacher. 'Lou is all the way from Virginia. Now, *there* is history,' Julie-Ann went on proudly. 'She's the mother of presidents. There! What about that?'

Eva stared and racked her brain. The old woman across the table must be the same age as Biden if she was a day and, culturally, she couldn't be Obama's mother. Trump then? 'Lou is Donald Trump's *mother*?'

'I beg your pardon?' Julie-Ann turned and stared at Eva.

'You said Lou was the mother of presidents?' Did Trump have a brother who'd also achieved high office? Eva didn't think so, but you never knew. Look at the president-prolific Kennedys.

'No, no, noooo.' Julie-Ann patted Eva's hand. 'You Brits – you're so *funny*: I just love your humour. *Virginia* is the mother of presidents. Eight Virginia-born gentlemen succeeded to the highest office in the land, including four – *four*, *waddayathinkaboutthatthen*? – of the first five presidents. Now, *that's* history! *That's* something to shout about!'

'Fabulous.' Eva nodded. 'Wow.' She nodded gratefully as Alicia offered more wine. God, she was missing her girls; she'd give anything to be back in Heath Green right now. Bathing Nora, allowing Laila to stay up a little longer than usual, as it was Friday night. And going off to Bolton Abbey with them all in the morning.

She loved Bolton Abbey. She and Rayan had first taken his parents there when his dad was still alive and Azra, having rarely strayed from the built-up, post-industrial urbanisation of Little Horton in Bradford, had fallen in love with the countryside in North Yorkshire. Had said, if, when she died, she couldn't be flown back to her native Pakistan, then she wanted to be buried up near Bolton Abbey. And they'd all be there tomorrow without her – Eva. Eva felt the same overwhelming panic she'd first experienced on the Eurostar the week before and reached for her water, attempting to steady her breathing.

'You OK, Honey?' Julie-Ann looked at her strangely.

'Yes, fine, thank you.' Eva breathed deeply, felt herself begin to calm and smiled at a waitress who was putting a starter of – according to the little menu card to her right – *Scallops and Chorizo with a Hazelnut Picada* in front of her.

'Mind you,' Julie-Ann was saying through a mouthful of scallops, 'it's the old historic houses we love, Evelyn...'

'Eva.'

'Sorry?'

'My name is Eva.'

'We've done Windsor...'

'More of a castle that, I think.' Eva smiled, forcing herself to eat.

'And Chats *Worth*.' Again, the American emphasised both syllables. 'And we just adored Castle Howard down the road from here.'

'Bit more than *just down the road*...' Eva began but Julie-Ann was tucking into her food and wasn't listening.

'So,' Eva eventually asked, once the starter dishes had been removed and she was being asked if she'd prefer the seabass, the lamb, or the vegetarian option, 'what would you think about doing an art course like this, but actually *held* in an old historic house?'

'This *is* an historic house.' Julie-Ann flung a hand out towards the ornate Georgian ceiling. 'Did you not realise that, honey?'

'I meant something more like Castle Howard?'

'To be honest, sugar, I think Lou and I are heading back to cruising again.'

'Cruising?' Eva had a momentary, if quite startling, vision of the two elderly Americans on the streets of South Carolina, leaning in through the windows of Chevvies and Dodge Impala Coupes and asking: *Show you a good time, honeypie?* 'Ah, you enjoy going on cruises?'

'Sure do, Evelyn. You meet such *interesting* people on those.' She sniffed, gave Eva an on-off smile, before turning pointedly to her neighbour on the other side.

An hour later, Eva found herself in an outside annexe with Andrea, three other women and a smallish lump of grey clay.

'So, ladies, I am Andrea Zaitsev.' The man spoke with an accent Eva couldn't quite place. 'I'm here to turn you all into artists.' He almost glared at his new class. 'First you must take off all rings you wear. And—' he looked pointedly at Eva's hands '—why you come with long red nails? You must forget about lovely manicured nails and soft hands. You must *think* like an artist. *Become* an artist in… *your mind…*'

Hang on, Buster, Eva thought, cross at being hauled out in front of the others. *You wouldn't be so bloody shirty with me if you knew my mother was Alice Parkes and my dad Yves Dufort. Ha! And that I've spent* most of my life *thinking like a damned artist. Well, when I wasn't doing root canals and fillings anyway…*

'…then you become an artist in *your body*.' Andreas' eyes raked Eva's own body and she suddenly had an inkling what Julie-Ann had been talking about.

Andrea Zaitsev, while not conventionally good-looking had, she realised, an undefinable presence. He wasn't overly tall – probably not quite six foot – but his brown eyes were incredible and, when he did smile, which certainly wasn't often, his teeth were white and even. His large hands had long, tapering fingers, the nails ingrained with clay, and Eva wondered what they would be like on her body, unbuttoning her shirt, inching their way up her leg…

'Tonight, I show you the basics; let you feel the clay: feel its heart, its soul, its potential. And then tomorrow we start properly.' Andrea Zaitsev stared across at Eva, and she thought, her pulse racing slightly, never mind his looking deep into the soul of a lump of bloody clay, he appeared to be looking deep into the very heart of her whole being. And she hadn't quite made up her own mind whether she wanted this man, wanted anyone, actually, to have the capacity to do that.

26

Eva slept badly, unable to find comfort in the too-soft bed and mountainous cloud of pillows. She'd also been unable to open her bedroom window much wider than a couple of inches and the night air had felt close and sultry after the heavy downpour of the previous afternoon and evening. She longed for fresh air, felt unable to catch her breath properly and, finding the heavy scent from the longiflorum lilies on the polished table in the room almost overpowering, eventually put the flowers outside, jettisoned all the pillows except one and finally managed to sleep.

She started awake, heart pounding, the remnants of the dream that had woken her just out of her grasp. And then she remembered it: Rosa was conducting a wedding ceremony in her church, lilies on the end of every pew and in great vases down the aisle and she herself, the bride, was holding the same lilies, breathing them in, turning to tell Rayan 'I do.' But just as Rayan was putting the ring on her finger, he turned in apparent absolute horror and said, 'You're Eva *Quinn*, not Eva Malik. You cruise the streets of Virginia. And that's why I don't want to have sex with you anymore.' And then suddenly the bride was no longer herself, but Dr Yasmin. She was wearing a white coat, had a stethoscope around her neck but a veil hid her face and Laila and Nora, in beautiful matching pink bridesmaids' dresses, were looking at her in adoration, patting her pregnant tummy and shouting, 'We love you, Mummy…'

Eva shot up in the bed, reaching down for the abandoned

pillows and sitting back on them while trying to measure her breathing. She was going to end up with high blood pressure, a stroke even, if she didn't find a way to stop this hyperventilating. Too much wine, she admonished herself; it always affected her sleep. She peered at her phone – just 4.30am – and the dawn chorus had already been at it a good hour. She got out of bed, went for a pee, searched in vain for a message or phone call from the girls, wrote them another message but didn't send it. She didn't want Rayan to know she was awake at such an early hour.

The previous day's rain had moved on, leaving a cerulean blue sky tinged with pink as the day began to prepare itself once more. Almost the longest day, she realised. Soon they'd be heading back to winter. And Christmas. Who would get the girls at Christmas? Her, surely, seeing as how Rayan – and presumably this Dr Yasmin – were Muslim and shouldn't be celebrating Christian festivities? Which, she conceded, as she slid out of bed once more and pulled on jeans and a T-shirt, was ridiculous and unfair of her. Rayan had always celebrated Christmas fully with her and then, when they came along, with the girls.

It was 5.15am. She was going outside. Outside into the grounds to walk. To breathe.

Eva made her way through the same reception area she'd arrived at the previous afternoon, letting herself out of the house's classic solid timber door, its six panels forming an elegant, symmetrical centrepiece. Apparently, according to the brochure, the art retreat boasted twelve acres of gardens and woodlands, as well as over half a mile of shore around the lake, and she set off down the beautifully kept gardens to the lakeside. The stunning mountain scenery to the south softened gradually to the gently undulating hills of the north and, as she walked, breathing in the early morning scents of oriental poppies, astrantia, and a mass of red and yellow roses she recognised but couldn't identify, she began to feel calmer.

The star of this summer show of flowers was undoubtedly a large bushy plant covered in white flowers and Eva stopped to watch the industrious community of both bees and butterflies, intent on their bonanza of nectar, before carrying on down to the water's edge of Ullswater Lake.

The happiest combination of beauty and grandeur. Was it Wordsworth or Coleridge who'd penned those words in celebration of the stretch of Z-shaped Ullswater? Eva couldn't remember, knew it was probably one of them, and sat down on the edge of the lake, her toes in the icy water. And, when she realised the seat of her jeans was wet through, thought sod it, took them off, pulled her T-shirt over her head and went straight in.

The cold made her gasp, sent her heart racing, but, always a pretty strong swimmer, she dived down under the lake's icy depths and attempted a somewhat showy if uncoordinated crawl along the margin of the shoreline. Two minutes were more than enough, and gasping with the cold but thoroughly exhilarated at what she'd achieved, Eva waded and stumbled to the shore, stones and pebbles hurting her frozen feet as the tiny waves lapped and sucked at her ankles before retreating once more.

Shivering, her hands and feet totally numb, Eva made to rub herself down with her jeans and T-shirt before attempting to pull on the now damp clothes over her sopping underwear with useless fingers. Another swimmer was making their way to the shore a good fifteen metres or so from her. The man walked from the water – stark naked – and Eva realised it was Andrea Zaitsev. He must have seen her, must have known she was watching him, but made no attempt whatsoever to cover his nakedness. Indeed, as she struggled to pull her own T-shirt down over her wet bra, he turned his face towards her, closing his eyes and lifting his arms to rub at the mass of black curls before tying it back up in one practised move. The same black hair rose in a line from his groin and Eva, whose advances towards her husband had, for so long, been spurned and rejected, felt a bolt of lust shoot right through her.

She was still struggling to pull wet skinny-jeaned denim up

her cold, mottled legs as Andrea walked towards her. Now fully dressed in white jeans and a tight black T-shirt emphasising the quite glorious body beneath it, he hunkered down at her side.

'You appear to be struggling, Mrs Malik.'

Eva still couldn't quite work out his accent. 'Just a bit,' she twittered. 'Nearly there.'

'Maybe if I pull here? And here? The back of your T shirt is caught up under your armpit.' He adjusted the damp, clinging material and Eva was able to immediately pull down the rest of the T-shirt over her breasts and, embarrassed, haul up her jeans.

'You couldn't sleep?' Andrea asked.

'My own fault – probably too much alcohol.'

'Kills all creativity.' He smiled, reaching for a pack of cigarettes from his bag and lighting up.

'And that stuff just kills,' she admonished. 'I don't think I know anyone who smokes anymore. Oh, apart from my mother.' She was calling Alice Parkes her mother now? Susan, her mum, would be terribly hurt if she heard that.

'My one vice,' Andrea said, pulling deeply on the cigarette. 'I allow myself just the one, these days.'

'MS?' Eva asked, glancing at the packet.

'Italian,' Andrea replied.

'You are Italian?'

'My mother is Italian but my father was Russian.'

'Was?'

'He die several years ago.'

'Hence the accent?'

'We live in Moscow for many years. I go to school there but, when my father die, we leave and we return to Milan. My mother is there, and it is my base, but she miss her life in Moscow.'

'And will you go back? Can you go and just live in Russia whenever you want?'

'No.'

'Right.' Eva didn't probe further. 'And how come you've ended up here?'

'Teaching spoilt rich women to make mug that they can put on shelf and have as souvenir?' He smiled, but there was no malice in his tone. 'I'm a sculptor.'

'Sculptor? I thought I'd enrolled on a ceramics course?'

Andrea laughed. 'I have an exhibition up and running. It take me several years to complete and I suddenly find myself with bit of time on my hands. I love the Lake District and agree to teach here on the course for the three months the exhibition is up and running, before I go back to my workshop in Milan.'

'So, you are a potter as well as a sculptor?'

'Sculpting is my love, my life, but my mother is *ceramista* in Milan. I watch her and learn from her. The level I teach here is not difficult.'

'So, where is this exhibition of yours? London?'

'No, you probably don't know the place. Yorkshire Sculpture Park? It has both indoor and open-air galleries. Near Wakefield? Outside of London, it is perhaps the best place to see the work of both British and international artists.'

'Including Henry Moore and Barbara Hepworth.' Eva came straight back at him. 'The park's collection of works by Moore has one of the largest open-air displays of his bronzes in Europe.'

'You know it? You like Hepworth?'

'I know very little about either Henry Moore or Barbara Hepworth,' Eva said, conscious of the man's arm occasionally brushing her own as he talked and explained his passion. 'But I live just ten miles or so from the sculpture park.'

'Oh? Really? You live so near and yet you know *nothing* about these artists? Damien Hirst is there too.'

'Well, I know *something* about them,' Eva retorted, stung. 'I mean, we've often taken the children to Bretton Park.'

'To feed the ducks?' Andrea frowned. 'But not to appreciate the incredible talent?'

'Well, yes, I've pointed things out to my daughters. Explained the ideas the sculptor is trying to get over…'

'And then you go for ice cream and they forget what Henry

Moore is saying with his work.' It was a statement rather than a question.

'Hang on. Nora's only just three. She'd much rather…'

'It never too early to teach your children. My father was Minister for Health in Moscow and always very busy, often not at home.'

'Blimey, I bet you're glad he's not there now.'

'I'm not glad my father dead.'

'No, no, I didn't mean…'

'I know, I know. But my mother took me from when I was little boy to the RuArts Gallery, the Pushkin and Tretyakov. We go always to see the work of Yuri Albert and Evgeny Antufiev.'

'I'm sorry, I don't know them at all.'

There was a silence after that until, out of the blue, Andrea suddenly demanded, 'Why you here, Mrs Malik?'

'Because I couldn't sleep.'

'No, I don't mean here, at edge of water. I mean why you *here*, by yourself, learning simple pots?'

'If I told you, you might sprag me up.'

'Sprag up?' Andrea frowned.

'Sorry, Yorkshire term. Means *tell on me*.'

'And is there something to tell?' Andrea actually stroked her arm and Eva shivered. 'You cold. You need hot shower.'

'I'm a spy.'

'Now you telling lies. You say this because my father was in Russian government?' Andrea actually laughed as he spoke. 'You taking piss?'

Eva laughed in return. 'I'm not taking the piss.' Oh, sod it, there was no reason not to explain her true motives in enrolling on his course. 'I *am* actually here as a bit of a spy,' she smiled. 'I'm in the process of setting up my own art retreat. In Yorkshire.'

'Ah, so you *are* potter? You *know* how to make ceramics?'

Eva shook her head. 'Nope, not a clue. I'm a painter. Oils preferably, but I'm not bad with water colours.'

'With these nails?' Andrea took her hand, examining the red varnish.

'Not usually like this.' She grinned. 'Most of the week they're covered in paint. Although I then have to scrub them like mad, as I'm a dentist.'

'A dentist? You're a dentist?' Andrea stared. 'Mrs Malik, I need to know more.'

'It's Eva.'

'Eva, after we work today, will you tell me more? I'm intrigued.'

'Is that a chat-up line you use on all your pupils?'

'You think I'm *chatting you up*?' Andrea raised an eyebrow.

Scarlet with mortification – here was another man who didn't fancy her, from whom she was reading the wrong message – Eva stood. 'No, of course not,' she lied. 'Right, off for a shower,' she sang gaily over her shoulder. 'Must get on.'

Andrea caught at her hand, taking a navy cashmere sweater from his bag and placing it round Eva's shoulders. Italian, she thought dizzily, as he tied the sleeves around her neck. 'Eva, *of course* I'm chatting you up.'

27

Eva found she was enjoying handling the grey lump of clay much more than she'd ever anticipated she would. She'd done some ceramics both on her GCSE and A-level art courses at school and college, but throwing pots had never really been her thing. Once she'd seen off the maths and sciences she was also, for some strange reason, very competent at, she was always to be found in the art departments, indulging her love of oils and little else.

So, it was with some surprise that she found she was really appreciating learning, and enjoying, this new skill and, glancing across at the efforts of the three other women – all American and all probably in their seventies – she realised she wasn't bad at all.

'You've done this before, Eva,' Cynthia from Cincinnati complained as her pot disintegrated on the wheel and flew off before she could save it.

'Just a little, Cynthia,' Eva agreed.

Andrea moved behind the other woman, placed another piece of clay on the wheel and guided her hands with his own. 'Slowly, slowly,' he intoned. 'Art, like good food and making love, should be taken slowly.' He glanced across at Eva who felt her insides turn to liquid as her face blushed pink. Hell, she might be good at throwing pots, but she felt totally out of practice in the art of flirting, of knowing whether this man *was* actually flirting with her or just charming his way through the repetitiveness of teaching the same thing over and over again to a bunch of amateurs.

After lunch with the others – Andrea didn't join the group this time and, when they returned to the annexe, he made no mention of where he might have been – the four of them were set the task of designing a cup and a plate. Eva enjoyed this bit immensely, finding and using watercolours that had been set out on the table to enhance the two mugs and plates she was designing to make for Laila and Nora.

'You have talent,' Andrea said, coming up behind her and watching as she drew and painted in their names on the planning paper. 'These are for your little girls?'

Eva nodded.

'And they're at home?'

'They're actually all at Bolton Abbey having a picnic with my in-laws.'

'And you don't want to be there? With them? This art retreat you are planning is more important than your little girls?'

Eva felt tears start and she shook her head, afraid to speak.

'It complicated?'

'It's complicated,' Eva agreed and then, regaining some composure she went on, 'I wasn't invited.'

'You don't get on with your in-laws?'

'I love my in-laws.' Actually, that wasn't strictly true. There were times when Azra, Rayan's mother, had driven her mad, arriving unannounced, taking over her kitchen and filling the house with spicy cooking smells.

'My husband and I have recently separated,' Eva finally admitted. 'I'm not finding it easy.'

'I would think, Eva, you need more than playing Happy Families. Your art is too important to you.'

'You can't know that.' Eva felt cross. 'You don't know me, and my girls are *everything* to me.'

'I'm sure they are.' Andrea moved to the side of her, blocking the view of Cynthia and Bernadette who were both earwigging. He lowered his voice. 'You don't say *your husband* is everything to you.'

'I...'

'You have outgrown him, maybe?'

'He's not a sweater I've shrunk in the wash,' Eva said angrily. 'I'm not finding this easy to cope with.'

'You're not being honest with yourself, I think?' He turned to the other women in the room. 'OK, we have planned our cups? We throw them. Not on the floor, Cynthia, please. We throw them and tonight I put them in kiln. Now, I demonstrate once more. Come, gather round.'

Andrea sat at one of the wheels and took fresh clay. 'OK, watch, Cynthia: centre clay on wheel; now push while centred to size; pull wall to dimensions...'

Eva found herself losing concentration. Was Andrea right in his prognosis of her marriage? Had she outgrown Rayan? Did her art mean more than saving her marriage? She thought of all the weekends and evenings over the past few years when she'd sloped off up to Heatherly Hall in order to paint in the little studio Bill had sorted for her. Bill knew. Bill understood. And yet Bill wasn't her father after all...

'...we smooth walls with rib; and we turn upside down for trimming...'

Andrea finished his demonstration and glanced at the clock on the studio wall. 'Afternoon tea, I believe?'

The three Americans' eyes lit up and they immediately started taking off aprons and washing hands.

'Eva? You want little sandwiches? Scones with cream and jam? English tea?'

'Actually no. I'm still full after lunch and I'd rather get on with this.'

'Ladies?' Andrea followed the others to the door. 'You have half an hour. We have much to get through if these are to be in kiln tonight.' He turned back to Eva once the others passed the window on their way back to the dining room. 'Shall we make a start?'

'A start?' Hell, what was he suggesting? She hoped desperately he wasn't going to kiss her. She hoped desperately that he was.

'The wheel? We only have three. We need to get yours started to give the others a turn when they get back. 'OK, sit.'

Eva sat.

He placed a lump of clay on the wheel and Eva started it spinning slowly with her foot, her hands concentrating on shaping, pushing and pulling.

'Not so fast, take it easy.' Andrea pulled up a stool behind hers and, sitting behind her, took her hands in his own, directing, persuading, pushing and caressing.

'Ghost,' Eva muttered, trying to concentrate on her pot rather than his breath on her cheek, his warm body on her own.

'The film, *Ghost*?' Andrea said and she knew he was smiling. 'You're right: *Ghost*.' He bent his head and she thought he was about to kiss her neck – was desperate for him to kiss her neck – but he simply redirected her hands to a better position and then stood, leaving her to it.

By six o'clock, Eva was buzzing. Despite her very early start and lack of sleep the previous evening, she was fizzing with excitement, and couldn't stop admiring the two raw cups and plates she'd made for her girls. The other three women had managed one apiece or, in Cynthia's case, some strange little vessel that didn't appear to know whether it was a vase, trinket box or mug. They'd all left half an hour earlier for cocktails and canapés but, determined to make cups for each of the girls, Eva had stayed behind to complete them while Andrea tidied up and switched on the kiln, waiting for it to heat up.

'You miss dinner if you don't go now.' Andrea smiled.

'I need a shower as well,' Eva said, picking up her bag and sweater, but reluctant to actually leave.

'I go to meet a friend now in Pooley Bridge,' Andrea said. 'I supposed to stay and have dinner and chat to guests,' he went on. 'Part of job description. But I have enough today.'

'OK.' Eva made to go, disappointed. She didn't, she realised, want to leave him. 'See you tomorrow.'

Andrea nodded and then, as she started to close the door behind her, he said softly, 'You want to have ride with me later, Eva?'

'A ride?' Eva's pulse raced. Did Andrea not understand the ambiguity of the word?

Andrea nodded again. 'You have shower and enjoy dinner. I'll be back around nine-thirty. We have ride and you tell me all about your art retreat. Yes?'

'Oh.' Eva hesitated. 'I believe there's a talk later on by some Lake District artist.'

'He very boring. Very paint-by-numbers artist. No excitement there.'

Eva immediately remembered Lachlan Buchanan pointing out that Alice Parkes had not become a world-famous icon through painting by numbers, and smiled at the recollection.

'You very beautiful when you smile, Eva.'

'Oh, thank you.' She went slightly pink. 'OK, nine-thirty then?'

Already late for dinner, Eva dashed back to her room and rang the girls.

'We're having a lovely time. Mummy, but I wish you were here.' Laila sounded plaintive and Eva's heart went out to her.

'Darling, I wish I was there too, but I've had to come and do my homework for the new art retreat Aunty Hannah and Aunty Rosa and I are going to set up at Heatherly Hall. You know, like you have to do your homework for Miss Worthington? Listen, I've learnt how to throw pots, Laila.'

'You're throwing them? Is somebody catching them?' Laila was puzzled.

'I'm learning to *make* pots,' Eva explained, laughing. 'I'm making mugs and plates for you and Nora.'

'Will you teach me?' Laila asked, excited.

'Yes, definitely.' And Eva realised she was going to do just that. She felt she really could teach total beginners the basics now, if needs be. She chatted some more to Laila, finding out just what they'd been doing all day and then, once she'd spoken to Nora, who'd sung her a song her Aunty Hadhira had taught her, asked to speak to Daddy.

'Are they OK, Rayan?'

'Yes, we're all fine. We're going to have dinner in the hotel, now. Are you OK, Eva?'

'Me? Do you care?'

'Of course I care.' Rayan hesitated. 'I can't stop caring for you, Eva, just like that.'

Eva felt tears start and she sniffed them away.

'You know we were washed up, Eva. We couldn't go on like we were, making each other so unhappy.'

She nodded, unable to speak.

'Eva?'

'I know, Rayan. I know.' It was time, she knew, to start being honest with Rayan. As well as herself.

Eva showered and towelled herself dry and then, realising she hadn't shaved her legs for weeks, jumped back under the water, using the complimentary plastic shaver supplied by the retreat. She was just debating whether to shave off her bush – what *was* the thinking on this, these days? – but realised she'd probably end up nicking herself or looking like a plucked chicken and anyway, she really liked her pubic hair; had never got why kids wanted to end up looking like pre-pubescents rather than women.

She hadn't brought any body lotion or perfume with her, but found her trusty tube of hand cream in her handbag and rubbed it into every bit of her skin. She sniffed at herself – hmm, slightly lemony – and cleaned her teeth. She dried her hair, pleased that she'd let it grow back to its longer length rather than the shorter bob she'd sported for a few years, did her make-up and went to investigate her overnight case in the hope that, she might, by chance, have packed some matching sexy underwear.

She hadn't.

She pulled on a clean pair of M and S knickers, berating herself for the ridiculous direction her thoughts were taking her, and went down to dinner.

'I thought it was a drive you suggested?' Eva asked when, at nine-thirty, she dutifully presented herself after walking through the almost hypnotically scented gardens towards the back of the house. It was still incredibly light, and Eva reminded herself that not only were they heading for the longest day but, up here in the far North of England, in midsummer, night-time descended even later than in Yorkshire. She looked round for the promised car.

'I'm up here,' Andrea smiled. He'd changed out of the white jeans and black T-shirt, exchanging them for Levi's and a white one. 'Come on.'

He led the way through a neat vegetable garden, through an orchard of apple, plum and pear trees, the tiny buds of fruit the promise of an abundant harvest in the months ahead, and through yet more well-tended rose gardens, alive with insomniac bees. 'You should be in bed,' Eva muttered to the bees as Andrea finally came to a standstill at a stable block.

'When you said a ride, you meant *a horse ride*?' Eva glanced in trepidation towards the stable block. She was not a horsey sort of girl; neither Rosa, Hannah nor herself had ever longed for a horse or asked to have riding lessons when they were kids. The nearest the three of them had got to anything horsey was mucking out the alpacas at the petting zoo up at Heatherly Hall when they were kids. And they'd hated that.

Andrea smiled, went into one of the stables and returned with a black hard hat, which he passed to Eva. 'I really don't think...'

she began to Andrea's back as he retreated into the stable, presumably to bring out some great snorting stallion she was going to have to get her leg over…

Leg over? Ha!

'OK, what you wearing? Trousers?' Andrea frowned as he came back out and handed her a leather jacket, before zipping himself into one of his own and reaching behind him for his own hard hat. 'You not afraid of speed?'

'As long as it's not on a horse.' She breathed a sigh of relief when she looked down properly at the hard hat and realised it was a bike helmet. 'Whose jacket and helmet are these?' she asked, pulling on the leather top and fiddling inexpertly with the helmet.

'Bella's,' he said shortly, as if that explained it all.

'Bella?' Eva stood still as Andrea moved to help with the recalcitrant fastening on Bella's (whoever she was) helmet. The heady smell of leather and the faint hint of a lemony aftershave mixed with the cinnamon waves from the many tubs of night-scented stocks gracing the front of the stables was making her weak at the knees for this man in front of her.

'There,' Andrea said, checking her (Bella's) jacket. 'Good to go.'

'Bella?' Eva asked again as Andrea returned to the stable and wheeled out one of the biggest motorbikes she'd ever seen. She was beginning to think the stallion a better option.

'Bella work here, but her days off. She leave for Manchester on train,' he said shortly, flipping the pillion foot rests on the bike before mounting and steadying himself, both feet squarely on the ground. 'OK, Eva,' he commanded, once she'd managed to mount the bike behind him. 'Put your hands around me. You need relaxed but firm grip and move with bike naturally. Just do what feel right. You OK?'

'Yep,' she squeaked. Shit, she thought, as the bike set off through the stable yard and down towards the large open wooden gate, before turning right onto the country road and accelerating at speed. Eva felt her heart and pulse escalate in unison with the bike as the Harley Davidson roared along, the warm summer evening breeze in her face and the rumble of the V-twin engine beneath and between her legs.

Andrea powered the bike through the village of Pooley Bridge before taking the main road that clung to, and followed, the margin of Ullswater lake to their left. Once on the main road, the bike gathered momentum and Eva realised they were probably well over the speed limit, but she felt totally safe in this man's hands, surrendering to the glorious experience of flying through the summer evening as dusk began to descend and a large strawberry moon rose over the lake itself.

Andrea slowed down completely as he took them through the villages of Watermillock and Glenridding where tents and B and Bs announced their popularity with tourists and then, leaving the A road, continued slowly down country lanes until he pulled up at a quirky-looking pub in the village of Patterdale.

'Where the dogs come from,' Eva said as, with slightly shaky legs, she dismounted the bike and waited until Andrea parked correctly in front of the pub.

'Dogs?' Andrea smiled, removing his helmet and unzipping his leathers.

'Patterdale terriers. No idea what they look like, but I guess they must have originated from here.'

'What will you drink?' Andrea asked. 'I'm just having Coke, but don't let that stop you.'

'Do you know, I really fancy a cider. Sorry, no money on me. Hang on, I've got my phone, somewhere.' Eva pulled a face of apology and patted at Bella's jacket pocket before unzipping it and sitting at one of the vacant tables outside.

'No worry.' Andrea grinned. 'You pay me back later.'

Pay him back? What the hell did he have in mind? Sweating slightly, her pulse racing once more, Eva shrugged off the other woman's jacket and, running a hand through her flattened hair, wished she'd at least brought a lipstick with her.

Andrea placed the glass of cider in front of Eva and sat squarely in front of her, before sinking half of his pint of Coke in one go.

'Bad for your teeth.' Eva, ever the dentist, smiled.

'Do you never do thing that is bad for you?' Andrea raised an eyebrow.

'I think I just did,' Eva said ruefully. 'I have two little girls at home. Coming off that bike at speed could have left them without their mother.' She took a long drink of the dry cider which was cold and utterly delicious. 'Having said that, there appears to be a new one waiting in the wings.'

'Oh?' When Eva didn't feel able to expand further, Andrea took the glass from her hand, placed it on the table and, instead, took her hand in his own. 'Eva, tell me. Tell me it all.'

And she did. Told this man, who listened, nodded, occasionally broke in to ask a question, everything. About Rosa and Hannah, about being a triplet – *you are tripletta? There are two more of you?* – and inheriting Heatherly Hall; about recently meeting her birth father, the break-up of her marriage; the planned art retreat. And, eventually, that her biological mother was Alice Parkes and her father Yves Dufort.

'*Oh, Dio mio*.' Andrea leaned back on his chair and stared at Eva.

'Actually, Andrea,' Eva said embarrassed. 'Forget I said that. I shouldn't have told you.'

'It is lie? You make it up?'

'No, it's true, but not something, at this stage, I want to be made public.'

'I would think you want to shout it from the rooftop?' Andrea continued to stare and then grinned, running a hand through his long dark curly hair. 'No wonder you good at drawing this afternoon. Alice Parkes? Yves Dufort?' He whistled, and then reached a hand to Eva's face, the ball of his thumb tracing the length of her full bottom lip. 'You sit for me, Eva?'

'Sit for you?' Eva stared in turn. 'What do you mean?'

'I would like to draw you. To sketch you.'

'I thought you were a sculptor?'

'Of course. But I need to sketch to begin with. Before I sculpt. You know?'

Eva nodded.

'Come.' Andrea took Eva's hand and together they walked back to the bike. She waited until he steadied the bike once more, jeaned legs across the seat, both feet on the ground but, instead of turning the ignition and reaching for his helmet, he turned to her. Reaching a warm hand up to her face, he threaded fingers through her hair before gently pulling her towards his open mouth and kissing the corner of her own with such expertise she thought she might just fall over, right there in the middle of the pub car park.

She most certainly hadn't been expecting anything like *this* when she left Yorkshire the previous afternoon.

28

'You actually live here? In the stables?' Eva took off the helmet and unzipped the leathers, handing them both to Andrea who, after wheeling the Harley back into one of the stables, had come back out to retrieve them from her.

'Not actually in stable.' Andrea laughed. 'I'm not horse. The staff quarters are above.' He nodded skywards. 'The stables are used for cars and bikes. And storage. Come.'

Andrea led the way up a flight of steps, which led to a corridor of white-painted doors. 'The stable boys used to live here, apparently, as well as some of servants when there was no space in attics across at house for them.' He took a key, unlocking and opening the third door along. 'You alright coming in here with me?'

'Alright?'

'I don't want you to think I bring you here to… you know…' Andrea suddenly seemed somewhat shy, unsure of himself. 'I need to sketch you.' He frowned. 'The light not the best now, but no time tomorrow. You go home tomorrow, I believe?'

Eva nodded. 'Just here for the weekend.' She looked around the room. While basically a fairly monastic cell, the room was clean and neat and Andrea had obviously endeavoured to make it his home for his three months' contract with Dame Bryony. A corner of the room, under the window, held a small sink and fitted microwave, a minute fridge and kettle. A complicated-looking sound system, laptop and books in both Russian and Italian almost filled one side of the room, while an Italian-inspired throw, in a dark-coloured, silky crepe de chine graced the single bed.

'You didn't carry all this lot up here to Cumbria on your bike?' Eva smiled, moving across to the books to find out what Andrea was reading. Amongst the titles she couldn't decipher, she found some she could. Several were in English: biographies of the Romantic poets – Wordsworth, Byron and Coleridge – as well as anthologies of their work.

Andrea moved towards her, stroking her face briefly before walking to a shelf from which he took a large pad and charcoal. 'No, I don't bring all this up on bike – an impossibility. I ride my bike from Milan to Sculpture Park in Yorkshire at the same time as my sculptures come in lorry. And then I ride up here, and my mother send my things I can't do without, on here for me.'

'You biked all the way here?' Eva was impressed. 'Goodness.'

'So, you go home tomorrow?' Andrea asked again, moving a chair to the door. He frowned, shook his head and moved the chair back to where it was. When he was happy with its position, he beckoned her over and she sat while he lifted and rearranged her hair from her face.

His touch was electric and, unable not to, Eva unconsciously moved into his hand slightly.

'Later, Eva,' he murmured, moving to sit on the bed opposite her with his sketchpad.

Embarrassed that her wanting him to touch her was so obvious, Eva stiffened.

'Eva, relax. You can't believe how much I want to kiss you again. But just give me ten minutes on this. Ten minutes to get you on paper…'

Ten minutes morphed into twenty and then forty-five, giving Eva ample time to study Andrea as he worked in silence, adding lines and marks to the paper, rubbing at the charcoal, frowning occasionally. How could she ever have thought, the previous evening when she first saw him across the table at dinner, that he was ordinary? Andrea Zaitsev was *anything* but ordinary. He was utterly beautiful, his smooth olive skin unmarked except for frown lines on his forehead and a scar – the mere whisper of a silvery white line – near the corner of his right eye. His facial hair – very similar to Rayan's she mused – was, like Rayan's, heavily stubbled and yet falling just short of a full beard. His clear, intelligent eyes were almond-shaped, very dark and, when he smiled, as he was doing now, full of humour.

'May I see?' Eva asked as he stood, placed the pad on the bed and went to the sink to wash his hands.

'Of course. Vodka?'

'Vodka?

'Every Russian worth his salt – is that correct English saying? – drink vodka.' He smiled in Eva's direction and then busied himself with glasses and a bottle while Eva crossed the room to look at the drawing.

'You like it?'

'It's very clever...'

'But?'

'But... you've made me look a bit... miserable?'

'Sad, Eva. I think you sad from minute I saw you last night. You are going through sad time in your life.'

'So, what will you do with the sketch?'

'I have commission for outside City Hall in Milan.'

'Oh? I don't know Milan at all.'

'It was originally beautiful palace designed by Galeazzo Alessi and built in sixteenth century for very wealthy Genoese trader called Tommaso Marino. Since nineteenth century, the Palazzo Marino is used as City Hall. Its *Sala Alessi* is usually reception hall for special guests of the city.'

'And you are doing a sculpture for them?'

'I've been approached. It at planning stage, but they are serious about my work. The corners of ceiling are decorated with paintings by Aurelio Busso representing the four seasons, and there are frescos and bas reliefs that show story of Perseus.'

Andrea smiled and tilted Eva's face up to the light. 'You very good model for the ideas I have for sculpture of Autumn.'

'I think I'd rather be Spring,' Eva grumbled. 'Or Summer.'

'Believe me, Eva, you are Autumn… Fall… Autunno… Na Osen. Call it what you like, you are Autumn.' Andrea picked up the pad, obviously pleased with what he'd achieved in the time. He drained the shot glass of vodka while Eva continued to sip at hers. She'd only ever drunk the spirit doused in orange juice and, without this addition, was finding it hard going.

'You want to return?'

'Return?'

'Back to your beautiful, overheated room that you have spent so much money on booking? You have very early start, this morning, swimming in lake. You must be tired?'

Eva glanced over her glass. Was he mocking her? Laughing at her? She didn't think so. 'No,' she said finally. 'I don't want to return.'

'That is good,' Andrea said softly, taking the shot glass from her hand and placing it on the table. 'Because, Eva, I would very much like you to stay.'

'To draw me again?' Eva felt ridiculously trembly even though she knew she was coming out with banalities.

'If that what you want, Eva?'

Eva felt Andrea coolly appraising her but she didn't answer. Didn't quite know how to say that she just wanted him to kiss her like he'd kissed her in the pub car park, without sounding either needy, tarty or like something from a Mills and Boon romance. He turned and reached for his pad once more.

'I…' Eva started. God, where was the confident girl she used to be? 'I… I'm not used to this…'

'This?'

'Being in a man's bedroom. I mean, who isn't my husband.' Eva felt the colour flood her face.

'And you wish you were with your husband? You miss him?'

'Andrea, my husband hasn't made love to me for the last two years.' Eva reached for her glass once more for something to do with her hands and took a long drink of the vodka, hoping it might give her some confidence. Unfortunately, it just made her cough. 'And...' cough cough... 'and... I've...' cough... 'forgotten how it all works. Forgotten where everything goes...' cough...

'Hey,' Andrea frowned, taking her hand. 'Eva, we just sit and talk if that what you want.'

'It's not what I want,' Eva said. 'And no, I don't miss my husband.' She realised she was speaking the truth on both accounts.

Andrea walked the few steps over to her and, taking her hand, brought her to her feet. He bent his head and, as he'd done in the car park, kissed each corner of her mouth before running the tip of his tongue slowly along her upper lip. He brought both hands up to her hair, holding her face and kissing each closed eyelid as Eva breathed in his scent – something citrus and yet totally masculine – until suddenly it came back to her what to do. It was like riding a bike: you never forgot how to react. She'd only had the cider and half the shot glass of vodka and yet she felt drunk. She was drunk on this man, she realised, every sense heightened.

Andrea gently pulled the flimsy cotton sweater from its anchorage in her jeans belt, kissing her all the while, and then two strong warm hands were inching their way up her back, stroking, smoothing until Eva felt her legs almost buckle. His hands were on the hem of the material, bringing it upwards to actually pull over her head.

But it was stuck.

God, Eva thought, almost in panic, my head's grown in the two years since I last did this, but Andrea was turning her round, undoing the zip that she had forgotten, and he hadn't realised, was there.

'You are very beautiful, Eva,' Andrea was now saying as, still behind her, she felt fingers tracing her backbone then his mouth on her skin, licking, kissing, caressing...

'Nearly forty and two children.' Eva gasped slightly as her bra was unfastened and her hair lifted from the nape of her neck, Andrea's stroking fingers replaced by his warm mouth. Unable to bear it any longer without almost mewing in ecstasy, she turned back to face him.

'I am artist.' Andrea smiled. 'Believe me, when I say you very beautiful.'

Emboldened by this, Eva brought her hands to his white T-shirt and, slowly, undid the large leather belt above the swelling in his jeans that told her everything she needed to know: this man really *did* want her. He wasn't going to reject her, wasn't about to stay her hand and turn away from her as had been the case for so long with Rayan.

Andrea's body was quite magnificent – but then, she'd already seen that for herself at the lakeside earlier that morning – and she ran tentative hands around his waist to his smooth-skinned back, moving them down to the tightly muscled backside.

'Goodness,' Eva breathed in admiration, any nerves gone as she stroked and delighted in such toned buttocks. 'I'm going to ask Santa for a Harley Davidson if this is what you get from riding a bike. You could crack a Brazil with these.'

Andrea laughed out loud at that. 'You talk too much, Eva.' He took her hands from the back of his jeans and pulled her down onto the floor before taking off his T-shirt and making love to her so thoroughly and selflessly and in probably – as Eva recounted to Hannah and Rosa once she was back at home – exactly the way one would expect from an Italian man.

Sunday morning and with it came the rain, coming down with such force and in such a deluge, Eva seriously began to look out for Noah and his mates. Andrea had walked her back to her room around 2am and for that she'd been grateful. Making love to someone she'd only just met was fine (and more than absolutely incredibly wonderful) but she wasn't ready for the intimacy of actually *sleeping* in the same bed (and a single one at that) with that someone.

Despite the lack of sleep, Eva felt refreshed, almost reborn. *Oh, give it a rest, Eva*, she upbraided herself as she helped herself to coffee and a croissant, eschewing the cooked breakfast on offer. *You've had sex for the first time in two years and with a new man, not climbed Everest.*

And yet she felt calmer, less anxious, less miserable and panic-stricken about her life without Rayan. A man – and not any old random fumbler from the village after three pints of Tetley's in The Jolly Sailor – had very obviously wanted her, found her attractive; most certainly hadn't been repelled by her own latent desire.

Eva looked round the breakfast room where other guests were filing in and filling up plates with eggs, bacon and sausages before sitting singly and in small groups at the smaller tables, which had replaced the long communal table at which guests had been previously invited to dine. This was obviously what guests wanted and expected: food, was, it seemed, just as important to would-be artists as the actual teaching and practical work. This was what she'd set out to find out. She would be able to report back to Hannah, Rosa and Lachlan and put forward more of her plans for the Heatherly Hall Art Retreat.

Retreat? Eva mused as she poured more coffee. Wrong word maybe, this 'R' word? Did *retreat* conjure up more an idea of some sort of monastic cell and plain food, with Rosa brought in to say an encouraging prayer over their bread and water repast in order to encourage their creativity? Art Experience? Art Adventure? This weekend had certainly been an adventure for her. Should she also, she frowned at the thought, be on the lookout for gorgeous, talented teachers like Andrea Zaitsev in order to hook the punters? And would she be able to keep her own hands off such gorgeous paid help? She smiled at that and poured yet more coffee.

'You smile this morning, Eva.' Andrea had come into the

dining room, his hair dripping, the shoulders of his faded denim shirt wet through from the rain. He poured coffee for himself before sitting across the table from her. 'You are slightly happier?'

'I think so,' Eva admitted. 'Thank you for last night.'

'Why you thank me?' Andrea frowned. 'It something I very much *enjoy* – not duty. And the sketch I make, Eva, that so helpful to my idea for Palazzo Marino. Now...' he looked round '...I *must* do my duty and talk to other guests or I get into trouble for spending all my time with beautiful ones.' And, without another word, he stood and moved across to sit with Cynthia from Cincinnati and Bernadette from Alabama.

The rest of that Sunday morning was spent painting and firing the beautiful mugs and plates Eva had created with the expertise she hadn't known was in her, adding with love the colour and decoration relevant to each of her little girls. She was, she knew, desperate to get back to them later that afternoon, but, at the same time, Andrea was keeping her from disregarding another meal in the dining room and setting off back to Yorkshire earlier than she was expected to.

At one o'clock, the four women in the group gathered around Andrea for a ten-minute plenary and to view each other's work. Eva was very obviously top of the class. 'You've done this before, honey.' Bernadette laughed, but her tone was slightly accusing. 'Or...' she glanced towards Andrea and back at Eva '...ah reckon you've had an unfair advantage over the rest of us girls. Right,' she went on, 'ah had so much breakfast, ah was fit to pop, but ah'm just about starved once again.'

The four women left the annexe, making their way across the rain-swept gardens to the dining room and lunch. 'You want to join them, Eva?' Andrea, leaning against a work table, folded his arms, looking long and hard at her until she felt the colour rise in her cheeks once more. As well as a longing for this man's touch on her again.

What I want, Andrea, is for you to unfold your arms and put them, instead, around me, Eva thought wistfully but instead, she said, 'I'm going to head back to Yorkshire, I think.'

Andrea took her hand in his own. 'Your manicure is gone,' he said, smiling. 'Good. That is good. Real artists don't have time for red nails. He lifted her fingers to his mouth. 'You have talent, beautiful Eva. I...' He broke off. 'Eva, I don't want you to go. I need to see you again.' He took her in his arms and she rested her head on his chest, hearing his heartbeat, so happy to be there. 'It is long, long time since I feel like this,' he added almost wistfully.

Eva breathed a deep sigh of pure happiness. 'Andrea...' she started, but broke off as the outer door to the annexe opened and banged shut. She stepped quickly away from him, understanding that the management of Dame Bryony would not be happy to see one of its paying guests in the arms of one of its teachers. She moved to pick up the girls' mugs and plates as the annexe's inner door opened and a young girl, perhaps in her late twenties, came in, laughing as she squeezed rainwater from her long blonde hair.

'I'm back, Andrea,' she called, moving to kiss his cheek. 'Had enough of Manchester after a day – missed the fresh air and blue skies.' She laughed, shaking her wet hair at him. 'And missed you of course.' She kissed his mouth this time, before turning to Eva who she'd obviously only just realised was behind her. 'Hi, have you been working with Andrea? He's so talented, isn't he?' She extended the free hand that wasn't snaking possessively around Andrea's waist, in Eva's direction. 'I'm Bella. I teach here at Dame Bryony as well.'

29

'*I can't do it anymore, Rosa, I just can't do it.*'

Joe Rosavina's words, shouted loudly down the carriage of the London to Leeds train almost a week previously, had reverberated round Rosa's brain ever since, repeating themselves while she tossed and turned in bed; there while she mowed the vicarage lawn and weeded the flowerbeds; even with her while taking the funeral service of ninety-year-old Joyce Taylor the previous week and certainly present while opening yet another tin of cat food for Elvis who, she'd discovered, had the incessantly voracious appetite of a teenage boy. At least Elvis appeared to have seen off the rat problem, and she was actually getting used to having the cat around, missing him when he was off on one of his night-time sorties, pleased when he made his reappearance back in his favourite resting place, scratching and settling down in a flurry of black hair onto the rug at the bottom of her bed.

She'd been planning on bringing Elvis into church with her this Sunday morning, had written her sermon around him, the central character in praise of all God's creatures.

Unfortunately, the star of the show appeared to have left: *Elvis has left the building*. She'd spent the previous evening watching the film *Elvis* on Netflix (drooling in a most unvicarly manner over the actor, Austin Butler) and had not only cobbled together some of the man's most well-known songs on the church's sound system, ably assisted by Nile, formerly known as Nigel, who had also promised to belt out Elvis's version of 'Glory Glory Halleluiah', in praise of the Lord above.

It would either work or be a total disaster.

I can't live in the same village as you, Rosa, and not be with you.

Joe's words were still crashing through her brain as she welcomed her brethren into church; were still there as she led the congregation in prayer and still firmly in situ like some insistent ear worm when, taking her eyes from the lectern as she stood in the pulpit and, glancing to her left, saw Sam Burrows had joined, and was sitting with, her mum, Susan, and sister Virginia, in their usual pew at the front of the church.

Having had to further assure Sam that she *really couldn't* marry him, *couldn't* continue their relationship, Rosa had finally told him gently – and then rather more firmly – that she was unable to give him the love he deserved. Any sighting of him since, whether in the village, when he just appeared to be passing by (which was a hell of a lot) or his presence in church, like now, made her feel terribly apprehensive.

Rosa left the pulpit and walked to the front of the church, anxiety at seeing Sam totally affecting her train of thought. What was she meant to be talking about? What sermon had she planned? Why the hell, when she turned to the choir behind her, was Nile Cartwright dressed in a strange white fringed outfit? She didn't have a clue. Her brain was an empty fishbowl, devoid of any relevant thought about her planned sermon. She'd no notes, no aide-memoire, nothing whatsoever to remind her what the hell she was supposed to be talking about. The congregation was getting restless, concerned even, as she stood there, frozen with stage fright. Someone coughed, another sneezed. A baby began to cry.

Still nothing.

And then, trotting down the aisle, tail erect, benevolent orange eyes seeking out the woman who'd latterly taken on the job of Keeper of the Whiskas, came Elvis.

Suddenly, like a ray of sunshine parting the clouds, it all

came back and Rosa was off, gathering up a compliant Elvis who settled placidly into her white-surpliced arms before telling the story of Elvis and the rats, of the verger's cat creeping and creaking up the vicarage's uncarpeted stairs; of watching the film *Elvis* the previous evening. Then watching as Nile Cartwright, to the entertainment of the congregation, gave the performance of his week, gyrating his hips in their white fringed trousers while belting out 'Glory, Glory Halleluiah', Daphne Merton bashing out the accompaniment on the organ while the choir swayed and sang in unison, convinced they were in Las Vegas rather than Westenbury Parish church.

Spontaneous applause and laughter broke out at the end of the performance and Elvis (the cat) put out that his slumber had been disturbed, stretched his unsheathed claws on Rosa's arm and jumped down in a flurry of cat hair before sauntering idly back up the aisle. He settled himself down halfway up its length, considering, before taking up the offer of another pair of arms from the adoring congregation.

Rosa smiled, stretching her neck to see who Elvis's new disciple was. Then her eyes met another pair, gazing back: blue eyes, beloved eyes, that radiated nothing but love for herself. And Rosa suddenly knew that it was time to forgive, time to accept she'd never stopped loving Joe Rosavina, that she never would stop loving him.

Time now, Joe, to not only forgive, but forget. For which blessing she could only thank the Lord.

Slowly, she walked down the church towards Joe and, as the congregation turned in surprise, unsure whether the morning's service was actually over or not, half standing and then, when Rosa started to speak, hurriedly sitting once again as their vicar said a final prayer to her brethren, to her friends, her family, her villagers; to her only one true love:

'I take my final thoughts from Mark 11:25,' she said in a clear voice, before pausing, smiling and intoning:

'"And when you stand praying, if you hold against anyone, forgive them, so that your Father in heaven may forgive you your sins also."'

'I would imagine Grandpa Cecil is turning in his grave,' Virginia snapped as she led her two gloomy-looking adolescent offspring down the aisle towards Rosa. 'It was like something out of *Sister Act*. Elvis, for heaven's sake? And that mangy cat in church? We'll never get its hair out of the hassocks...' She stopped abruptly when she saw Joe sitting to her left. 'Oh... forgiveness? Oh, that's what that affected little prayer, halfway up the church was all about, was it?' She sniffed, drawing herself up to her full height of five foot three. 'Well, on your head be it, Rosa. I hope you know what you're doing...'

Virginia suddenly reversed back down the aisle, like a car in the wrong gear, grabbing at Barty and Bethany as she went. 'Have some thought for Sam,' she hissed back at Rosa, before bumping into and attempting to manoeuvre the man in question along the empty pew and down the left-hand side of the church.

Sam, however, had caught sight of Joe, the much-maligned Elvis sitting smugly on the other man's knee; and he'd caught sight of Rosa who'd now moved to sit at Joe's side, holding his hand, instead of at her usual post outside the church shaking hands with her departing congregation. In a fit of obvious uncontrolled anger, he suddenly launched himself at Joe, grabbing him by the shirt collar and twisting in fury.

'For *heaven's sake*, Sam.' Rosa was on her feet, trying to get between them, while Virginia, in turn, pulled at her sister's cat-hair-covered white surplice. Elvis (the cat) scarpered in disgust at the disturbance while Elvis (Nile – formerly known as Nigel – Cartwright) seeing his one best chance to get his hands on Rosa, flung both his arms around her, hauling her off protesting back down the aisle and away from the departing congregation who, realising something was amiss, were craning necks and rubbernecking for Britain.

Virginia then made a grab for Sam as the fight appeared to go out of him out of him, turning and launching him like a propelling pencil in front of her and down towards the vestry and the back exit away from both Joe and Rosa.

Finally, Rosa managed to extract herself from Nile's clutches, dust herself down and walk calmly to the church door, reassuring the departing churchgoers that all was well.

'Go in peace.' She smiled, shaking hands and patting heads, asking after Mr Harper's prize onions, Mrs Lindley's bunions and Ellen Blake's new great grandson in Canada before ushering them out into the rain-splattered churchyard and off to their Sunday dinners.

'Go in peace?' Hilary Makepiece was already breathing down her neck. 'Not overly *peaceful* in there, was it? You know, Rosa, I totally had your back, was the one who really insisted the parish committee take you on when we interviewed you…'

'Not now, Hilary,' Rosa sighed, running a hand through her hair.

'Look at you, Vicar, covered in cat hair.' Hilary tutted, attempting to brush her down. 'The thing is, there's already a bit of talk…'

'Talk?'

'Gossip, I suppose you'd call it. You know, the church stalwarts, the *oldies* not quite convinced about your, shall we say, *modern* approach to your work here?'

'Cut that out, right now, Hilary,' Sandra Butterworth, collecting and replacing hymn books, censured crossly. 'The church has never been so full as it has with Rosa in charge. The vicarage garden has never been in such good shape. The villagers love her sermons; Denis and me love her sermons. In fact, Denis and me love Rosa herself. So, if you don't like it, Hilary – shame on you – then bugger off…' Sandra raised her eyes skywards. 'Sorry, God… but, as I say, Hilary, if you don't like it, get yourself on up to St Luke's in Almast village. There's plenty of room up there for complainers and busybodies who don't know when they're well off.'

'It's just,' Hilary said, chastened by the verger's wife's censure in a way she'd never been cowed by the teachers at Westenbury Comp, 'if the Sunday papers get hold of this…'

'What, a bit of jealousy? Come on, Hilary there's always been jealousy. And yes, ending in fisticuffs too as I recall when your Darren took a pop at Billy Dyson in the church hall last harvest festival over who's got the best bloody leeks.'

'I don't think…' Hilary started.

'And,' Sandra was still in full flow, 'the only way the Sunday papers will *get hold of it*, is if someone tells them. And I'm sure, Hilary, as churchwarden you will do your utmost to make sure that doesn't happen? Hmm? Right, I've a treacle sponge needs putting in the steamer if our Denis is to get his pudding today.' She turned to Rosa, patting her arm. 'Great sermon, love. Our Jess would have loved it.' She winked at Rosa. 'And, good choice, love.' She nodded in the direction of Joe who was still sitting in the pew, head in his hands. 'You'll have your fill of Rosavina's pizzas for life.'

'It's a good job Chiara wasn't in church with you,' Rosa said, handing Joe a big mug of strong tea.

'I think I need gin,' Joe replied ruefully, gingerly feeling at his neck, which was red and chafed. 'My sore head from the damned cows was just beginning to feel like my own again. And now, I feel it's back to square one. Gin would be good!'

'It's Sunday and I'm a vicar,' Rosa replied piously. 'It's tea from now on.' And then, smiling, reached for a bottle of Merlot. 'I thought we could share this later,' she added, almost shyly. 'If you're able to stay to eat with me?' Why on earth was she feeling shy? She'd known and loved this man since first coming across him when they were both sixteen, earning holiday money up at Heatherly Hall. 'So, Chiara?'

'At Florence McLean's for the night. My mum's picking her up later, taking her and Florence down to the restaurant for pizza.'

'And *Mrs* McLean?' Rosa's heart missed a beat. 'The last thing I need is another thwarted lover in my church.'

'I love it when you say *my church*, Rosa. You're filled with such passion for it.'

'And is that a problem?'

'A problem?' Joe frowned. 'Why would it be a problem?'

'That I have passion and love for something other than you?' Rosa was serious.

'As long as you can fit me in somewhere and still feel love for me as well?' Joe was equally serious. 'I know I need to earn it back…'

Rosa didn't reply to that but, instead, sat down with Joe and sipped at her own tea. 'Mrs McLean?' Rosa finally asked.

'Rosa.' Joe shook his head. 'There was really nothing much there to begin with. It started because the girls were friendly and we kept bumping into each other in the school playground. I told her, right from the start, I loved someone else, that really we could only be friends.' He grinned. 'At Daisy's supper do, Melissa thought it was Hannah I was still in love with. That Hannah ended up in the trifle because Melissa was there with me.'

'And she knows now?'

'Knows what, Rosa?' Joe stroked Rosa's face with his thumb. 'Knows I've never stopped loving you? Knows that I can't be without you?' Slowly, he began to kiss her.

For Rosa, it was like coming home, instantly recognisable as *Joe's* mouth, *Joe's* lovely smell of clean, ironed shirts, of Dior aftershave. Of Joe. Just Joe.

Only ever Joe.

Rosa drew away gently. 'Mrs McLean's not going to be descending on me, twisting my surplice round my neck and kicking Elvis into touch?'

Joe laughed. 'She made it pretty clear to me, when I dropped Florence off yesterday evening, that she was dating some bloke. Some actor in *Emmerdale*, apparently.'

'Really? Blimey? Which one?'

'Rosa, I don't care. OK, get your jeans and walking boots on; I've a dog in the car needs exercising.'

'The naughty Ron?' Rosa laughed. 'Is his leg OK now? You always wanted a dog, didn't you?'

Joe nodded. 'Apparently, the younger a dog is, the quicker it takes for a fracture to heal and it wasn't as bad a break as we suspected. Having said that, we have to watch him. Sometimes end up having to carry him home. He's actually Mum and Dad's; no point in me and the kids getting attached to one of our own, although I was so tempted to bring home Ron's brother as well. No point if we were all going to Australia.' Joe looked at Rosa, his eyes questioning.

'Why Ron?'

'After Ronnie Biggs. He's always trying to escape out of the garden.' Joe looked at his watch. 'And the car. He's probably eaten half the upholstery by now.'

'And Australia?'

'Two emails written on my computer at the moment: a letter of acceptance…' Joe took Rosa's face in both hands, kissing her open mouth '…and another turning down the job, one or the other ready to send in the morning. Your decision, Rosa. I meant it when I said I couldn't live in the village and not be with you.'

Rosa felt Joe tense as she stood, picked up her mug and moved towards the sink. She turned, staring down at him and, for a few seconds, appeared unable to speak. 'Stay, Joe,' she managed finally to get out. 'Stay with me. I don't want you to ever leave me again.'

The rain had cleared by the time Rosa had changed into jeans and T-shirt and found her walking boots. She fed Elvis, locked up the vicarage and made her way with Joe across the road to where his car was parked.

'Hell, that's not *The Sunday Clarion*, is it?' Rosa nudged Joe's arm and pointed to where a man with a professional-looking camera was taking photos of the church. 'That's all I need.'

Joe laughed. 'No, you daft thing. It's James Hampshire. He was in our economics class at sixth-form college. Don't you remember him? Big into the architecture of historic buildings nowadays. Lectures at Midhope University, apparently.' Joe stopped to return the photographer's wave. 'And don't worry about being in the gutter press. It'd bring the punters in.'

'Punters?' Rosa frowned. 'Not funny, Joe. According to Hilary Makepiece, I could be out on my ear. Especially, as a single woman, I appear to have ditched one lover and am immediately being seen…' Rosa broke off, embarrassed.

'…about to take another?' Joe squeezed her hand, finishing her sentence for her. 'Just take your time, Rosa, there's no rush…' Joe added, seeming suddenly as awkward about their situation as herself.

No rush? Rosa wanted to stop him right there, turn him round and kiss the life out of him.

'We need to get to know each other all over again,' Joe said. 'A lot's happened in the seven years since we were together in London.'

'So, is this walk with Ron a bit like a first date then?'

'Why not?' Joe was laughing. 'Sounds sensible to me. A first date with me and Ron.' Joe made to unlock the car door. 'I hope he's not peed – it's been a good forty minutes since I deserted him to creep into church at the end of your service. I did leave him in the shade and a window open for him…'

A bundle of blonde fur flung itself joyfully at Joe before dashing towards a nearby tree. And then Ron was back, jumping up at Rosa, barking hysterically and wagging his tail in appreciation at being released from the car.

'No damp patches.' Joe felt at the back seat. 'Come on, Ron, walkies with Rosa. Do you remember Rosa, Ron? And, just so you know, I love her.' He bundled Ron back into the car before turning to Rosa and, not caring who might see him kissing the village vicar in full view of the church, proceeded to do just that.

'Ooowwfff,' Rosa finally managed to get out, before going back for more.

'You sound like Ron when he wants attention.' Joe grinned, kissing her eyes, her nose, her mouth once again. 'Come on, let's go.'

The rain had totally cleared by the time the three of them had driven out to Bilberry Reservoir above Holmfirth and, although it was wet underfoot, it felt so good to be out in the clean fresh air on a cool June Sunday afternoon.

'Mum used to bring us all out here to pick bilberries,' Rosa remembered. 'And then we'd make Bilberry pie and our tongues would be bright purple. I remember, one year, Eva being in a strop about something – maybe Hannah, Virginia and I had picked more than she had – and she deliberately squashed her bag of berries. I think it's the only time I remember Mum losing her rag with her.' Rosa sighed. 'She's very unhappy at the moment – frightened she's going to lose her girls to this new woman who's having Rayan's child.'

'I've met her.'

'Who?' Rosa stared.

'Dr Amir.'

'You've been to see her? As a psychosexual counsellor?' Rosa actually stopped walking.

'No!' Joe laughed. 'Rayan introduced us – he was in the restaurant with her a few weeks ago. Rosa, she's really nice.'

'There's no reason why she shouldn't be,' Rosa said almost crossly. 'Although it doesn't make it any easier for Eva. In fact, her being nice probably makes it a lot harder. You know, can't call her a bitch, a husband stealer.'

'I get the impression Eva gave up on Rayan,' Joe said gently. 'He loved her, but he just wasn't enough for her. You know Eva, she'd frighten the bejesus out of Hannibal Lecter.'

'Bit unfair, that, Joe. There is an amazingly loyal and protective side to her. She, particularly, was the one who helped me through my cancer treatment even though, at the time, she was pregnant with Laila. And I think if she'd had a gun on her when you left me for Carys, she'd have probably shot you.'

'I deserved it.' Joe smiled.

'You had a drunken one-night stand with Carys when I refused to go to some works do with you. I now realise she'd been determined to have you probably from the minute she saw you.'

'I was an utter fool.'

'You were drunk. *I* was more interested in Rosa Quinn investments: I was taking uppers to keep going, supplied by Carys who I always thought was on my side. And, Joe, you wanted children. I didn't. The thought of being pregnant and hampered with childcare terrified me – I was just obsessed with my business, wanting it to be even better than it was. I don't know what was driving me, but I do see I must have been hell to live with. I put Rosa Quinn Investments before you and me, Joe. And Carys helped me all the way.'

'Rosa, you had cancer.'

'You didn't know that. Carys set her cap at you, was fixated on having you and suddenly she's pregnant with the child you always wanted and which I was not prepared, at that point, to discuss with you, never mind setting out to have a baby of our own.'

'I shouldn't have married her. It was a disaster from start to finish.'

'You had a baby on the way. You wanted children. I didn't.'

Joe was quiet for a moment. 'I'm frightened I might lose Chiara, Rosa. Carys rang me again this morning from Sydney. That's why I was late for church. One in the morning over there apparently. She'd obviously been at some party, some do. She loves her life out there. She wants Chiara and Rhys out there with her.'

'Well, I guess Rhys is almost sixteen and can make his own mind up. Last time I saw him, he was eager to go and stay with her. Although, you know, since he's been in trouble with the police, got a record, they might not let him in.' Rosa held up her hands. 'I honestly don't know how it works, Joe. Does it make a difference if his mum's out there, to sponsor him and vouch for his good behaviour? I don't know. But Chiara?' Rosa trailed off. 'Where do you stand legally?'

'Not sure. Now I know I'm not setting off out there myself…' Joe turned to Rosa for confirmation and she squeezed his hand in affirmation '…I need to get some legal advice.' Joe sighed. 'She's determined to get her daughter back.'

'What does Chiara want?' Rosa asked gently.

'Carys has been talking on Zoom with her a couple of times a week. Showing Chiara her room, the pool, the beach, even the school she'd go to. Not sure I can compete.'

'She *is* her mum, Joe.'

'And I'm her dad,' he retorted crossly. 'Carys left her when she was just four years old – over three years ago.'

'I know, I know, but Carys is Chiara's mum and if Chiara wants to go and be with her.' Rosa hesitated but eventually blurted out, 'Joe, be very sure that going out to Australia with the kids isn't your best option. Think hard before you email that letter tomorrow.'

'Rosa, look at me.' Joe turned her towards him and the elderly couple walking past looked on with interest. 'I'm not going *anywhere* without you. I'm staying *here* with *you*. I love you…' Joe's voice was raised and the couple turned their heads, smiling. 'Marry me. Rosa, marry me.'

'Alright.'

Joe stared. 'Yes? You will?'

'Yes.' Rosa started to laugh. 'Yes. Yes please.' She flung her arms round this man she'd adored for most of her life and he lifted up all five feet of her, burying his mouth into her neck, kissing her and laughing.

'When?' he asked. 'When shall we do it?'

'Whenever.' She laughed. 'Next week. Tomorrow. Whenever.' But then she remembered. 'Joe, I probably can't have children of my own.'

'But you want them now? You've changed your mind?'

'Desperately,' she admitted. 'I think once I was ill and then saw Eva pregnant with Laila – though at the same time with the cancer treatment saw my chances of ever becoming a mum going down the drain – then I realised: I'd left it too late. It's the one regret I'll have to my dying day.'

'Rosa, you're well? You're not dying?' There was real fear in Joe's eyes.

'Joe, I'm fine. Well, at the moment. Who knows if it will come back?' She shrugged. 'All I'm saying is that if you're wanting more children, especially if you're going to lose Chiara, then I'm afraid my chances are slim.'

'You froze your eggs. You told me that.'

'I did. There's ten of them in the clinic in Wandsworth.'

'We can look into this together. You're not alone with the decision. And…' Joe kissed her once more '…if it's not to be, so be it. It's you I want, Rosa. Any children we may eventually have together is a bonus. It's you, Rosa. It's only ever been you.'

30

While Eva was making her way back south from Ullswater and Rosa separating the two men fighting for the woman they loved, Hannah, out of bed since 5am, was up to her ears in a surfeit of new piglets. Daisy the vet had promised to look in to give advice as well as, hopefully, a hand with the new offspring but had phoned to say her father, Graham Madison, the village vet, was struggling with the calving of some prize cow and she'd had to drive over to Barnsley to assist him. And, as there was only one sow still to go into labour, she was sure Hannah, helped by the petting zoo staff, was more than capable of being a brilliant midwife if called upon.

The farrowing 'rooms' for the five pregnant sows had been prepared by Lachlan and Lachlan's new assistant, Geraldine ('call me Ger') a fiery-haired young Glaswegian who'd recently graduated from the local agricultural college and had more knowledge of animal husbandry in her little finger than Hannah had in her whole body. With a voluptuous figure to die for – undisguised even in her dungarees, overalls and toe-capped boots – a mass of beautiful red wavy hair and always fully made up, (was it for Lachlan or the pigs?) Ger strode the perimeter of the pig and the alpaca pens, as well as the boundary of the hall itself, like a Valkyrie. She'd only been in situ since graduating four weeks earlier, but was already showing her contempt for Hannah whom she patently regarded as an amateurish townie, as well as her respect for Daisy and utter devotion to Lachlan

Buchanan with whom she was very obviously in love. If not already shagging, Hannah thought crossly.

The only reason she, Hannah, had been left in charge of the pigs this particular weekend was that both Lachlan and Geraldine had booked off the time for family weddings – Geraldine back in Glasgow and Lachlan somewhere in North Yorkshire. Geraldine had pinned up a ten-point plan that Hannah had been instructed to refer to at all times: this ranged from recognising that, prior to farrowing, a sow will become restless and lie down and get up constantly, and may urinate frequently, ('*I* was never off the loo through both of my pregnancies,' Eva had confirmed cheerfully before zooming off up to her art retreat) to reviving a piglet that didn't appear to be breathing and, in huge block capitals, a reminder of Daisy's phone number.

Before setting off on her weekend jollies, Geraldine had cornered Hannah with more porcine instructions until Hannah's head was spinning. The previous seven days she'd assisted Lachlan, Geraldine and Daisy, watching carefully and trying to take it all in but, with Daisy held up over in Barnsley, Hannah herself was in charge this Sunday morning. While not convinced she was actually *in control*, she comforted herself with the fact that there was only the sweet little sow, Beyoncé, still to produce, and hopefully she'd cross her legs and hang on until Lachlan was back later that evening.

Geraldine had shouted a final piece of advice from her snazzy little two-seater, revving impatiently on the gas, eager to be off back to Scotland. 'As long as you respect the sow's instinct to protect her offspring, and are careful never to give her cause to become concerned for the litter's safety, you needn't worry too much about her becoming violent.'

'Violent?' Hannah had managed to get out.

'You must realise, Hannah,' Geraldine went on, her long red flowing hair a perfect match for the green sweater and tight white jeans she was wearing for the journey north, 'that there's *always* a certain amount of risk involved in handling a pig, and that *you'll* be no match for a pissed-off 200-pound sow.'

Thanks, *Ger*.

But the previous day and this Sunday morning had gone well, Hannah told herself as she hurried back to the hall to grab something to eat. Leaving Leah and Patrick – two of the students she'd taken on to help temporarily at the farm once A levels were over – in charge of the nursing sows, she made her way back to the flat via Tea and Cake to make sure everything was running smoothly there as well.

'Ham sandwich, love?' Maureen Hardcastle called, grinning as Hannah peered in through the open door of the café, checking the state of the tables and the length of the queue for lunch.

'I don't *think* so,' she grunted. Blimey she was beginning to sound like a bloody pig now. 'Brie and chutney please. To take out. Oh, and table four needs clearing,' she instructed quietly to another of the students manning the café. 'And could you tie your hair back properly please?'

Hands full of sandwich, coffee and a particularly enormous slice of Heatherly Hall cheesecake, Hannah climbed the steps to the staff side door and made her way back up to the flat. The thirty new piglets from the four farrowings in the last three days all appeared to be thriving, she thought proudly; they were really quite cute. What they were actually going to do with all these piglets was a decision that still had to be made, which she wasn't going to think about until Lachlan forced her.

'Oh, you're back?' Hannah looked up from her computer as Eva walked into the office. 'I thought you'd be going straight home for the girls?'

'I am in an hour or so. Rayan's taking them back to Heath Green for me to take over. I can't wait to see them and give them the pots I've made for them. I just called in to pick up my iPad. I'm sure I left it in here.' Eva scanned the room.

'It's in the drawer. Right, while you're here, we need some help with the pigs.'

'You're joking?' When Hannah just looked at her, Eva went on, 'I think *everyone* here could do with some help. There's a hell of a queue waiting to get into Tea and Cake, and one ice cream van obviously isn't enough. We need another at the far end of the gardens, by the petting zoo.'

'I hope you're not getting at me, Eva, about the need for extra staff?' Hannah scowled crossly. 'It's a summer Sunday afternoon. Daisy's hopefully coming over in an hour or so to check on the pigs...'

'There you go then, Hannah, you don't need me to help as nursemaid.' Eva grinned.

'...and Tiffany and I and HR are interviewing in the morning for more temporary staff. We've at least another two and a half months of summer to see out, and just about every area needs extra help. You might need to get your pinny on yourself, next weekend.'

'What about Lachlan?' Eva asked, ignoring Hannah's suggestion of helping out in Tea and Cake as they'd always done as school kids on Saturdays and during the school holidays. 'Isn't he over there with you?'

'Gone off to some wedding do – a friend of his in Harrogate or somewhere apparently, although, to be honest, I can't believe anyone would want to be *his* friend.' Hannah shook her head. 'And Ger also has a family wedding back in Glasgow. Bloody selfish I reckon, their families and friends getting married when there's piglets popping out at every turn.'

'I think, if you remember, Hannah, it was you who provoked this pig proliferation.' Eva laughed at her alliterative response. '*You* who let the randy old boar in with the sows. Mind you, good for him, that he's still got it in him at his age. So, what are you doing here if there's so much going on up there?'

'I just came back for a quick sandwich and coffee and I'm off back there again.' Hannah turned from the computer and Eva could see she was in her oldest jeans and sweatshirt. A distinct smell was wafting across the office from her. 'Had a good time? Been worth going?' she asked, still concentrating on whatever she was writing on the computer.

'Oh, Hannah…'

'What?' She stared at Eva whose face was animated. 'That good?' She tutted. 'Hell, I get to spend the weekend playing midwife to thirty piglets and you swan off to paint and pot and eat wonderful food? In that case, you can make me another coffee. And find me a custard cream.' Hannah waved her mug at Eva who didn't seem to be listening. 'Eva?'

'Oh, Hannah, it was wonderful.'

'Good, I'm glad. Make sure you're ready with a presentation at the next meeting.'

'I can't tell you how wonderful it's been.'

'Try,' Hannah said drily, turning back to her computer.

'I swam in the lake at five in the morning. And, Hannah, I *did it*.'

'Swam in the lake? Good for you. Hey, maybe we can do something with the Stratton Lake? Wild swimming's all the thing at the moment.' There was excitement in Hannah's voice. 'But listen, wait until I tell you about Rosa and the goings-on in church. Both Mum and Virginia have been on the phone…'

'I did it! I had sex.'

'Blimey. Is that what's expected on an art retreat nowadays?' Hannah was all ears. 'We have to provide sex on tap as well as art materials and fabulous food…?' She broke off as the office door banged and Rosa appeared.

'I just had to come and tell you.' Rosa, still in walking boots and mud-splattered jeans was as animated as Eva.

'We've heard. Mum and Virginia already on the blower. Probably be in *The Sunday Clarion* next week. Or at least in the parish mag. Fighting between your current lover and your old one in your church, in front of your brethren? Ooh juicy stuff. You'll probably be excommunicated.' Hannah began to laugh.

'Isn't that just Catholic popes?' Eva frowned.

'Catholic anybodies, I think,' Hannah opined.

'I'm getting married,' Rosa finally managed to get out.

'Again?' Eva laughed. 'Is it all back on then? Did he get the infamous horrible emerald back on your finger? Let me see it.' Eva reached for Rosa's hand.

'Joe?' Hannah smiled. 'Mum told me.'

'Joe?' Eva wasn't smiling. 'Oh, Rosa. You *are* joking? Have you thought about this properly?'

'I love him. I've never stopped loving him.' Rosa beamed. 'Time to forgive and move on. I don't want a life without him any longer. He's asked me to marry him and I've said yes.'

Hannah went over to Rosa, hugging her hard until Rosa, spluttering, had to come up for air. 'You stink, Hannah.' She laughed. 'I mean, *really* pong.'

'I know, I know. Pig pong.' Hannah looked glum. 'Even once I'm showered and changed, I'll still be wafting eau-de-porky around. I'll never find a man who either isn't a farmer or has anosmia... Oh, Rosa, I'm so happy for you. You two were always meant to be together.' She turned to Eva. 'And *you* need to get on board with this for Rosa's sake, Eva. No sneery remarks when you see Joe; no flippant comments about Carys Powell.'

'Rosa, if it's what you really want? If you think it's right and you can't see your life without Joe then, OK, I promise, I'll be the perfect sister-in-law.' Eva went to Rosa in turn, holding her and hugging her until Rosa had to come up for air once more. 'Thanks, Eva.'

'She can afford to be magnanimous.' Hannah grinned. 'Eva here, has broken her two years' stint without sex.'

'You're back with Rayan?' Rosa said hopefully, her eyes wide, but then, remembering, frowned. 'But what about the baby on the way?'

'I had an epiphany this weekend...' Eva started.

'Well, that's a new word for it,' Hannah sniffed. 'Is that what we have to call it these days? And, did the earth move for you?'

'I finally realised I wasn't making Rayan happy and need to let him go.' And then, taking a deep breath, she added, 'My teacher was called Andrea and we made love.'

'Andrea?' Hannah stared. 'A woman? You've changed sides? Well, fair enough, if that's what floats your boat.'

'An-*dreya*.' Eva split the name into two syllables as Julie-Anne from South Carolina had done, two evenings previously. Just two evenings ago? So much had happened since then. 'Andrea Zaitsev. He's half-Russian half-Italian.'

'Well, there's a novelty,' Hannah said, feeling envious. Once again, Eva appeared to have come up smelling of roses. While she just smelt of bloody pigs.

'Sounds exotic.' Rosa smiled, pleased that Eva appeared in a better place than when she set off up to the lakes. 'And was it just, you know, sex? Which,' she added hurriedly, not wishing to appear to be preaching, 'you know, is absolutely fine. Or will you see him again?'

'I'm taking it for what it was – a chance to get back in the saddle, as it were. A man fancied me. Wanted to have sex with me. An exceptionally attractive man at that.'

'And?' Hannah urged. 'And now?'

Eva hesitated, not wanting to spoil the wonderful picture of her encounter with Andrea by confessing to her sisters he was already spoken for. She sighed. 'His girlfriend came back from a weekend away just as I was about to leave. I came home earlier than I'd intended, once she appeared on the scene.'

'Oh, Eva!' Rosa was distressed.

'History repeating itself, then?' Hannah raised an eyebrow. 'Did she find you at it and come after you with a knife like with Yves's wife and Alice?'

'Sorry to disappoint you, Hannah, but absolutely not.'

'Par for the course, anyway,' Hannah said. 'Men are genetically wired to be unable to keep it in their pants. Look at Joe.'

'One night, Hannah,' Rosa protested. 'One night.'

'With catastrophic consequences,' Hannah insisted. 'Dreams

shattered. Lives ruined. And then, of course, we have the cheating neurosurgeon.'

'Hannah, Ben was a persistent philanderer,' Eva snapped. 'Joe Rosavina is different. He made one, just one, *very big* mistake. He'd never looked at another woman until Carys Powell set her cap at him. I do hope you're not going to bring up Joe's mistake every two minutes.' Eva, for once appeared to be on Joe's side.

'*You've* very quickly changed your tune,' Hannah said. 'On Joe's side.'

'I'm on *Rosa's* side,' Eva put in quietly. 'We, as her sisters, need to give them both every help to make this work.'

'As I said, 'Hannah sniffed, 'magnanimous after getting laid. Hopefully, getting your leg over will stop you being so bad-tempered and bossy, Eva.'

'*Leg over?*' Eva glared at Hannah. 'That's such a revolting turn of phrase, and you appear determined to – *vulgarise* – what I've just shared with you. I wish I hadn't now. I'm *not* one of your boars in the petting zoo,' Eva snapped again, all magnanimity evaporating at Hannah's words. 'You know, aggressive if deprived of sex.'

'Interesting though, isn't it?' Hannah insisted. 'Aggression's a striking feature in male seasonally breeding mammals, associated with the end of the mating season. I've just been reading all about it. That's the extent of *my* Saturday night's excitement,' she added gloomily, 'while you're swanning off over the hills with some oligarch. And,' she went on, determined to have another go at Eva, '*your* mating season, Eva, you have to admit, came to an end years ago. Totally understandable then, why you've been so foul.'

'Right, OK, you two, stop it.' Rosa brought up both hands in protest. 'Two lovely things have happened this weekend and we shouldn't be arguing the toss over them.'

'So, where's Joe now, Rosa?' Hannah asked.

'He dropped me back home. He's gone to pick up Chiara and Florence from the restaurant.'

'Florence McLean?' Eva's ears instantly pricked up. 'For heaven's sake don't let Laila know or I'll never hear the end of it. There'll be tears before bedtime if she knows her best mate's deserted her for another.'

'Joe's taking Chiara home,' Rosa explained. 'Sorting her out, and then when his mum's back from the restaurant, he's coming back to eat with me. I just had to dash over here to tell you both.'

'Right. No chance of any help from you then, re the pigs?'

''Fraid not.' Rosa laughed. 'I've a date with a long hot scented bath and then supper with Joe.'

'Well just be careful,' Eva said as Rosa made to leave. 'You're a vicar: no hanky-panky before your wedding day. Hang on, I'm coming down with you.' Eva picked up the recovered iPad and keys and followed Rosa out.

'Right, Brian.' Hannah sighed towards her dad's decrepit sleeping cockerpoo who Richard had just deposited with her for the next couple of days while her mum and dad set off somewhere. Liverpool, was it? She hadn't really been listening. She stood and drained the cold dregs of her coffee before reaching for the opened packet of custard creams. 'Looks like it's just you, me and the Lugubrious Laird of Balmoral then. If he ever gets back, that is.'

31

'Hannah, I think Beyoncé's about to have her piglets.' Patrick, obviously anxious, was hovering at the gate of the pig area. 'I was just going to come and get you. Leah's in there, but she's acting strangely.'

'Who?' Hannah asked, eyebrows raised? 'Beyoncé or Leah?'

'Sorry?' Patrick, always of a slightly anxious disposition, gave a nervous bark of laughter.

'Most females do act strangely when they're about to give birth,' Hannah said, attempting humour, not wanting Patrick to see the panic she herself was feeling. 'Actually, Patrick, can you try and find the spare warming lamp in the office?'

'Righto.' Patrick set off in the direction of the tiny office, obviously relieved at having a job to do.

Hannah made her way to the pen that had been given over to the one remaining pregnant sow. 'Blimey, who's made all this mess?' Hannah stared at the vandalised farrowing box whose wooden sides had been destroyed, the hay and shavings thrown around. 'What's going on, Leah?'

'I don't know,' she said, eyes wide with shock. 'I think she's nesting.'

'*I* made her a lovely nest.' Hannah frowned, put out.

'She obviously doesn't like it. Look, she's trying to make her own out of the bits of wood she's chewed.' Beyoncé was moving the remaining straw with her snout, adding it to the pile in the corner before collapsing heavily onto it and throwing Hannah a mournful look over her shoulder as if to say: you got me into this mess, Buster.

'OK.' Hannah nodded a confidence she wasn't feeling. 'We're here if she needs us. All we can do is be here if she needs us. Actually, Leah, can you go to the office and try Daisy the vet's number again?'

Two minutes later, Leah ran back in. 'Hannah,' she was shouting almost hysterically, 'Madonna's got Patrick up against the wall.'

'Shit.' Hannah flew across the yard, Leah on her tail. Were they insured for porcine GBH against six-formers? He was off to Oxford to do medicine, as well – the UK and the NHS couldn't afford to lose this one. When she arrived, an obviously terrified Patrick was up against the wall of the pen, warming lamp clutched protectively in his hand, while Madonna faced him, her body tense, tail flicking from side to side like an irritated cat. 'Patrick, what the hell are you *doing* in there? I've warned you before about...' The sow turned as Hannah tried to speak calmly. 'It's OK, Madonna. It's OK, Patrick, she's not grunting or screaming. You're just in her personal space...'

'*You* fucking well sent me into it, Hannah,' Patrick snapped, his face white, his eyes never moving from the angry pig blocking his way to safety.

'*I* did?' Had she? Surely, she'd asked Patrick to find the lamp in the office, not in Madonna's pen? 'Hang on.' Hannah grabbed a long-handled yard brush and moved cautiously between Patrick and the sow, talking in a low voice, soothing the angry mother as she'd seen both Lachlan and Daisy do on previous occasions. Madonna eyed Hannah, felt the tip of the yard brush on her flank and started to swipe her head from side to side. Shit, Hannah thought, not a good sign. Taking a deep breath, she moved the pig backwards slightly, allowing Patrick to run behind her towards the pen door. 'Don't rush,' Hannah hissed furiously. 'Just keep calm.'

'Hannah!' Leah's panic-stricken voice came through the open

door, but Hannah didn't dare turn in her direction. 'Shall I ring 999?'

'Police or ambulance?' Hannah hissed again. 'To arrest the damned pig or cart me off to hospital?'

'Can you get out of there?' Leah was really panicking now. 'Two of Beyoncé's piglets have been born, but neither are breathing.'

'I'm trying my best *to effing well get out of here*!' Hannah shouted, her heart racing, any attempt at calm leaving her as Madonna backed away from the brush before, with a squeal of rage she advanced once more onto it, pushing Hannah towards the back of the heating area.

'Shh, Madonna, shh, it's all alright.' Food and soft music she'd read, just the night before, were the best way to calm an angry sow. In desperation, Hannah felt in her pocket for the custard creams she'd squirreled in there and, singing softly: '*like a virgin, touched for the very first time, like a vir... ir... ir... ir... gin*,' over and over again, she offered a biscuit to the sow. Madonna stopped in her tracks, glared suspiciously at the hand offering custard creams before sniffing at, and finally accepting the bait. Crunching noisily, she swallowed, grunted and eyed Hannah, waiting for the next one. Hannah felt her pocket. She had two to go. What then?'

'*Get into the groove, yeah, you got to prove your love to me, yeah*,' Hannah warbled in desperation as Madonna knocked back the last of the custard creams and looked questioningly at her through sandy-coloured eyelashes.

'Hannah, get the fuck out of here.' Lachlan Buchanan was suddenly in between herself and the pig, grabbing at the yard brush and allowing Hannah to slip behind him to safety. Madonna, obviously recognising a pro when she saw one, gave a final scream of fury but gradually allowed Lachlan to edge her backwards before turning to her six squealing piglets in the main part of the pen. She lay down with a martyred whump, gathering hungry piglets like iron filings onto a magnet.

Once outside, Hannah sat on the grass, head between her knees, legs like jelly. She was going to be sick; she shouldn't have wolfed all that cheesecake at lunchtime...

Taking deep breaths, her chest heaving, Hannah suddenly felt a cool hand on her neck. 'Keep your head down, Hannah. It'll pass.' Lachlan was bending over her, not allowing her to stand.

'I don't know *why* Patrick was in there.' Hannah was shaking her head. 'I told him to go to *the office* for the spare lamp, not into Madonna's heating area. I know I did.'

'He's nearly in tears. Says you're always on at him to use his initiative, show a bit of aptitude.'

When Hannah didn't reply, Lachlan went on, 'Patrick wanted to show you he could use his brains: when he couldn't find a spare lamp in the office, he knew where there was one.'

'Oh Jesus.'

'He's just a kid, Hannah. He wanted to please you.'

'Oh...' Hannah found she couldn't speak as she tried hard to control the tears she'd managed to keep at bay ever since she'd thrown Ben Pennington out of her life. 'But I'm a youth worker,' she sobbed. '*Was* a youth worker. It was my job to understand kids; to know why they were behaving as they were doing; what was making them tick.'

'Stop beating yourself up, Hannah. You're shattered, you've been taking on too much.'

'I'm fine,' she snapped crossly, wiping away tears with her filthy sweatshirt, embarrassed at Lachlan's condescending tone. Or was it one of sympathy? She suddenly sat up, remembering. 'What about Beyoncé's piglets? Leah said two weren't breathing?'

'She managed to save one,' Lachlan said. 'She'd been with me when I managed to get one of Adele's breathing last week, and just went for it with Beyoncé's piglet. 'Fraid there was nothing we could do with the other. Leah and Patrick are in there with her while she delivers the rest.' Lachlan helped Hannah to her feet. 'Don't have a go at Patrick, Hannah, he was only trying to help. I'll take over here now. Go and get a shower. You look all in.'

'OK, OK.' Distressed and embarrassed at the turn of events: that she'd been outed as bullying Patrick, that one of the piglets had died on her midwifery watch, that she'd almost thrown up over Lachlan Buchanan, Hannah wanted nothing more than to retreat to lick her wounds. She made her way to Beyoncé's pen where three healthy little piglets had already been moved to the warmth and safety of the heating area by Leah and Patrick, while the sow was obviously resting before giving birth to the others.

Hannah took Patrick's arm. 'Patrick, thank you so much for trying to get the other lamp for me. You put yourself in danger, but I understand why you did it. Thank you so much. It was a very brave thing to do.'

Patrick went scarlet. 'It was nothing, honestly. You were pretty brave yourself in there. Madonna could have really gone for you.'

'Listen, you two, carry on with Lachlan now; he's taking over. Once the piglets are all out, get yourself showered in the staff rest room and then there's a drink over at Astley's, the wine bar, for you both.' Hannah looked at her watch. 'They'll be open at six. I'll tell them the drinks are on me. OK? And thank you again. You've both been brilliant.'

Hannah walked back to the hall and found she was crying again, great sobs that she couldn't stop. She so desperately wished Bill was still here; that she could go and find him up in his apartment, that he'd pour her a glass of his best port and tease her and tell her she was doing OK. But then, if he was still alive, *she* wouldn't be living at the hall and would still be travelling the motorway every day to her job at the youth court. And, obviously just as rubbish at understanding how kids tick, given the disaster she was turning out to be when left in charge at Heatherly Hall.

More tears, more sobs, more self-flagellation for being no good at anything. Thank goodness she still had her dad, Richard, to have a good chat with, but then she remembered he and her mum had gone off to Liverpool for the weekend leaving Brian, the dog, with her. She needed to let him out and go for a walk though he was so geriatric these days he was happy to snooze his days away behind the sofa. More sobs that her mum and dad weren't there for her. And that Brian was probably on his last legs. And Rosa, loved up with Joe, wouldn't want her descending on the vicarage full of self-pity and angst. And Eva? Well, she and Eva were always sniping at each other. Or was it that she, Hannah, was constantly getting at Eva because she was jealous of her sister's determined ability to just get on with her life no matter what it threw at her. Oh, envy was such a tiring, dispiriting emotion.

Hannah walked quickly, pulling up the hem of her sweatshirt to mop at her eyes, which wouldn't seem to stop spouting tears like some out-of-control watering can. Then, remembering she'd no T-shirt underneath, and was flashing her safety-pin-strapped bra to wide-eyed Heatherly Hall Sunday visitors, she sobbed even more. She realised she probably hadn't grieved properly, or enough, for Bill, excited as she'd been at taking over the running of Heatherly Hall. She was lonely, missing Bill and wanting the Ben Pennington she thought she'd fallen in love with; distressed that she'd been such an awful judge of character over Ben, but acknowledging that he was a total cheating pillock and she really didn't want him back in her life anyway.

She was so tired, and longed for a shower and a lie-down in a darkened room. She felt a familiar low-down cramping pain in her middle and was conscious of a wetness down below. Oh God, now she had her period on top of everything else.

And, she knew, there wasn't so much as the sniff of a Tampax in the bathroom cabinet.

32

Hannah ran a hot bath (there was always plenty of hot water on tap at Heatherly Hall) and lay in it for a good hour, washing and conditioning her hair and replenishing both the water and the heat several times over until, as pink as if she'd been lying out on Scarborough beach on an unexpectedly hot day, she hauled herself out, found clean jeans and T-shirt, as well as two somewhat battered Tampax loitering with intent at the bottom of her handbag, and went to find Brian. Martyrish at being left by Pack Leader Richard, as well as abandoned behind the sofa by Hannah, Brian was in the middle of a massive sulk and could only be persuaded onto the lead with many chunks of Wensleydale.

'Come on, Bri,' Hannah coaxed. 'I need cheering up, not depressing even more. I'm sorry I left you for a couple of hours, but I need you on my side.' The dog finally deigned to accompany her down the stairs and out of the hall towards Stratton Woods. 'I need *some* fucker on my side…' she muttered under her breath as the pair of them entered the cool green of the trees, and she let Brian off the lead.

She'd only walked half a mile or so, before the weirdest thing happened. One minute she was on solid ground, the next one leg was down a hole up to her gusset. For some reason the words of Susan came immediately to mind: whenever, as kids, the three girls were trying – unsuccessfully – to do the splits, Susan would wince, telling them to stop it; they'd split their gussets. For years Hannah had thought your gusset was your *down below bits* and it had come as something of a relief to know Susan had been mindful, not of their maidenheads, but of their Marks and Spencer's white cotton pants.

Jesus, what on earth had happened to her? One leg was down a deep hole, while the other still on solid ground, pain shooting not only up the stranded leg but searing her *down below bits* in a way that promised any sex life she *might* have had in the future was now well and truly out the window. How the hell was she going to get out of this hole? Literally.

'Brian!' Hannah wailed at the dog. 'Brian!' Any hope that a thirteen-year-old decrepit cockerpoo was suddenly going to metamorphosise into Super Dog, his red cloak and underpants a beacon of hope and rescue, were hopelessly dashed as Brian cocked a leg, peeing long and thoughtfully, before wandering off in the opposite direction.

'Brian!' Hannah yelled again. Maybe if she could just grab his collar, she could persuade him to reverse and help pull her out.

'Oh, deary me.' Lachlan Buchanan was suddenly standing at the side of the hole looking down at her in some amusement. 'You've fallen down a badger hole. Have you no regard for badgers, Hannah? Or their holes?' MacDuff, Lachlan's collie sitting obediently at Lachlan's feet, was obviously thinking otherwise.

'I thought you estate management lot were trying to exterminate the entire badger population?' she snarled, a combination of exhaustion and relief at potential rescue making her say things she might be better off keeping to herself.

'Dairy farmers and the fear of Bovine TB. Get your facts right,' he added while bending down and threading a muscular arm underneath her armpit. Hannah wondered if there was going to be an accompanying squelching noise when she was pulled out, like a wellington out of mud.

There wasn't. Instead, there was pain in her right leg and horrible discomfort in her nether regions, amalgamating chummily with the griping pain in her tummy she always experienced on the first day of her period. Once every bit of her was back fully on terra firma, Brian obviously thought better of his initial abandonment and came back to sit at her feet, attempting to demonstrate he could be just as well-mannered as this other dog. 'No good sucking up now,' she told him, rubbing at her leg and ankle. 'Hell, that hurts.'

'Can you stand?'

'Dunno.'

'Lean on me. There, you've not broken it. Maybe twisted your ankle? Where were you trying to get to?'

'Nowhere particularly. I used to walk in here with Bill.'

'You miss him?'

Hannah nodded, not trusting herself to speak and tried to set off. She stopped immediately, unable to put any weight on her foot.

'Come on, Hannah,' Lachlan said kindly. Kindly? Since when had Lachlan Buchanan ever been kind? 'Lean on me and I'll get you back. Just think yourself lucky there's not a badger attached to the end of your foot.'

Despite herself, Hannah started laughing. 'Like the man who goes to the doctor and asks him what he should do with the mole on the end of his penis and the doctor looks over his glasses at his patient and asks should he be reporting him to the RSPCA.' Despite the pain in her foot Hannah started really giggling and found she couldn't stop. Must be the shock, she told herself, as she continued to utter little squeaky giggles while hobbling painfully towards the hall and, glancing towards Lachlan, realised he was also laughing. Lachlan Buchanan laughing?

Hannah took another surreptitious look to her left and admitted, not for the first time, that Buchanan was rather good-looking in a military sort of way: probably around her own age though certainly, with his auburn hair and brown eyes, not her type. She thought of Ben Pennington with his dark hair and blue eyes and faltered, as Lachlan grabbed hold of her arm more firmly. 'You know, I reckon you're too young to be the estates manager,' she said, thinking not only of old Jim Mitchell, who'd finally retired from the job, but also that actually the red hair was rather lovely and he himself was a rather nice cross between Damian Lewis and that wonderful *Outlander* actor in his kilt.

'Do you want to go back to your flat?' Lachlan asked as they approached the gates of the hall once again. 'You need a cold bandage on that ankle.'

'Not got such a thing as a bandage,' Hannah replied. 'There'll be one in the porter's lodge, I guess.'

'Come on, I've got a whole medical cabinet of stuff.'

'Have you? Why?'

'Oh, you know, legs caught in barbed wire, shock from electric fences, folk falling down badger holes – the usual stuff.' Lachlan led the way to his little studio apartment, which had once been part of the original coach house.

'I've not been down here for years,' Hannah mused, hobbling and hanging on to Lachlan's arm. 'We used to love playing in here when it was in its original state. Bill kept his cars in here and there were a couple of old Victorian carriages; we adored sitting in them and pretending we were royalty.'

'Well, welcome to Staff City.' Lachlan smiled, unlocking a door and leading the way. 'It's actually not bad at all. Bill did always try to make sure his employees had decent accommodation if they needed to live in.'

'And do you *need* to live in?' Hannah was curious. 'I mean, do you own a house somewhere? Sorry, look, you don't need to tell me if that's a rude question. You know, like asking how much you earn or what your politics are?' Hannah felt herself blush.

'I live here at the moment. I'm happy to be here at the hall while I work out what I'm doing. I have a house in Ballater in Aberdeenshire; just debating what to do with it, to be honest.'

'Work out what you're doing?'

'Whether I'm staying down here in Yorkshire.'

'Right.' Why on earth was the possibility of Lachlan

Buchanan's leaving Heatherly Hall making her feel strange? She couldn't stand the man. Better off without him, surely?

'OK, Hannah, sit yourself down there and I'll fetch a bandage.'

While Lachlan was gone up the white-painted metal spiral staircase that had been installed once the coach house had been developed into staff accommodation, Hannah looked round curiously. Everywhere was exceptionally neat and tidy, (maybe he *had* once been in the military?) fairly basic, but with an amazing number of books – poetry, biographies as well as classic and more contemporary novels. Well, who would have thought Lachlan Buchanan was into poetry?

More surprising were the saxophone and violin left somewhat carelessly on the sofa underneath the window. Lachlan Buchanan a musician? She'd always loved sax music, had even attempted to play the instrument at school, but it had come to nothing.

Like so much of her life, her attempts at learning the saxophone hadn't ended in any satisfactory conclusion.

'You've got that *I'm feeling sorry for myself* look on your face again.' Lachlan smiled, kneeling at her feet and deftly wrapping her bruised ankle in a damp bandage. 'It will be pretty black by tomorrow,' he added.

'Feeling sorry for myself?' Hannah quickly tried to rearrange her features, but Lachlan just laughed. 'Right, is that better?' she asked, the rictus of a smile on her face.

He laughed even more. 'Now you look like Donald Duck.' He put the final touches to her ankle. 'Not too tight?' he asked and, for some reason Hannah couldn't quite work out, realised she rather liked the idea of his hand staying just where it was on her leg.

'OK.' He stood, looking down at her. 'Tea or something a bit stronger?'

'I've sworn off alcohol.' Hannah frowned. 'Had a bit of a session at Daisy's place a couple of weeks ago.'

'I heard.'

'Oh?'

'Daisy told me. Head-in-the-trifle stuff?' Lachlan smiled but there was obvious concern in his voice. Lachlan Buchanan, concerned?

'She didn't!' Hannah flushed. 'Wait till I see her.'

'I asked.'

'Did you? Why?'

'It's pretty obvious to anyone that you've being going through a stressful time lately.'

'It was all going to be so lovely,' Hannah sniffed. 'I just thought I could waltz in and take control and everyone…' Hannah raised an eyebrow at Lachlan '…*everyone* would be with me in my vision for Heatherly Hall.'

'It doesn't work like that.' Lachlan smiled again. 'There's always got to be someone in a team whose job it is to put the brakes on. And Hannah, it's been eight months. *Only eight months* for heaven's sake. You've achieved so much in that time: the wine bar, taking on new staff, Eva's up-and-coming art retreat. Some bloody *silly* ideas, I grant you… I mean, *Westenbury*?' He shook his head before moving into the tiny kitchen, coming back with a bottle and two glasses 'As well as a plethora of piglets we weren't expecting.' He poured a measure of amber liquid and handed it to Hannah.

'Napoleon was looking a bit lonely. Actually off his food. I just thought I'd give him a treat by putting him in with the girls for a while. I never thought he'd get a new lease of life and… you know…' Hannah looked suspiciously at the glass in her hand. 'What's this?'

'Medicinal,' Lachlan said. 'Sip it slowly. It will help.'

'Help what?' Hannah eyed Lachlan over her glass but sipped at the smooth amber liquid.

'That's lovely,' she said. And it was. She felt the warmth of the alcohol immediately seek out her bruised ankle, her period pain and the headache that had come on from crying so much.

'Finest dram from the Royal Lochnagar Distillery. Slowly, sip it slowly,' he commanded once more. 'Let it do its work.'

They sat in mutual appreciation of the whisky, Hannah on the sofa, leg up on a cushion, Lachlan on the floor in front of her, his long jean-clad legs out in front of him, his head resting against the sofa's arm. His hair, Hannah saw from her vantage point above him, was the most incredible shade of deep red: burnt toffee, autumn leaves, a young vixen's brush, and she realised she was having to stop herself from moving her hand towards it. Bloody hell, he must look magnificent in a kilt: he really could be a stand-in for Jamie Fraser in *Outlander*.

'You could be a stand-in for Jamie Fraser in *Outlander*.' The words were out before she could reel them back in. Hell.

'*Outlander?*' Lachlan turned his head.

'Oh, just someone on TV,' Hannah mumbled, embarrassed.

'I don't have one.' He smiled.

'You know, Mr Buchanan,' Hannah said slightly tipsily, the whisky making her talk, 'I've come to really like your accent, especially with all that rolling of your R's. And your name – Lachlan Buchanan – I mean, you could be in a Jilly Cooper novel with a name like that.'

'There's not one R…' Lachlan rolled the consonant long and hard '…in my name. And Jilly Cooper?' Really?'

'I'm sorry.' Hannah wanted to laugh. 'It's a lovely name. Lachlan Buchanan: all those short consonants. "Cu" and "nu"…' She spat out the sounds, grinning at him somewhat inanely. 'Really, really fabulous… and…'

Lachlan Buchanan put a hand on her arm. 'I should quit while you're ahead,' he said drily. 'So, Hannah, apart from the mess you think you're making of running this place, what else is going on in your life? Where's the neurosurgeon when you need him?'

'Oh, you know about him?'

'Can't help but, when you've been flaunting him at every turn like a prized possession.' Lachlan's tone was sardonic but his smile, when he turned towards her was sympathetic.

'Flaunting him? I wasn't *flaunting* him,' Hannah said crossly. 'Anyway, it's all over.'

'He wasn't right for you,' Lachlan said bluntly.

'Wasn't right for me? And how do you know that?' Hannah felt indignation rise. Typical Lachlan Buchanan to be so bloody sneery. 'When did *you* come across Ben Pennington?'

'He was always in the Stratton Arms across the road, or in the new wine bar,' Lachlan said. 'Chatting up the bar staff as well as the customers.'

Hannah felt as though she'd been stung. 'Really?' she asked, sadly. 'Was he? Honestly? I didn't know.'

'No, you were too busy trying to show how brilliant you are at running this place: in the pigs, in meetings, helping out at the wedding venue and conference centre as well as getting your pinny on in Tea and Cake if someone hasn't turned up for work.'

'Anyway, it serves me right,' Hannah sniffed, trying not to cry again. She buried her nose in the whisky, loving its peaty fragrance.

'Serves you right?' Lachlan really turned now. 'No one deserves to be treated like that, Hannah.'

'I'm a terrible person,' she wept as Lachlan listened. 'I had an affair with Ben when he was still married. For almost a year, Lachlan. I knew he was married, knew he had children, and now I deserve everything I've had thrown at me – including a potty full of pee that Alexandra – his wife – once threw over me.'

'You're shivering,' Lachlan frowned. He took off his own sweater and passed it to Hannah who took it gratefully.

'Not that I blame Alexandra,' Hannah hastily added. 'I mean, he actually left her and the children for me.' Hannah looked Lachlan in the eye. 'Although, if I'm being honest, I reckon she threw him out. He had nowhere else to go.'

'Stop beating yourself up,' Lachlan said seriously. 'We've all done things we wish we hadn't.'

'I bet *you* haven't.' Hannah managed a smile. 'You'rrrre a strrraight-talking, dependable man frrrrom the Highlands.' She affected a Scottish accent, rolling her R's and shortening her vowels.

'Get your accent right, Hannah.' Lachlan smiled back. 'You sound like that old bloke off *Dad's Army*. And your geography's off as well: I'm from south of Aberdeen. Which, to be fair,' he relented, '*is* bordering on the Highlands.'

'And will you go back there? To Scotland?' Hannah asked, suddenly hoping for him to say, no, he was staying right here.

'Hannah, I left Balmoral for the same reason you're berating yourself right now.'

Hannah stared and then, attempting levity when she saw Lachlan was embarrassed at what he'd just admitted, said, 'What, *you* were having an affair with Ben Pennington as well?'

Lachlan smiled at that. 'You know what I'm saying, Hannah. I was having an affair with a married woman on the estate.'

'Bloody hell, not Princess Anne?'

'Hannah, will you stop trying to make me feel better by making a joke of everything?'

'I'm sorry. It's my worst trait; Eva and Rosa are always telling me off for it. You were hurting?'

'Hmm. I didn't know she was still married: as far as I knew she was separated. But then she went back to her husband. So, I applied for several posts, got this one, packed up and came south.'

'And are you feeling a bit better?' Hannah asked hopefully. 'Is time a healer?'

Lachlan smiled. 'When I first saw you back in November, your dog off his lead near the sheep, you know, on the day you discovered Bill had died, I was feeling pretty low to be honest. I missed being in Scotland; didn't think I'd ever get over Bridget.'

'The woman you were in love with?'

'Hmm. I think, after just two months here, I was ready to throw in the towel. And then, with Bill dying, I reckoned it was a good enough reason to move on again: couldn't bear the thought of some bloke from California lording it over us. I assumed Jonny Astley, Bill's son, would inherit.'

'As we all did. And, instead, you ended up with us three

nutters in charge.' Hannah laughed as she remembered the look on Lachlan Buchanan's face when he'd been advised to whom the Marquess of Stratton had left his majority shareholding in Heatherly Hall. 'I'm amazed you weren't heading for the hills, once the will was read,' Hannah added.

'My bags were packed.' Lachlan smiled. 'Then I decided to stay, see how it would all pan out.'

'And now?' Hannah held her breath, hoping against hope Lachlan Buchanan might want to stay on in his role. At least for a little longer.

'And now, Hannah, I'm not planning on going anywhere.'

'Really?'

'Really.'

They grinned at each other somewhat nervously, and then Lachlan put down his empty glass and reached to smooth back a lock of Hannah's long dark hair before leaning in to kiss her. It was such a good kiss, soft but meaningful, and Hannah felt her pulse race.

'God, I must smell of pigs.' Hannah reluctantly pulled away first, remembering.

'Well, if you do, so must I.' Lachlan smiled and stood up. 'Come on, Hannah, you're bushed, I'll walk you and Brian back up to the hall. Get a good night's sleep.'

And, despite lust coursing through every bit of her, from her fingers to her toes and right down to where it really mattered, Hannah knew, if this was to go any further, she wanted to take it slowly, like people in a real, legitimate relationship usually did.

33

After leaving Hannah at her computer that Sunday afternoon, Rosa and Eva had made their way outside to their respective vehicles, Eva to get herself ready to welcome back her girls from their weekend with Rayan's family at Bolton Abbey, and Rosa in order to dash back and prepare a wonderful supper for Joe and herself.

Joe and she had, Rosa knew, so much to discuss, so much to talk about if they were going to have a future together but, for this evening, at least, she just wanted to be with him, to touch him, to breathe him in, know he was actually there with her, that she wasn't going to be without him ever again. That he loved her, as he always had done ever since their eyes first met in the alpaca pen up at the hall and then, a few weeks later, at sixth-form college.

She'd called in at the supermarket on her way back through Midhope and bought duck breasts and figs, which would go beautifully with the new sprigs of rosemary just waiting to be picked from the tub outside her kitchen door; but then, in an agony of indecision, she'd made her way to the fish counter and thrown hake and clams into her basket, knowing there was a bottle of cider in her pantry to make a sauce which, with a splurge of dill oil, would be absolutely divine. She dithered over what pudding to make and then, telling herself to stop being so ridiculous, bought lemons and cream to make a simple – and light – lemon posset. The last thing she needed over a candlelit dinner was to have to undo her jeans buttons after a huge jam roly-poly.

Jeans? She wasn't going to wear jeans, she admonished herself as she drove back home. It was summer, the morning's rain had cleared and the mid-June afternoon was shaping up nicely. Maybe, they could even sit outside? Her little pink cotton shift dress would be just fine. Simple, understated and her favourite.

Rosa pulled up in the vicarage drive and was hauling her shopping out of the boot when some instinct made her glance across the lawn and flower beds towards the front door where a figure was waiting.

Sam.

When he saw she was laden down with bags, he hurried towards her. 'Rosa… I…' He took two of the shopping bags from her but then seemed rooted to the spot, unable to speak further. He was gazing at her with such a baleful, hurt look in his eyes, her heart plummeted.

'I shouldn't have had a go at your ex, Rosa,' Sam said, shaking his head. 'But I don't regret it. He deserved it. And, can't you see, it's just because I love you so much? Doesn't it show just how much you mean to me? That I'm not going to let him come between us and spoil what we have?'

'I'm so sorry, Sam,' Rosa said firmly but continuing up the path so that he was forced to follow in her wake. 'I never wanted to hurt you,' she added as she put down the bags on the doorstep and hunted for her keys. 'I'm so sorry it didn't work out for us.'

'But you're a vicar…' Sam took her hand. 'You shouldn't hurt anyone.'

'I'm a human being first.' Rosa smiled. 'I'm human: I make mistakes.'

'He'll hurt you again,' Sam said almost sneerily. And then added, 'There's nothing I can do to make you change your mind?' He dropped her hand, waiting for the answer he obviously didn't want.

Rosa shook her head. 'I'm sorry.'

'Right, that's it then, is it?' Sam gave her a hard stare. 'We really have broken up? You're determined to go ahead with all this without discussion?'

'But Sam, we discussed this. You *knew* it was broken and over, weeks ago.'

Sam continued to stare at her but, eventually, seeing there could be no going back, no further discussion, dropped his eyes and made to leave. 'I hope it… you know… all works out for you.'

'Thank you, Sam. And for you too.'

He gave her one last lingering look before walking, a solitary figure, back down the garden.

Rosa took a deep breath and unlocked her door.

Once she was in the kitchen, she sent a message to Denis to check he was taking Sunday evensong as had, lately, become the norm, and when his reply was the confirmation she'd been praying for, she tied her apron firmly round her waist and started cooking.

Joe was wearing a deep blue shirt, which matched his eyes, and chinos. He was nervous, Rosa could tell, as he stood in the kitchen pouring them each a glass of the wine he'd brought with him.

'Joe?' Rosa walked from the work surface where she'd been chopping the ingredients for a salad. 'What is it?'

'I'm frightened.'

'Of what?'

'That you're going to turn round, Rosa, and tell me this afternoon was a mistake. That you've changed your mind.'

'A mistake?'

'That you were just having me on. You know, that you don't think we can make a go of things?' There was real fear in his eyes. 'The thing is, Rosa, I don't think I could bear to lose you again. These past seven years or so without you have not been the best. I've…'

'It's OK, Joe, really.'

'…I've woken up from the same dream so often, Rosa: you're there with me, none of the stuff with Carys ever happened, you're beside me…' Joe broke off, unable to go on. He took a gulp of his wine. 'And then I wake up and you're not there… and I remember what I did, what happened…'

'Listen Joe, this isn't going to work…'

Joe closed his eyes.

'…unless you can forgive yourself as I have. Joe, I love you. The past years were there for a reason: you have Chiara. So, unless you can forgive yourself, accept that I've never stopped loving you, then…'

Joe took the knife she still held in her hand and, placing it on the kitchen counter, took Rosa's face in his hands, looking deep into her eyes before bending his head to kiss her. Oh, that remembered kiss: Joe's mouth, Joe's touch, Joe's skin on her own.

'Stay with me, Joe,' Rosa managed to finally get out as he wrapped strong, steady arms around her.

'I'm not going anywhere.' He smiled. 'Ever, ever again.'

34

August and the long summer holiday still had a couple of weeks to run before Laila was back at school and Nora about to start part-time at Little Acorns nursery. The plan was that either she or Rayan would drop the girls at school each morning and Jodie, who'd fallen in love with one of the local farmers and put off, yet again (to Eva's relief) her intended return to Australia, would be around to pick up Nora at lunchtime as well as carry out her nannying duties every afternoon.

Eva had finally met Dr Yasmin and been most relieved to find her not the ravishing sex goddess of her worst nightmares, but an attractive, extremely intelligent woman who plainly adored Rayan and did her best with the girls, both of whom preferred to spend the majority of the week and alternate weekends with Eva, and the rest of the time with Rayan and Yasmin.

'The girls need the stability of being with their mother in the home they're most familiar with,' Eva had argued. And with Rayan spending so much time at Malik and Malik, now that Sam Burrows had given just six weeks' notice before leaving to take up a new position nearer his mother in Sheffield, as well as being on the point of moving himself and Dr Yasmin into a brand-new house just a few miles away from Heath Green, with all that that entailed, he'd reluctantly agreed to the custodial arrangements for the girls Eva had suggested.

It was quite possible that once her and Rayan's divorce had come through, Rayan might ask for more time with his daughters but, with Yasmin still to go through the second half of her pregnancy (and Eva recalled how knackered she herself had been in her own pregnancies by then) while moving her consultancy business from Leicester, as well as the coming upheaval of being a new mum, she couldn't see Yasmin being desperate for two extra little girls to look after on a more permanent basis. So, for the moment, Eva felt able to breathe a little easier and, as well, to keep Rayan sweet, had agreed to continue her two days at the surgery once the girls were back at school and while new staff were interviewed and appointed to take the place of Sam and, eventually, herself.

Eva was trying very hard to see her two days in the Lakes with Andrea Zaitsev as just that – two wonderful days with a talented and charismatic man who had enabled her to retrieve some of the self-confidence she'd lost through the two years of Rayan's sexual rejection. But it wasn't easy. Two months on and her dreams were often of him, of reliving the exhilaration of that bike ride around Ullswater Lake on a balmy midsummer evening; of making love on the floor of his room; of the most intense climax she'd ever experienced. It was the stuff of dreams. And dreams, she knew, were not reality.

When Bella had so unexpectedly appeared in the annexe, and it was pretty obvious the girl was involved with Andrea, an embarrassed Eva had taken possession of the beautiful mugs and plates she'd designed and created for the girls and made a hasty exit back to her room, quickly packed up her few things and headed for reception. She had absolutely no desire to come between Andrea and this girl, Bella, and simply wanted to be out of there as quick as she could.

But when she'd made her way to her car, at the bottom of the car park, he'd been waiting for her.

'You go without saying goodbye?' Andrea asked.

'I'm sorry, I didn't realise you were with someone.' Eva felt unable to meet his eyes, didn't want to see any guilt or misgivings there that would have spoilt what she'd had with him. She wanted to remember him as he was, as he'd been, the time spent with him when she hadn't known he was already taken by another woman.

'If I'd told you, you wouldn't have spent time with me.'

'Probably not.' She smiled. 'It was lovely. Thank you.'

'Eva...'

'I need to go.' She threw her overnight case into the back of the car, but placed the precious ceramics carefully on to the front seat beside her.

'Eva, don't...'

'Don't what?' Eva concentrated on packing her sweater and jacket around the precious pots.

'The friendship I have with Bella – it is not serious.'

'*Friendship?* Right, OK, fine. But does Bella know that?'

'I tell her weeks ago.'

'Fine.' Eva finally finished packing her things into the car before looking Andrea directly in the eye and was surprised to see something she couldn't quite work out. Regret? Integrity? Surely not the latter if he'd been cheating on this young girl? She needed to see it for what it was: an amazingly wonderful, erotic two days. Now she must get into her car, go home and get on with the reality of life.

'Eva, I need to see you again,' Andrea said simply.

'My life is complicated enough, Andrea...' Eva had closed the passenger door of the Evoque before moving round to open the driver's door and get into the car. 'It's been lovely.' She'd driven off, accelerating too fast from the car park, scattering elderly Americans as they made their enthusiastic way to lunch, leaving the Ullswater retreat behind and heading for the motorway home.

So why, now, two months on, was she unable to stop thinking about Andrea Zaitsev? Eva had just about come to terms with the fact that she'd failed as a wife, putting all her energies into being a much better mother than she'd perhaps been in the past few years. She'd loved having the girls at home for the summer, spending time baking with them, teaching Laila the basics of pencil sketching, giving them each a patch of the garden to sow quickly sprouting calendula, candytuft, godetia and larkspur, which both Laila and Nora inspected for progress religiously every morning of those sunny summer weeks.

Together with Richard, Susan and Brian, the dog, she and the girls had spent four days in an apartment in Filey. They'd eaten fish and chips on the front, walked to Filey Brigg and played crazy golf as well as searching in rockpools for crabs, long-spined sea-scorpions and even finding, one morning, a starfish, albeit pretty deceased and somewhat ragged-looking. Rosa, together with Joe and Chiara, had joined them for one of the days, bringing a very upmarket picnic made and put together by Rosa, that they all ate while sharing a bottle of good wine provided by Joe, sitting on gloriously sandy Filey beach.

Eva had found herself relaxing, enjoying just being with her girls without worrying – as she had for years, she now realised, that her marriage wasn't right. It wasn't, Eva was now able to admit, and there was a relief in coming clean about it and moving on.

With the girls overnight at Rayan and Yasmin's new house, Eva had had a couple of dates after signing up on Hinge and E-Harmony. One dinner date had even ended up being given a second and third outing, but had concluded in attempting such ridiculous sex – the rather attractive younger man obviously feeling it his duty to try out every sexual position in the book – that Eva had felt she was taking part in a gymnastic display rather than a loving, sexual encounter, and went home before she ended up at the Olympics. Though part of her did feel she deserved a medal for endurance.

She didn't see him again after that.

And then one Sunday in the middle of August, Rosa had rung

to say she, Joe and Chiara were off to the Yorkshire Sculpture Park with Hannah and Lachlan and why didn't Eva and the girls come along as well? They were going to walk, feed the ducks and Lachlan, particularly, wanted to see *Network*, the three-metre-high bronze by Thomas J Price on the upper lake.

Eva had demurred at first, not wanting to see anything that might remind her of Andrea but, knowing that his exhibition at the sculpture park had now concluded and she wouldn't be faced with anything that might pull at her heartstrings, she'd agreed to go with them.

It was another glorious summer day, with just a hint of something autumnal in the air, a harbinger of the season to come. Laila was delighted that Chiara was with them again, storing up the events of the day in readiness to relay back to Florence McLean once Florence was back at school after spending the summer in Paris with her father and his new family. They'd walked around the upper lake, seen the bronze Lachlan had particularly wanted to see and then, with Norah complaining 'my feets hurt, Mummy, my legs tired,' they'd cut across the Cascade Bridge to the lower park for their picnic.

They'd just sat down on the grass, spread the white table cloth (actually, Rosa had confessed, an altar cloth from church) on the very dry and parched grass and were tucking into Rosa's fabulous quiches and Hannah's cheese and tomato sandwiches, when Eva froze, a piece of quiche stilled on the way to her mouth.

'What's up?' Hannah stared at an immobile Eva and then, when Eva didn't appear able to speak, turned to follow her line of vision.

'Don't let him see me,' Eva squeaked, burying her head in Rosa's picnic hamper.

'Don't let *who* see you?' Hannah asked loudly and pointedly, while the others all turned in Eva's direction.

A man, looking incredibly like Andrea Zaitsev, was standing thirty metres or so in front of them, arms folded and deep in conversation with a very trendy-looking woman, his white-shirted back and black curly hair drawn up into a high ponytail, towards the picnic party.

'Is that your sculpture man?' Hannah asked, while Laila and Chiara both stopped eating to stare. 'Go and say hello, Eva, go on.'

'Who is it, Mummy? Do you know him?' Laila was now gazing with interest at her mother whose face, Eva knew, had gone quite pink.

'He's *going*, Eva. Go and say hello,' Hannah urged. Her own relationship with Lachlan Buchanan blossoming into something rather more than friendship, Hannah was in a position to be magnanimous.

The man stood talking for a few more seconds, pointing something out to his companion, and then both of them set off in the other direction.

'Go after him,' the others were now saying, laughing and encouraging. 'Stop acting like a love-struck teen, Eva. Go, girl!'

'It wasn't who I thought it was,' Eva said, feeling silly as the man walked quickly into the crowd of, and was soon lost in Sunday afternoon dog walkers and sculpture park visitors.

'Who did you think it was, Mummy?' Laila asked, more interested in the packet of Jammie Dodgers she was struggling to open.

'Oh, just someone I used to know.' Eva laughed, still embarrassed at the little scene she'd created for no reason.

'In the biblical sense.' Hannah grinned knowingly.

'What's the biblical sense, Mummy?' Laila wasn't to be put off.

'Ask Aunty Wosa,' Nora lisped. 'She's got a big Bible book in her church.'

Eva turned her attention back to her slice of quiche. Had Andrea Zaitsev been so much on her mind, she'd conjured him up in the place she knew he'd latterly spent time? How embarrassing. And what did that say about herself?

*

Tired out with the fresh air and walk, Eva's girls were both spark out by 8pm despite Laila arguing that she wasn't a bit tired and, as there was no school the next day, she surely had the right to stay up, like Eva, and watch TV.

'You have the right to be in that bed and fast asleep in five minutes, young lady.' Eva had laughed, amused at her elder daughter's demanding of her rights. God, she was going to be a handful when she was a bolshie adolescent, Eva mused. She'd be shipping her off to Dr Yasmin at every opportunity, in a few years' time.

Eva had just poured herself a rather large gin and tonic, kicked off her sandals and was rifling through the *Sunday Times*, when the front doorbell went. She did hope it wasn't the Jehovah's wanting to convert her: she'd had it with organised religion, what with Rosa turning to *her* God and Laila and Nora turning to *Azra's*. She picked up her gin, (surely if the religion-peddlers on her doorstep saw she was into a lovely gin and tonic, they'd accept she was a lost cause and beat it round to Steve and Annie's next door?) before having second thoughts and, replacing the glass on the table, (maybe more chance of them insisting on staying on the doorstep if she was a lost cause) walked through the hall to the front door.

'Oh?' Eva stopped short, not, for a split second, able to quite work out who it was and then, when she realised it was Andrea Zaitsev, unable to get her head round why he was standing there, in her garden, motorbike parked on the drive behind him.

'I saw you at the park,' Andrea said, not smiling.

'It *was* you?'

'It was. I'd seen you earlier, but you were with your family. I didn't want to embarrass you, didn't know if your husband was there.'

'No, no, my husband and I are on the point of divorcing.' Eva frowned. 'How did you know my address? Did Dame Bryony give it to you?'

'No,' Andrea said seriously. 'That would be very impossible. She die, I believe, over fifty year ago.' He stared at her hard and Eva, felt her pulse race. 'Would you prefer it if I go?'

'I'm sorry. Please, come in.' Eva led the way through the sitting room and out into the orangery where the last of the late summer evening sunshine was dipping to the west.

'So how did you know where I was?' Eva asked, seemingly unable to put Andrea at his ease by asking if he'd like to sit, rest his helmet or whether he'd like a glass of wine, gin or coffee.

Andrea stood somewhat awkwardly in front of her. 'May I?' he asked, placing his helmet on the floor and starting to unzip his leathers.

'I'm sorry, I'm sorry, of course. Let me get you a drink?' Flustered, Eva moved towards the kitchen. 'Can I get you a glass of coffee or a cup of wine?'

'I'm sorry?' Andrea smiled and made to pull off the jacket over his head. 'Zip stuck,' he apologised from the muffled depths of the black leather, his white T-shirt caught, and pulled loose, from his jeans belt before ascending in the same direction, along with the jacket.

'Or a cup of gin?' Eva breathed, taking in the tanned, muscled six-pack and the line of black hair rising from the depths of Andrea's low-slung jeans.

'A *glass* of gin perhaps? And some tonic maybe?' Andrea asked as he emerged from battling the jacket, running fingers through his black curls.

'Right. Righto. Absolutely.' For once in her life, Eva was glad she wasn't a man, with any evidence of lust on show in his jeans. 'Make yourself at home.' She went to the kitchen, ran cold water over her wrists, dashed to the metal fridge where she added Coral Dawn to her reflection before reaching for ice cubes, gin and tonic.

'So, Andrea,' Eva spoke deliberately slowly and a couple of

semitones lower than usual to avoid the rush of squeaky words tumbling out at will. 'So,' she started again, 'how did you find my address?'

'The gin?' Andrea asked, smiling and nodding to the glass, seemingly stuck of its own accord in Eva's hand. 'May I?'

'Of course,' she said, sounding like Margaret Thatcher, and handing him the drink.

'I left sculpture park and rode up to Heatherly Hall. Your sister – Hannah, is it? – told me how to find you.'

'Oh, did she? Right. That was kind of her.'

'Eva, you need to know. When you and I… you know…'

'I know…' Eva said going slightly pink.

'When you and I make love, it had been over with Bella for weeks. I wouldn't have… you know…?'

'Are you saying that she wasn't your… you know…?'

'Was I still sleeping with her?' Andrea looked directly at Eva. 'Absolutely not. I have *integrity* – is that right word? I do have some integrity.'

'She seemed to think you were still together.' Eva frowned. 'She came in and kissed you. On the mouth.'

'I know. She still want it to be all on, I'm afraid.' Andrea took a long drink before screwing up his face. 'Is there *any* tonic in this, Eva?'

'Tonic?' Eva pulled her own face, turning round and looking for any manifestation of a bottle of Fever-Tree. 'Sorry, tonic, yes.'

'Eva, I had to see you again. I try to explain about Bella. You weren't prepared to listen to me. You were off out of car park like bat out of heaven.'

'Hell.'

'Sorry?'

'It's a *bat out of hell*.'

'Look, Eva, if the other weekend mean nothing to you, then I'll go. I've a couple more weeks with Dame Bryony and then I'll go back to Milan.'

'You're going back?'

'Only if there's nothing for me here.'

'You were with some woman at the sculpture park.'

'I was.' Andrea smiled and then relented. 'My mother.'

'Your *mother*? Goodness she must have had you when she was ten-years-old.'

Andrea laughed. 'Nearly as young – just eighteen. My exhibition is finished there, and I either take it back to Milan or move it on to Churt in Surrey. I don't like the idea of it being in one country while I'm in another. But coincidentally, my mother is about to exhibit her latest ceramics in Yorkshire. She flew in from Milan to Manchester and I drove her over to Sculpture Park; we were just organising best way to go about it.'

'So, where's your mother now? She's not waiting out in the garden, is she?' Eva's gaze turned automatically to the window.

Andrea laughed at that. 'Last time I saw her she was off to a wine bar. On the estate? With your sister and a man speaking Scotch? I'm afraid I couldn't quite understand what he was saying all the time.'

'Scottish.' Eva smiled. 'Lachlan. My sister appears to have fallen in love with him after almost a year of disliking him intensely.'

'It is often the way. He seem very much in love with her too. Anyway, they take my mother off for drink and dinner, giving me instructions on how to find you. I go and pick her up in an hour or so.' Andrea paused. 'What you think, lovely Eva? We have an hour?'

'What are you suggesting?' She smiled.

'I think, maybe, it good idea to introduce me to *these two*?' Andrea smiled in return and nodded towards the open orangery door.

Eva turned quickly to see both Laila and Nora, who'd obviously heard the front doorbell go and snuck downstairs, now on the floor and peering round the door.

'That will take ten minutes,' Eva said, grinning and moving to pick up Nora who was having a fit of shy giggles. 'That leaves a good forty, I reckon…'

35

December

'So,' Alice Parkes began, gazing round and up at the lofty ceilings of the newly refurbished suite of attic rooms in some wonder and, for once, seemingly lost for words. She hesitated for a few seconds more, watching as the weak midday December sunshine put its rays through the long bank of windows to the side of each of the six workrooms, as well as through those overhead. 'I never realised,' she eventually went on almost dreamily, 'just how *very* conducive to the artist the light in this part of the world is, even in winter. You know, the intensity and quality of light will affect how you perceive and develop the value in your art. If the light is too intense, then you're likely to overcompensate and create drawings and paintings that are too dark. Similarly, if the light is too weak, then you've the possibility of producing artwork that is also too weak; washed out even. I'm sure Bill Astley, twelfth Marquis of Stratton, was totally aware of this and while, as a young girl, I was very much seduced both by the artist and his work, I was not fully aware, at the time, of the man's very great talent.'

'*Young girl?*' Susan hissed from her vantage point three rows back, 'Alice was thirty, if she was a day, when she jumped on Bill.'

Alice cleared her throat, longing, Eva could tell, for a cigarette. She broke into a bout of coughing and then, flexing her arthritic fingers, continued. 'Today, ladies and gentlemen, I am so delighted, so *proud* to not only be back here in Westenbury, the village of my birth where I learned so much…'

'Yes,' Susan whispered loudly, 'learned to *get out* the minute she could, and then not come back until it was to her own advantage...'

'...but am just as proud to be here to support my own three daughters, Rosa, Hannah and particularly Eva, whose brainchild this wonderful art retreat is.'

'*Whose* daughters?' Eva heard Susan mutter in undertones behind her. '*Just* like Alice to take all the credit for *my* girls, now that they're out of nappies, no longer moody teenagers, and... and... *artistically interesting*.'

Rosa, who was standing with Joe next to Susan and Richard, reached across to squeeze her mum's hand and Susan shot her a grateful look before turning back to scowl in Alice's direction.

'You OK?' Joe whispered, smoothing back a lock of Rosa's dark hair before bending to leave a kiss on her cheek.

Rosa nodded in the affirmative, feeling happier and surer of herself than she had for years. She glanced down at the simple gold band on her left hand as she did so many times, every single day, remembering the ceremony in her church, six weeks previously, surrounded by just her own family and Joe's, and officiated by Ben Carey, now Bishop of Pontefract, but formerly incumbent in Westenbury village.

They had walked hand in hand over from the vicarage that Friday morning, Rosa in a cream midi dress and brown suede boots and Joe in a dark suit. Rosa Rosavina: how she loved her new name, this perfectly clever combination of her and Joe, joined now in the presence of God.

Joe simply took her hand and dropped another kiss on her head before returning to Alice's speech.

'Ladies and gentlemen,' Alice was saying, 'I can't tell you how wonderful it is to be back home once more, to be here with my own very dear family: my daughters, my sister – Susan – and my niece – Violet...'

'*Virginia*,' both Susan and Virginia, standing near the front with Barty and Bethany, hissed in unison.

'... and my granddaughters, Laila and Nora, who – I'm led to believe – are already following in the family tradition of showing great artistic potential.'

'*Granddaughters?*' Susan just about exploded. 'Since when have *my* granddaughters become *hers*, for heaven's sake...?'

'But, of course, we also have with us this afternoon, not only local artistic talent in the guise of ceramicist Kate Maddison and my own daughter, Eva Malik...'

'She's *not* your daughter, Alice,' Susan hissed crossly, 'she's mine. *Mine*. All three are *mine*.'

'...but nationally and *internationally* talented artists as well. We're lucky to have with us, today, the Italian ceramicist Adalina Zaitsev as well as sculptor Andrea Zaitsev, whose work will be back at the YSP in Wakefield next year before returning permanently, I believe, to Milan. But I know—' Alice broke off to survey her audience '—guests here this afternoon, as well as invited press, are gathered in anticipation of meeting – maybe, with *one* exception – a man who could be viewed as Europe's greatest living artist today...'

'One *exception*?' Susan was like a coiled spring on the point of release. 'Does she mean *herself*? Alice always was so full of herself... even when she was a little girl, she...'

'...Yves Dufort from Paris who is going to join with me...' Alice waved an imperious hand in Yves' direction as he moved to join her at the front '... to formally open *The Dame Alice Parkes Art Retreat at Heatherly Hall* this afternoon. Yves?'

Yves, looking dapper and much younger than his actual seventy-five years, took Alice's hand and kissed her on both cheeks before turning to the gathered guests and national, as well as local, press.

'Ladies and gentlemen,' he said with a smile, speaking in almost perfect English, 'it is my very great pleasure to not only open this *superbe* new art retreat up here *dans le ciel...*' Yves waved a hand towards the windows where a cerulean blue sky portrayed a very different season to winter's actuality '…in this amazing historic hall, but to be welcomed to Yorkshire by these three beautiful sisters who have worked tirelessly to make this art retreat the best it can possibly be.'

And then, together with Alice, he turned, pulling at the cord, which drew back the little red velvet curtains on the plaque mounted on the newly painted wall.

THE DAME ALICE PARKES ART RETREAT
AT HEATHERLY HALL

OPENED DECEMBER 2022
BY DAME ALICE PARKES AND YVES DUFORT

'Trust Alice to be given a damehood just in time for the plaque going up,' Susan sniffed over her cup of tea as the guests mingled, talked, met the artists and took photographs of Bill Astley's oil-painted murals on show to the public for the very first time.

'And just look at her, Mum' Virginia was equally scathing. 'She's practically got her hands on Eva's Italian man's *bottom*.'

Hannah, overhearing her big sister's muttered words to Susan laughed. 'Ah, Virginia, Andrea Zaitsev may be in danger of having his bum fondled by Alice but, I tell you now, his eyes are only for Eva.' The three of them turned to the right, firstly to see Andrea reach to take Eva in his arms and then to the left as Lachlan Buchanan brought cups of tea over for himself and Hannah, bending to kiss Hannah's open mouth, regardless of Virginia's obvious pained expression.

'Goodness me, you three are *all at it*.' Virginia nodded towards Rosa who was now openly kissing Joe Rosavina while laughing at something he was saying. 'And her the *village vicar* as well. Grandfather Cecil would be quite horrified at such a public show of…'

'Ladies and gentlemen.' Yves Dufort was back at the front of the room, holding up both hands. 'I give you The Girls of Heatherly Hall.'

To a long and loud round of applause, the three Quinn triplets – Eva, Rosa and Hannah – joined hands and moved to join him at the front.

Acknowledgements

A big thank you to all the fabulous members of the editorial team at Aria, Head of Zeus, who have helped to make *The Girls of Heatherly Hall* the best it can possibly be.

Thanks, as always, to my lovely agent, Anne Williams at KHLA Literary Agency, for her unstinting help, advice and loyalty.

And of course, to all you wonderful readers who read my books and write such lovely things about them, a huge, heartfelt Thank You.

About the Author

Julie Houston lives in Huddersfield, West Yorkshire where her novels are set, and her only claims to fame are that she teaches part-time at *Bridget Jones* author Helen Fielding's old junior school and her neighbour is *Chocolat* author, Joanne Harris. Julie is married, with two adult children and a ridiculous Cockapoo called Lincoln. She runs and swims because she's been told it's good for her, but would really prefer a glass of wine, a sun lounger and a jolly good book – preferably with Dev Patel in attendance.

You can find Julie on Twitter or on Facebook
Twitter: @juliehouston2
Facebook.com/JulieHoustonauthor